GOOD LITTLE MARAUDER

GOOD LITTLE MARAUDER

MATT COOK

Aura Libertatis Spirat

GOOD LITTLE MARAUDER

Braveship Books

www.braveshipbooks.com

Aura Libertatis Spirat

The Library of Congress Cataloging-in-Publication Data is available upon request.

ISBN 978-1-64062-092-6 (hardcover)
ISBN 978-1-64062-095-7 (ePUB)
ISBN 978-1-64062-094-0 (Amazon Kindle)

First Edition: 2019

Printed in the United States of America

0 9 8 7 6 5 4 3 2 1

Jacket illustration by Houston Sharp
www.artstation.com/houstonsharp

Jacket design by Ivica Jandrijević

Book design by Alexandru Diaconescu
www.steadfast-typesetting.eu

Jacket illustration includes the following works of art:

Alma-Tadema, Lawrence (1895). *A Coign of Vantage.*
Bouguereau, William-Adolphe (1891). *The Broken Pitcher.*
Bouguereau, William-Adolphe (1900). *The Little Marauder.*
Delacroix, Eugène (1830). *Liberty Leading the People.*

To Cousins Mel and Muriel Engelman,
Brave heroes of World War II and its aftermath.

Acknowledgements

This book would not have been possible without the inspiration and support of many people—some distant, others near and dear.

The camoufleurs of Operation Bertram—Geoffrey Barkas the filmmaker, Jasper Maskelyne the magician, and many others, several of whom are named in this book—helped win the Desert War by way of their creativity and bravery. They inspired this story. French artist William-Adolphe Bouguereau's masterpiece prompted the title of the book and namesake of its main character.

My agent Victoria Skurnick, editor Julie Mosow, and copyeditor Sue McClung helped shape and polish the prose. Alexandru Diaconescu, Houston Sharp, and Ivica Jandrijević created the interior design, jacket illustration, and jacket design, respectively. Rossa O'Keefe-O'Donovan and Isla Smith helped ensure authenticity of British dialect in parts.

While often disquieting, Jon Zhang's habit of raising hypothetical questions and playing devil's advocate helps to exercise divergent thinking. That consistent exercise aided the development of this book's subplots.

Fidel Hernandez is a design perfectionist. His exquisite attention to detail remains a perennial lesson in the importance of getting the facts straight. No easy task when it comes to history.

Espen Teigland enjoys identifying patterns throughout history. Our discussions involving political, social, and economical connections between national and global communities helped me explore and interpret a multitude of historical texts. This facilitated a more comprehensive understanding of wartime issues than otherwise would have been possible.

My mother, Sharon Cook, continues to demonstrate how experiences and events are clarified or distorted depending upon the prisms through which they are viewed. In writing this book I relied on many.

A First Lieutenant in the Army Nurse Corps, Cousin Muriel P. Engelman wore the Star of David while serving behind the front lines at the Battle of the Bulge in America's first mobile hospital unit. In September 2018, President Macron appointed her Chevalier dans l'Ordre National de la Légion d'Honneur (Knight of the French Nation, Order of the Legion of Honor). The rank of Chevalier includes such luminaries as Douglas MacArthur, George Patton, Colin Powell, Chester Nimitz and Charles Lindberg.

Muriel's husband, Cousin Melvin A. Engelman, LCDR, USNR (Ret.), requested assignment with the Marine Corps and served in Nagasaki with Marine Occupation Forces and in North China with the 2nd Battalion, 5th Marines. He retired after 39 years in the Navy Reserve.

Both 98 years old, they recently celebrated their 70th wedding anniversary. The free world owes these and all heroes of World War II and its aftermath an immeasurable debt of gratitude for their courage and resolve.

GOOD LITTLE
MARAUDER
MATT COOK

1942

Ralf

Ralf Speer fastened a row of buttons on his overcoat as he searched the Berlin sky for bombers. There had been few air raid alerts that year, none of them serious, but still the Vice Minister of Propaganda had made it part of his routine as he left the Ministry for home.

A crowded trolley chimed as it passed, and he caught his reflection in the moving window. I look grim, he thought, hoping the dark circles under his eyes were merely an illusion caused by the dirty glass. Punishing as his work schedule was, surely the past year hadn't taken this terrible a toll.

A coworker had recently said he had an imperial look about him, but it could have been flattery, something a man in his position must learn to discern. He might have appeared more youthful than his fifty-two years were it not for his solemn expression. The deep bags under his eyes didn't help either. Any worse, he thought, and his daughter would be afraid to hug the ghoul disguised as her father.

The trolley stopped, and he glanced twice at a passenger stepping off. The man drew his scarf around his face and turned away, clearly trying to avoid Speer's gaze.

Speer called out to him as he headed up the stairs of the Ministry building. "Heinrich?"

The man stopped. "Hallo, Ralf."

"What are you doing at the Ordenspalais? I thought you'd be at the workshop by this time."

"I'm to interview for a position as a radio broadcaster." The answer took a moment too long in coming. "A new day job."

"I see," Speer said. They could not be seen together for too long, and certainly this was not the place to ask Heinrich more questions about his plans. "Good luck, then."

A drill siren went off, and they parted ways.

It was early evening, and the street was bustling with people headed for home. For Speer, though, the workday was just beginning. He crossed the park, walking with the slight hobble that had stuck with him since his service in the Great War. A trail of steam escaped his lips. The ground was wet from a drizzle, the sky the color of concrete and getting darker. The first ten days of October had seen no variation in this kind of weather, and with winter coming, it would only get colder.

He passed a rundown building from which men in gas masks were carrying dummy bodies on stretchers toward ambulances. Young boys on bicycles were out in full force, unintimidated by the drill sirens as they rang their bells and shouted out the price of their newspapers. Those who rode too close to the men in masks were shooed away.

Speer kept his distance. He was replaying the conversation he had just had during a meeting with Joseph Goebbels and a former Abwehr officer. While they had been reviewing proposals for a new line of school propaganda posters, the officer had shared an account of an Irishman who had risked his life to defect to the Axis and spy in the Western Desert. Apparently, the man had arrived in Cairo after circumnavigating the African continent. He was now assumed to be in deep cover within the British Eighth Army. The Irishman was a promising asset, and they expected to hear from him soon.

As Speer entered a residential area, his thoughts turned to his daughter, Katharina. Coming home to her was the highlight of every day. He quickened his step toward a house at the end of the cul-de-sac. There was a small garden outside, with a young cherry tree, making it one of the more cheerful homes in the neighborhood. He was glad to see she wasn't climbing its branches, as her knees already had picked up more scrapes than he could count. He kicked the mud from his boots and opened the door. A sweet little voice called out to him.

"Papa!"

As usual, his heart melted. She sat at the top of the staircase, dark curls draped over her cheeks. She was beaming. Eight-year-old Katharina stood up and practically leaped down the stairs into her father's arms.

She was one of the few children in her class at school who hadn't been evacuated to the countryside for the *Kinderlandverschickung*. A third of a million children had been relocated in the past two years to protect them from the risk of air raids in major cities.

"How's my little marauder?" he said, picking her up in her white lace dress.

She kissed him on the cheek, then pointed to an alpine snowbell flower in her hair.

"Look!"

Speer gasped. "It's beautiful! Who gave it to you?"

"Karl," she said. "He likes my painting."

"You wear it like a princess."

She grinned. "I'm hungry," she said. "When is Heinrich coming back?"

"Heinrich? Why?" His guard went up, though he couldn't say why. He would have to have a long talk with Heinrich when he returned.

"He was going to pick up a treat for me."

"I don't think he'll be back tonight," Speer said. "What would you like to eat?"

"*Eintopf*," she said.

"All right. Come into the kitchen, love, and I'll cook some stew."

As he set her down, there was a smack against the pane of a nearby window.

"What was that?" she asked.

They walked outside together, and he knelt in the grass beside a fallen bird with a chipped beak, its wings flapping on the ground beneath the panel. It was trying to right itself.

"A sparrow," Katharina said, watching her father scoop up the bird in his palms. It struggled to escape, but he folded the wings into its body, holding it still. "Is he hurting?"

"I'm sure. It hurts to fly into a window."

Her lips puckered, and as he saw the moisture welling in her eyes, eyes with irises as dark as her pupils, he said, "We'll take care of it like a doctor and nurse. Maybe it will heal."

She followed him back into the kitchen, where he set the sparrow in a cardboard box on a bed of wrinkled tissue. He spread a light towel over its body, pinning its wings down so it couldn't flap and hurt itself any more. Using a wet cloth, he wiped the blood from its forehead.

"What if he doesn't get better?"

"We'll do our best," he said.

"When Heinrich comes back with the treat, I'll give it to the sparrow."

He saw the same look of sadness she had worn the week before. His neighbor had complained that she'd kicked his six-year-old in the jaw without provocation. It turned out the boy had been frying ants with a magnifying glass, and Katharina had decided to end his reign of terror. Later she had scooped up some of the remaining ants and taken them on an adventure along the street gutter in her paper boat.

Ralf knew she would worry for weeks unless he took proper care of the bird.

"There," he said, tucking a thin layer of cloth under its head. "We'll come back later tonight and see how it's doing."

"Okay, Papa."

"Now, before I do any cooking," he said, "why don't you show me the painting you've been working on?"

"Okay!"

He followed her down the hall, where she opened a closet door to a wall of cubbyholes stacked with linens. She reached through a pile of pillowcases and sheets into one of the cubbyholes, finding a knob. She twisted it, and the wall gave way, swinging out to reveal a hidden staircase.

They descended into an underground chamber. The room was a conflagration of color; over a dozen men and women were inside, juggling palettes and paintbrushes. Each had a canvas on bedsheets. The table in the center of the room was covered with jugs of water and tubes of paint. Propped on little stands were photographs of the classic artworks that were in the process of being replicated. Katharina was allowed to be down here, but she was *never* allowed to speak of this workshop away from home.

The painters, all working swiftly and with great skill, greeted Speer as he entered. He said hello to them as he followed Katharina to her private workspace. Her canvas stood on an easel whose legs had been cut down to match her height.

"See, Papa?" she said.

He studied her painting: a human form with blue wings, set against a woodland under a shining orange sun. Except for a rather knobby face, the figure lacked the crudeness one might have expected from a child her age.

"It's fantastic," he said. "Such wonderful detail and colors. Madame Le Brun has competition."

"What is it, what is it?" she challenged.

"Isn't it obvious? She's a fairy."

Katharina looked at the canvas proudly.

"If I had to guess," he added, "I'd say it was your great aunt's Snowfall Queen."

"That's right!" she said.

Speer had read Katharina bedtime fables since before she was old enough to understand words. Earlier this year, he had begun reading her the short stories and poems written by his aunt, which featured the Snowfall Queen, a fairy living in the Alps. Katharina had become enchanted.

He was pleased that she was growing up around art. She would never really know her mother, Florentine, who had died of tuberculosis when Katharina was four, but at least their home was always full of people. The artists in the hidden workshop were not just family to her; they also fired her imagination, giving her sketches of goblins, pixies, genies, and other fantastical creatures.

When she wasn't outside climbing trees, she was in the studio, painting beside her favorite artist, Karl Decker. Karl had no children of his own, but he treated Katharina like a daughter.

"Did you paint this by yourself?" her father asked her. "No one to hold your hand?"

"Mhm," she said, with a guilty glance at the painter closest to them, a skinny man in coveralls flecked with paint. He might have been nice-looking with some grooming, but Karl was too much of an artist to care about how anything looked if it weren't on his canvas.

"Is that right, Karl?" said Ralf.

"She's talented. I hardly helped," the man said, with a wink at Katharina.

"We should frame it, then," Ralf said. "Now I'm going to have a quick talk with Karl. In a few minutes, I'll start cooking. Will you go to your room now, my good little marauder?"

"Okay, Papa," she said, and ran up the stairs.

"She has a good mentor," Speer said. His attention turned to the painting on Decker's easel. "And a busy one. How's the Bouguereau coming?"

"I should finish by this evening."

Speer leaned in with a magnifying glass for a closer look.

The painting showed a young girl sitting on a slab of stone, wearing a white dress. She took center stage, on a grassy hill or plain, holding a pear in her right hand and clutching her forehead with her left, poised to sweep her fingers through her wealth of dark brown hair. Most likely, she was a peasant girl, but she might have passed for a rebellious daughter of aristocracy. She was barefoot, her feet crossed beside a weed. It was hard to identify what was in the background: mountains probably, or maybe an ocean. The child's skin had an ethereal glow, just like the fabric of her dress, and her eyes were deep, black, and wise—and rich with the possibility of mischief.

Speer's brows came together, as they often did when he fell quiet. "No one captures the tenderness of Bouguereau like you do, Karl," he said.

"With Bouguereau, it's not about mimicking technique or seeing through his eyes. It's about understanding his sense of life."

"Whatever your methods, don't stop. I expect our output will have to increase in the coming weeks." Speer noticed the chair next to Decker's was empty. He lowered his voice a few notches. "Speaking of, has Heinrich Jecklyn's output been up to standard lately?"

"I tend not to notice. Why?"

"I ran into him at the Ordenspalais on my way home."

"That's odd."

"He said he was applying for a new job as a radio broadcaster."

"Hmm." Decker seemed uninterested. "How are things at the Ministry, anyway?"

"I had a meeting with Goebbels and a former Abwehr officer today."

"How was it?"

"The first half was dull. We spent hours discussing a poster the Ministry is developing for primary schools. Their proposal shows an institution for the dull-witted on one hand, and a community of beautiful houses on the other. It will inform students that the annual cost of schools for feeble minds will pay for seventeen homes for good German families."

Decker's face remained neutral. "And the second half?"

"The officer told us a few stories that have crossed his intelligence desk lately. One was about an Irishman who has risked his life to spy for Germany. He was trained at the Abwehr school before returning to England. The British sent him sailing around Africa. He's now in deep cover, somewhere in Egypt."

"Did you get the operative's name?"

"Damien Bray."

Speer wrote out the name on a card and handed it to Decker, who said, "You think he's worthy of our courtesy?"

"Hitler himself has met this man. It seems the Abwehr are really counting on him."

"I see."

Decker slipped the card into his pocket.

"Keep this one to yourself," Speer said.

"Understood."

Speer patted his colleague on the shoulder and said, "Now I'd better report to the kitchen and take care of my hungry child."

Katharina

They had finished dinner an hour ago, and Katharina had slipped into her pajamas. Her father lifted her onto the bed and tucked her in, unfurling the blanket up to her chin. As he pulled up a chair, she wished there were room for him to climb in next to her. She loved to lay her cheek against his side and feel the vibrations in his chest as he read to her. She only half-listened to the stories, anyway. What mattered was his voice.

"Papa?" she said.

"Yes, love?"

"When will the National Socialists beat the Allies?"

She rested her head on the pillow and tried to decipher his expression. He was making a grown-up face, one that looked troubled by emotions she couldn't comprehend.

"Why? Are you still afraid of the Allies?" he asked.

"No," she said, but as he moved to stroke her arm, she realized he knew she was lying. He could always tell.

"Just because you're afraid, that doesn't mean you aren't brave," he said. "Just the opposite. Being brave means doing something when you *are* afraid to do it."

"Is the Führer brave?"

"Very," he answered.

"We're going to beat the Allies, then?"

"Undoubtedly."

"Are you hurting, Papa?"

"Why do you ask?"

"You look like you're hurting."

"If I look that way, it's because I was just thinking about the poor little bird, darling. But I'm happy because I'm with you." He pinched her cheek. "You don't still have nightmares about the Allies, do you?"

"Sometimes."

"They're regular people. Men and women, most of them in uniforms, just like people in Berlin. Except the uniforms look different. They don't have spiders on them."

"Why not?"

"They're afraid of spiders."

"I'm not."

"You're braver than they are. See? There's no need to worry about the Allies. If you ever think about them, just imagine them doing naked jumping jacks in the rain. They'll look so silly that you won't be afraid."

"All right," she said, relaxing.

"What do you say we continue your great aunt's story?" he said, sliding on a pair of spectacles and opening a leather-bound book with an earmarked page in the middle.

"Yes, please!"

She could smell the book's musty fragrance, one with hints of grass and vanilla. Her eyes narrowed to half-mast, keeping her father's profile silhouetted against the lamp on the nightstand. She liked to watch him read.

"The Snowfall Queen descended from a gray and windless sky,
And scarce upon her visage fair were traces left of mirth.
The shimmers of her sapphire wings did through a forest fly,
As far as Nixie's Pond, by which her slippers touched the earth.
'Awake, my Nixie,' said she, and from 'neath the surface stirred
A maiden of the water who did swiftly heed her call.
'Beware,' the Snowfall Queen exclaimed, 'for I now carry word,
A nachzehrer apparition roams our mountains tall!'"

Katharina wasn't sure when her eyes had fully closed, but they had grown heavy, and she was now drifting off to the white forest, guided by the voice of her father and floating in a blanket that couldn't have felt warmer.

. . .

She awoke to heavy rain and a black room. Papa usually left on a night-light, and she wondered if maybe the electricity had gone out.

Hearing a faint chittering downstairs, she began to worry about the sparrow. She didn't normally get out of bed when it was this dark, but tonight she shoved the blankets aside and tiptoed out of the room. She stopped at the top of the stairs, where she could see down into the kitchen. A light was on.

Papa was there, reaching into the cardboard box, cradling the bird in his palms. Katharina sat on her haunches to see what he was doing. He touched a finger to its head, probably to check for bleeding. Then he set the bird on the counter, having removed the towel from its body. The sparrow let out a raspy tweet as it tried to stand on its two feet. It fell over on its side and tried to balance by flapping a wing. Her father tried to help it into the air, but his touch seemed to make it panic. It quivered, confused, digging its head into the counter. Then it stopped fighting with itself. Katharina knew it was giving up. The sparrow trembled and chirped, a creature in pain, as if it knew it would never fly again.

Papa sighed. She wondered if he was still as optimistic as she was. If it can't fly, she thought, it must learn to walk.

But her father must not have seen it that way. He picked up the sparrow, pinning its wings to its body, and gave its neck a sharp twist.

Her heart clenched at what sounded like the snap of a twig. She didn't want to feel angry with Papa—he had nursed the sparrow, and it was kinder to end its pain—but couldn't he have given it one more day?

She went back to bed, trying not to cry into her pillow. Her father passed her room in the hall outside, heading to sleep himself. Tomorrow, she would ask him about the sparrow, and he would tell her it had healed and flown away. She knew that. Grown-ups invented stories like that, but she was smart enough to realize there were aspects of life that adults didn't want children to see. At least not yet. They would shade the truth, or hide it. She didn't understand why. The world worked a certain way, followed a set of rules, and truth was truth, so why did grown-ups feel the need to disguise it? If she were to make her life the best it could be, it seemed she should understand the rules and see reality for what it was. As for the world her father wanted her to see, she could always paint it.

The pillow had gotten moist under her eye. She flipped onto her other side, using a sheet to soak up the wetness. A tree rustled by her window on the second story, scraping the glass, and she listened to the patter of droplets on the leaves. The rain was getting heavier.

Was that all she heard, or were there voices, too?

She did not want to climb out of bed again, but if she was really hearing something, she had to tell Papa. She stared out the window a little more, watching the movement of the tree.

She remembered what her father had said about bravery. Pushing back the covers, she wedged herself against the nightstand and scrambled up to the window ledge so she could see outside.

She wanted to scream but couldn't find her voice.

A group of uniformed men stood outside their house, clustered by the front door, holding pistols, whispering. Then one of the men pointed his gun at the doorknob and fired. She heard the blast from inside the house as the guard kicked down the door.

Maybe the darkness had obscured them, but she didn't see any spiders on the uniforms of the men now pouring into their home. *Allies!*

"PAPA!"

Downstairs, she heard shouts and gunfire. She ran to the doorway and saw men filing through the vestibule. One was barking orders at the formation of uniforms approaching the foot of the stairs.

She looked toward her father's bedroom. The door flew open, and Papa dashed out. Katharina had never seen him so distressed. When he spotted her standing by her open bedroom door, his face became something wild.

"Get under your bed and don't come out!" he said to her in a controlled whisper. "I love you more than anything in the world. Go!"

She took a few steps back, not daring to look away from him as he stood on the landing and drew his pistol on the intruders.

"You are trespassing on my property!" he shouted. "Do you know who I am?"

Silence. Katharina stayed hidden behind the door, eyes darting between her father's face and his weapon. She could feel the image of him searing into her memory like a branding iron. He stood still. His anger frightened her, and she took comfort in her fear, knowing the strangers must have felt the same way about him.

"You have no right to be here," he said. "Leave at once."

There was a loud *crack*.

Her father clasped his chest.

Then she saw the hole in the back of his pajamas.

"Bastards," he said.

Collapsing to one knee, he began shooting at the men crowding the base of the stairs, striking two, one in the skull, before the riptide of return fire swept him. His body slackened, and he toppled over.

This was all beyond Katharina; she couldn't grasp what was happening. She crawled under the bed, her world dissolving under a heavy flow of tears. She felt like she was drowning. The house had lost its shapes and contours and become a mix of sensations and sounds—cold air, hard wood, bellows, gunshots, boots coming up the stairs.

The door flew open, and she could see black boots enter the room. The floor creaked against her ear. The man threw her closet open and tossed her newly pressed dresses out like they were trash. Finding nothing, he opened an armoire—empty—and he said a word her father had forbidden her to use. Two more men came in. The first said something to the others, and they moved down the hall toward her father's bedroom. Katharina stayed completely still. After a few minutes, the three men headed back downstairs. She couldn't be sure, but it sounded like they had gone to the backyard.

She had to warn Karl!

Katharina crawled out from under the bed and peeked downstairs. The way was clear, but the Allies would surely come back and continue their search. She bounded down the stairs and nearly tripped over a dead body. This must have been the man Papa had shot, his skin a ghastly white. She ran toward the linen closet, opened it, reached through the stack of sheets, and twisted the knob.

There were still over a dozen people in the underground chamber, painting as usual, oblivious because the walls were soundproof.

"Allies! Allies!" she shouted.

The artists turned.

"Strangers!" she said. "They killed Papa!"

The room stirred as the painters abandoned their work and tried to make sense of her words. Some gathered paint cans as makeshift weapons.

Katharina ran to find Karl Decker. He was by her side in seconds, his face pale.

"How many were there?" he asked.

She didn't know, but she held up all her fingers.

"Stay by my side, okay?" he said.

She nodded as he wiped the wetness from her cheeks.

Karl rolled up the painting he had finished—the dark-haired, barefoot girl on the plain, holding the pear—and slid the canvas into a cardboard tube. Holding Katharina's hand, he sprinted to the top of the subterranean staircase and peered out. Two of the intruders had already come back into the house and were talking under an archway between the kitchen and living room. He picked up Katharina in one arm, carried the tube with the other, and sprinted for the home's main door. The intruders must have heard him. They called out to their comrades and rushed back down the hall.

Several of the other artists had begun to pour from the hidden cavity. Behind her, she heard a flurry of shouts and scrambling footsteps, followed by muted screams. As Karl ran out the front door, Katharina heard the clamor of the boots descending into her father's secret chamber—followed by more *cracks*.

"They found Papa's workshop!" Katharina cried.

Karl didn't respond. She bounced in his arm, and his grip on her was painfully constricting. He only set her down when they were safely across the street outside.

"Go hide in the brush," he said, pointing to a tangle of foliage. "Don't move until I come out."

She scurried off, and he returned moments later, dragging the body of the uniformed intruder that Papa had shot through the skull. Over his shoulder was her red wool coat, and in Karl's other hand was the dead man's pistol.

"Put it on and follow me!" he said, passing her the coat. She had never heard him speak with this kind of urgency. He ran toward an intersection while she followed him as fast as she could. She thought she heard him say something about praying there were no police nearby, but she missed his exact words over her own pounding heart and heavy breathing.

Karl glanced toward the end of the cul-de-sac to make sure they weren't being pursued. Traffic was thin at this late hour. A BMW 319 convertible came by, and Karl ran into the street with the handgun, pointing it at the automobile.

"Get out of the car!" he said. The gun shook in his hand.

The driver, alone in the two-seater, threw up his hands and pleaded for his life, offering the vehicle.

"Get in," Karl said to Katharina. She did, and watched as he stuffed the dead man into the folded canopy behind the passenger seats, using it as a body bag.

"Look!" she said, pointing to her house.

Handguns raised, three men burst through the front gate and bolted after the car. They were already firing. Karl hit the gas, and the tires spun against gravel on the pavement before catching. The BMW accelerated as the intruders closed in at thirty yards. Katharina turned in her seat and saw three of them climb into a Mercedes-Benz, which quickly came up behind them. "Drive faster, Karl!" she screamed.

Katharina hung on to her seat for balance as the car gained speed and veered into an alley. The men who had been following them disappeared, and she could see nothing outside but the whizzing streaks of streetlights. The windshield wipers thumped and swooshed, barely keeping pace with the downpour.

The car dipped and bumped as they sped over ruts and cracks in the road, jolting Katharina in her seat. Hearing a siren, Karl yanked the steering wheel, but the police lights never appeared. On a dark side street, he hit the brakes and jockeyed the car into a gap between two other vehicles parked at the sidewalk.

He cut the engine and the headlights. Katharina was relieved, but Karl seemed to be holding his breath, peering into a side mirror as the Mercedes-Benz rounded the corner behind them and screamed by. Another vehicle stopped at an intersection. "Get down," Karl whispered as he ducked in his seat.

When the street fell quiet again, Karl dragged the body out of the automobile canopy. Hiding behind a tree, he stripped the dead man of his uniform and swapped clothes. Up close, Katharina shuddered to see Karl wearing the same uniform as the men who had killed her father. The cuff band and right-side collar patch were plain black, without insignia. His shoulder board, denoting rank, was piped in green. No spiders.

"We have to get another car. They'll be looking for this one, and with all the bullet holes, it's easy to spot. Let's go, sweetheart."

"What about *him?*" She pointed to the corpse on the sidewalk.

"We leave him," Karl said.

He took her hand. Finding a nearby boulevard, he stopped another vehicle using his pistol. This car was a 1938 Opel Admiral. Behind the wheel, he revved the engine and found the nearest busy street heading northwest through the city center.

He turned the car into Potsdamer Platz and parked near a vacated building.

"Come on," he said to Katharina, checking his watch.

They ran toward a concrete structure across the street and followed a colonnade into the main complex. It was crowded inside. She dared not let go of Karl's hand as they entered the hubbub. All she could see was a muddle of fast-moving umbrellas and overcoats.

"Where are we?" she asked.

Echoes of voices, bells, rumbles, and whistles filled the concourse. She had to listen hard for his answer. Karl did not stoop down to reply. He was searching for something.

"A train station," he said.

"Are we going to take a train?"

"No, I have to make a delivery. Please, I know it's hard, but try to keep up, sweetheart!"

He spotted a track through an archway and doubled his pace.

"Up you go, Katharina, into my arms!" he said, lifting her. He broke into a run, still clutching the cardboard tube.

Near the track, a ticket collector stopped him and asked for his boarding pass.

"I'm not getting on the train," he barked at the collector. "I'm delivering this tube to a passenger."

"You have blood on your shirt, a child in your arms, and you're soaking wet."

"Damn it, the train leaves in one minute!"

"That's right," said the collector, "with or without your item."

The collector called over a guard, who asked, "What's inside?"

"A painting."

"All luggage is subject to random inspections," he said. "Open it."

Karl slid the canvas out of the tube and unfurled it. The guard took a close look at the scene of the girl with the pear. "This looks like degenerate art."

"Look at my uniform, you idiot," Karl said. "This is a delivery from the Vice Minister of Propaganda to a wealthy art collector in Munich. You insult the Ministry by accosting me here. Step aside, or count on an official complaint. If this painting is not delivered on time, Goebbels himself will hear about it. He'd be happy to recommend an overhaul of this station's security."

Karl gave him no time to reply. He stuffed the painting back into the tube and walked on, while Katharina clung to his neck.

He stopped outside the penultimate carriage, scanning the passengers. Katharina also looked at the drawn faces, not quite sure what they were looking for. The train hissed as pressure was released from the brake pipe. A steam trumpet blared.

The train began pulling away. Karl waved and shouted, and a passenger—a bespectacled man in a tweed coat—rushed to the open window. Bouncing in Karl's arms as he ran to keep pace with the carriage, Katharina saw fear and determination on the passenger's face.

"Here," Karl shouted to the man in tweed, "grab the tube!"

The passenger took hold of the painting and drew it into the car.

Karl set Katharina down and took a few moments to catch his breath as the train outstripped him. He took her hand again and guided her back through the melee of people in the atrium, avoiding a file of guards that had entered from the far end. She looked at him and could see his eyes darting about the room as he choreographed his next move.

"Walk fast," he said. "You've been the bravest girl tonight. Your father is proud of his darling. He's watching over us."

She heard a tremor in his voice. Why was Karl still afraid?

They merged with a mass of people and avoided the guards' notice by moving back toward the colonnade. Karl led her across the street, and they took the Opel onto a busy road. In the time it took them to leave Berlin, the rain never stopped. The city lights gradually disappeared, and a waxing moon cast its glow across the countryside. For the first time that night, she began to feel safe under Karl's protection.

"Where are we going?" she asked.

"To Wangerland, northwest of Bremerhaven. It's not safe for us here."

"Who was that man on the train?" Katharina asked.

"A friend of mine and your papa's," Karl said.

"What happened to the other artists?"

"Sweetheart, must you ask so many questions?"

"Sorry." She decided to sit in silence unless spoken to, and her eyelids started to droop as the motion and warmth of the car soothed her to sleep. She pictured her Papa watching over her.

. . .

Katharina woke as the car slowed and the headlights illuminated the red, black, and white stripes of a guard booth. The road ahead was blocked by a horizontal pole. Five soldiers wearing field tunics, Stahlhelms, and calf-high jackboots kept watch around a sentry box. The leader, a man in a black leather trenchcoat, stood sheltered under the triangular roof, smoking a cigarette, while the others weathered the rain. His station was equipped with a tank, three Nimbus motorcycles, and a *Kübelwagen* support vehicle that to Katharina looked like a bathtub on wheels.

The leader put a hand on his Luger as the Opel slowed to a halt. Karl rolled down the window.

"Names and destination."

"Karl Otto Josef Decker, with Katharina Marie Speer. I am on official duty, transporting the daughter of Ralf Speer to Denmark. The girl is to be evacuated from Berlin for the *Kinderlandverschickung.*"

That was a lie, Katharina realized. He had told her they were going to Wangerland. Papa had said never to lie. But as the guard in black leaned in through the window, she heard coldness in his voice and decided that Karl must have a good reason to be economical with the truth.

"There are no camps in Denmark. Why aren't you taking her to the Sudetenland, or Austria, or Bohemia and Mor—"

"Perhaps you did not hear me," Karl said. "She is the daughter of the Vice Minister of Propaganda, and will go to no camp. The girl will live with a host family in Esbjerg."

That terrified her. "No!" she blurted.

They were talking about her as if she weren't even there, and Karl kept on lying. At least, she hoped that he was lying, and he didn't really plan to leave her with strangers. Her friends from school had slowly vanished from Berlin during the past two years. Her father had explained that they had gone to the countryside so they would be safe from air raids. She didn't want to be one of them.

The guard arched an eyebrow. "No?"

Karl stayed calm.

"As you can see," he said, "she is frightened to leave home."

"Show me your papers," the guard said.

Karl reached into his new uniform and handed the man a thin sheaf of documentation. The guard reviewed the material, and then he looked at Katharina.

"You are the daughter of Ralf Speer?" he asked Katharina.

She nodded, listening to the pitter-patter of rain on his helmet and wishing he would go away. If her Papa was dead, was she still his daughter? Her eyes welled with tears as she wondered.

"How old are you?"

"Eight."

"And your father works at the Ministry of Propaganda?"

She nodded again.

"Does he do anything else?"

"Mhm," she said.

"What does he do?"

"Paints."

The guard handed back Karl's papers. She had passed his test. No eight-year-old would know that Ralf Speer was an accomplished German painter unless she were family.

The guard gestured to the others, who lifted the bar from the road.

"Proceed," he said.

Soon the lights of the military post became tiny dots in the nightscape of farmland behind them. "Katharina, I must tell you something very, very important," Karl said as they sped through the darkness. He reached over and touched her arm. "Are you awake?"

"Yes," she said sleepily.

"After tonight, you must never tell anyone about your father." Katharina felt wide awake all of a sudden. "You must never say that you are his daughter."

"When will he come for me?" she asked, even though she had promised herself she would not ask any more questions. She dreaded the answer, but she had to know the truth.

"Your father is with the angels," he said. "All the painters are now."

Katharina turned away from Karl and curled into herself. She could barely remember her mother, and now her father was gone, too. She pictured his face, the way he had stroked her arm, and his last words to her: "I love you more than anything in the world."

"When people ask, say your father and mother were Austrian farmers, not involved in the war, and that your family was killed in an accidental bombing during a Luftwaffe drill. That is why you speak only German. You were the sole survivor." He put his hand on her shoulder again. "Promise me, no matter what."

"I promise," she said.

She soon fell into a deep sleep, only waking once or twice when they passed through checkpoints. They reached Bremen before dawn and stopped for gasoline at a filling station before the road turned sharply north, toward the municipality of Wangerland.

Daybreak found them passing the small village of Hohenkirchen on the North Sea coast. Katharina awoke in her seat from a fitful slumber full of nightmares. Karl still watched the road with sleepless, dilated eyes as the sun's first rays began to stretch over a sandy beach and pier. He turned toward the pier and parked the car near a grassy hillock by the shore.

"We're here," he said.

Katharina yawned and watched Karl get out of the car. He was staring at the ocean.

"What are you looking for?" she asked.

He picked her up, pointing to a tapered, half-submerged black shape that reminded her of a whale coming up to breathe, except longer, smoother, and capped with a turret. She figured that was a chimney. It had been well concealed by the wharf, hidden under nets and screens, but it must have been preparing to leave, as groups of men were pulling away the shielding.

"See that?" he said. "It's a submarine, a British U-class. It's going to take us to England."

She gasped. "*Allies!*"

"Do you remember what we talked about?" He set her down and knelt beside her. She nodded. "You don't need to be afraid. I'm not sure what they will do to me, but they won't hurt a child."

"I don't want them to hurt you!"

"Sweetheart . . ."

He jumped, startled, as a bullet shattered the window of the Opel. Three SS motorcycles zipped down the road toward them. Another shot rang out, and he shrieked, falling onto his side and clutching his thigh.

"Karl!"

"They must have sent out radio alerts from Berlin," he said through gritted teeth. "Katharina, listen to me! Run to the submarine and go to England. They will find a safe home for you. You must never mention the name of your papa, or his position. Do you understand? You're Austrian, and your parents were farmers killed by a bomb. Repeat it back to me."

"But Papa said lying is—"

"The people in England . . . they're afraid of your papa, and may not treat you well if they learn you are related to him. But that's no reason not to love him."

"I want you to go with me!"

"Run to the submarine! *Now*, Katharina!"

She turned toward the pier and dashed, her legs unsteady and unbalanced. She fell twice, scraping a knee and elbow through the pajamas she still had on, but despite the smarting in her limbs, she ran across the beach and onto the wharf. The black vessel wasn't far.

Over the sound of her own chokes and snuffles, she could still hear the barrage of gunfire hitting the Opel. She knew Karl had taken shelter behind the car and wondered how he would fend off the attackers.

When she reached the submarine, half a dozen men wearing a different kind of uniform, one she had never seen before, were hustling about their work on its deck, apparently spurred on by the gunshots.

"She has no living family," Karl shouted to them from the hillock. "Take her!"

Katharina spun around and looked across the wharf, seeing him one last time. Three men who had parked their motorbikes were encircling him. One of them took out a pistol and fired a single shot—a quick, echoless pop—and Karl fell onto the knoll.

She screamed.

The three men started down the pier after her, but they were met by return fire from the submariners. They backed off for the moment, but Katharina knew they would come back before long.

One of the submariners lifted her from the dockside and set her on the deck. The deck was narrow: one step too far to either side, and she'd fall into the water. The entire submarine stretched almost two hundred feet in length.

"No identification, no possessions," the man said in a language she couldn't understand; it must have been English. "Just her satin jim-jams."

Her new caretakers opened a scuttle near the conning tower and passed her down to an officer. The room below was dark and sterile, accessed by two cramped hallways that looked more like cave tunnels. Overhead, powder-green pipes and cables careened every which way. Hatches clanged around her. She smelled all sorts of odors: amine, diesel, sweaty people. The men hardly seemed to notice their new passenger. Some were operating dials and gauges or turning valves, while others merely walked by in a hurry, crouching and sucking in their stomachs to fit past each other through the tight walkways.

After a while, an officer took her into a room full of beds, set her on a mattress, and muttered something indecipherable before closing a curtain.

Ten minutes passed, and then the bed began to vibrate. Not just the bed, but the walls and the pipes, too. Sitting in her closed-off cell, she shivered. She had never set foot on a boat before, let alone the kind that could travel underwater. She heard and felt a heavy rumbling, as if the vessel were speaking with the voice of storm clouds. There was a rush of water through the piping as the trim and drain tanks were flooded for diving. The hull groaned, and the walls started to tick around her, like the sound of a cooling engine. Then came the high-pitched whine of pumps and generators. Eventually the deep rumble waned and died as electric motors replaced the diesel engines.

Katharina felt for the snowbell flower in her hair, the one Karl had given her, and realized it must have fallen out during the night.

She no longer fought her sobs—only her dizziness. The world had begun to tilt.

THE DIARY OF DAMIEN BRAY

My Days in Camouflage Company

First Three Letters

31 August 1942

My darling Evanna,

The thought of hurting an old man makes me sick. I respect the wisdom of the elderly. Where others see decrepitude, I see choices that have stood the test of time.

It has been hard to take my mind off the inevitable. Cigarettes don't help much anymore. Perhaps you can soothe my nerves. This diary will help me feel closer to you.

I've finished my shift at the anti-torpedo gun and come out for a smoke that I hope will ease my nausea. In the six weeks since leaving Liverpool, my stomach hasn't complained about anything but the *Andorra*'s poor excuse for a galley. Now I feel like a first-time sailor in a hurricane.

I've tried to let the view of Venus calm me the past few nights. Sometimes I lean out over the railing and listen to the water churning under the steamship. It's a soothing sound. Constant, fresh, best heard right here, astern. No one knows this spot better than I do. I've manned the gun since our escort went away and left us vulnerable to U-boats. I asked for the night shift so I don't have to run into officers and make small talk or accept invitations to play cribbage or deck tennis. On occasion, they ask me to censor letters in the lower decks, but usually I stand watch by the gun.

We've sailed twelve thousand miles along the west coast of Africa and north to the Red Sea, all to avoid the Mediterranean. It's too dangerous for a merchant vessel there. At last we're creeping up the Suez Canal. We make port in two days, which is why I must act tonight. Looking west toward the banks, I can already see the sprawl of the Allied army. Miles of depots, store dumps, workshops, huts, tents.

Seeing those camps makes me wonder why I fought so hard for us to leave Galway when the war started. I don't have to close my eyes to picture the sandstone cliffs or the sea stacks or the hills by home, hills I fell in love with long before I even met you. Truth is, I didn't want to leave, but I thought it would be impossible for people like us to keep our peaceful life in the long term. Not unless we all did our part and joined the war effort.

Seems absurd now, to think I was convinced the British army could use a Saharan archaeologist and amateur stained-glass artist. I should be damned for letting them find a way.

It's my fault things happened as they did. If I weren't so stubborn, you'd still be with me, and the sun would still rise each day.

But they had a hand in it, too.

I hope you have it in you to forgive me for what I must do. It's the only way I can begin to reconcile the greatest mistake of my life.

I love you with all my heart and always will.

Your Damien

1 September 1942

My darling Evanna,

He didn't make a sound as he died.

The old man lived in one of the first-class cabins. I knew which one was his from the passenger manifest. He was an Englishman traveling to Cairo to start a shipping company and personally deliver some cash investments. I learned this while censoring his letters.

It happened this morning before dawn. I struck a few matches and slid them under the crack of his door. After they burned out, I knocked and waited for him to answer. He woke up, and I heard him say this better be bloody important. I told him this was an emergency, that a fire had started in one of the coal bunkers and would soon spread to his stateroom. He unlocked his door for me as soon as he smelled the smoke.

The poor bloke must have been eighty-five. He stood there in his pajamas and nightcap, ready for me to escort him to a muster station. I retched when I saw him standing so helpless and sleepy-eyed. But I knew what I had to do. I gagged him and forced him to open his safe. Then I smothered him with a pillow. They'll think he died in his sleep.

There's no telling what this journey will bring. I have to be prepared, and the Germans were too damned cheap to give me anything but counterfeit bills. He had five thousand pounds with him, but I took only five hundred. If my bags are searched, questions will be asked.

I've never felt so horrible. As a pilot, I must have killed at least a dozen men, but I never saw their faces. I never held them down and felt their bodies tremble. They were faceless men behind windshields. This man had flesh.

Looking out my cabin's porthole, I see the sky's turned red. The sun will soon rise, and we've nearly reached Port Said. Time for me to get whatever sleep I can. I doubt it will be much.

If you're watching me from above, darling, know that I took no pleasure in this. His death makes me deeply ill, truly, as does every casualty of war. I hope you can forgive me as you watch from heaven.

Your Damien

2 September 1942

My darling Evanna,

The most tedious chapter of my journey is over. The *Andorra* reached Port Said this morning. When I stepped off the gangplanks, I realised I'll never again be forced to endure the reek of engine oil for hours on end or search the sea for periscopes.

The train ride to Cairo was hotter than my mother's oven. The floor was dirty as an ashtray, and the carriage stank to high heaven. People kept packing in and packing in until I thought the floor might collapse. I'd have preferred first class and could have afforded it now, but it would have been a mistake to reveal my wad of cash. We passed several villages on the way. Little mud-hut slums where children came running out of their shanties, hooting and chasing the train with sticks. If there's something to envy about life in places like that, it's the simplicity.

I finished my canteen after the second hour of the trip, and my throat felt like papyrus by the time we pulled into the Cairo station. My fellow camoufleurs and I stepped off into a madhouse of soldiers and civilians. There were uniforms everywhere here, with colors from all corners of the earth.

Our orders were to report to GHQ Cairo at No. 10 Tomolbat Street. We flagged a cab, if you could call it that. The windshield was cracked, the wipers were attached to a string. The car had big dents and sagging tyres and no headlights, but I looked around and saw the other cabs—not much better, and I figured an engine was better than a mule because . . .

You wouldn't believe the roads in this city. Army lorries, staff cars, bicycles, tanks, sheep, donkey wagons, camels laden with heaping bags—they're all one giant soup of traffic. Horns blare continuously. It's mad!

We entered the Garden City district, and our cabbie stopped at a guard post in an apartment block known as "Grey Pillars." It's the heart of command of Churchill's C-in-C Middle East, the hub from which the Desert War is being fought.

The guards checked our papers and let us through. It was hard to hear anything over the *tick-tick-tick* of typewriters and the buzz of telephones and the clerks shouting at each other inside. I told a staff officer we'd arrived from the No. 4 Camouflage Course at Farnham Castle. Reporting for duty. He took us into a bedroom that had been converted into a workstation. They've converted everything into workstations here, even the kitchens and tiny bathrooms.

The major there had our orders. He told us we're to join the Camouflage Unit at Helwan. 'E' Camp, they call it. We'll be under the command of Lieutenant Colonel Geoffrey Barkas, an English filmmaker. He's popular for his pamphlets and demonstrations on the importance of military camouflage. His Camouflage Unit is made up of artists of all kinds—sculptors, painters, architects, poster artists, illustrators in woodcut, even a restorer of Old Masters. I fit right in.

Our Humber is rounding a dune now. Ahead I see sixty or so huts materialising in the heat haze. We'll be pulling into 'E' Camp in a few minutes.

I'll write again tomorrow.

Your Damien

1962

Katharina

Kate Atwell swirled her paintbrush in a palette, mixing the reds and yellows of the autumn landscape below. Her easel straddled a boulder atop a ridge in Snowdonia, the first national park in Wales. From her perch in the mountains, she could view nearly a thousand square miles of rolling terrain. Her brush glided along the canvas, coloring a valley far below the summit of Snowdon, the tallest mountain in the country.

In her painting, a fairy flew over the peak of the mountain. It was a scene she had painted over and over since childhood. The fantasy world she carried inside her had sustained her during her first years in England, and now that her heart was broken, she had returned to the images and stories that had comforted her as a girl. This was her favorite spot to come and paint: remote, far from the trail, a place where she could be alone with her thoughts. She knew every crest and lake in the park. Snowdonia had been her sanctuary for the past twenty years—a place that knew her laughter, her tears, and her secret.

Even though she and Alfred often had sought out this spot to picnic and be alone together, she refused to stop coming here just because he had broken off their engagement. The place had been hers before it had been theirs, and now it would be hers again. Never mind that every time she heard pebbles rolling down the mountain, her heart leaped and she looked for him to appear. She knew that he would not seek her out again. Alfred loved her, but he had been clear: He couldn't start a life with her, knowing what he knew.

For the hundredth time, she cursed herself for telling him the truth. She had kept her promise to Karl Decker for twenty years. She had never spoken to anyone of the little she knew or remembered of her father and had told herself the story about being the daughter of Austrian farmers until she practically believed it herself.

As a teenager, she had often come here to reflect on her life before she came to England and the night of her escape from Berlin. She could still recall bits and pieces: her father reading to her and tucking her in, the way the tree knocked at the window in her room, and the magical, secret workshop where she had painted with the artists who she now understood had conspired with her father. She remembered too the gunfire in her own home, running through the streets of Berlin with Karl, a bustling train station, and the strange scene of Karl giving a painting to a passenger as the train pulled away. When she had first arrived in England, she thought often of her father's admonition to always tell the truth, and then of her promise to Karl. In time, the story that Karl had invented for her became her truth, and the details of her old life began to fade.

Especially because after the horror of that night, fortune had swung her way.

When the sub docked in mid-October 1942, she had been bused to London, where she spent weeks at an orphanage. In December, she was adopted by Lord George and Lady Lona Atwell, Baron and Baroness Trefwyn, a Welsh couple whose first child had died during infancy. They said to her that first year, and every year since, that she was their greatest Christmas gift.

The woman who oversaw the orphanage had changed the child's name from Katharina to Katherine, or Kate. But the matron had not been able to change what was in Kate's heart—at least not at first. Kate had hated the other girls in the orphanage, the food, and the gray winter skies of London, but when she went home with the Atwells, they made her the center of their universe. They taught her English, Welsh, and French and enrolled her in a primary school where she learned to read and write. It hadn't taken long for her to understand the depth of their love and compassion.

School had been a different story. The children taunted her while her English skills were still poor, pointing at her and shouting things like, "Heil your Hitler, Germ!" Always mindful of what Karl had said, she would shake her head and yell, "Austrian, not German!" but they were always ready with, "What language do you speak?" She felt loathed and isolated. She could not understand what she had done to deserve their enmity, especially when her life had become so miserable overnight. Not that she needed their pity, but all she wanted for a long, long time was to go back home, even though she knew it was impossible.

Lona told her it was because they feared her, and she couldn't help but think of how she had been taught to fear the Allied Powers. At the beginning, she would come home from school on the verge of tears, afraid to share her feelings with the Atwells. She didn't have the right words yet, and she didn't want to look fragile or demanding after they'd brought her home from the orphanage; they could always send her back.

Life improved when the war ended. She had become fluent in English, and her peers seemed to have forgotten she was a foreigner. New friends thought she was Welsh. When Kate was thirteen, George and Lona enrolled her in boarding school at Cheltenham Ladies' College in Gloucestershire, England, where she focused on art history. She came back to Beaumaris as often as she could throughout her teens. By then, she could barely remember growing up in Berlin, and the solitary hikes through Snowdonia helped her shake off the gloom she felt when she thought of her origins. She found peace in the mountains and would bring her canvas, easel, brushes, and palette into the open spaces, far from civilization, from people. The Atwells had even built a mountain cottage for her on the edge of a lake called Glaslyn, where she could spend days in creative privacy. That was where she first met Alfred. And where he told her it was over when she confided in him about her father.

She was twenty-eight now. Her friends were all married. Many even had children. But Kate was still living with her parents. She was still alone. She looked out to the northeast of the Snowdon Massif, over the rural villages of Nant Peris and Llanberis, as she filled in her canvas. Her neck was draped with beads of turquoise, her skin fair and porcelain but for a small scar cutting into her left eyebrow. It had healed to look like a fading pockmark. Waves of dark brown hair, almost black, matched the color of her eyes.

She heard the crunch of footsteps on pebbles.

"Miss Atwell?"

Over the ridge, she could see the balding head of Clive Mountjoy, her father's chauffeur and house steward.

"If you've come to steal me from these mountains, Clive, you can't outrun me."

A breeze picked up, causing her turquoise blouse to billow.

"I'm nimbler than I look for a man in his sixties."

"I'd like to see you make a go of it."

"Your father sent me to fetch you. We're to pick up Ms. Fossey at the estate and drive to the runway to meet the plane your father has chartered."

She sighed, then packed her equipment and went down the slope to greet him.

She followed him to a silver Jaguar a mile away. A twisting path through the mountains took them out of the national park, and soon they were crossing a bridge over the River Menai toward the island of Anglesey. The ruins of Beaumaris could be seen ahead, where the strait opened to the sea.

Kate remembered the first time she had been driven to this house. She had been a terrified, confused eight-year-old, sitting in the backseat with two strangers who called themselves her new mum and dad. She barely spoke English. And, at first, she hadn't really believed them when they told her that she would live with them in their castlelike château on Anglesey. Nothing about her life had felt permanent yet.

George and Lona had hired her first art tutor when she was ten. They had watched her lose herself in drawing and painting, taken her to galleries throughout Great Britain and to homes of affluent collectors. These visits fueled her creativity in ways a playground never could. She'd stay for hours without getting restless, then come home and paint for days on end.

During one of her earliest visits, she spotted a painting she recognized from her father's studio. She had been so excited at first, but after asking careful questions of George and Lona, she had come to understand that her father had been a thief. The paintings in his studio had all been forgeries. Around that time, she also learned what the war had been about: that the *Axis* had been fighting for genocide and totalitarianism, and the *Allies* for life and freedom. She had seen the cold light of fact: Ralf Speer had been a high-ranking Nazi official and a war criminal complicit in mass murder. Alongside his public career as Vice Minister of Propaganda and his dealings with Goebbels and Hitler, he had led a criminal personal life, operating a forgery workshop from his home. *Her* home.

She put away her few sweet memories of him. Fact was fact: Her father was a key figure in Hitler's regime. No matter what she remembered, he was a monster. His voice had once soothed her to sleep every night. Now it haunted her. He appeared in her nightmares, issuing orders of execution in the same tone he'd used to tuck her into bed: *This is art, my good little marauder.*

By age twelve, she had shivered to think her blood ran with his genes. While her friends sought to distance themselves from their parents, Kate only wanted to be closer to the Atwells, only wanted to reassure herself that she was *their* daughter, not Ralf Speer's. She never told anyone how she felt in her own skin, or that when she looked in the mirror, she saw a face like a killer's. Now she understood why Karl had made her promise, why she had rehearsed the story of being an orphan from Austria. Even after she knew what her father was, she told no one, not even the Atwells, of his identity, his role in the Third Reich. Only Alfred. And he had rejected her. Now she had to keep the secret of why.

From secret reading and research, she understood that Karl Decker had also been a forger and a close confidante of her father's. As far as she was concerned, Speer and Decker had deserved to die, even if it had been at the hand of the SS or Gestapo, who she'd believed were Allied soldiers at her young age. She had read the story of their end in her art history classes, but no one had ever learned how Nazi intelligence had discovered her father's forgery workshop. Kate didn't care. Justice—if there were such a thing in Berlin at the time—had been served by the bullets that had taken Karl Decker and Ralf Speer.

But one thing about that night still troubled her. It was the one of the few things she remembered clearly, and she thought of it every time she boarded a train. What had been so important about that particular painting, the oil of the brunette young girl with the pear, that Karl would risk his life and hers to deliver it to a man at a train station? She probably would never know, but that didn't change the fact that October 10, 1942, had been the luckiest night of her life. Her escape from Berlin had led her to Lord and Lady Atwell, and away from a genocidal fraudster.

Mountjoy turned into the driveway. Kate had never painted the château, and she wished now that she had time to bring out her watercolors. The gardenia bushes bloomed with their white flowers, and the bright walls and masonry had yet to take on the gray hues of winter. In a style inspired by the Loire Valley of France, the architecture emphasized vertical ascension, sweeping the eye along its windows and up to its spires. The chimneys and turrets formed an elaborate roofscape that reminded her of the skyline of a town. A pole jutted from the stonework of the south tower, waving the pattern of a red dragon *passant* on a green-and-white field—the flag of Wales.

"See you in a few," she told Mountjoy as he parked.

Down below, Lona Atwell was pruning a hedge of azaleas in a garden that sloped down to a private beach on the river. Kate wondered where George was. Most likely, she'd find him in the tea room or his library.

Inside, the household staff were scattered about the kitchens, storerooms, and laundry areas. On days the Atwells expected guests, they'd be polishing silver for the dining rooms, heating and scenting the steam room, and clearing leaves from the tennis court in the upper garden.

As she thought, George was in his library study, where he often read and smoked over a blend of Scotch whiskey. Kate had the fondest memories of her late-night talks with him in this room.

She could smell his fragrance as soon as she entered, a very particular concoction of old books, polished leather, whisky, and tobacco.

"Hello, Papa."

"Darling," he said. He was dusting his collection of ivory pipes on the fireplace mantel. The mantel itself was coated in copper. George had inherited and expanded his family's copper-smelting business based in Trefwyn, a growing industrial town in South Wales. He had promoted the building of a railway that would connect the copper mines of Trefwyn with the Swansea Bay ports. A former Conservative member of Parliament for Aberavon, he had championed the merits of Welsh copper in parliamentary debates and grown his father's fortune by helping Trefwyn become a major industrial center. "Mountjoy seems to have found you quickly."

"He knows my best hiding spots near the cottage."

"You should be careful spending all that time in the mountains, or you'll sprout the tail of a troll." His expression turned serious, and he pushed her hair from her face. "It's his loss, my love. Paris will help you forget him. And maybe you'll even find someone new."

"I don't want to find someone new," she said. "Maybe I'm meant to be alone."

Though never seen out of a suit in public, Baron Trefwyn preferred the comfort of his pajamas at home. He looked more like an academician than a business tycoon, with a head of unruly white hair and a look of permanent focus, like a mathematician seconds away from proving a theorem. He took her in his arms and held her as if she were a small child.

"What is your friend Colette up to?" he said, leading her to sit in one of the armchairs flanking the fireplace. "I haven't seen her all morning."

"I'm not sure anyone has ever seen her conscious in the morning."

"You'd better wake her. Make sure she packs everything. Last time I checked, her room looked like a hurricane had gone through it. I'd rather Mountjoy not have to send a new parcel to Paris every week."

"I'll go check on her."

"Be quick. The pilot will be waiting."

She headed upstairs. She'd met Colette Fossey in Worcester College at Oxford while studying the History of Art. After completing their postgraduate studies together at Oxford and attending art school, they had worked at a high-end art auction house in London. Thinking that she was moving back to Wales to marry Alfred, Kate had quit her job several months earlier to prepare for the wedding, but now that the wedding was off, she was left with no fiancé, and no job either. When her parents first suggested a fresh start in Paris, she had said no. But when they mentioned there was a position waiting for her at Pendelfarr Gallery with the renowned art consultant Victor Maxence, she had changed her mind. Especially because Monsieur Maxence had a job for Colette, too. The two young women would begin their new life in one week, sharing an apartment in Paris.

That was, if she could drag Colette out of bed. Kate knocked on the guest-room door. There was silence at first, but when she knocked again, she heard whispers, the ruffling of sheets, and a series of French-infused vowels that sounded like, "Just a minute."

When the door opened, Colette stood in the middle of the room, wrapped in a towel. She was a petite, buxom, natural blonde who dyed her hair a cabernet color. Her lips were pouty and full, her sleepy eyelids splattered with freckles.

"What time is it?" Colette said.

"Noon," Kate said. "I hope you're packed."

"An extra hour wouldn't kill us."

"How could you sleep with that window open? It's drafty in here."

Kate stepped inside before Colette could protest. Reaching for the window, she spotted a man climbing down from the balcony. She watched him slink through the garden, pulling up his trousers.

"Who is he? The tennis instructor my mother and father hired for you?"

"A bartender from the village."

Kate lifted an eyebrow.

"You're supposed to take my side on these things," Colette went on. "Help make sure the coast is clear, not give me a sermon."

"He looked a bit young. That's all I was thinking."

"You only saw his backside."

"I thought you'd go for the tennis instructor. He fancies you, and he aspires to be a great athlete."

"He's too polite, which makes for a dull athlete where it counts. Listen, I'm going to find you a gorgeous man in Paris. Then you'll bring him back to this house and discover what the steam room and tower bedrooms are for."

"I need time to be alone for a while," Kate said.

"Just because Alfred was an idiot doesn't mean there aren't a million men out there who'll love you!" Colette took a seat on the bed. "I wish you would tell me what really happened, but even if you don't, I just want to say, since we're starting a new chapter together today, that whatever's holding you back . . . from being yourself and loving life . . . it's idiotic."

Kate bristled, but only because she knew Colette was on to something.

"There's nothing holding me back. It's just that I imagined one life for myself, and now I have to plan for another. It isn't easy starting all over again."

"Well, we're starting all over again together," Colette said, "and I wouldn't have been able to have done half the stuff I have since I met you without you and your parents. You have everything. You can do and be whatever you want, and maybe you feel guilty about that, maybe you feel . . ."

"Feel what?"

"That you don't deserve to be happy."

"That's ridiculous," Kate said, but she knew her friend was right. She'd had the great good luck of being George and Lona's daughter, but her biological father had been responsible for a vast number of deaths. Ever since she'd learned the truth about him and the war, she felt morally tainted, like someone born with a debt she could never pay. She had tried to clear her conscience by telling Alfred the truth, but look where that got her. Now Kate knew for sure that she could never discuss her past with Colette.

Colette came from a lower-middle-class family in Barfleur, a small town on the Normandy coast. Her parents had been killed by Nazi forces. Before they became close friends, Kate had told Colette her cover story, and the two young women bonded over the fact they had both been orphaned during the war. It was a strong bond, Kate knew, and one that transcended their temperamental differences. Over the years, Kate had considered telling Colette the truth, but now she was glad she hadn't.

She wondered whether their friendship would survive if Colette knew Kate's true father ranked among the Fosseys' murderers.

"Alfred was crazy to break it off, but now you can go out and find someone else. You don't have to feel bad about that. Leave those feelings behind when we fly off to Paris," Colette said. "And if you can't right away, at least maybe you'll tell me what really happened between you two."

"One step at a time," Kate said. "You haven't even packed yet, and we're leaving in less than an hour."

Kate started to close the door.

"You can tell me anything," Colette said. "Don't forget it, Kate."

Anything but this, she wanted to say.

"That's why you're my favorite conspirator." Kate smiled. "Now pack your damned suitcase. I'm going to Paris with or without you."

Kate headed downstairs, wondering how someone so different had become her soul mate. At first, their shared experience had made her feel less alone in the world. But now it was more than that. Maybe it was because Colette helped her feel connected to people and the pleasures of living. Colette was a social butterfly with a fearless approach to life; Kate was a disciplined introvert. Living vicariously through her friend, she could forget the baggage of her past and imagine what it was like to be a free spirit.

Kate waited by the Jaguar with her family and Clive Mountjoy, who helped Colette with her bags as she came out the front door.

"Bon voyage to you both," Lona said. "Travel safely."

"I'll miss you, darlings," George said. "Work hard. Find us more paintings."

"Write from Paris," Lona added.

Kate hugged her father and then her mother, bidding one final farewell as she got into the car with Colette. She looked toward Snowdonia and bid Alfred a silent goodbye once and for all.

Mountjoy drove the young women to a private airfield in the woodland, where a pilot awaited their arrival and helped them board a Cessna 170. Kate had been taking flying lessons in this plane recently, but she was not yet proficient enough to fly solo or handle passengers of her own.

The propeller buzzed into a spin, making a racket in the cabin as the aircraft aligned with the runway and gained speed. The wings quivered and steadied. As they lifted from the asphalt, Kate replayed Colette's words in her head.

We're starting a new chapter today.

Whatever's holding you back . . . from being yourself and loving life . . . it's idiotic.

Leave those feelings behind when we fly off to Paris.

If only Colette knew how hard that was.

Colette

A week had passed since Kate and Colette arrived in Paris and moved into their apartment on the Rue Dauphine. They'd had three days to settle in before they started their jobs at Pendelfarr Gallery, and used them to find a rhythm to their days and nights in Paris. They woke early, stopped at the corner bakery on their walk to work, and opened the gallery before the brokers arrived around ten. They spent their days manning the reception desk and serving as secretaries for the sales agents, who shared one large office in the back. It had been two weeks, but they still had not met Victor Maxence.

Colette couldn't say which made her happier—that Paris was her territory, or that it was *not* Kate's. If it hadn't been for Alfred breaking up with Kate, she never would have had this job. At first, when the Atwells called her about moving to Paris, she had been insulted that George and Lona were buying their daughter companionship and comfort. But the more she'd thought about it, the more she realized that any job was better than the one she'd had in the gallery in London. Besides, she had spent so much time in Wales being treated like the fortunate recipient of the Atwells' generosity that, at least in Paris, she could take the lead again.

Colette had not been nearly as lucky as her friend in the aftermath of the war. After her parents were killed, she had grown up with her aunt and uncle, owners of a small shop that sold groceries and periodicals. They had made her start working at the store when she turned seven. She had been a nuisance to them otherwise.

As a child, she'd been fascinated by fashion magazines from Paris. She loved flipping through the pages, choosing favorite outfits, and inviting the neighborhood girls to dress paper dolls with cutouts. They talked about the glamorous lives they imagined they'd live in the capital, and Colette spent her days dreaming of moving to the big city. Meanwhile, her aunt and uncle disapproved of her infatuation with an industry they called shallow and forbade her from collecting the fashion magazines.

During the summer of 1953, a photographer for a modeling agency, passing through Barfleur, had spotted Colette in the shop and asked if he could take her to Paris, where she could model. Her uncle had refused on the grounds that she was too young and corruptible. But Colette found the opportunity so alluring that she left home at once, accompanying the photographer and moving in with him as his girlfriend.

She spent the next two years modeling in Paris, rising through the ranks until she achieved a moderate degree of celebrity in fashion circles. She had enjoyed the lifestyle—money, sycophants, men, the chance to be photographed in fine clothes. Still, the creative process intrigued her more than the runways. Colette wanted to be a designer.

But the photographer belittled her artistic ambitions and, upon taking to the bottle, began physically abusing her. Fleeing his residence at eighteen, she went back to her aunt and uncle in Barfleur. They refused to take her in, telling her she had turned her back on her family, and they didn't accept strangers or charity cases.

She'd been desperate. She'd known her modeling career wouldn't last but a few more years, and having lost her aunt and uncle's support, she needed to invest in an education. The editor of a fashion magazine for which she'd modeled, one of the few men who'd shown her kindness, had been a graduate of Oxford and a friend of the provost of Worcester College. He'd managed to secure her a spot and a small scholarship. She worked hard to overcome her educational deficiencies as she pursued a degree in the History of Art.

She met Kate in college. They became good friends, and she deeply admired Kate's artistic ability. Despite her introversion and cautious attitude, Kate was known at the university as the "lucky one," thanks to her family's fortune—and her looks. Colette had admitted to herself, not without difficulty, that Kate was the true beauty of the two of them; she simply hadn't learned to use her gift like the weapon it was. The poor girl didn't invite any risk, danger, or complications into her life.

That was where Colette came in. From the first night they had gone out together, she had made Kate bolder and brighter than she ever would have been on her own. When Colette learned that Kate had been orphaned during the war, she began to see her friend differently. Soon they were inseparable. Colette knew in her heart that she had initially latched on to Kate because she enjoyed all the trappings of Kate's lifestyle, but over time, she actually came to love the girl whom she now called her best friend, though Colette remained conscious of their difference in wealth and status.

On their first day of work, Kate emerged from her room in a conservative black dress and black pumps, carrying a pocket-size guide to Paris.

"You can put the map away," Colette told her confidently. "Follow me."

The gallery was tucked away in a complex of buildings between the Quai Malaquais and the Rue Bonaparte, near a famous art school, the École Nationale Supérieure des Beaux-Arts. Term was starting, and all around, students flocked to their classrooms.

As Colette opened the door to the gallery, a church bell pealed nine o'clock. They were supposed to arrive at 8:30, but it had been a slow morning, and she'd had a fight with her hairspray.

"*Bienvenue.*"

Colette swung around to see where the voice had come from, and Kate stepped up beside her.

The man before them was tall and gaunt, dressed in a white shirt and black vest, a black tie with white polka dots, and a beret. Seeing his mustache and thin, triangular beard, Colette imagined him mounted on a horse, carrying a lance and shield, followed by a pudgy sidekick as he chased a windmill. She held back a chuckle. Her amusement gave way to discomfort when he spoke again. His voice had the gravity of a man who had forgotten what it meant to laugh.

"*Je suis Victor Maxence et vous êtes en retard.*"

"*Je suis très désolée, Monsieur Maxence,*" Colette said immediately. *I'm very sorry, Mr. Maxence.* "It won't happen again." She kept her eyes down, waiting for him to say something else. It was no surprise he was intimidating. Maxence was famous in France not only for his own paintings, but for his acclaimed biographies of Degas, Matisse, Cézanne, and several German artists. He was a respected historian and art critic who had taught at the art school for thirty years, in addition to being a world-renowned art consultant.

"See that it doesn't," he said, his voice icy. Colette stole a glance at him, but he had turned his attention to Kate. "Ah, Mademoiselle Atwell." He oozed warmth all of a sudden and held his arms out. "It's a pleasure to meet you. I've worked with your parents periodically. Lovely people."

Kate stepped forward awkwardly, and Maxence kissed her on both cheeks before linking arms with her and starting to walk her around the gallery. Kate looked at Colette, who had gone to tidy up the reception desk and was trying to be invisible. She rolled her eyes and gave an almost imperceptible shrug, but Colette barely noticed. She was seething, and in that moment she resented her best friend, even if Maxence's partiality wasn't Kate's fault.

"I have a proposal for you and Mademoiselle Fossey," Colette overheard him saying. She glanced up, but when Maxence looked at her, she lost her nerve and sat down at the desk. "I've been working with Monsieur Pendelfarr for many years, but we only opened this gallery a year ago."

"You have wonderful pieces," Kate said. Flattering the man as best she could, Colette thought. "Colette and I feel lucky to work here."

Colette softened a bit toward her friend, but as she checked on the brokers' office and began to make coffee, she sighed. As long as they were together, she would be overshadowed by the Atwell name. On the upside, her job was safe, at least for today. At twenty-eight, she couldn't go back to modeling, and she had no marriage prospects on the horizon. Without this position, she wouldn't be able to stay in Paris. And if she fell out of favor with Maxence, it would be difficult to find another place in the art world, at least in Europe.

". . . As with my research into the life of Ernst." Colette wandered back into the gallery as Maxence droned on. He had shifted into professor mode, and his voice was a heavy dose of morphine via the ears. ". . . Similar to what she had learned in Sicily, from her instructor and lover . . . with a delicate treatment of chiaroscuro as to approach the style of his master, Vermeer . . ."

Colette watched as Kate dutifully nodded and smiled while Maxence brought her to the next painting on the wall. It should have been easier to listen to a man who knew so much, but Colette's mind had begun to drift as the old man went on about the prominent artists he'd been so fortunate to meet.

". . . Much like the post-World War I originals of a man I admit I had actually, rather astonishingly, respected as an artist: Ralf Speer. I even wrote a biography of him."

She saw Kate stiffen and pull her arm away from Maxence.

Colette walked over, her anger evaporating in the face of Kate's uneasiness. Her friend's face had blanched. She was clenching her fists so hard the blood had left her knuckles.

"I heard you say you had a proposal for us, Monsieur Maxence," Colette said, boldly drawing his attention away from Kate and whatever he was saying about German artists.

"I most certainly do," he said, clearing his throat. "I'd like you to throw a first anniversary soirée for this gallery in Paris."

Colette couldn't help herself. She clasped her hands together with delight. As she looked at Kate, though, her enthusiasm dimmed. "You okay?" she whispered as Maxence started to explain his vision for the soirée.

"I'm fine," Kate said shortly.

But Kate had always been a terrible liar. Colette wondered what was the matter.

Katharina

The moment Maxence pronounced Ralf Speer's name, it was as if a firecracker had exploded inside the room. Kate's heart started pounding so hard, she was afraid someone would hear it. She spilled coffee over the papers at the reception desk and stayed in the gallery instead of going to lunch with Colette, who Kate worried had noticed her odd behavior.

Colette returned abuzz with ideas for the soirée. Kate tried to listen and focus, but her mind wandered, brooding over Maxence's remark. So, he had written a biography of her father. Kate tried to make herself indifferent, but there was no cheating the curiosity that had taken hold of her.

It was only when the brokers had left the building and Kate and Colette were finishing for the day that her nerves finally subsided. Colette turned to her and asked, "What did Maxence say to you? You turned white as snow this morning."

"My breakfast must not have agreed with me."

"You promised you'd tell me the truth from now on," Colette said. "The whole truth."

"I am," she said as they walked home past the groups of students gathered at the sidewalk cafés. As they passed the library, she glanced through the open door to a beautiful courtyard. For a moment she longed to be a student again, to go back to the time before she had met Alfred, when all things were possible.

They walked in silence for a while, and Kate felt relieved her friend didn't press the issue.

"With or without Maxence's permission," Colette said, "I'm going to invite my modeling friends to the party. I want it to be full of the most beautiful art and the most beautiful people in Paris."

"Just don't get carried away," Kate warned. "It should be elegant, not brash."

She felt the flash of annoyance from Colette before hearing the steel in her friend's voice. "I know you have elegant covered. All I have to offer is brash."

"Oh, Colette, I didn't mean it like that." Kate rushed to keep up with her friend, who had started walking faster. "Invite your friends. Invite everyone you know. It can be elegant *and* fun. Just like you."

Colette looked at her, and Kate could see her decide not to stay upset. "It's going to be a party no one will forget. We'll get the jazz ensemble from last night. Hor d'oeuvres from Le Grand Véfour. Vintage Moët. We'll open up the back garden." Kate only half listened as Colette chattered all the way home.

Kate poured herself a glass of wine and sank down on the sofa; Colette was still talking. "I have a date tonight," she called from her room before emerging in a shimmery gold dress, an updo, and dramatically lined eyes. Her transformation had been breathtakingly quick. Colette giggled. "With Philippe. One of the brokers."

"You sure that's a good idea?" Kate arched an eyebrow.

"It's a *great* idea," Colette said, taking Kate's wineglass and finishing the last few sips. "If he has a friend, I'll call you to come and meet us."

Kate couldn't help but smile at her friend's exuberance. "Not tonight. Tonight's all yours."

"I'll let you off the hook this once," Colette said, turning slightly more serious, "but you have to get out more."

Kate helped Colette into her coat, secretly delighted to be left alone for the evening. She could contemplate Maxence's words in peace. The door closed, and Kate listened to the clicking of Colette's heels as she traipsed down the stairs to the street.

As many times as she had looked for information about Ralf Speer in art textbooks, she had found very little, even in the library at Oxford. Perhaps she would find Maxence's biography in Paris. She had always dreaded what she might discover, and today was no different. But now that she knew such a volume existed, she had to get her hands on it. There were three bookshops on her walk to work. None of them specialized in art or history; it would be difficult to find something so obscure.

The library of the École Nationale Supérieure des Beaux-Arts, she thought. She had seen into its courtyard this afternoon. She would find a way to go tomorrow.

. . .

The next day, when one of the brokers sent Colette on an errand, Kate saw her chance to slip away unnoticed. She took a piece of Pendelfarr Gallery stationery and typed a quick note:

> *I hereby certify that Katherine Atwell is an employee of the Pendelfarr Gallery. Please allow her access to the École Nationale Supérieure des Beaux-Arts library.*

She glanced around at the empty gallery. No one was paying much attention to her. She signed Victor Maxence's name at the bottom of the letter, grabbed her coat, and practically ran out the door. She knew she didn't have much time.

When she arrived, she slipped her note to the librarian.

"I'm looking for Victor Maxence's biography of Ralf Speer," Kate said, practically whispering her father's name. The librarian didn't bat an eye as she walked to the card catalog, flipped through the cards, and noted the book's call number on a slip of paper she passed to Kate.

"Down three levels on the left," the librarian said. "If you need more help, I'll be here."

As Kate stepped off the elevator and into the dark stacks, she was reminded of the library at Oxford. She had loved it there, but this library was tailor-made to her interests, and she thrilled to think of the treasures within. She flipped on light after light, stopping at the end of a long shelf marked with numbers that corresponded to those on her paper.

She trailed her finger along the shelf until she found it. It was a slim book, no doubt reflecting the small amount of information available on her father. She sat down, leaned against one of the bookshelves, and opened to the introduction:

> *Ralf Speer was born in 1890 in the Pomeranian town of Stolp. His father, Helmut, was an iron foundry worker and sculptor by hobby. His mother was a strict Calvinist. Both were from Döbeln, Saxony.*
>
> *In 1908 Speer enrolled in the University of Bonn, studying art history, psychology, psychiatry, and literature. In 1910 he spent time in France visiting museums and copying many paintings. He came to*

admire Rubens, Rembrandt, and Blake, as well as Northern European artists of the early Renaissance and late Middle Ages, namely Dürer, Grünewald, Bosch, and Bruegel. As a frequenter of artistic circles in Paris, he met fellow art students as well as some masters, and took trips to Italy and the Netherlands to cultivate his network. In 1912 he met August Macke, with whom he traveled to Thessaloniki, Mount Athos, and various other Greek sites, capturing seaside villages on oil canvas. In 1914 he was invited to accompany Macke and the artists Paul Klee and Louis Moilliet to Tunisia, where Macke painted some of his greatest masterpieces of the luminist approach and influenced Speer's prewar style.

In late 1914 Speer was drafted into the Kaiserliche Marine *(German Imperial Navy) for the Great War. He joined in August as an officer cadet and served on torpedo boat units, and as a watch officer aboard Kaiser Wilhelm II's yacht SMY* Hohenzollern*. In December 1914 he was reassigned to the* Seydlitz*, a battle cruiser of the I Scouting Group of the High Seas Fleet, and participated in a number of coastal raids of English seaport towns. In early January 1915 he fought in the Battle of Dogger Bank: During morning battle, the* Seydlitz *was struck by a 343-mm shell from the British* Lion *in her forecastle, and then by another shell, which breached her rear barbette and detonated the propellant charges within the chamber. Speer was injured and nearly lost his leg, incurring instead a lifelong limp that would soon force him to walk with a cane. Despite his injury he continued serving at sea through the Battle of Jutland under the command of Admiral Franz von Hipper. This ended July 1, 1916. Speer was awarded the Iron Cross, 2nd Class.*

Kate realized how little she knew about her biological father. All she had were memories of a gentle voice reading bedtime fables, memories made by a little girl who had yet to learn the meaning of evil. Even the cause of his limp was news to her. More than that, she had forgotten he'd had one. Now she remembered it well. She continued to read:

After Jutland, and as a result of his injury, Speer was to be transferred. When he listed his primary skill as "painting," he was sent to the Tuchola prisoner-of-war camp to process prisoner documents. Until his discharge in 1918, Speer lived in a guardhouse outside a row of barracks. He describes his experience in his memoirs and attributes his artistic transformation to the horrors witnessed at Tuchola. Speer was appalled by the mistreatment of the predominantly Russian and Romanian prisoners, and the smaller fraction from Western Entente countries. He despised his post and was initially outspoken about the exploitation of inmates, but was later threatened into silence by fellow guards.

Speer's chronicles of Tuchola tell us that he had befriended a distraught Romanian prisoner, a man who had lost the last remaining photograph of his daughter, "Catina," in battle and wished to see his child's face before he died. Speer offered to paint a portrait based on the man's physical description of her, but before he could present his completed work, the prisoner was shot. The man's death epitomized the horrors of war to Speer who, in the throes of a depression that would last years, wrote: "I felt I had come to know the girl in my painting, and had wanted to hear her father say: 'That's her, my Catina.' I knew that, should I one day father a girl, I would name her Katharina in tribute."

A shiver ran down her spine as she learned the origin of her name. So, her war criminal of a father had known compassion once. Had he been born with a conscience and lost his humanity with age? Had something changed him when Hitler rose to power?

After his service in the Great War, Speer's art developed a distinctive expressionist style, wherein he distorted and blackened physical reality for emotional effect. His paintings reflected his altered vision of himself as a tormentor, and guilt over having fought for the Central Powers in the Great War. He began painting men as either oppressors or oppressed, the former having monstrous faces and the latter appearing frail and vulnerable.

There had been a time when her father had believed in right and wrong. But then, every criminal was innocent at some point in life. There was always a story of decline, a fall from grace. What was his?

In the early 1920s, a series of retrospective exhibitions in Munich and at the Kunsthalle Mannheim earned Speer fame and official honors during the Weimar Republic. His art appeared in a range of publications. In 1928 he was chosen to teach a master class at Städelschule Academy of Fine Art in Frankfurt, and in 1931 the National Gallery of Berlin purchased several of his paintings. It was at one of his exhibitions that he met Florentine Hess, a schoolteacher and admirer of his work. She moved into his home in Berlin.

Hitler became Chancellor in January 1933. At the time, his regime was popular with the German people, in whose eyes the failures of the Weimar Republic had discredited democracy. In April 1933, Ralf and Florentine were married. On May 22, 1934, Florentine gave birth to their daughter, Katharina Speer. Florentine died of tuberculosis in 1940.

In 1939, Speer was appointed Vice Minister of Propaganda under Joseph Goebbels. Speer and over a dozen artists were executed on October 10, 1942, during an SS raid on his home ordered by Hitler. It was discovered that he had been operating an art forgery workshop from a hidden basement.

She flipped through the pages, where his later paintings were printed —windows into a disturbed soul, all of them. They made her shudder. Finally, she arrived at a photograph of Ralf Speer himself.

Though she would not have been able to describe him before, in that moment, she remembered his face well, down to the details—the way the lines, planes, and crags came together with grave solemnity. There was a quiet pride in his expression, too, as if about the Nazi uniform he was wearing. The photograph must have been taken soon before he died. She looked for more images, a candid photo that might have included her mother, or perhaps even her. Nothing.

She read through the short biography once more and then flipped back to the photo. With a glance at her watch, she realized she had been gone more than an hour. Impulsively, she ripped the photo from the book and put it in her purse. She put the book back in its place on the shelf and started toward the staircase, turning off the lights as she went. The aisles behind her went dark.

Victor

Victor often had been asked to hire the children of collectors, but this was the first time he had taken on a family member *and* her friend. The Atwells were important clients, so he had little choice but to accept, but now that he had met them, he had misgivings. Kate Atwell certainly looked the part of an elegant, refined young woman, but the redheaded friend had a certain rebellious disposition that was sure to draw the wrong kind of attention. Which was the last thing the gallery needed.

He heard a tapping at the door as he started to gather his coat to head home for dinner.

"Come in."

"Monsieur Maxence? I'm sorry to bother you, but I wonder if you could tell me more about Ralf Speer." It was Kate Atwell herself.

"Have a seat, mademoiselle," he said. "Quickly. I only have a moment."

He was surprised she would bring up the topic again. When he mentioned Speer's name the day before, he couldn't help but notice that her entire body tensed.

"I was an early fan of his work," the professor went on, "and in 1928, I attended Speer's master class at Städelschule Academy of Fine Art in Frankfurt, unaware that he would become . . . well, you know."

"What was he like?" She was looking at the artwork on the walls of his office. There were a few icons, and a pair of framed reproductions of fifteenth-century oils. One depicted a humanlike form with a single large leg, screaming under a red-hot iron; the other was a Naiad being raped on a riverbank by a goat-headed creature. She twisted her hands in her lap.

"I only met him briefly. He was a calculating individual." She was clearly steeling herself for something. For what, he couldn't guess. "What exactly do you want to know?"

"How it felt to meet him," she said.

"The subjects of my biographies don't make me 'feel' one way or another. My interest is academic." He considered her for a moment. He was accustomed to young people being nervous around him, but never this nervous. "Come with me. I want to show you something."

He led her down a narrow hallway into the supply closet. Pulling out a cart, he revealed a hidden door that opened to a spiral staircase.

"We don't keep much down here," he said as they descended together, "but I do have a few pieces from my personal collection. And since I see you have some interest in German painters . . ."

He walked to the corner and stood before a dark painting depicting a father holding the lifeless body of his daughter. He watched her face twist with distaste.

"What is this?" she asked.

"A Speer original. His work is valuable for those who are interested in this kind of thing."

"It's a horrible piece," Kate said. "No wonder you keep it in the basement."

"The horror is what makes it wonderful. I'm interested in the psychological transformation we see through his work. The shift from the lighter tone of his early pieces to the darkness later in his career, when he became an art forger and Nazi official. He painted portraits of this Romanian prisoner of war and his daughter until soon before he was killed himself."

"Catina," she said under her breath. "Frankly, I don't see much to appreciate here."

"So, you read my book," he said. Perhaps there was more to Kate Atwell than he had first believed.

"What happened to his daughter?" she asked. The young woman stared, mesmerized, at the painting, in spite of the fact that it obviously repulsed her.

"The man in this painting died in a POW camp with Speer, and his wife and daughter were killed during World War I."

"No," she said, turning to look him in the eye, her gaze severe. "Speer's own daughter. Katharina."

Maxence felt the hair on the back of his neck stand up. What was this woman playing at?

"No one really knows. After her father was killed, she was spirited to England, where she must have been adopted like many war orphans.

Many people were interested in her whereabouts after the war, but in the years since, interest has died down. We may never know where she is or who she is."

The young woman nodded and then walked to the staircase, leading the way back up.

"Thank you for talking with me, Monsieur Maxence."

They stood for a moment in the darkened hallway. "Why so interested in Ralf Speer, mademoiselle? The man was a monster, after all. An exceptional artist, yes, but a monster."

"Was he an exceptional artist, monsieur, given the number of works he copied? A forger is simply a thief, after all."

"Certainly," he agreed, but something stirred inside him. Kate Atwell was young and inexperienced, but there was something more there, something he wasn't seeing. At least not yet. "A talent, yes. But still a thief."

. . .

Victor Maxence locked the gallery door after Kate Atwell. He sat at his desk in silence, nearly certain that her interest in Ralf Speer was personal. He thought of the way she looked and sounded. Her eyes had been glassy, her voice shaky. Her dark hair and eyes floated before him, and suddenly he was struck by the strangest idea.

He picked up the phone. "This is Victor Maxence. Have I reached the admissions office at Oxford? . . . Please connect me. . . . Yes, hello, I've a favor to ask. . . . I'm looking for information on a young woman working at my gallery. Could you please look up a file on a student by the name of Kate Atwell? . . . Yes, I'll wait. . . . Good, now see if the application lists her nationality. . . . Welsh? Does the application list what languages she speaks? . . . What are the four languages? . . . I thought so—French, English, Welsh, and *German* . . . Okay, *merci*."

He dialed another number.

"Victor Maxence here. This is the financial department, correct? . . . All right, I have a request. Please check your records for the names George and Lona Atwell. . . . Wealthy Welsh art collectors, who I'll be meeting with, and I'm curious about their background—what pieces they might buy, what they've bought, anything you might know about their family. . . . That's right, Lord and Lady Atwell. . . . Good, that's promising purchase history. . . . What do the records say about family? . . . Please look some more. There should be some notes on file, detailed notes, even on personal things. We keep these for all our clients. I want to come to this meeting prepared. . . . A former Conservative member of Parliament? Then his family records should be a bit more public. . . . I thought so. Do the Atwells have children? . . . A daughter? You said she was adopted? You're certain? . . . From where? . . . I understand, not everything is listed. What year did they adopt? . . . Yes, I know you only have limited information on each collector, but this is important. . . . 1942, you say? Is that all you have? . . . That's all right. You've been helpful. *Merci.*"

He hung up.

The more he thought about it, the more it made sense.

With a sheet of stationery on his desk, he composed a telegram:

Conrad,
I think I've found her.
Victor

Katharina

September came and went, and though she hadn't thought it possible, she began to think less about Alfred. October found Kate often strolling along the Seine or reading in parks and gardens, trying not to think of Maxence's writings on her father. The account of Speer's early life had given him flesh and blood, showing her the man beneath the malice, reminding her he'd been a real person. Luckily, she had Colette's obsession with Parisian nightlife to keep her distracted. Not to mention the anniversary celebration they were planning for the gallery, which was only eight weeks away.

By November, the two of them spent most of their time, at work and at home, discussing ideas for the party, which they had decided would be a Christmas soirée. Temperatures had bottomed below freezing that month, and the cold weather had kept even Colette at home more often than before. By December, if they did go out, they spent their time with Philippe and his cohort. While Colette's circle of friends widened daily, Kate was content with the city, her work, and time with Colette alone. She had refused steadfastly the few brave suitors who had tried to spend time with her. She also had purchased a Renault Floride and driven it through the hills of Epernay now and again—but never with company, and with decreasing frequency. It seemed Colette used the car for weekend trips more often than she did.

Kate didn't mind. She loved Paris. She watched France in the process of rebuilding its identity and reclaiming its great power status; the nation had only begun to emerge from World War II and the Algerian War. The streets blazed with a sense of optimism and Christmas spirit. The Champs-Élysées was festooned with tinsel and garlands, impromptu dance scenes could be seen by the river and in ice skating rinks, and luxury specialty shops stayed open well into the night. The spirit of the students going to and fro near the gallery was not at all dampened by the weather. Kate enjoyed watching them, and although she still passed the library every day, she had not gone in again.

Finally, the night of the soirée arrived. It was a Friday, and Kate and Colette had spent all day attending to the final details. They had left themselves an hour to come home and get ready.

Kate waited anxiously for Colette, who was fifteen minutes behind schedule when she finally emerged from the bathroom wearing a scarlet, backless dress and velvet gloves. Her cheeks were tinted with rouge, her hair done in a low beehive with bangs and adorned with a rhinestone brooch.

Kate grabbed her car keys, but Colette stopped her.

"Taxi, no Renault," Colette said, dropping a cigarette case into her clutch. "I told Philippe you own a Ferrari."

"Why on earth did you do that?"

"There are expectations that go along with your wealth." Colette's references to the Atwell fortune always made Kate uncomfortable.

"You mean my parents' wealth," Kate said. "And a car is just a way to get around."

"Would you accommodate me this one night?"

Kate didn't feel like fighting, and besides, they were already late. They hailed a cab.

"Musée de Montmartre," Colette told the driver. She turned to Kate as if to reassure her. "It's going to be a fabulous evening. You know how I know?"

"You managed to put your eyelashes on perfectly the first try?"

"Because we're young and in Paris. Because we look ravishing. Because we've spent months planning this party. And if you aren't in the arms of a man by midnight, I'm forever losing hope. You know Stefan? The broker who works at the desk next to Philippe? I know he wants to get to know you. Not to mention all the men who try to talk to you wherever we go. None have the courage to ask you to dinner. You're a wall of ice."

It was one of those things Colette would never understand. Part of the peace Kate had found during the past three months had come from her decision not to start anything romantic. What was the point, if she could never be honest without scaring a man away? *By the way, my father was worse than a serial killer, and if we ever had children together, they'd have his genes*. My *genes*.

Out the window, she could see the illuminated dome of the Sacré-Coeur Basilica. They had begun climbing Montmartre on their way to the Christmas soirée. In the end, the guest list had grown far too large for the gallery, and Victor Maxence's assistant had suggested that they have the party at the museum there.

"I think you'll like my game," Colette said.

"What game?"

"You'll see. Something I made up to help the guests mingle."

"As long as you're not playing matchmaker."

"I can't predict what will happen. At least you've dressed well tonight. All that money, and you never indulge in glamour. You're a waste, you know. Try to take advantage of tonight. Talk to everyone. Don't stay too long with any one person. If someone tries to corner you, say you have to refill your glass. Treat the attractive men like you haven't seen them in ages and everything they say is funny or fascinating. Charm. Glow."

"Are you quite finished?"

"It's not only about meeting a man," Colette admitted. "You have the world at your feet. Everyone knows your parents. Doors will open wide for you if you want. You could even have your own gallery someday. Now I'm finished."

Kate considered what Colette had said during the few moments they had before the taxi pulled to the curb and she paid the fare. Colette was right, but somehow it still felt like an insult rather than an encouragement. Colette often spoke as if Kate's name and wealth precluded the possibility of her earning or achieving anything on her own merits.

There was quite a crowd inside, and for a moment, Kate worried that something wasn't done, that there might have been an important task that she and Colette had forgotten. But that was impossible, and she reminded herself that her job was to charm, to mingle, to represent what was beautiful and desirable about Pendelfarr Gallery to the patrons. She smoothed her turquoise cocktail dress and stepped out of the taxi. A natural five-foot-nine, she was positively statuesque with heels on. Her white earrings matched her lace and pearl fascinator and drew out the dark hues of her hair. As the cab drove away, for an instant Kate saw Colette staring at her with an expression that was hard to decrypt. Her eyes had narrowed, and she seemed distant, as if taking Kate in, from head to toe, as a rival rather than a friend.

Colette's expression gave way to a smile, and she said, "Shall we dazzle?"

"As ever."

Inside they were greeted by carolers—the gentlemen in top hats and overcoats, the ladies in plaid dresses and bonnets—crooning traditional French Christmas melodies. The gallery was brightly lit and full of photographs and paintings. The art on display was the one thing Colette and Kate had not been responsible for. Maxence had chosen the most exquisite and most expensive pieces to show clients that night.

Guests milled about the exhibition, chatting and laughing. An art student she and Colette had hired passed by, handing out slippers stuffed with candies and trinkets—"Treats from *Père Noël*!" She saw Colette across the room kissing the cheeks of what could only be her model friends. Determined to relax, Kate made her way to the bar, where she ordered a martini and gazed absentmindedly around the room as the bartender mixed it.

"May I ladle you some mulled wine?"

She turned around. Philippe's friend, Stefan, was standing there. Even though they had worked together for almost three months, Kate wouldn't have recognized him on the street. Broad, muscular, and square-jawed, he flashed a forceful grin.

"This will be perfect, thank you," she said, picking up her drink and tapping the rim of her glass against his. "Cheers."

"You're the Atwell girl, Colette's roommate?"

"Right."

He was a bit wobbly on his feet, probably a few drinks in.

"How'd you two meet?"

"At Oxford, for History of Art. We also worked together at a London auction house."

"I played rugby for a team in the Belgian Elite League, but tore a ligament in my knee." She smiled a bit at the non sequitur, wondering how long until she could get away.

"Sorry to hear."

"Yes, well, it forced me to change career paths and pursue my secondary passion for the visual arts, but I'm very happy now."

"It must have been quite a switch."

"It was. I played fullback. Most of my family was glad about my decision," he said. "They were happier to see me holding a paintbrush than catching kicks and punting balls. I come from a family of artists, see."

"Oh?"

"A long line, actually. You might possibly have heard of my not-too-distant cousin, René Magritte."

She wished she could say no, due to the pompous way he had said "might possibly," but she knew she couldn't get away with it.

"Really?" she said.

"Funny old man . . . though I prefer a more abstract sort of surrealism. Anything that's abstract, really. There's no sense in having a painting resemble reality, don't you think? That's what photography is for. I tell you, most artists are too . . . bound in the objective. Too dependent on visual reference. Too logical. I want color without form. Take Russian Constructivism, for instance. That's brilliance."

"You think so?"

"Those artists made their works become . . . well, life itself. Objects of the spirit, to help us find where we belong on this earth, if anywhere. Take Malevich, for instance: Have you ever seen something as remarkable as his *Red Square?*"

"As a matter of fact—"

"Or *Black Square?* Or *White on White?* And such eloquent words to describe his own art. He said, 'I have transformed myself in the zero of form and have fished myself out of the rubbishy pool of academic art. I have destroyed the ring of the horizon and got out of the circle of objects, the horizon ring that has imprisoned the artist and the forms of nature.' What's so amazing to me is the reduction of art from the conscious, conceptual level to . . ."

He made a grandiose gesture, searching for the right words.

"A soup of colors and smudges?" Kate ventured.

"When you put it that way, it sounds uninspired. But you must understand."

"I think I do. Is that the kind of painting you sell? Like the *Red Square?*"

He kicked back his head in laughter and took the opportunity to glide a hand over her shoulders, maneuvering himself away from the wall and sealing her in the corner.

"That's what speaks to me, but I try, I really do, to open myself to other influences. Like abstract expressionism. And I've tried painting myself, some drip-style. But I don't only do abstract. If I feel uninspired, some semblance of human form might come through. It must be in my subconscious, but that's how my human figures usually are. I guess it's my rejection of the idea that man could ever rise to his proclaimed ideals or be anything but a beast at the core. That's what we are, after all. Animals. So that's how I paint us. I'll show you my studio sometime."

"I *would* accept," she said, lifting his arm away, "if our philosophies of art were compatible. Thank you for the conversation, Stefan. I'm going to listen to the carolers."

His cheeks turned pink as she freed herself and walked into the other room. She suddenly missed Alfred terribly, in spite of everything. If these were the men available to her, perhaps it would be better to continue concentrating on work and owning her own gallery.

Colette, who had been watching, broke away from her own conversation to speak with Kate.

"He's interested in you," Colette said. "That's Stefan Wijnandts, a reputable broker and a sophisticate."

"A sophisticate with a childish sense of art and an appalling view of mankind."

"He comes from a family of famous artists."

"Should that matter?"

"At least admit he's attractive," Colette said. Kate took another sip of her martini, refusing to answer. "I know what will lighten you up. We'll play the game now."

Colette took two cloth bags from under the dessert table, then clapped her hands and called for everyone's attention. The crowd gathered in the largest room. When they fell silent, she held up a bag in each hand.

"Thank you all for coming this evening," she said. "I was going to ask if you were enjoying yourselves tonight. Then I saw the eggnog bowl on its third fill." There were laughs. "I'd like to introduce a Christmas game. In these bags are a collection of short, famous verses. They have each been cut in half. The beginnings are in one bag, the endings in the other."

As Colette spoke, Kate had the feeling she was being watched. Maybe it was just Stefan. No, he was laughing with a group of friends across the room, making himself the center of attention. She swept her gaze over the guests, spotting a man at the far end of the gallery. Dressed in a camel-hair overcoat, he was tall and motionless, hands in his pockets, features silhouetted by a ceiling light. She couldn't be sure he'd been staring at her, but he seemed removed from the revelry, standing by himself. He did not have the relaxed posture of the other guests, and he glanced away when she looked at him. She had never seen this man before.

She returned her attention to Colette, who went on, "The ladies will pick from one bag, the gentlemen from the other. Now, mingle to find your counterpart!"

There were cheers, nods, raised glasses. Colette passed the bags around. Kate reached in one and pulled out her half of a verse:

I met a traveller from an antique land,
Who said—"Two vast and trunkless legs of stone
Stand in the desert. . . . Near them, on the sand,
Half sunk a shattered visage lies, whose frown,
And wrinkled lip, and sneer of cold command,
Tell that its sculptor well those passions read
Which yet survive, stamped on these lifeless things,
The hand that mocked them, and the heart that fed;
And on the pedestal, these words appear:

Kate finished reading her segment when a handsome older man edged up to her and extended a hand.

"*Bonjour*," he said. "I'm Ludo."

"*Bonjour*, Ludo. Kate."

"Would you like to read your half?"

She did, and he continued with:

What is love? 'tis not hereafter;
Present mirth hath present laughter;
What's to come is still unsure:
In delay there lies no plenty;
Then come kiss me, sweet-and-twenty!
Youth's a stuff will not endure.

They exchanged funny glances, then chuckled.

"Non sequitur, I'm afraid," he said.

"Good luck finding your match," she said.

He wandered off and was replaced by a young man in a green sweater:

"*Bonjour*, pretty lady, shall we see if it was meant to be?"

Kate read her portion again. He delivered his continuation in a theatrical voice:

How cheerfully he seems to grin
How neatly spreads his claws,
And welcomes little fishes in,
With gently smiling jaws!

She laughed at his Shakespearean performance, nearly spilling what was left of her drink.

"You're quite a thespian," she said.

"Why, thanks. Though I'm afraid . . . Percy Shelley and Lewis Carroll . . . it wasn't meant to be."

"Star-crossed, we are not."

As her would-be suitor drifted away, she noticed the man in the camel-hair coat standing near her. Had he been listening? She dismissed the idea when she saw him exchange verses with another guest. When he finished reading, she kept a watch on him, still failing to get a good view of his face.

Two women approached him. He stopped for both, and she could hear their amusement over their mismatches, but he did not stay to chat. He circled the room, listening, as if filtering through the voices on a search. She saw him pause near Stefan, who was reading his verse to a young woman. Disappointment appeared on her face. She shook her head and walked away. The man in camel hair approached Stefan and said something. Then Stefan shrugged, and they traded papers.

The man looked around the room again. Kate turned her back to him and hoped not to be seen, and then lost sight of him. She would ask Colette who he was, but not now. Her friend was standing by a Christmas tree, surrounded by male guests. Other men came up to Kate, eager to swap verses. She did so halfheartedly, thinking about the fact that she could no longer find the man in the overcoat and feeling slightly annoyed with Colette for setting up this game, which likely had been designed with Kate in mind. Even though her friend had the best intentions, Kate didn't approve of the way Colette threw herself in the path of available men and expected Kate to do the same. She straightened the trays at the dessert table while surreptitiously glancing around for the man in the camel-hair coat. He was a curiosity, a reason to watch and wonder, but he must have left the party.

Then she heard his voice.

"Pardon me."

She turned around.

"Care to trade lines?" he said.

She wasn't sure why, but her words stopped in her throat. The stranger stood there, awaiting an answer, with a grin on his dimpled face that seemed to mock her. He was trim and swarthy and must have been about twenty-seven. His hair, the color of midnight, was combed into a low and understated pompadour. He struck her at first as too clean, too tidy. He might benefit from a day without shaving, or a windstorm to tousle his hair, she thought.

For no good reason, she didn't trust him, nor did she feel like playing Colette's game any longer. She wanted to ask why he had been staring at her earlier, but she was also a bit frightened of him for some reason, so she simply nodded and said:

"Right, okay."

She read her portion, and then he continued:

'My name is Ozymandias, King of Kings:
Look on my works, ye mighty, and despair!'
Nothing beside remains. Round the decay
Of that colossal wreck, boundless and bare,
The lone and level sands stretch far away."

"It's a match," he said. "Percy Shelley at his best."

Kate tried to hide her unease. She had watched him switch poems with Stefan to engineer a match.

"What's your name?" he asked.

She didn't care to tell him but saw no way out of it. "Kate. Yours?"

"Kate . . . ?"

"Atwell."

She had the odd feeling he already knew that.

"Nice to meet you, Kate. I'm Moritz Dahl."

"You're a collector, a broker, a fine arts student?"

"All of the above," he laughed. Kate felt annoyed at his evasion.

"You don't look familiar. Have you been into the gallery?"

"Apparently, not during your work shift," he said. "What's your story, Kate?"

His eyes were a pale, husky blue, shocking against his darker complexion—and they focused only on her, as if trying to read her thoughts.

"My story?" she said.

"You could start by telling me where you're from."

"A place called Beaumaris. It's in Northwest Wales, on the Isle of Anglesey."

"It must be beautiful."

"It is."

"Well, that's a start. There must be more. What's your artistic specialty?"

"Watercolor," she said. "By trade and by skill."

The music of the carolers had faded to a distant hum, as had the general chatter in the room. In fact, the whole soirée seemed to evaporate as she became further determined to unravel the intentions of this man.

"What about you?" she asked.

"I'm from Denmark," said Moritz.

"What brings you to France? The Royal Danish Academy of Fine Arts is an excellent school, and Copenhagen is filled with new galleries."

"I prefer the charms of Paris. And you?"

"My friend, Colette. We plan to start an art consultancy together."

"You'll make an excellent partnership, if this party is anything to judge by. Speaking of which, do we get some sort of prize for matching poems so quickly?"

"Not if we cheated."

"What do you mean?"

"I saw what you did with Stefan. You manipulated the game."

He laughed and said, "Were you spying on me?"

"Not spying, but I did see."

"You wouldn't blame me if you had read the Whitman piece I drew from the bag. Free verse has no lyrical quality. I'm loath to call it poetry. Heard your friend Stefan read the end of 'Ozymandias' and had to ask to switch. Good thing, or we'd not have met."

She offered a cautious smile. "Right."

"Hope you don't mind, but I'm going to serve myself a drink. May I bring you another?"

"Still working on the martini," she said.

He nodded. "It was nice meeting you, Mademoiselle Speer."

Her heart skipped a beat.

Did he—?

The room had the illusion of closing in on her.

"I'm sorry, what?" she said.

"I said it was nice meeting you."

"You have me confused. I didn't say . . . I gave you my last name. It's Atwell. Kate Atwell."

"My mistake," Moritz said, bowing.

Those blue eyes of his gripped her and wouldn't let go. There was a reined-in violence in them. He smiled as the color left her cheeks.

He turned away and made for the beverage table. She watched, transfixed, as he mixed a French vermouth with kirsch and raspberry syrup, shook his cocktail with ice cubes, garnished his glass with a cherry, and inserted himself into a group of other guests, never again glancing her way.

. . .

Kate's hands shook as she ordered her second martini. Moritz Dahl had disappeared, but their conversation had left her rattled. As many times as she told herself she had imagined him calling her "Mademoiselle Speer," she couldn't shake the sound of his words from her memory, or the feeling that he had been testing her—and that she had somehow failed.

Who on earth was he?

As the night went on, the room swelled with the sound of laughter and conversation. Seeking a moment of refuge from the revelry, Kate made her way over to the alcove, where the gallery's curators had hung the chosen artwork for the evening. She had seen guests eyeing the paintings and had even heard one man say, "That's mine!"

A Matisse. That's what the man had been excited about. She leaned in closer to study the individual brushstrokes that comprised the whole. The work was worth millions and a favorite among Maxence's clientele, but its crude simplicity and coloration were not her cup of tea. Nor did she care for the cubist still life beside it, a Braque. She was attracted more to the rococo palette of the portrait on the opposite wall, a Vigée le Brun. She walked closer to it, surveying the room, stopping at a small surrealist piece on the way. It was familiar to her somehow, and she panicked for a moment, thinking she might have happened upon a painting she remembered from her father's studio. But then she remembered. She had seen it once before, in a private collection while traveling with her parents.

"Klee." The voice came from directly behind her. "You seem to have an affinity for German painters. Or in this case, Swiss German, I suppose."

"Monsieur Maxence," Kate said, startled by his proximity. "*Joyeux Noel.*"

He took her hand, bent at the waist, and kissed it. She was happy to be wearing gloves.

"I must commend you and Mademoiselle Fossey," he said. "The party has been *un grand succès*. All of these paintings are spoken for."

"May the new owners be happy," she said. "Did you acquire this painting from Lord and Lady Russell?"

His face clouded over. "It's been part of the Pendelfarr collection for over a decade. Now that there's such demand for Klee, the collectors clamor for them. The prices keep going up and up."

Kate looked at the work again. Lord and Lady Russell wouldn't have sold it for any price, and she was sure it was the same painting. She and her mother had stood discussing Klee's visual allusions to poetry and music. Her memory was crystal clear.

"I do worry that modern art is so much easier to copy, unlike the work of the great masters," she said. "The war has made it easier to create legitimate provenances for paintings that may not be originals. Hence, the market is flooded with forgeries." She glanced at him, noting his darkening expression. "The greater market, of course. Not at Pendelfarr."

"No, not at Pendelfarr," he said coolly, with a sip of his drink. "I commend your concern for authenticity, mademoiselle. Though I understand you're something of a forger yourself."

Kate froze, not understanding his meaning.

"*Pardon?*"

"I attested to your employment so that you could enter the library, did I?" He smiled. "Or perhaps not, but who's to say, now that the deed is done and you found what you were looking for?"

"I'm so sorry, Monsieur," she said. "I . . . no one was around to sign the letter, and I needed to . . . research a piece. For tonight."

"The ends justified the means." He was staring at her appraisingly, with an almost suspicious look on his face. All she wanted was to get away from him, but now that he had confronted her, she had no choice but to finish the conversation, wherever it was headed. "Besides, art, like truth, is in the eye of the beholder, no?"

Kate dared not look directly at Maxence. Her eyes swept across the rest of the exhibition, and she wondered how many of the paintings on view were real. She examined the painting more closely, shaking, then looked at the unsuspecting patrons mingling at the party.

"You must go to the police and report whoever sold this to you."

His grip on her arm tightened, and he turned her to face him. "You'll not speak of this painting again. I'll not have everything I've built here unraveled by amateur speculation and innuendo."

Kate stood silently. She would not agree to his demand, but she had nothing more to say in the moment. Finally, he released her.

"*Auf Wiedersehen*," he said. "Enjoy the party."

The martinis and their confrontation had gone to her head. The same words almost formed on her lips by instinct, but she caught herself before saying them. If he was making a joke, it was in poor taste.

Katharina

Kate knew she had to leave immediately. The way Maxence had looked at her, had gripped her arm, frightened her to the core. She was determined to go to the police the very next day to report her suspicions.

She looked around for Colette, who was engaged in conversation. Her friend would be reluctant to believe her, she thought, but she would have to break the news soon—not here, not now, but in the morning, she decided. Right now, she simply had to get out.

The party was far from over, but she made a quiet exit, walking to the nearest semi-busy street to hunt for a cab.

One thing was clear: Her job at the gallery was finished. She would have to return to London, perhaps even to her parents. Kate felt a sense of dread. Walking briskly, she had nearly reached the Boulevard Barbès when someone shouted behind her.

"Kate!"

When she turned around, it was Moritz Dahl. After the conversation with Maxence, she had forgotten about him. He must have been following her. Who was this man, and how did he know her secret?

She walked faster.

"Kate! Wait!" The sound of his footsteps grew closer. "I have something to show you," he said breathlessly. "If you want me to leave you alone after seeing this, I'll go away. Forever."

She slowed. Desperate as she was to get away from him, he had practically caught up to her. No way to ignore him.

"Who are you?"

"Let's find some light," he said, his voice gentle but insistent as he avoided her question. "Sacré-Coeur, up the hill. Great view of the city at night. And good light."

She knew it was a terrible idea to accompany this stranger, but curiosity got the better of her. She was already terribly shaken. Her past was a mystery to everyone she knew—and even herself—but this Moritz man knew her secret, and maybe more. She kept her guard up as they wound their way back toward the basilica along the narrow streets of Montmartre. Soon she could make out the church's portico and three arches, and the bronze equestrian statues of Joan of Arc and Saint Louis IX. The main white dome towered over the city.

"Take my coat," Moritz said. "It's freezing out here."

"Tonight has been the strangest of my life, and now I'm walking in Montmartre with a stranger who thinks I'm someone else. Temperature's not my main concern."

"Suit yourself," he said, and she wondered if he could tell that she was shivering to the bone.

They strolled through a garden. The air was chilly and quiet but for the far-off medley of horns honking and blaring. She looked out at the streets glowing red and white below, veins of a city pulsing with traffic. A few miles out, the Eiffel Tower pierced the sky. A cloud swept low from the northwest, eclipsing the Arc de Triomphe in a maroon haze.

"What is it you want to show me?" she said.

Moritz leaned against the basilica and removed a cap from a cardboard tube protruding from his coat pocket. He pulled out a canvas, approximately two feet by four feet, and unfurled it on the ground. The light around them was strong enough for Kate to make out the oil-painted image.

It looked like something she had seen before.

But after all these years, it couldn't be.

The girl in the painting was wearing a white dress and sitting on a stone slab surrounded by weeds and shrubs. She clutched a pear in her right hand and held her left hand to her forehead, as if to brush aside her full head of hair. She was young and barefoot, most likely a peasant girl out playing.

God Almighty, Kate thought. This was Karl Decker's painting. The one he'd brought to the train station in Berlin twenty years ago, before he was shot dead helping her escape to England.

"Have you ever seen this?" Moritz asked.

She realized her throat had gone dry. She tried to relax, to think of something, anything, to say. She was tempted to run as fast as she could away from this stranger if it would keep her secret safe.

Finally, she tried to say with resolve, "No."

"Are you sure?" he said. "Will you take a closer look?"

Memories of that night came flooding back. The invaders in their home. Her father's lifeless body. The dark, smelly submarine. Herself, curled up in a ball on a mattress with the curtain pulled tight. She didn't want to look at the image anymore, but it was just as hard to look at Moritz and hide her shock.

"I don't recognize it and don't know why I should," she said. "How do you have it?"

"You really don't know?"

"Why would I?" she asked.

Moritz rolled up the canvas and tucked it back into the tube. A shadow crossed his face. She couldn't quite untangle his expression. It was as if he had withdrawn from her in that moment, trying to keep whatever was running through his head from showing in his eyes.

He might be afraid of me, too, she suddenly realized.

"Take the painting." He handed her the tube. "Take it and go, Katharina."

"That's not my name—"

"Don't argue. I need closure. Please."

She looked at him one last time, searching his face for a clue as to what he meant.

Then, without saying goodbye, he walked away.

This was lunacy. What was going on? Her mind flooded with questions as she stood there in the garden holding the cardboard tube. She might have called out to him, but she didn't have the courage to be Katharina Speer again. Not after tonight, and not so soon after meeting him, even if it meant getting answers.

Watching him become a small silhouette in the distance, she began to walk briskly down the street, holding the tube at her chest.

He stopped a moment, turned back.

"It's a forgery," he called from down the street. She paused to listen. "A forgery of *The Little Marauder,* William-Adolphe Bouguereau."

Then he turned a corner and disappeared down the hill.

Moritz

Moritz stepped into the car waiting for him near the Rue Becquerel, a dimly lit street with no foot traffic. The man at the wheel wore a black knit cap pulled down to the flat line of his eyebrows.

"It's her," Moritz said.

The other man didn't turn to face him; he kept his eyes fixed on the windshield.

"You're sure?"

"I'd bet my life on it, Yehuda, and I'm not a gambling man."

"Did her roommate give you their address?"

"Just the street: Rue Dauphine."

The man he had called Yehuda turned the key in the ignition and pulled away from the curb. He was fiddling with his short, neatly groomed beard. They passed another vehicle at an intersection, and for an instant, the flash of passing headlights gave Moritz a clear view of the man's angular features and aquiline nose.

Yehuda was of average height, with a slight bone structure. If it weren't for the fact that he was a weightlifter, he might have even looked petite. His arms were thick, his chest squared out by muscle, his skin a ruddy shade of leather. Now and then they'd pass a lamppost, and shadows would flit around the cuts and sinews of his physique.

"When will we search her apartment?" Moritz asked. "I assume tomorrow?"

"Tomorrow we'll keep her under surveillance, learn her patterns. We'll go in when the time is right."

Moritz heard a clinking noise as Yehuda stepped on the brakes to avoid a pedestrian. He glanced at Yehuda's feet in time to see him dislodge a glass bottle that had wedged itself against the gas pedal. It must have fallen from his lap or pocket.

As Yehuda picked it up and concealed it from view, Moritz added this to the list of strange behaviors he'd observed over the past week or two.

Yehuda was hiding something. An addiction of some sort? Was there alcohol in the bottle?

They were supposed to be a team, but these past few days, Yehuda seemed to be of a different mindset. He'd been independent in his work and opaque about his intentions. Moritz had even heard him place a call to someone named "Victor," and later Yehuda lied to him about it. After all Moritz had sacrificed to be here, he decided he would draw the line tomorrow, when he had the energy, and ask what was going on.

Yehuda turned onto the Rue Royale and drove southwest through the Place de la Concorde. Out the window, Moritz saw the Luxor Obelisk and the ornamented fountains. A pair of lovers sat kissing at the water's edge. A few other people ambled about the square, but not many. By his watch, it was 2:06 a.m.

"You passed the street to our hotel," Moritz said.

"I'd like to see the Rue Dauphine."

"This may not be the best time. Kate will be getting home soon. It would be counterproductive if she saw me."

"I'll be careful."

Yehuda flipped on the car's AM radio, and a voice came through the speakers, in French, washed out by static: "*As motorists wend their ways home along the crowded and soon icy streets, people forget the invisible, uninvited passenger in their vehicles. That passenger is hazard. The hazard of a traffic accident. You can help decrease the fatalities in our streets. Extreme speed on slippery roads is a cause of motor accidents. Control your speed to keep within the safety limit, not just within the legal limit.*"

He searched for a different station.

"*. . . Needs the inspiration and solace of faith, for it is religious faith which binds our families together and builds moral character. As the spirit of Christmas grows, so does the need to turn to the path of enduring principles and eternal light.*"

Something flickered on Yehuda's otherwise flat expression. He left the channel where it was. They stopped at a traffic signal, and Moritz suddenly knew why the man had switched on the radio: to hide the noise as he prepared his move.

Moritz saw it coming right before it happened. Just enough time to suck in a deep breath.

Yehuda's right hand shot out at Moritz's mouth, holding a rag soaked in liquid from the bottle. The odor of the cloth was pungent and sweet. He could feel an etherlike substance creeping into his nostrils. He dared not breathe more than necessary as he tried to shove Yehuda's arm away. It was impossible. The man's grip was too powerful, too well placed.

He rotated to face Yehuda, throwing a fist at the man. Yehuda deflected the punch and grabbed hold of Moritz's hand, bending it backward. He felt a growing pressure as his wrist was inverted, until it seemed the tips of his fingers could have touched his forearm. Pain lanced all the way up to his shoulder. He let out a few wisps of air while trying to draw his hand back and pry Yehuda away. Somehow this only seemed to strengthen the man's hold on him.

One more second of warning, and Moritz might have stood a chance, but Yehuda's attack had come out of the clear blue sky. Now the sweet smell of the rag was beginning to overcome him. He resisted, or at least that's what he told himself to do as he reached for the door handle. He fumbled, unable to see what he was doing, though he managed to find the lock. It came up with ease, but not before Yehuda dragged him in closer by the collar. Moritz thrashed, trying to gain control. Yehuda had him by the lips and nose and was not letting up with the rag.

The buildup in his lungs was getting painful. He had to breathe soon, and the harder he fought, the more he needed the air. He tried to bite Yehuda's hand but couldn't get past the rag.

Yehuda pulled him closer still, throwing his neck back. A sharp pain seared down his spine, costing him leverage. He tried one final time to wrench away the man's arm and whack him in the throat, but Yehuda's profile was starting to look fuzzy.

Moritz couldn't hear anything anymore; his ears were vacuums. A tingling feeling had begun to course through him. He'd taken several short but unavoidable breaths and could feel the moisture of the rag running along his nose and down to his chin. The cloth was soaked all the way through.

He wasn't sure what he was seeing. It was dark outside. Dark in the car. There were no more visible lampposts.

The rag was gone. He no longer registered a struggle. Only that he was spinning, or levitating.

As the traffic light turned green, Moritz slumped in the passenger seat.

. . .

He reached for a light in the void. He couldn't say which came first: sight, sound, or awareness—nor could he say how much time had passed.

His eyelids were heavier than sandbags. With an effort, he cracked them open to a world of ill-defined shapes. A dull noise droned in his ears. He felt as if he were washed ashore under a receding tide. The waves came back now and then, tempting him with sleep, but the horrible throbbing in his neck kept him awake.

He tasted blood. Most likely, he had bitten his tongue when he'd blacked out. His cheeks were cold, pushed flat against a moving, vibrating surface. The ground was unsteady, rocking and jouncing. Maybe this was the residual effect of the vapors he'd inhaled, but it hardly felt that way; vertigo could make the world spin or sway, but not bump and jitter.

A minute passed, and he managed to summon the capacity for rational thought, or a semblance of it—enough to sort through the sensations. His body was shivering in a cold, bitter wind. He felt an occasional spray and splash of water.

He realized he was sprawled on the floor of a motorboat. Yehuda was at the helm.

Moritz checked his watch—no sudden movements, as Yehuda had to think he was still unconscious. It was 2:21 a.m. Only fifteen minutes had passed. They must have been zooming somewhere along the Seine. He tried to string his memories together in chronological order as they trickled back to him. They'd reached a traffic signal. His partner had sprung a chloroform rag on him. He'd seen the attack coming but had succumbed to the chemical. He'd managed to take a deep breath before the attack and fight the urge to inhale for a while. Maybe that was why he had emerged from his blackout so quickly. He'd had that instant to prepare.

The sound died, and the vibrations stopped. Yehuda must have cut the motor. Moritz closed his eyes and relaxed his body, faking sleep. He could hear Yehuda clambering over to him and kneeling at his side. Then he felt his ankles being pushed together and bound in rope. There was no use resisting. He was in no shape to fight, and Yehuda would only further sedate him.

Something metallic, most likely an anchor, clanged against the floor. Yehuda's boot dug into his chest and rolled him off the boat, over the motor and into the water. He stayed near the surface at first. Then there was a sudden yank at his feet, and the water surged up around him.

Katharina

Kate put a kettle on the stove when she arrived home. Her bedroom sprang to life as she turned on a lamp. Her shelves were lined with art volumes bookended by pots of primrose. On the wall beside her closet, half a dozen comical scenes from *Don Quixote* were hanging in frames, in tribute to her favorite book. Plantlets bloomed by the window and crawled up the sill. The vintage travel chest leaning against her bedframe was laden with photographs of George, Lona, Colette, and other friends. She had yet to frame her recent watercolor rendition of the Snowfall Queen, which lay on her desk, pinned by crystal paperweights.

She removed her dress and slipped on a comfortable silk robe, waiting for the water to boil. When the kettle began to whistle, she poured her tea and sat by the fireplace to clear her head and to start to make a plan. At least that's what she told herself she would do, but the desire to unfurl the Bouguereau forgery got the best of her.

Sitting there, staring at the painting, she recalled the way her father used to sweep her into his arms, making her feel secure. How dangerous those arms had been in retrospect. She could hear the voice he had used when he picked her up; it was coming through in the crackles of the fireplace: *How's my little marauder?*

She'd often wondered why he had called her that. The answer was clear now. As a little girl, she must have reminded him of the subject of this Bouguereau painting, with her big brown eyes and tumbling dark hair.

She went into her room and removed the back of a picture frame, where she had concealed the photograph of Ralf Speer from Maxence's biography. Maxence. She would have to deal with him, too. She had cut the photograph from the page so she could hide it easily. Looking at the *Little Marauder* forgery, she remembered her first easel and painting alongside Karl, who had helped her so much. Karl had been working on this painting when he died, died for her father and for the ideology that had nearly torn the world apart. She would never understand her father, never be able to reconcile the two men he had been. She wanted to hate him, but what she really hated was how much power he still had over her. She looked forward to the day, if it ever came, when she could see the picture and feel nothing personal about it.

The chamomile did little to quell her nerves. Moritz had done more to fire them up than even Maxence had. She had too many questions to sleep tonight. Who was this Moritz Dahl? How had he found Karl's painting? How had he found *her* after twenty years? She thought of Alfred. He didn't want to marry her, but he wouldn't have betrayed her, would he? She hadn't mentioned the name "Speer" to anyone but him since boarding the submarine as a little girl.

What did Moritz mean by wanting "closure"?

She returned to the fireplace, huddled close to the flames, and took a swig of tea, which burned its way down her throat. She had begun to sweat. If there was one thing she knew, it was that the truth about her past was threatening to rear up like a horse and kick everyone she knew with its flailing hooves.

Yehuda

Yehuda revved the motor and steered the boat in a U-turn, crossing back over the site of the splash. The walkways by the quay were empty. It had been a clean dump.

He pulled back on the throttle and began coasting northeast along the river, gliding beneath the arch of a bridge. The Seine snaked its way through the city and all the way to its mouth at the English Channel. He was traversing a section that ran northeast and would soon curve due east. He heard the groan of a high-pitched motor behind him and spotted a boat heading his way. Damn. Was it official? He looked over his shoulder, unable to tell in the darkness. Had the body surfaced? He kept a solid grip on the wheel and reached for his knife, keeping it handy at his side as the craft gained on him.

He heard laughter, and the other boat came close enough for him to make out its two passengers. Male and female, lovers, perhaps newlyweds. Joyriding in the moonlight.

"Hey! Hey you!" the male passenger hollered in French. He and his lady were locked arm in arm and laughing. "Want to race?"

Yehuda hoped the man would keep his distance. The fewer loose ends, the better; he preferred a low kill count.

"Your engine is stronger," Yehuda called back. "It's not a fair race."

The other man swayed on his feet, obviously inebriated.

"Chicken!"

Yehuda felt a rising dread as the man jockeyed his boat closer, about to make himself a witness should the police discover a body in the area.

"You're drunk," Yehuda said. "Don't hurt yourselves."

"Don't hurt yourselves!" the man jeered. His girlfriend found this hilarious.

"Scratch my boat, and I'll call the police."

The other craft continued to drift nearer. Yehuda's fingers tightened on the knife.

"Come on, race us to the Pont du Carrousel!"

The bridge was located between the Quai des Tuileries and the Quai Voltaire, not far from the fine arts school or, he guessed, the street where Kate lived. He was headed in that direction, but he dared not risk a confrontation with the authorities.

"Like I said, I'm handicapped."

"You can have a ten-second lead."

"Let it go," Yehuda said. "No race."

"He's afraid we'll hurt ourselves!" The man began clucking. "*Cot cot cot codet!*"

"No race," Yehuda said. "Have a good night."

"Move out from the dark, so we can see a coward's face!"

The woman sniggered. He could see she was carrying a bottle of gin. They seemed intoxicated enough to forget his face if they saw it, and they would continue to make a scene until he went along.

"Fine," Yehuda said. "But no handicap. Just let's go."

The man held up his fists in triumph, then clapped his hands. He sped off, and Yehuda pretended to race him for a few seconds before falling back. Their laughter faded under the whine of an engine growing distant, and soon the couple disappeared beyond the bend.

Yehuda slipped the knife into its sheath and strapped it to his calf. He pulled into a dock, moored the boat, and found his car in the parking spot where he'd left it. He opened a map of Paris and located the Rue Dauphine.

Moritz

Moritz thought his eardrums might rupture under the pressure. Hitting the river's bottom, he waggled his jaw to equalize. He opened his eyes a crack and turned his head around, searching for light, seeing nothing in the murk. Not a glimmer. Needles of cold began to prickle and numb his skin.

The buildup of carbon dioxide in his lungs had a sobering effect, countering the fumes he'd inhaled. Uncertain which way was up, he blew out a thin stream of bubbles and felt the direction of their movement along his cheeks for a clue. He still had no gauge of depth. He pushed off the river floor with his legs, testing whether he could overcome the weight of the anchor, but he was jerked down again.

He bent his knees and reached for the ropes with both hands, pulling at them. They didn't budge. He dug his fingers between the cords at his ankles, following their spiral. One loop, two, three . . . how many loops were there? A current swept over him, and he drifted to the side, blown down against the slimy floor, losing his hold on the rope, disoriented again. The drug in his system seemed to amplify the feeling of rotation.

If he could slow down his heart, he'd be able to hold his breath longer. But the thrumming in his chest quickened, bringing him closer to his pain threshold. He could taste the muck, feel the silt on his skin. He wrestled harder with the ropes, this time trying a more methodical approach, hard as it was to think clearly. Maybe there was an alternative to untangling the mess around his legs. He followed the cord to the anchor and tried to heave it up with his hands. It felt like a cannonball.

His fingers explored the anchor's surface; they were abraded by rust. There was a ring through which the rope passed. He pried at the knot where two ends of the rope came together, feeling his fingers slip and lose dexterity in the cold.

His chest lurched forward as if he'd been hit from behind. He had to breathe. The pain was excruciating, the spasms uncontrollable. He might have been seeing black spots if it weren't so dark already. He determined to give the knot another try. Wedging his thumb into a crevice, he tried to create slack with his other hand. The knot slipped a millimeter. Two millimeters, three. The cords began to slither apart.

He exhaled as slowly as his lungs would allow. His head was engulfed in bubbles. Finally, the cords came free of the anchor. He pushed off the soft silt, rocketing upward, finding the river to be deeper than he'd thought. It must have been nearly thirty feet. He followed the bubbles for what seemed like an eternity and thought he might lose consciousness on the way to the surface. But then came the lights above him, twinkles from the world he missed, giving him reason to add strength to his dolphin kick.

He breached the surface and gasped for air, sucking in water by accident. He choked it out and gasped again. His lungs were desperate. He splashed in the river, using his arms to stay afloat; his legs were still bound. God, it felt good to breathe. He crunched his abdomen tight, forcing blood to his brain before paddling to the riverside. He lifted himself up to the quay and took a moment to free his ankles, letting the water drip from his clothes.

He could finally take a minute to think.

Why Yehuda had betrayed him, he couldn't imagine, but if Yehuda had used and deceived him so easily and then tried to murder him, the next victim was almost certainly Kate.

Ordinarily he wouldn't have cared much, but now she was the only person who could help him understand his partner's betrayal. That was, if she could be trusted, and if he could get to her first.

He ran to the nearest street and asked for directions to the Rue Dauphine.

Katharina

Kate pulled back the covers and slipped into bed, wishing she felt even an ounce tired. She thought about pulling a textbook from the shelf. At Worcester College, textbooks had been the best soporific. She had even jotted her thoughts on paper tonight, using fragments and shorthand so as not to fill an entire journal. Writing your worries down was supposed to help unburden the mind and pave the way to sleep. Let your anxieties go until tomorrow. That was the logic, but it didn't help her much. She kept thinking of more things to write down. Her mind was bubbling with questions that led to more questions.

Thanks to Moritz, the conversation with Maxence had taken a backseat. Memories from her early years in Germany were marching back in rank and file: a handwritten note sitting on her father's desk, wishing him a happy birthday, signed by Goebbels and Hitler—the time she'd met Josef Mengele, who performed monstrous experiments on prisoners, at a Christmas party at home—shaking hands at the same gathering with Odilo Globočnik, liquidator of several of the world's largest Jewish communities, who had patted her head and called her cute—staring out the backseat window at the pale, sullen faces as her father drove his compatriots through a Jewish ghetto in Italy—speaking with Hitler's former chief architect, Albert Speer (a man who shared her surname, but thankfully no relation, as it would be unimaginable to have two Nazis in her family)—and as the battle for sleep went on, she rolled onto her side, trying to shut it all out.

An hour passed. Finally, she felt herself getting tired. Her dreams usually didn't arrive until morning, but tonight they came early. She didn't know exactly where she was, but knew she didn't belong, because she had never liked dark or crowded places. There must have been a few hundred people standing around her. She was eight years old again, no taller than anyone else's hips. So many hips, sharp as blades. The ceiling was so low that some of the people had to crouch. No one had much hair, not even the women, and what little they had was thin as spider silk. The walls were concrete. The room had no lamps and no windows; the only light came from the outside corridor. Access to the corridor was closed off by a sliding metal door. There was a round hole in the ceiling about the size of an electrical socket.

She could see the ribs of the people around her. They were all naked. Their arms and legs looked like wires. Most of them stood where they were and didn't try to move, even as the chamber got even more crowded. She didn't know what was going to happen, but she knew she had to get out. She began running through the forest of legs, ducking and dodging, trying to weave her way to the sliding door, which had not yet closed. The ground was slippery. She fell and scraped her knees, got them bloody. All she had to do was stand up and keep running, but the pain in her knees made them buckle whenever she tried, and all the legs around her kept knocking her aside. Refusing to be trampled, she began to crawl. It felt like the skin was peeling right off her knees—and at the same time, the floor was becoming more slippery and difficult to move along—almost frictionless, in fact. She had to keep going forward. She reached out and clasped the ankles around her to drag herself toward the exit. She could finally see the sliding door. It was starting to close. She yanked and pulled harder as the man guarding the exit started sealing off the room. He had deep purple circles under his eyes. He was tall, his forehead wide and fit for a crown. There was a regal solemnity about him.

She knew the man.

Papa, she said.

Where are you going? he asked in a voice he'd use with a stranger or an adversary. He was looking in her general direction, but not directly at her. She needed him to see her!

It's me, Papa! Let me out!

She saw recognition on his face. But it meant nothing to him. He reached into his pocket and tossed her a small object. It landed at her feet. She picked it up—a dead sparrow. The door rumbled along its groove as he sealed the chamber. When she turned back, the people trapped inside with her were chirping. Feathered and beaked, they no longer had human faces.

Outside, there was an accelerating ticking noise, like something metallic hitting the spokes of a spinning bicycle wheel. The sound ran for a long interval, growing louder, clacking as a motor roared to life outside the walls and caused a breeze to waft down from the hole in the ceiling.

She jolted upright in bed.

She was dreaming, she told herself. Just dreaming. She sat there a moment, letting the comfort of reality take hold. But she had to wonder if she had reached the dream's natural conclusion, or if something else had awakened her.

A rattling at the front door gave her the answer. Colette must have come home. That was surprising. When she went out for drinks, she usually didn't come back until late the next morning, but she'd been out only a few hours tonight.

The rattling continued. Kate lay back down in bed, listening. Colette seemed to be taking a long time to let herself in. Maybe she'd had more than a few cocktails. Doubtful, as the rattling was faint, not like the work of a heavy-handed drunk.

Kate got out of bed, wobbly at first, and opened the bedroom door to the living room. The streetlights spilled through the window. The rattling seemed to suggest that the person behind the door did not have a key, but was rather trying to bounce the lock's pins into place with a pick.

She grabbed a knife from the kitchen, tiptoed back into the bedroom, picked up the phone on the nightstand, and stared at the rotary dial. What was the emergency number in France? She couldn't remember. She set the handset back on its cradle and considered raising the windowsill to cry for help, but there was no one to be seen outside, and yelling would only signal her intruder that she knew he was there. She couldn't climb out, either; it was a five-story drop.

The rattling of the doorknob became violent. She looked for possible places to hide. Was there an attic? Not that she knew of. No space under her bed, either. She could hide in the closet, but if someone had come for her, surely the closet would be the first place he would look. Her eyes fell upon the travel chest. She cleared away the picture frames resting on the lid and squeezed herself inside, crouching into a ball and keeping the chest open a crack so she could see out as the front door swung open.

The man who walked in was built like a middleweight boxer, a black knit cap pulled down to his brow. He stopped near the doorway and reached down to his calf, unsheathing a knife of his own before proceeding into Colette's room at the other end of the residence.

He moved quickly, quiet as a cat and clinging to the shadows. It seemed he had done this before. He left Colette's room in a matter of seconds—a bad sign, she thought; if he were here to steal jewelry, he would have found plenty in there.

He crossed the main living area, and she kept still, watching, as he entered her room. The intruder's back stiffened at her bedside as he realized the bed was empty. He must have expected to find someone sleeping in at least one of the bedrooms. As she thought he might do, he threw open the closet.

She tempered her breathing, so loud to her own ears. He felt his way through the closet, reaching between garments. Finding nothing of interest, he closed the door and made his way into the kitchen, where he found the kettle on the stove. He lifted its lid and swirled a finger through the water.

"Katharina," he said. "Your tea is still warm."

She could feel fear pumping through her. Should she burst out and run for the door?

"Where are you?" he said.

Her finger was getting tired. She thought about letting down the chest lid, but didn't want to miss what he was saying.

He went on, "Katharina Marie Speer, born in 1934 to Ralf and Florentine Speer in Berlin. I know all about you, Katharina. If you want your secret to stay safe, I suggest you come out."

Right, Kate thought. That's what your knife is for, to keep me safe.

The floor creaked under his feet. Her finger slipped, and the chest lid fell a half-inch, making a slight noise. She froze, her stomach sinking. He must have heard her. His footsteps came closer and stopped beside her trunk. She was trapped, curled into a ball, without hope of flight.

The man flung the lid open, and she sprang out like a jack-in-the-box, slashing at him with her own blade and lacerating his abdomen. She'd hoped to cut him in the neck, but it was dark, and she was panicking; his lower torso was the best she could manage. She ran for the front door. He lunged at her, catching the hem of her nightgown and pulling her down. Her knee struck the floor with a painful *thud*. God, did that hurt. She scrambled back to her feet and dodged a swipe of his knife. He advanced, hunched over, clutching his wound with one hand. She tried to attack him again, aiming for his thigh, but despite his injury, he was quick enough to sidestep her. Her eyes had long since adjusted to the darkness, or she'd never have been able to tell where he was. They circled each other in slow, sure steps, eyes on each other's blades, which reflected the light of the streetlamps.

He stalled a moment, then pounced. His hand shot toward her wrist and knocked her weapon aside. She could feel his immense strength. The fight was over; she knew it. He picked her up by the waist and forced her onto the bed. Leaning over her with one hand, he pinned her palms back against the sheet. She tried to squirm out of it, but he was too powerful, and her knee hurt too much. With his other hand, he took his boating knife and pressed the blade against her throat over the carotid artery. She winced at its coolness.

"What do you want from me?" she said. He was so close that she could feel the blood trickling from his gash onto her bare leg. She tried to turn away, so his breath wouldn't feel so close to her cheeks, but his knife only dug in harder, keeping her where he wanted her.

"It doesn't matter what *I* want," he said.

He changed his grip on the knife, prepared to slice. Then, unexpectedly, his grip loosened, and he let out a muted groan. He rolled over and jumped upright. Now free, she sat up from the bed to see what was happening.

There was someone else in the room.

Colette?

No, the figure was tall and broad, definitely male. As he stepped into a shaft of light from outside, she recognized the man as Moritz. He had kicked her attacker's lower spine, and now he was shuffling about the floor in search of her fallen knife.

"Kate, run!" he said.

She swiped her keys from her desk and bolted toward the front door. Bypassing the elevator for the staircase, she took the steps four or five at a time. On the bottom floor, she pushed through a set of doors that led to the street. She wasn't sure which hurt more—her knee or the pebbles of the sidewalk jabbing into her bare feet as she dashed toward her Renault parked nearby.

She opened the driver's door, shoved her key into the ignition, and turned it.

"Wait!" she heard Moritz say.

He had come through the doors and was running after her.

She didn't care that he had helped her. He had withheld information from her and was not to be trusted. She started to pull away from the curb, but he came around and pounded on the passenger-side window as she eased her car out of its tiny spot.

"Kate, stop!" he shouted. "Let me in!"

His appeal was noise to her. She didn't bother looking at him as he knocked at the window.

"Sod off!" she yelled.

She backed up the Renault and spun the wheel. Two more swivels, and she'd be free of him forever.

"I know who that man is," he said. "He tried to kill me, too. I need your help finding out why. I'll tell you everything I know. And who I really am."

She flipped into reverse and hit the accelerator hard, nearly striking the car behind her.

"For God's sake, Kate," he said, "I saved your life. He's coming back, and I can only hold him off a few seconds in this state."

Battling tears, she opened the lock on his door. It was stupid, but she had to know what was going on. Moritz got in.

The intruder had reached the base of the stairs. In her rear-view mirrors, she could see him sprinting toward the car.

She blinked, and a memory flashed through her. She was escaping with Karl Decker. The SS soldiers were nipping at their heels . . .

"What are you doing?" Moritz said. "Lock your door and drive, or he'll slash your tires!"

She tapped the gas, twisted the wheel, then reversed again. The running man was within a few yards of the sidewalk when Kate floored the gas and sped off along the Rue Dauphine.

Conrad

The snow blanketing the Llao Llao Hotel was bathed in golden light. Seated in the Andean foothills of Bariloche, Argentina, the resort crowned a hilltop between lakes. It looked like a small village of chimneys and sloping rooftops.

The grounds were nestled within a forest of Patagonian evergreens in the heart of a triangle formed by Mounts López, Capilla, and Tronador. To the immediate south and west, a mantle of shrubs and foliage climbed up toward the rock faces and cliffs that marked the range's boundary.

The windows within the hotel's lodge-style Grand Salon offered a 270-degree panorama of the highlands. The room was quiet but for the clatter of silverware and the voice of one man. Guests at banquet tables watched as Conrad Pendelfarr, their host and master of ceremonies, paced the spotlighted floor alongside a life-sized sculpture of Diana. The marble huntress had drawn her bow and stood poised to fire, aimed at a stuffed dear head mounted on the far wall.

"Eighty thousand from Dr. Floyd," said Pendelfarr. He was a practiced auctioneer. His voice rolled and halted, alternating between a poetic legato and a snarelike staccato. "Eighty thousand for this magnificent piece, and do I hear a—ninety from Mrs. Armitage, that's ninety, ninety thousand going on—one hundred thousand, folks, one hundred thousand dollars for this magnificent Diana. Let's keep—a hundred and ten, everyone, that's a hundred and ten thousand and it keeps climbing for—one hundred and twenty from Mr. Davenport, one twenty, and remember we're talking about a fine piece, so keep up the momentum. Yes, folks, a sensational statue originally on display at the Pitti Palace, so do I hear one thirty? . . . That's one hundred thirty thousand from Dr. Floyd again. . . . Now going *once* for any higher bids. Take a look at this marvelous piece of history here, folks, and think twice about the value. . . . Going *twice* for one hundred thirty thousand from Dr. Floyd . . . three times, and *sold* to a new proud owner."

The applause filling the salon showed restraint as two tuxedoed assistants carted the statue offstage. The piece was replaced by a pair of jeweled elephants carried in on palanquins, each animal about the size of a beer cask. Around the room, a staff of waiters had begun to clear the finished entrées. They were now setting up to prepare a bananas flambé dessert, served tableside.

"Congratulations, Dr. Floyd," Pendelfarr said. "We move now to an extraordinary pair of works that no doubt please you all. These two elephants once graced the Mandalay Palace, the last royal palace of the final Burmese monarchy. During World War II, the palace citadel was requisitioned for military use by the Japanese and turned into a supply depot. Before it was destroyed altogether by Allied bombing, some of its finer artistic pieces were salvaged, these precious elephants among them. They are carved from wood, prepared with gesso, and embedded with gemstone cabochons once used as currency in Burma."

Pendelfarr gave his spectators a moment to admire the elephants. He was addressing an international audience of several dozen private art collectors who had gathered in the Río Negro province for his company's annual auction. Tonight's event was exclusive—top-tier clients only. Every guest had purchased a minimum of three truly rare items in his collection. Naturally, he knew them all by name. They were the most loyal patrons of Pendelfarr International, a broker of fine and decorative art since the late 1940s.

He was proud of his company and his ability to run a high-class operation. To him, salesmanship was about creating an unforgettable experience. His collectors weren't buying art; they were buying *him* and the memories he provided, even if he was a bit of an odd-looking man.

His hair had thinned and receded, showing a prominent forehead that had begun to take on the gray pallor and wrinkles of a smoker. With small lips, a narrow nose, and an elflike chin, it was as if every feature was a bit too compact for his face, except for the excess skin on one of his eyelids, which hung low enough to be magnified by his spectacles.

Looking through those lenses, one did not notice the imperfections so much as his self-assuredness. He spoke with the drama of an illusionist in a large theater, and tonight, he had his audience in the palm of his hand.

"We'll begin with a starting bid of two hundred thousand for the pair. Would anyone like to start us off with—two hundred from Mrs. Armitage. Do I hear three? . . . Three hundred thousand from General Hernández—four from Mrs. Armitage . . . Not surprisingly, folks, we're already at twice the starting bid; do I hear four fifty? Think about how far you all came. Don't lose out on this opportunity. Please speak up—four fifty from Mr. Davenport, followed quickly by General Hernández to four seventy-five—that's four hundred seventy-five thousand going once, going—half a million from Mrs. Armitage. As you can see, ladies and gentlemen, three rivals have emerged, and they seem determined to win these jeweled elephants . . ."

He trailed off as a young woman tapped him on the shoulder. It was his newest executive assistant, a girl in her early twenties. He wondered what could be urgent enough to merit the intrusion.

"Señorita de la Fuente," he whispered to her. "We are in the middle of an auction."

Her answer was soft, spoken like a woman eager to avoid his disapproval.

"A telegram," she said, handing him a note. "Important, I think."

He opened the message and read:

Girl got away with help from MD. Pursuing.

He simulated a smile for the crowd to see, and said to her, "Sounds like a promising investment opportunity. Please tell the sender I hope he does indeed pursue and close the deal quickly."

She nodded, tossing her pale, blond hair, and he watched her as she walked offstage, enjoying the sway of her hips and letting her exotic scent stay with him. With a silver sequined dress that emphasized her bosom, she had a sensuous glamor that was sure to make her the focus of every male eye in the room. Having an attractive female at his side could never hurt, particularly at his age.

The recommendation letters from Isabel's previous company in Buenos Aires had been glowing. He had been so impressed by her drive and professionalism that he'd hired her halfway through her interview. He realized now that he knew little about her personal background; he couldn't even say where she was from. Her accent wasn't quite Argentinian.

But she was a lovely girl, Isabel de la Fuente. Intelligent, graceful. She would make a good candidate for a special position he had in mind. He would inquire more about her later.

"Forgive me," he said to the audience. "That was half a million for the elephants, half a million from Mrs. Armitage."

Katharina

"Wake up," Kate said. "We need to go to the police."

It was eight o'clock in the morning in Paris. She had parked her Renault along the Quai du Marché Neuf, near Notre Dame Cathedral, so she and Moritz could catch a few hours of sleep. They had stretched a blanket across the front two seats of the car.

"I told you last night," he said, yawning. "They'll never catch your intruder."

"How do you know?"

"He's too clever."

"Fine. But you need to start answering questions. Like who you really are. Who that man was. How you found my apartment."

"He found you before I did," Moritz said, rubbing the sleep from his eyes. "I told him you lived on the Rue Dauphine after hearing that from your friend Colette. He must have asked your neighbors. I came afterward and heard the struggle."

The tiredness in his voice made her impatient.

"Why in God's name did you tell him that? So he could hunt me down?"

"I had no idea he would try to kill you. We were supposed to surveil your apartment. He was a partner. At least I thought. Then he tried to kill me, too."

"Who is he?"

"His name is Yehuda Uzan. He works for Mossad."

"*Mossad?*"

"Long story. I don't have all the answers."

"And you? Who are you?"

He looked at her with skepticism, as if regretting his promise to tell her anything.

"I guess I owe you that," he said. "My name really is Moritz Dahl. Or, I should say, it is now. It wasn't always. I'm from Egypt originally. Moved to Israel eleven years ago."

"Are you also a Mossad agent?"

"No," he said. "I did join the Israeli Defense Forces, but let's backtrack. In 'forty-eight, as the end of the British Mandate of Palestine drew near, the Haganah's leadership—"

"Haganah?"

"The Jewish military organization before the IDF," he said. "They had drafted Plan Dalet, a set of procedures whose stated purpose was to defend the territory and people of the Jewish state against invasion by Arab armies. The plan divided the Field Corps into five regional brigades. I was assigned to one, but not for long. A team of fifty men was put together. I was one of them. Had the right skills in my favor. It was called Unit 101. A small special forces team."

She learned from Moritz that the team had been organized by Ariel Sharon, under orders from Prime Minister David Ben-Gurion, to address recent Arab *Fedayeen* attacks against the Israelis. The formation of Unit 101 was catalyzed by a five-day battle after a Syrian patrol had entered a demilitarized zone near Tel Mutilla. The men were put through intense training day and night, engaging the enemy in cross-border exercises and executing reprisal operations.

"My time there was brief," Moritz said. "The unit merged into Paratroopers Battalion 890 in January of 'fifty-four, under the command of Lieutenant Colonel Sharon."

"I suppose this is all leading up to how you got your hands on *The Little Marauder* from my father's workshop."

"I'll get there," he said.

She wished he would get there faster but appreciated his mind for detail.

The IDF General Staff, he explained, was petitioned to create a top-secret intelligence-gathering unit three years later, comprised of athletically and intellectually gifted Israeli youth who could penetrate deep into hostile territory. Modeled after the British Special Air Service and adopting its service motto of "Who Dares Wins," the group soon became independent. Fighters were held to the highest standards, trained in reconnaissance, martial arts, camouflage, navigation, and survival behind enemy lines. They would even be instructed by Bedouin trackers to help them understand the thinking of their Arab enemies.

"They were called *Sayeret Matkal*," he said. "In the IDF, they became known as 'the Unit.'"

"I've never heard of the Sayeret Matkal."

"Because they're good at what they do."

"I'd like to know how I ever crossed paths with a member of the IDF Special Forces, born in Denmark. Or did you say Egypt?"

"A former member," he corrected. "And yes, I was born in Alexandria. Moved to Cairo when my mother relocated her hat shop there. She was a well-known milliner in Egypt. Iris Taha. Everyone knew her. Her hats were in vogue throughout Egypt. She met my father while traveling to Copenhagen for a women's congress. I only saw him once, when I was four or five. He was a Danish sailor named Rasmus Dahl."

"You said your name wasn't originally Moritz?"

"It was Anwar," he said. "Anwar Taha. I changed it before joining the IDF. Told them I was a Jewish immigrant from Denmark, to help my chances of military service. Anyhow, when Rasmus didn't come back to us after the war ended, my mother spent years looking for him, trying to contact people in the Royal Danish Navy who might have known him. She took lots of trips to Europe."

"Did she ever find him?"

"Nope."

"I'm sorry," she said, though she didn't think she heard much sadness in his voice—and she didn't trust him enough to care yet.

"Three years ago, I was asked to be part of an operation in Argentina, working with Mossad and Shin Bet agents. Mossad was capturing escaped Nazi war criminals. They'd gotten intelligence from the Nazi hunter Simon Wiesenthal and other sources that Adolf Eichmann was living in Buenos Aires under the name Ricardo Klement. We arrived in Buenos Aires in April 1960, after Eichmann's identity was verified. Spent days keeping him under surveillance to learn his routine. We got him on the eleventh of May outside a bus stop near his house, close to where he'd been working as a foreman at a car factory."

"Are you saying you were part of the team that captured Eichmann?"

"Yes."

"How'd you smuggle him out?"

"We brought him to a Mossad safe house to confirm his identity, then flew him out of Argentina. The plane stopped in Senegal before our arrival in Israel later in May. He arrived under heavy sedation. I would have had reason to celebrate, but when I got home, I learned my mother had died of meningitis three weeks prior."

Kate said again, "I'm sorry."

"She'd gone traveling again. She never lost hope of finding my father."

"She must have loved her husband deeply."

"They were never married," he said. "Well, he was—just not to her. I was conceived from their affair. The only time I saw him was when he visited years later. All I remember are bits and pieces. Good things. He hugged me, told me I'd make a strong soldier. I assume he's gone now, like my mother. It's been a year and a half since she passed. She left me a very strange inheritance."

He handed her a note. She read the portion he had underlined:

I leave you a bank vault in my name. You are to take what is found inside and bequeath the contents to a woman named Katharina Marie Speer. Finding her will not be easy. She'll likely be in England, where she was taken by submarine during the war. Honor this wish of mine, son. The gift is a symbol of my gratitude and appreciation of her family legacy.

"And in that vault," Kate said, "you found the painting?"

"The Bouguereau, yes."

"She was clearly looking for another person. I told you, I'm not . . ."

She wavered, wondering whether it was worth the effort anymore.

"No need to keep up the act," Moritz said. "I saw your face when I called you 'Mademoiselle Speer,' and later when I showed you the painting. You don't have to worry about my knowing, Kate. 'The son shall not suffer for the iniquity of the father.' Ezekiel 18:30. Nor shall the daughter."

She found this less than reassuring. "So, you know the kind of man he was."

"I do."

"How could your mother have left anything for me? We come from different continents. We never met. Where's the connection?"

"It can't be coincidental that the painting means something to you."

"But why give it to me, a stranger? Did she have any idea who Ralf Speer really was?"

"I don't know," Moritz said. "By the time I learned of the bank vault, she had passed. I never had a chance to ask her about her instructions, or anything else for that matter."

"She was obviously misguided about my 'family legacy.' Ralf Speer was a monster."

"Like I said, no idea what she was thinking."

"Karl Decker painted this *Little Marauder* forgery," Kate said. "He was an employee of my father's." She told him about her escape from Germany, and how Karl Decker had delivered the painting to a man on a train before bringing her to the sub. "Ralf Speer thought there was something special about the painting. I think the girl reminded him of me. He called me his 'good little marauder.' "

"Was there a resemblance?"

"I suppose so." She then reminded him, "You still haven't said anything about the man who tried to kill me."

"Yehuda Uzan. I met him in 'sixty, around the time of Eichmann's capture. He was an agent for Mossad. We became friends. I told him about the strange letter my mother had left me and asked if he had any idea how I could track down this Katharina Speer. Then, a few months ago, in September, he came to me and said he was almost certain he'd found you. He suspected you were living under the name Kate Atwell in Paris."

"How'd he figure that out?"

"He said the intel had come from within Mossad. He told me who Ralf Speer was, and he said you were aiding former high-profile Nazis, ratline escapees. That you were helping them build new lives."

"Why would he say those things?"

"I don't know. But at the time I had no reason to doubt him. He told me all the intel had come from Mossad and that he'd been assigned to surveil you. He knew I had the painting you might recognize, so he wanted my help in identifying you. It was all supposed to be off the books."

"You're off your trolley. Why would Mossad have any file on me, let alone a pack of lies?"

"Either Yehuda's acting on his own, lying to me, or the Israeli government is hiding something from me."

"How did Mossad locate me?"

"I don't know, but Yehuda and I came to Paris to monitor your activities. Or so I thought. He knew about the party Pendelfarr was hosting at the museum in Montmartre. I switched the poems last night so I'd have an excuse to talk with you and see how you'd react to being called 'Mademoiselle Speer.' Sure enough, it shocked the hell out of you."

"And when you unfurled the painting . . ."

"More proof. After our meeting by Sacré-Coeur, I went back to Yehuda and told him we had the right woman and that you were living on the Rue Dauphine. We started driving. Then suddenly he sprang a chloroform rag on me and dumped me in the Seine. I managed to make it through. That's when I came after you. His story had to have been a hoax."

"If I really had a connection to any ratline escapees," she said, "he wouldn't have tried to kill me. Interrogate, maybe, but not kill." She didn't trust Moritz enough yet to tell him about her conversation with Maxence about the forgeries, but she had to believe that somehow it was all connected, even if she didn't know exactly how.

"You'd have gone to trial. That's why I came for you. We have to share information so we can get to the bottom of all this."

"Aside from what happened on October 10, 1942, I have nothing to add. I barely remember that night, and I've been Kate Atwell ever since."

"It's still a piece of the puzzle," he said.

She searched the lines of his swarthy face for dishonesty or malice. He seemed to be doing the same with her; after all, if he was telling the truth, he'd been led to believe she was a Nazi abettor.

"I assume we'd both like to learn why this former partner of yours tried to kill us," she said, "and to prevent any further attempts. If either of us uncovers anything, we should alert the other. How can I contact you?"

He grinned, morbidly amused.

"That's your plan?" he said. "Go back home and continue life as normal? Let me know if anything happens and hope I return the favor?"

"Aside from taking this to the police, I don't have any other plan."

"You don't want the French police involved. They'll slow you down, and they can't protect you from Yehuda," he said. "I think we should work together."

She folded her arms. "This is daft. But I suppose . . . well, how do you see that happening?"

"We're both looking at the same puzzle, and we can try to fill in the blanks together. If that doesn't sell you, the fact is, you're safer with me."

"Might be a half-decent idea if we had a place to start."

"We do." He reached into his pocket and pulled out a small leather book. The pages were still soggy from his trip to the bottom of the Seine.

"There was something else in the bank vault. A diary of my mother's first few years of travel. She wasn't only searching for my dad. She also spent some time looking for you."

"Your mom looked for *me?*"

Bewildered, Kate began flipping through the wet pages. Much of Iris Taha's writing had become smeared and illegible.

"Don't worry if you can't read it," Moritz said. "Most of it was indecipherable anyway. Random notes scrawled here and there. I couldn't make sense of it. Only thing I managed to get was an address surrounded by exclamation points, toward the middle."

He showed her the page and the section that read:

! ! ! ! ! ! ! !
! W. G. K. *!*
! believes saw K. M. *Speer Oct '42—!!! !*
! interviewed Bahnhofstrasse 8251, Zermatt !
! ! ! ! ! ! ! !

The entry was dated 17 May 1947.

"Your mother wrote that fifteen years ago," Kate said. "Any idea what 'W. G. K.' means?"

"Someone's initials, maybe? I couldn't say whose."

"This is our only lead?"

"As far as I know."

"You're not exactly brimming with useful information."

"Can't argue with that," he said. "But I'd like to know why someone used me to try to kill you."

She thought it through and made a decision. It was mad, but she had to know why someone had tried to stick a knife in her throat.

"I suggest we return to my apartment, carefully, so I can get the painting and pack a bag."

"Pack a bag?"

"Does my bedtime attire look suitable for Switzerland, Monsieur Dahl?"

THE DIARY OF DAMIEN BRAY

My Days in Camouflage Company

Final Three Letters

3 September 1942

My darling Evanna,

We've reached 'E' Camp. We were greeted by the sergeant in charge and told to offload our bags and rest for an early morning tomorrow. I took a stroll around the perimeter of the testing site here and found a nice place to lie back in the sand. There's a dry, dusty wind here. I can feel it now, tickling my arms, and like to think that I'm feeling you with me in the warmth of the breeze—that it's you stroking me.

Do you remember our conversation when I got my first pilot's assignment? We were deciding on a constellation to look at during our time apart. That way we'd know we were both seeing the same part of the sky every night. I remember it like it was yesterday:

'Cassiopeia is the clear choice', I said.

'Why, you fancy a vain queen?' you said.

'No, I've already got one of those. It's because the stars make a W, easy to spot'.

'Not as easy as Aries, whose three brightest stars make a near straight line', you said. 'That's my favourite'.

'Simple favourite for a simple lass'.

'Hey! If you want simple, I say we choose Venus, the brightest speck in the sky'.

So we did, and we held its glow in our sights every night I was away.

Well, I'm gazing up there again. Can't help wondering if that's you twinkling back at me, or if it's merely the sky's most luminous reminder that I'm alone now.

Your Damien

26 September 1942

Evanna, my love,

I've spent almost a month at Helwan and have been impressed learning about the camoufleurs' devices of the past year.

Among the cleverest successes was the defense of a desalination plant during the Siege of Tobruk. The plant was large and impossible to conceal, but processed forty thousand gallons of seawater daily. Without the water, the British would have had to surrender the fortress. To protect their supply, they painted an oozing shape of black tar on the roof and walls of the plant. Seeing pictures from recce cameras, the Germans thought they'd bombed the structure and caused it to cave in.

They also managed to hide a rail complex at Misheifa, complete with a depot, marshaling yard, locomotive facilities, sheds, and sidings. They did this by creating a decoy railhead and tank delivery spur that stretched for miles. The idea was to divert aerial attacks and confuse the enemy on the timing of a real attack. Dummy locomotives were made from canvas, false tanks built of palm fronds, petrol cans hammered into track, and even cookhouse stoves transformed into smoking fireboxes for the locomotives. The dummy headquarters had tents, huts, kitchens, and straw soldiers. Over two weeks, the Germans attacked the site with nearly a hundred bombs that would have otherwise been aimed at the real railhead.

Apparently, there's more to come.

Today I was awakened in my hammock at 6 a.m. by a subaltern. After a rather cheerless breakfast of hardtack biscuits and Marmite, I was taken to see the chief instructor with my colleagues.

The instructor said a telegram arrived from Grey Pillars: Something big is underway at Eighth Army HQ.

I wondered if the news would be worthy of my first transmission. I reined in my excitement and let the others ask for details. The instructor didn't know much. Apparently, this one's hush-hush, even at Grey Pillars. It's some sort of plan to be carried out by our chief camoufleur, Barkas.

They're calling it Operation Bertram. By the sound of it, our commanders think we'll hit Rommel for six out of Africa with this one.

The instructor told us Barkas has requested that a member of the No. 4 Camouflage Course be sent to Eighth Army HQ at Borg-el-Arab. This is a massive-scale operation, and he worries they're shorthanded in leadership. I told the instructor I had experience with desert travel,

Saharan archaeology was my field of study, and I've never been afraid of a bivouac.

He told me to pack my duffel and ride with the next lorry bound for Borg-el-Arab. I've tried to prepare myself for arrival at Eighth Army HQ. I'll need to find a safe place to radio the *Afrika Korps*.

We're en route to Borg-el-Arab now. I'm sitting in the back of the lorry, crammed in here with supplies. We've headed up the coast. The signs say we've entered the Western Desert. I managed to glimpse the Pyramids and the Sphinx before we turned off the main road.

The Mediterranean blues sparkle to the north. To the south, it's a different story. All you can see are shrubs, endless queues of military vehicles, dune fields strewn with fallen tank parts, and tens of thousands of tons of *materiel*. Even some shot-down German recce planes.

I miss Galway almost as much as I miss you. Talk to the angels up there, will you?

Let Bertram be my ticket home.

Your Damien

27 September 1942

My darling Evanna,

I am now deep within the Eighth Army at Borg-el-Arab HQ.

This will be my final entry.

The British have found a way to make soldiers out of artists, and vice versa.

Today I was briefed on Operation Bertram. The plan is mind-boggling.

This morning I was summoned by the Director of Camouflage himself. I found him in his hut. He looks to be in his early forties, uniform tucked in, hair slicked into a part. He was all pep.

Geoffrey Barkas offered a salute and said, 'So you're the Irish stained-glass man'. I told him it was by hobby, not by profession. He said most of us wouldn't call ourselves professional warfighters either, yet here we are.

He led me inside, pointing to a wall pinned with maps of the Alamein line. It was marked up with Allied and Axis positions. He began with a general overview of the importance of the North African campaign, saying the Eighth Army is all that's keeping Rommel's forces from advancing past El Alamein to Cairo, Alexandria, and the Suez Canal. With the Suez Canal, control of the Mediterranean would fall to Hitler, and with Egypt, Hitler would gain access to Middle Eastern and Persian oil fields.

As I stood by listening, I felt my pulse rise; I couldn't wait for him to get on with it and tell me about the extraordinary project that's underway.

The *Panzerarmee* has retreated to a strong defensive position, he said. Recce planes report that the German and Italian tank corps stretch for twenty miles, from the sea down to the Qattara Depression. That's an impassable area far below sea level, filled with salt pans, cliffs, and fine sand. The depression's escarpments form a boundary on the battlefield, preventing either army from outflanking the other.

He went on and on about how in the north, 15th Panzer has support from the Italian Trieste and Littorio Armoured Divisions. In the south, 21st Panzer has the Ariete and Bologna Divisions. Between them, they've got a formation of paratroopers known as the Ramcke Brigade. And plenty of 88s, the German antiaircraft and antitank artillery guns that everyone dreads over here. He also said the Desert Fox is deepening his 'Devil's Garden' minefields, a belt of desert sown with millions of mines and entanglements of barbed wire, deadly to tanks.

I studied the markings on the map, more interested in the scribbles to the east of the Alamein line.

The British plan.

I told him I'd heard he had intentions to see off Axis forces from the desert in some sort of large-scale deception. He confirmed this to be true and said it was top secret, that loose lips anywhere—including Grey Pillars—could jeopardise the whole thing. I told him that having censored letters on the RMS *Andorra*, I've learned discretion is a virtue in wartime. When he told me I was ready to hear about Operation Bertram, I was almost too excited to speak.

There's going to be a two-pronged, simultaneous attack, he said. The real one will be in the north. The other, a trick attack in the south. The attack will take place on 23 October, but they'll make the Germans think it will be a week or more later.

That's only twenty-eight days from now, and in that time a *complete* phantom armored corps is to be built in the south: six hundred dummy tanks and support vehicles. An entire army conjured from nothing—hey presto!

To the north, they plan to transport thousands of tons of armor, artillery, and *materiel* without the Germans realising.

In two days!

On the map, I studied a field of operations spanning fifteen hundred square miles of desert and asked how all this was to be done.

He explained, to make the Germans turn their attentions south, they plan to build up false stores made from whatever comes to hand. Sticks, canvas. Dummy tanks will be made from reed, bedframes, cardboard barrels, and frond hurdles from around the Nile Delta. From the air, it will look like the accumulation of an army. All from makeshift, ad hoc production lines.

They even have a plan to convince the Germans of the supply dump's importance: by building a dummy water pipeline into the area, with the help of local laborers. The pipeline is to be called 'Diamond'. It will be five miles long, built at a speed the engineers say would match a real job. It'll have embellishments, too: water towers, control boxes, scarecrow men.

I asked how he planned on moving the tanks and munitions north under the nose of the Luftwaffe. He told me about a stage magician among the camoufleurs who had developed a device called the 'Sunshield'. It's essentially a frame of canvas and black steel tubing that can disguise a tank as a lorry. No surprise the inventor's an illusionist.

They intend to transport an entire army of tanks using these Sunshields. In the weeks leading to battle, real lorries will be openly parked in what's to become the tank assembly area on the front line. Real tanks will be openly parked at a great distance, an apparent two days away. Forty-eight hours before the attack, they'll use Sunshields to disguise the tanks, and drive them up to the front line under cover of night, where they'll look like lorries. Where those had been, they'll put dummies. From the air, it will look as if nothing has changed.

At first glance, I thought the plan sounded ludicrous, that I could let it fail on its own. But as he went on, I realised they'd thought through every detail. They'd even devised little ruses like generating false radio traffic to give voices to their straw men. Besides, the camoufleurs have been successful so far; I have to believe that Operation Bertram has merit.

He gave me a role. I'm to help disguise the army's larger field guns and ammunition limbers, and direct a dummy-tank production line in the south.

Construction began today. My head's still spinning. They're determined to see this through. I've been to the workshops. I've studied the blueprints. I watched the laborers dig the first trench. Bertram is underway.

In all likelihood, the Desert War will be decided in twenty-eight days, at the next battle of El Alamein.

Looking out into the Blue, as the men call it—the vast desert—I can imagine the lineup of the *Panzerarmee* many miles beyond. They're a straight shot west.

Somehow, in the coming weeks, I must contact Rommel and warn him of the grandest magic trick ever attempted.

My love, as long as you watch over me, I won't fail you.

Your Damien

1962

Colette

The pulsations in Colette's head continued to beat, beat, beat at the hand of a sadistic drummer. After all the water she'd guzzled when she woke up, she'd expected her hangover to be gone by now.

Stepping off the sidewalk, she crossed the street toward home and walked into the path of a car. The driver honked and swerved, missing her.

"Idiot," she said, and almost mustered the energy to kick his rear fender.

Her voice was hoarse. She wondered if she was still a bit drunk, or whether it was her usual morning grogginess clouding her brain. She checked her watch—make that *afternoon* grogginess. It was one o'clock.

Rubbing her temples, she decided she didn't mind the pain as much as she might have. Last night had been a smashing success, and even though she and Kate had planned the party together, she had done the lion's share of the work. The compliments had flooded in, and a few of the brokers, including Philippe, said it was the best event of the year. Perhaps she could finally move out from behind Kate's shadow. Maybe she would even get a promotion, or at the very least, get to do more than answer the phone.

She pieced her night together. She couldn't find Kate at the end of the soirée, so she'd gone straight to an after-party with Philippe. At some point the cognac had come out, and she didn't remember much after that. This morning she'd awakened in his apartment, but he'd been comatose at the edge of the mattress when she got up, and too far gone to hear her getting dressed, scrambling eggs on his stove, or leaving for home. She decided to leave him in peace. They would see each other at work the next day.

She looked for her keys in her handbag and let herself into her apartment, too bleary-eyed to notice the man stepping out of a car as she arrived.

"Kate, I'm home," she said.

There was no answer. She peeked into her roommate's bedroom and saw the covers were still a mess. Strange. Kate's room was usually pristine.

"*Bonjour?* Kate?"

She hadn't been home five minutes when she heard a knock at the front door. Looking through the peephole, she saw a handsome, bronze-complexioned man in a three-piece suit. A Middle Easterner, she guessed. He had the purposeful look of an executive, and she wondered if he had been at the party the night before.

As if sensing her proximity on the other side of the door, the man said in French, "Mademoiselle Fossey, my name is Yehuda Uzan. I'm an investigator working for a foreign government. I've come to ask you some questions about your roommate, Kate Atwell, if you don't mind."

Her heart quickened. Had something happened to Kate?

"Is she okay?" Colette asked.

"That's what I'm here to discuss with you."

He spoke excellent French, colored with a hint of an accent she couldn't place.

"I'd like to see your identification."

"Certainly," he said, opening a briefcase and removing a sheaf of papers from a folder within. He flashed a page in front of the peephole. Colette squinted, unable to quite read it.

"Slide it under the door," she said.

He did, and she studied the page with his full name, birth date, picture, and brief description of his vocation following the title "Investigator." Some of the writing was in Hebrew.

"You're from Israel?"

"That's right, Mademoiselle Fossey."

"So, what are you doing here?"

"If you'd like, we can have this conversation on two sides of the door," he said, "but it's chilly in the hallway, and I'd love some coffee."

She swung the door open. "Come in." She invited him to take a seat at a couch. "Where is Kate?"

"I'm hoping you'll be able to tell me."

She made coffee for both of them and took a seat.

He said, "I want to preface this by saying what I share with you will be hard to believe, but the information comes from my country's highest intelligence circles."

Ouah, Colette thought. Intelligence circles? Where could this be going?

There was nothing unfriendly about her visitor, but the presumption of an infallible higher order rankled her. He'd spoken of these intelligence circles as if they should not have to earn her trust.

"Who do you work for, Monsieur Uzan?"

"Our national intelligence agency," he said. "Mossad."

"What are you doing in France?"

"Trying to locate your roommate, Kate Atwell. I'm afraid she's not who you believe her to be."

"What in God's name do you mean by that?"

"We have evidence that Kate has been aiding Nazis and other fascists who, following the Second World War, fled Europe via ratlines to escape justice."

Colette tried not to show any reaction aside from irritation at having her life disrupted by what was obviously a bureaucratic mistake in a foreign office.

"That's preposterous," she said. "You must have crossed files or something. You've got the wrong person."

What bumbling imbeciles.

She reminded herself that he had no right to be here, and she could ask him to leave at any time. That was another thing she hated about "authorities" like these. You had to remind not only them, but also yourself, of your rights when you were around them, or else they would run roughshod over you.

"Get out of this apartment now, please," she said.

"You don't want to hear the evidence?"

Getting involved with this detective's mix-up would be a futile and hopeless pursuit, she knew. "Your story doesn't make an ounce of sense."

"Do you know who her father was?"

"I've asked you to go." She stood up and walked toward the door.

"Answer this one question about her father."

He had some gall to stay sitting there, drinking her coffee, after she'd asked him twice to leave. He wasn't even a French authority. She could call the police on him if she wanted. She might have resisted on another day, but she felt her headache coming back in waves, wearing down the fight in her.

"Yes," she said. "He is George Atwell, a wealthy copper—"

"I mean her biological father," he said.

Where was this going? "She never speaks of her earliest childhood."

"Why not, do you think?"

"It's probably unpleasant. I don't talk about mine very much, for the same reason."

"What has she told you?"

It was none of his business. "Will telling you make you leave?"

"If you want me to."

"She came from a family of Austrian farmers who were killed during an accidental bombing, some kind of Luftwaffe drill," Colette said. "So, you see, it's natural she wouldn't want to talk about it. Now run back to your mighty intelligence circles and tell your people they've made a ridiculous error."

"Does it sound plausible to you that the eight-year-old daughter of farmers, living in the Austrian countryside, would somehow make her way onto an escape submarine on the other end of Germany, by herself, following the death of her family?"

"She was evacuated."

"I asked if it sounded plausible."

He was right—it didn't—but she asked, "Why would Kate lie about it?"

"To hide the truth about her real father. He was Ralf Speer, Vice Minister of Propaganda for the Third Reich." This piqued her interest, not because she believed him, but because she recognized the name from her art studies. "He worked closely with Joseph Goebbels, regulating culture and mass media to enforce Nazi ideology."

"Ralf Speer, the famous forger?"

"It seems Kate inherited her painting skill from him."

"You don't seem to know how ludicrous you sound."

"I know this comes as a shock."

"I'm not shocked because it isn't true. Why would you even say such a thing?"

She didn't believe this man at all, but she couldn't help remembering the moment in the gallery a few months ago when Monsieur Maxence had mentioned the name Ralf Speer, and Kate had turned deathly pale.

"Kate's name was given to us by Adolf Eichmann. He told us she was a key player."

"Adolf Eichmann used Kate's name?"

She really wanted to see him back this one up.

"Not only that, but a second Nazi war criminal, one we captured last year, corroborated Eichmann's account."

"But there must be a lot of Kate Atwells. It's got to be a common name in Britain."

"Look at this picture, and tell me if we haven't found the one."

Yehuda removed a photograph of a man from his briefcase and slid it across the table. The picture had been taken on a winter's day; the subject's black overcoat was dusted with snow. He was standing with his arms behind his back, halfway up the stairs to an official-looking building, facing the camera for a portrait shot. He had a regal countenance and a look of unquestioned belonging, like a man who thought of his workplace as his one true home.

As Colette studied the nose, mouth, and jawline, she felt a flutter in her chest. *Mon Dieu*, she thought. She looked at the photo a good while, noting every likeness between the man on those steps and the girl she had known for ten years. She was no expert in genetics, but by any standard, the resemblance couldn't be a coincidence. She had no doubt she was looking at a biological relative of Kate's.

The caption at the bottom of the photo read: *Ralf Speer at the Ordenspalais, 1941*.

Still, the investigator hadn't proved a thing.

"I don't understand," Colette said. "Even if it's true that Kate is his daughter, why would she help these ratline escapees?"

"It's hard to say," Yehuda answered. "She was born to a Nazi family. Family gives us roots, definition, something we always carry with us and cling to. The bonds of blood run deep. She may be motivated by legacy as much as ideology."

"Do her adoptive parents, George and Lona Atwell, have any idea about what you claim she's doing?"

"We don't think so."

"She hasn't told me anything about this. Not anything, ever."

"Forgive me, Mademoiselle Fossey, as I know the two of you are best friends, but of course she wouldn't tell you. Why do you think she wanted to come to Paris?"

"Her fiancé dumped her. She wanted a new start."

"How do you know that story's even true?"

Colette thought about all the times she had asked why Alfred had broken their engagement and how evasive Kate had been. "I don't, but this is wrong. *So* wrong. Wrong for me to even consider this is anything but a giant mistake. What business do you have coming to my apartment to say these things?"

She realized her saucer was soaked in spilt coffee.

"I was assigned to find Kate and bring her to Israel for questioning. We want to use her to get the names and locations of the ratline escapees she's associated with."

"She's innocent. I know it with every fiber of my being. And I won't help you detain an innocent person."

"But she's not innocent," Investigator Uzan said. "She's stolen a painting from Monsieur Maxence, and we think she's going to sell it to fund her activities."

Colette laughed out loud. "That's totally ridiculous. Do you even know who she is? Who her parents are? They're rich. She wouldn't need to steal anything, even if she was doing what you say she's doing. She didn't do anything wrong. And I hope to God . . . I hope to God you find the right person eventually, so you see it wasn't her, and so you can give the real perpetrator the noose."

Colette saw in the living room mirror that her face had turned red. She had begun to think about her mother and father's murder by Nazi soldiers. She had never had any sympathy for Germany or for the Germans themselves. She wanted anyone even remotely linked to her parents' deaths, or any of the atrocities committed during the war, to suffer. But that didn't include Kate. Her involvement in helping those pigs was unthinkable.

Yet there was no denying the facial similarity between her and Ralf Speer. This proved, at the very least, that someone was trying to fool her using advanced photographic trickery—or that Kate's story about her family of Austrian farmers had been false. Still, even if Kate had lied about her childhood, who would blame her? And who knew how much Kate actually remembered? Colette's own memories only existed because her aunt and uncle had always talked about her parents and kept photos of them around the house.

She said, "I want to read transcripts of the accounts given by Eichmann and the other war criminal you claim she was helping."

"Certainly. Right here."

The man reached into his briefcase and handed her two stapled sheaves of paper. She skimmed the lines of dialogue that were apparently recorded during trial, stopping now and then at any phrase that stood out: *Katharina shipped food packages overseas to scores of my former colleagues,* Eichmann had testified. *She had dozens of addresses in Argentina, Brazil, Paraguay, Chile, Bolivia, Uruguay ... assisted with bank transfers and transportation logistics within each nation and across South America ...* She leafed through the other testimony. *Provided false identities to at least seven escapees, among them the commandant to a midsized extermination camp ...*

Colette felt a cramp in her stomach even seeing the words, still nowhere near ready to start believing this man, but now she was at least more willing to listen.

"Any idiot with a typewriter could have pulled these transcripts out of his ass," she said.

She expected the accusation to put him on the defensive, but instead, he seemed to appreciate her desire to exhaust every possibility that worked in Kate's favor.

"That's true," he said. "I can't prove their authenticity here in your living room by any means, but I do have a third compelling piece of evidence. Would you like me to leave now, or would you like to see it?"

He had not tried to peddle his story like a salesman. He had shown her the facts and helped her piece them together, like a teacher. She had asked *him* for the transcripts, and now he was offering additional information. Painful as this conversation had been, she didn't see any harm in taking a look.

"Show me," she said.

Investigator Uzan finished his coffee and set it on the table. He presented another photograph, this one taken near Sacré-Coeur. She could see the lit domes of the basilica in the background. It was underexposed and blurry, taken at night, though she could still make out the two faces. One was Kate's. The picture was in black and white, but she recognized the design of Kate's favorite turquoise dress, as well as the earrings and pearl fascinator—the outfit Kate had worn to the soirée last night. The other person in the photo was a man who looked to be in his late twenties. She couldn't see much more than his profile, but he was holding some sort of tube-shaped object.

After a few seconds, Colette remembered she had seen this man at the party. Then, when it was time to go, Kate was nowhere to be found.

"This must have been last night," she said. "Who took the picture?"

"I did. The film was developed this morning."

She tried to guess when it was taken. Colette had looked for Kate for almost twenty minutes before leaving with Philippe, but Kate must have rendezvoused with this man. It appeared to be a clandestine meeting.

"You were following her?"

"Now I have proof that she's active. She may have already sold the painting and left town."

"Who's that man she's with?"

"A dangerous criminal named Moritz Dahl." He handed her a file on the man that included a mug shot, a brief biography, and a detailed list of offenses. "A member of her network."

The photograph hurt Colette terribly. Whether or not Kate had been lying about her past, it proved incontrovertibly she was keeping secrets again, all while living with Colette.

Colette tried to reverse course. Despite all the evidence he had shown her, this investigator was still a total stranger, and if his story turned out to be an elaborate fabrication, she could never forgive herself for buying it. But there was no way to falsify the third photo. It had to have been taken last night. Was Kate really hiding something?

No. Colette felt a pang of guilt for even considering it. Had she been too eager to believe this detective? It was a question for deeper introspection, she realized. Had she been looking for a reason to judge Kate and challenge her friend's integrity? A voice within her tried to confess, yes, she wanted Kate—on her pedestal of wealth, talent, promise, beauty, and morality—to sell out, to prove imperfect, to give Colette even one reason to look down on her.

Her inner confession was hardly loud enough to be heard over the throbbing in her temples. The investigator's visit had only worsened her headache.

"What do you want from me?" Colette said.

"Take me to George and Lona Atwell. If Kate is communicating with them, they may know where she is. Once we find out, you'll lure her to me. She trusts you."

"Why go to the Atwells? She lives here. Wait for her to come home."

"She's with Moritz now. She won't be coming back any time soon. My theory is that she sold him the painting, and he's warned her that we're on her trail. We've been trying to hunt him down for some time. He covers his tracks well."

There was no way she could help this man, Colette thought. She'd never get over the guilt. It would be an outright betrayal, and despite all the compelling evidence this man had shown her, none of it could outweigh her firsthand experience. She knew Kate better than anyone else. This had to be a mistake.

"I'm sorry," she said, "but I can't believe it. I don't think you're a liar. I mean, I think you honestly believe everything you're telling me, but someone's made a mistake. I know you must be thinking there's no substitute for facts, but there's no substitute for knowing someone, either."

"Okay, Mademoiselle Fossey," Investigator Uzan said, standing. "I understand your position." If he was judging her for refusing to consider the evidence, it didn't show. "I'll leave you in peace and continue my search. Thank you for the coffee. If you change your mind, give me a call."

He jotted down a number.

As he stood and made for the door, Colette said, "Don't forget your photographs."

"I have copies," he said, and showed himself out.

Colette shut her eyes, and at once a montage of her fondest memories with Kate began to play on the backs of her closed eyelids like a film reel. The scenes transitioned from the residence hall at Worcester College where she met Kate for the first time, to the auction house in London, to their walks in Paris, and even to the party last night—an evolution of scenes filled with joy and laughter, leading to their dream of starting an art consultancy together, all compressed into a few microseconds of mental footage.

Then she played all the memories back again. They were darker this time, shaded by an alternative truth. What if her entire friendship with Kate was a lie?

Stop, she thought. Her imagination was running wild. Surely, Kate would show up in the next hour and prove this was all one giant mistake.

. . .

It was the longest day of Colette's life, not only because of the headache, but because there was no sign of her roommate as the afternoon passed into evening. Colette sat unmoving on the couch without turning on a light, as her hopes that Kate would come home with an explanation slowly faded. At midnight, she was forced to go to bed. She had work the following day. All these months, she had dreamed of the triumphant Monday morning after the party, when she finally would be noticed and celebrated. Now that dream was turning into a nightmare.

She tossed and turned without falling into a deep sleep, and she decided to get out of bed before the alarm rang. Her only hope was to pull herself together, go to work, and figure out what to do at the gallery.

After a long shower, she carefully applied her makeup, dried her hair, and put on her favorite green dress. Aside from the bags under her eyes, she almost looked herself. What if this investigator was telling the truth? As the hours passed with no word from Kate, the possibility slowly crept into her psyche.

She made her usual walk to the gallery, peering into the bakery looking for Kate, anticipating her on every street corner. Until today, she had delighted in the Christmas decorations and good cheer on the streets of Paris, but not anymore. A sense of dread had taken hold of her.

She unlocked the gallery and flipped on the lights. As usual, she went to the back to start coffee and turn up the heat for the brokers who were due in an hour. She shivered. It was chilly in the old building.

Victor Maxence stepped into the hallway from his office, and she jumped with surprise.

"*Bonjour, mademoiselle,*" he said. His voice was even colder than the air in the room.

"*Bonjour, monsieur,*" she said with false cheer. "How did you enjoy the event?"

"A painting was stolen," he said. "I would contact the authorities, but I was hoping to speak to you first. And to Mademoiselle Atwell."

Colette didn't know what to say. So it was true. A painting was missing, and so was Kate. "What painting?"

"A minor work," he said. "But one I hope to recover with your help."

Colette hadn't looked at the artwork on exhibit at the party. She had been preoccupied with the party itself. But why steal? It didn't make any sense. Her parents already owned priceless artworks and could have easily afforded anything Kate deemed worthy. She brushed up against the investigator's story in her mind, but retreated instantly.

"What can I do?" Colette said.

"I've been contacted by a Monsieur Uzan, who seems to be looking for Kate for his own reasons," said Maxence, "but our interests are aligned for now."

Colette said nothing. She still couldn't believe that Kate was helping Nazis, and she had no intention of telling Maxence about any of Yehuda Uzan's allegations.

"He tells me that he's already spoken to you, but that you were reluctant to help him."

"Kate's my best friend."

"You *will* help him."

"What he said about her seems so hard to believe."

"Well, believe this, Mademoiselle Fossey. Until Kate Atwell is found, there's no place for you here."

"But I didn't do anything wrong," Colette said, desperation surging into her voice.

"If she is found, if the painting is found, I might be forced to admit I was wrong about you," he said with a sinister tone, "but as you said, you're best friends, and I find it hard to believe you knew nothing of her plans."

"I didn't," Colette said through tears. "I swear!"

"And I swear that if you step foot in this gallery again without a direct invitation from me, I will have you arrested for trespassing. You may go now."

. . .

Colette returned to the apartment feeling dejected. Today was supposed to have been joyous, but it was turning out to be the worst day of her life. The Atwells were paying the rent on the apartment, but once they realized Kate had disappeared, that would stop, and Colette would be homeless. She could never have afforded such a place on her own. Without a job, she wouldn't be able to find a place to live even on the outskirts of the city. Unless Kate turned up, and unless the painting turned up, she would never work in the art world again.

Even if it were true, even if Kate had taken the painting for some reason, her parents would step in to protect their darling daughter. That's what the wealthy did. They looked after their own. Colette would be collateral damage at the end of the day. The Atwells had been good to her, but she wasn't their daughter, and they wouldn't look out for her welfare. Not anymore.

For the first time, Colette considered the investigator's story. If he was telling the truth and Kate had run away with this man Moritz, she would not be returning home at all.

She stared at the photographs that Uzan had left there, spelling out explanations that could absolve Kate: a bureaucratic mix-up, an intricate prank, a vicious attempt by one of their colleagues to get Kate fired or to make her parents look bad. Anything to make her ignore her gut, which said the simplest answer was usually the right one. But all those explanations were implausible.

Eventually Colette wandered into Kate's room to check for signs that she'd left in a hurry. She found Kate's collection of framed pictures, which were usually arranged on a travel chest, stacked on her desk. Colette looked at the photos one at a time: a photo of Kate standing with George and Lona in the garden of their estate—the two of them smiling proudly in their graduation robes at Oxford—Kate as a young girl, holding Lona Atwell's hand outside the English orphanage where she was adopted . . .

She brought that picture closer. The edge of the photo had been bent, and something was tucked behind it. Removing the frame to see what it was, she discovered another photograph. It fluttered to the floor and landed face up.

"*Mon Dieu!*"

A chill went through her.

It was a photo of Ralf Speer. It looked as if it had come from a history book.

Oh . . . my . . . God.

She picked up the photo and gave it a closer look. Without a doubt, she could see Kate in the man. Even more telling was the fact this photo had been hidden there in the first place—a picture of the man Colette now had no doubt was Kate's biological father.

One of the men responsible for her parents' death.

Someone Kate was still clinging to.

Colette couldn't accept it. She didn't want to. But too much of Yehuda Uzan's story was true for her to completely dismiss the rest. If she went with him to talk to the Atwells, maybe they could find Kate, and Colette could discover the truth once and for all—for better or worse.

She ran to her room and, with a shaky hand, dialed the number he had given her.

"Detective Uzan," she said. "It's Colette Fossey. I'll take you to see Kate's parents, but that's it. I still don't believe you, but I want to know the truth."

"I thought you might come around."

"Lord and Lady Trefwyn live in Wales," she said. "On Anglesey, which you can reach by ferry from Le Havre, there's a small town called Beaumaris. They have a manor house there."

"How far is Le Havre from here?"

"A two-and-a-half-hour drive." She cleared her throat. "If I come with you . . . well, I know Kate, how she thinks."

"Are you saying you can help me track her down?"

"No, but I can get the Atwells to tell us what they know. They trust me."

"And I know Moritz," he said. "It's not such a terrible idea to start in Wales."

"Pick me up here when you're ready."

She went to her room, pulled out her overnight bag, and laid the picture of Ralf Speer at the bottom. When she saw Kate, she would ask her about her father, about the Nazis, and about the stolen painting. No matter what the answers were, if there was any consolation, it was that Colette would never have to envy any aspect of Kate Atwell's life again.

Katharina

As the cog wheels of the train began to turn and mesh with the rail, preparing for steep grades ahead, Kate gazed out the window at the white slopes of the Pennine Alps. The drive from Paris had taken one full, exhausting day. She and Moritz had spent the previous night at a ski lodge in Täsch, three miles north of their destination. They left the Renault there and boarded the shuttle train at sunrise.

They disembarked at a station in Zermatt. Comprised of three main streets and a maze of offshoots, the town lay at the southern end of the Matter Valley, among several of the tallest of the Alps; the steep walls and crooked summit of the Matterhorn soared from the clouds in the distance. A river crisscrossed the valley, rising from the Gorner and Zmutt glaciers on the east and west sides. Little hamlets could be found tucked in the neighboring valleys among the forests of fir trees.

"I could never get used to living here," Moritz said as they began walking north along the Bahnhofstrasse. "Too much damned snow."

"To my taste there's never enough. I like it here. My mum and dad will be jealous when they get my telegram."

"What telegram?"

"I sent a message before we left."

"Did you say you were going to Zermatt?"

"Only to tell them I'm safe, and not to speak to anyone other than Colette."

"Kate, you can't be so naïve," he said. "The man we're up against . . ."

"What about him?"

"If you leave information for him to find, he'll find it. No more mistakes like that." He seemed paranoid, but she knew he was also right. "Let's do what we need to do here and then get out of Zermatt."

"I'm sorry," she said. "My experience outfoxing assassins is limited."

"Watch, learn, and don't be thick," he said.

The cobbled main street bustled with pedestrians passing between stores and bars and chalets, many with skis slung over their shoulders. Bells jingled as a horse-drawn sleigh glided by. Groups of children stood in lines behind vendors melting fudge over roasted chestnuts. Kate looked up at the steeply scarped mountains enclosing the valley, following the perimeter, and came to rest on the pyramid of the Matterhorn. She imagined the fun she would have setting up her canvas and easel, mixing the various shades of snow on her palette, from shiny to pearly to powdery.

The road wound in a slight spiral and led to a small, less populated neighborhood. They checked the house numbers until reaching 8251.

"This is it," she said, apprehensive. There were so many unknowns. Coming to Switzerland had been a grasp at straws, but the entry in Iris Taha's journal was their only lead. It had taken them to a chalet nestled between two hills. She felt silly knocking on the door, not knowing who lived here, or who, or what, was denoted by W. G. K.

They heard activity on the other side, and the door opened a crack. The woman who greeted them looked to be in her early thirties. She was wearing an oven mitt and came accompanied by pleasant aromas presumably wafting from her kitchen.

"*Guete Morge*," she said. *Good morning*.

The falter in her voice suggested a reluctance to receive strangers. Kate could also tell she was no natural Swiss-German speaker.

"*Hallo. Sprechen Sie Englisch? Für meinen Freund*," Kate asked her in German, which she guessed was the lady's natural language. It felt strange to speak it after all these years, but the words came easily to her. *Hello. Do you speak English? For my friend*.

"Yes," the woman said. "Can I help you?"

Kate offered a hand, which the woman accepted tentatively.

"My name is Kate Atwell. This is my friend, Moritz Dahl. We've come to you under unusual circumstances." Moritz showed her Iris's notebook and turned to the relevant page as Kate continued to explain, "His late mother bequeathed something to me. It's a replica of a painting by Bouguereau called *The Little Marauder*. We don't know why she left this for me, but in her journal, she mentions my name, as well as your address and the letters W. G. K. We came to you hoping you might be able explain the connection."

The woman took the diary. Moritz pointed to the initials.

"If W. G. K. is a person," he said, "I think my mother met him or her long ago in some kind of interview."

The woman at the door handed the diary back, her eyes darting between them as if to gauge their intentions.

"Who was your mother?" she asked Moritz.

"Iris Taha was her name. She was a milliner. A designer of fashionable hats."

Kate saw the dim light of recognition on the young woman's face.

"An Egyptian lady," the woman said. "It was a long time ago that she came here. At least a decade."

"Fifteen years, based on the date of the entry," Kate said.

"I'd almost forgotten about her. She knocked on this door as you did. She was looking for two people. One was her lover. The other was a girl. A Kathy . . . or Katharina. She had a German surname."

"Do you know why?" Kate said.

"I'm afraid I can't help you," said the woman. "I don't really remember much more than that she came here."

"May we ask a few questions anyway?"

The woman was uneasy. "I can't make any promises."

"That's okay," Kate said. "It still helps if you let us try."

"We'd be so grateful," Moritz said. "I suppose I should start by asking, do you know why my mother would have come here to begin with? Or why would she have surrounded this diary entry in exclamation points? She must have learned something valuable."

"I told you, I don't know."

"Are you W. G. K.?" Kate asked.

The woman shook her head.

"No." Their disappointment had just begun to settle in when she added, "But I know who is."

"You do?"

"The hatmaker who came here so many years ago spoke with a man named Werner Gottfried Kunze."

Progress, Kate thought.

"And you are . . . ?"

"Petra. Werner's granddaughter."

"Well, Petra, you've already told us something we didn't know. Is there any chance we could speak with your grandfather?"

"That wouldn't be practical. He broke a hip recently, and in his advanced years, the recovery has been hard. He's resting in a hospital a mile away."

"I'm sorry to hear that," Kate said.

"On top of that, age has not been kind to him. He suffers from dementia. I was just now baking pastries to bring to his bedside. The last two times I brought pastries, he didn't even recognize me. His own granddaughter."

"It must be hard to see him in that state."

"It's hard to see any good man in a miserable state," Petra said. "Our family owes everything to him. He helped us escape from Berlin to Switzerland during the war. I was a little girl."

Kate smiled, feeling something in common with Petra.

"You must have been terrified." Sharing her own story might have earned the woman's sympathy, but she couldn't bring herself to do it.

"Yes, well, it was a long time ago, and I don't remember much. Now, I have to get going. The pastrics I'm cooking are for him. If they're not brought fresh, he won't eat them."

"Would it help if I told you," Kate said, not without a struggle, "that my name is actually Katharina Speer—and that I'm the person the hat-maker was looking for fifteen years ago?"

It was the first time she had willingly shared her identity with anyone. When Moritz met her eyes for a brief second, he looked proud, even if she didn't feel he had any reason to be.

Petra looked at her for a moment in disbelief. "Speer, that *was* the name," she then said. "I remember. Is it really you?"

"In the flesh."

"This is very out of the blue," Petra said. "I don't really know what to say."

"That makes two of us," Kate said. "Three, including Moritz. We didn't really know what to expect in coming here. It was a shot in the dark."

"Maybe you should meet my grandfather," Petra said. "The nurses have encouraged me to bring visitors. I doubt you will get anything useful out of it, but you can come along if you want."

Kate and Moritz traded hopeful glances.

"You're sure it would be okay?" Moritz said.

"They say it's good for his brain."

"In that case, we'll accept. Thank you."

"Just don't expect him to be coherent."

"As Kate said, we had no expectations coming to Zermatt," Moritz told her. "We'd appreciate the opportunity to meet Herr Kunze, even if he's not as clear-headed as he once was."

"Wait here, then," Petra said. "As soon as I finish wrapping the pastries, we'll walk to the hospital."

Lona

Lady Lona Atwell found her husband reclined on a sofa in his library study, smoking a pipe and reading *A Study in Scarlet* over whisky. He was wearing a loose bathrobe.

"It's clear why you love those pipes," she said. "Look at all the Conan Doyle you read."

"I was Sherlock in another life," George said, swirling his glass.

"In this one, all you inherited were his vices."

"At least your husband will admit he loves a simple crime story. What brings you up from the garden, darling? I imagine everything's rather windblown after last night's storm."

Lona was still panting from the climb up the slope, where she had been trimming the hedges by their beach. She brushed some of the leaves from her hair, which was still dark and full. She looked beautiful even when covered in twigs and dirt; her eyes still had a youthful sparkle under their long, healthy lashes. During a trip to America a few years back, someone had said she looked like a mature Ava Gardner, and that Ms. Gardner would be lucky to look like Lona at seventy.

"Clive brought me a bewildering telegram from Kate," she said.

"Oh?"

She handed him a piece of paper.

Dear Mum and Dad,

An unusual turn of events at work has led me to take a holiday in Zermatt—Monte Rosa Hotel. If you hear from Colette, please tell her I am okay. If you hear from anyone else, say nothing at all. I will be home likely after Christmas. Do not worry about me.

Love,

Kate

"What's the problem?" George asked.

"It's not like Kate to leave work and go gallivanting around Europe," Lona said. "And what does she mean 'tell Colette I am okay'? Why wouldn't she be?"

"Maybe she's met someone."

"She would never chase after a man or be so decadent as to take a spontaneous trip to Switzerland. George, I don't think this has anything to do with a romantic prospect."

"She's a grown woman, darling. Capable of making her own decisions."

"But why leave Paris so suddenly? And why didn't she tell Colette? She tells Colette everything."

"So, our daughter went to Zermatt. What's the worry?"

"She'll miss Christmas."

"Doing what she wants to do. If she's done something spontaneous, well, this is Kate we're talking about. I think it's the sort of behavior we'd like to encourage."

Lona sighed. For such a savvy businessman and politician, at times George could be an oblivious father. As much as she admired him, she had learned that you couldn't expect to know a man for fifty-two years and stay a stranger to frustration. She had been more than his wife and best friend; she also had been his closest advisor on matters of business and state. He trusted her counsel on practically every subject and always had—except where their daughter was concerned. On that front, he stubbornly insisted that any problem would work itself out.

Rearing a child hadn't been on her mind when she'd met George. She had been eighteen, working as a librarian, while he had been staying in Beaumaris to scout a copper mine outside a neighboring village. He had come asking for books on the flora and fauna of the Snowdonian Mountains, intending to plan a hiking trip. As the trails had been her playground growing up, she'd offered to be his guide. Their romance had blossomed in a matter of days. She had fallen in love with his boundless ambition. Much to the chagrin of George's father, who had wanted an aristocratic bride for his highborn son, they had married after a single year.

Having grown up in the small fishing town next to Beaumaris Castle, Lona had spent her childhood by the water near the foothills of Snowdonia, mapping the mountains and romping through the forests. The geography was ingrained in her soul. Moving to Trefwyn as a baron's wife had been a bold and bittersweet adventure. Awed as she was by her husband's ability to transform a village into a major industrial center, she could never get used to the smell of molten copper over fir trees and fresh fish, or the idea of having a title. It was in her nature to adapt by making herself productive, even if she had no need to work. She had studied to become a teacher of English and Welsh, and she organized a day school for the children of Trefwyn's copper workers. When George finished his political career in Parliament, they had moved back to Beaumaris, and she had almost felt whole again. Spending time with the youngsters had left her desperate for a child of her own.

She was certain George would be a good father, and he was that to Kate. She had him wrapped around her little finger the moment he'd laid eyes on her.

But he had never been one to pick up on subtlety.

She put the telegram on his desk, hoping to take the conversation further when their house steward tapped on the library door.

"Lady Trefwyn," Mountjoy said. "Miss Fossey is here."

Lona strode to the front door and threw it open.

"Colette!" she said, ushering her in. "What are you doing here? And where is Kate?"

"She's missing–disappeared overnight," Colette said. "I'm trying to find her."

Before Lona closed the front door, she noticed someone sitting in a car outside. Colette had not come alone. Lona escorted Colette into the library, and George stood up, finally paying attention. "Did you come with Kate? We've had a strange telegram from her just now saying that she's gone to Switzerland."

"Where in Switzerland?" Colette asked.

Lona did not answer her, but instead asked, "Is Kate in trouble? How can we get in touch with her?"

"I don't know how to tell you this," Colette said, taking a deep breath before continuing, "but Monsieur Maxence has accused Kate of stealing a painting from the gallery. I came here with an investigator to try to find her."

"Why would Kate steal? It doesn't make sense." None of it made sense to her. Not the telegram, and certainly not Colette's surprise appearance.

Lona was trying to figure out what to do next when Mountjoy, the family steward, stepped into the library.

"There's someone at the door. He says he needs to speak to you about a private matter."

Clive Mountjoy waited for her instruction with his usual outward indifference, but Lona knew he would share an opinion if asked. She liked that about him.

"What do you think he wants?" she said.

"I couldn't say, but in light of Kate's uncharacteristic telegram, it may be good to receive him and see that all's well."

Lona followed Mountjoy to the front door with Colette trailing behind her.

"Lady Atwell," the visitor said, bowing slightly at the waist.

"How may I help you?" Lona asked her visitor.

"My name is Yehuda Uzan, and I work as an investigator for Pendelfarr International," he said. "Monsieur Maxence reported a very valuable piece of artwork missing several days ago after the company's Christmas soirée, and since then, no one has seen your daughter. Kate didn't say she was going anywhere. She left behind no travel plans."

Lona tried to prevent her imagination from coloring in the worst possible scenarios. The man's story did not jibe with Kate's message or nature.

"Why didn't you call me immediately?" Lona said to Colette.

"I don't have anything to do with this," Colette said. "I've been fired from my job because of Kate. And now I'm trying to help her, despite . . ."

"Despite what?"

"Despite the fact she's been lying to us. All of us."

"What do you mean?"

Colette pulled the photo of Ralf Speer from her purse. "Do you know who this is?"

Lona looked at the photo. She hadn't thought of the man for a long time, but from the first day Kate had picked up a pencil, Lona had suspected that she hadn't learned to draw so skillfully on a farm.

"Some Nazi," she said. "What does this have to do with Kate?"

"He's her father," Colette said, and Lona noticed the investigator look at her with surprise.

"George is her father."

"They're saying Kate stole a painting. A Klee."

"Why would she?"

"To finance the aid she provides a community of former Nazis in South America."

"What kind of joke is this?" Lona said, looking between Colette and the investigator. "I'm not laughing."

"Where has she gone?" the inspector asked.

"I've answered your questions," Lona said sharply. "There's no need for further detail, Mr. Uzan, unless you have a warrant."

She tried to close the door, but he caught it with a boot.

"Move your foot!" she said.

"Baroness," he said. "If we don't find her within twenty-four hours, we'll be contacting Interpol. If you tell us where she is, we can save her and your family a great deal of embarrassment."

"She isn't here." Lona stepped closer to him, her expression fierce. "Now get off this property."

Mountjoy tried to help contend with the visitor. "Sir, allow me to escort—"

Yehuda shoved the door inward; it hit Lona in the jaw and slammed against the interior wall. She tottered back. When she found her balance, he had a boating knife in his grip.

"Clive!" she shouted. "Warn George!"

But Mountjoy wasn't quick enough. Yehuda Uzan's hand shot out and grabbed him by the collar. He tried to fight, but his opponent had twice his strength and looked half his age. Uzan seized one of Mountjoy's arms and twisted it behind his back, forcing him against the doorframe by nearly ripping his shoulder joint in two.

The house steward gritted his teeth as Uzan toyed with him, dragging the tip of the blade along his shiny, bald scalp.

"Stop it, *stop it!*" Lona screamed. "What are you doing?"

"I could carve in the alphabet," Uzan said. "Or maybe I could write 'Property of the Atwells' in case anyone forgets. He's got a nice smooth head, like slate."

"Don't hurt him!" Colette shouted. "Kate's in Switzerland!"

"Where in Switzerland?" said Uzan through bared teeth.

Mountjoy said, "Don't tell him!"

A trickle of blood began to roll down Mountjoy's scalp.

"Yehuda, let's go!" screamed Colette, pulling on his arm.

"Stop it! Stop!" Lona pleaded.

"I see you don't care for your manservant much," Yehuda said. "I should show you how serious I am, then find someone you actually care about."

He drove the knife through Mountjoy's carotid artery. The steward heaved a cough of blood and spittle. His body slumped against the door.

"No . . . NO . . . CLIVE!"

She ran to his side, holding his face, and watched the life drain out of him.

"God, no, you bastard!" she cried. "Colette, what have you done?"

"Do we understand each other now?" Uzan said. Colette stood shaking behind him.

Lona shouted down the hall: "Run, George! Get out of the house!"

The visitor grabbed Lona's arm and pulled her into a headlock, holding the knife at her throat as he dragged her down the corridor.

"Stop it!" Colette shrieked. "Let me talk to her!"

"Go back to the car and stay there, Colette," Uzan said. She bolted out of the room. "Now, Lord Atwell. Where will I find you?"

"Run, George!" Lona tried to say. "He's got—"

He tightened the pressure on her neck, muting her words.

"What's going on?" came George's voice from the library.

Uzan practically leaped toward the sound, keeping Lona's writhing body in tow. He turned a corner into George's study room, where Lord Atwell had risen from his settee, still wearing his pajamas. He rocked on his feet a bit, beset both by the commotion and by the scotch saturating his veins.

"What's going on?" he said again. It took him a moment to register the sight of his wife in the clutches of this stranger.

"George . . ." Lona managed to cough.

"Bloody hell!" he said. "Let go of my wife! What's going on?"

Uzan held up the blade for him to see, then slapped its cool against her cheek.

"This could have been easier," he said. "And it still can be. I want to know where your daughter is."

"Get out of here, George!" Lona squealed.

"Listen to me!" he said. "You let go of her. We won't call the police. You can be on your way."

"Not without the information I need."

George reached for a ceramic lamp and lunged at the visitor. Uzan stepped aside, letting the baron's momentum carry him forward. He kicked the old man behind the knees. They buckled, and George dropped the lamp, falling on his rear.

"Stop, please," Lona begged. "This clearly isn't about a painting. There may be another way for us to give you what you want."

"Is it money you're after?" George said, struggling to sit up. "We can end this—"

"Shut up," Uzan said. He threw Lona to the floor. She landed by the fireplace, hard, feeling a spear of pain in her side, maybe a broken bone. "Tell me where Kate is!"

"You expect a mother and father to give up their child to a madman?" George roared.

"You're not her real parents."

"Go ahead and test that hypothesis. Torture us all you want. If we tell you where she's gone, we're fakes."

Uzan knelt between them, running the knife along each of their legs, nearly puncturing skin.

"Don't do this," Lona said. "Please."

She glanced at the fire iron, wondering if it were within reach, deciding it wasn't. But maybe she could reach the spade.

"I'm losing patience," Uzan said.

"I'll tell you," Lona said. "I'll tell you where she's gone."

Uzan held the knife in place on George's leg and looked her in the eye. "I'm listening."

"She's gone to London."

"Why?"

"We don't know. I swear it. She didn't tell us."

"How do you know she's gone there?"

"She wrote us a letter from London."

"You're lying."

"It's true, she—"

"I saw her the other day in Paris," Uzan said. "Not enough time to get to London and write you. Your lie is going to cost you."

"I meant by telegram, it's—"

Using one hand, he pushed George's forehead down to the floor. With the other, he slashed George's neck open.

"*No!*" Lona cried. "George!"

A sharp burst of air was expelled from George's lungs. Uzan held him down as he squirmed, until finally the loss of blood left him unconscious.

While he was distracted, Lona lunged for the spade. She swung it by the long handle, hoping to drive the edge into her assailant's head. He saw it coming and moved, a moment too late to dodge or deflect the blow altogether. When the blunt face struck his chest, he teetered backward, startled by the power behind her wallop.

Knowing he would soon bounce back and overtake her, she scrambled to her feet and ran for the front door. She had enough presence of mind to swipe Kate's telegram from George's desk, and then she unhooked a key dangling in the foyer, and ran as fast as she could down the circular driveway. The bruise from her fall—coupled with the early arthritis in her hips and knees—began to scream at her, but she plowed on, never once looking back at the visitor's car, where Colette was sobbing in the passenger seat.

She shoved the key into the ignition of her sedan. The car rumbled, and the tires spun through gravel as she laid into the gas. Finally catching friction, the sedan began to accelerate as Uzan came dashing out the front door after her.

The nearest police station was across the strait, four miles away. She turned left onto Beaumaris Road, speeding toward the Menai Bridge.

Colette

Yehuda Uzan stepped into his car. Colette was trembling. Her cheeks had lost their color and taken on the shine of tears.

"What's the matter?" he said, laying into the pedal and watching Lona's vehicle ahead.

"You killed Clive," she said. Her eyes were red. There was loathing in her voice, tinged with the fear of expressing it too candidly. "I knew him. He was kind. He was good. Who the hell *are* you?"

"I killed Lord Atwell, too. He also seemed kind."

Her chest heaved. She was hyperventilating.

"Getting information is not always pleasant," he said.

"You can't be who you say you are. No government official would do that!"

"I am exactly who I say I am."

"Then tell me what the hell you're doing!"

"I'm doing the work of justice, and I thought you wanted to help me," he said. "I thought you wanted to bring down the people who played a part in killing millions, including your mother and father. Kate is our connection. You'll either help me track her down, or you'll hold me back. Which is it going to be? Tell me right now. Commit to an answer."

"I didn't know you were going to murder anyone. And I didn't know—" Colette looked at him in the driver's seat, suddenly terrified that if she said no, he would kill her just as quickly and heartlessly as he had killed George and Clive.

"What?" he said. "That it would be so hard?"

"That you were . . . that it was so second nature to you. Slitting his throat like you were swatting a fly. You said you were an investigator."

"Did it scare you?"

She sniffled.

"What *should* scare you," he said, "is life in a prison cell. That's where you're headed if we don't find Kate. Maxence will see to it. And I don't imagine your aunt and uncle will visit much."

"How do you know about my aunt and uncle?"

Yehuda turned to her. "You said it yourself. 'I'm an investigator.' Why don't you think about honoring your parents? And protecting yourself? You think the Atwells will look out for you? Wake up, Colette. You must handle this yourself. Look out for your own welfare."

"Not like that. Not by killing."

"You think Kate thinks about anyone but herself? And those murderers she helps? It's hard watching someone die in front of you. Especially the first time. And if the victim was a good person, a person who showed you kindness, then it's even harder. But think of the victims from 1939 to 1945."

She stared out the window, her expression vacant.

"You're going through shock," he said, "like a soldier on a battlefield after the first shot is fired. You hadn't realized how important it is for us to find Kate. Now you do. Your feelings will pass."

"What are you going to do to Lona when we catch her?"

"I will get the information I need. You don't have to watch."

"And if I told you I'm done helping you?"

"I would be disappointed. You're an asset. You can get inside Kate's head."

"But you would let me go?"

"I'd have nothing to gain by harming you."

He sounded sincere enough, though she couldn't be sure of her own safety around this man. Her thoughts went to Kate, and her chest clenched again with the pain of betrayal—their friendship cast into the cold . . .

"What was your mother's name?" he asked.

"Jacqueline," she said.

"What's your earliest memory of Jacqueline?"

"Hearing her sing to me in her rocking chair."

"What did she sing to you?"

"All kinds of songs."

"Like what?"

"I dunno . . ."

"Name one."

"*Frère Jacques*."

"Sing it right now," he said.

"Why?"

"I want to hear it."

Ahead, Lona had turned onto the Menai Bridge. Yehuda had narrowed the distance between their cars by about half.

"*Frère Jacques, frère Jacques*," she sang. "*Dormez-vous? Dormez-vous?*"

"Imagine yourself in that rocking chair, in her arms," Yehuda said as she continued:

"*Sonnez les matines. Sonnez les matines. Ding, dang, dong. Ding, dang, dong.*"

She was finding it difficult not to keep crying.

"That's good," Yehuda said. "Now imagine her dead on that rocking chair. Picture the men who fired the bullets that killed your mother. Can you see them? Those men may still be alive. If not them, their compatriots. And Kate, your good friend, is sending them food."

"She's not my friend," Colette declared.

"She never was. Liars are not friends."

Colette found herself more and more willing to believe him.

Staring through the windshield, she dried her eyes.

"Okay," she said. "Let's go."

Katharina

Kate and Moritz followed Petra Kunze into the lobby of the local hospital, where a nurse escorted them to a room. The door opened to a rollaway bed. A half-eaten bowl of porridge and a full pitcher of water sat on the bedside table. There had been attempts to bring cheer to the room and its institutional green walls: flowers on the windowsill, a pastel painting of children riding bicycles, magazines beside the telephone on the nightstand.

The man lying on the bed did not turn to size up his visitors. His clouded eyes were droopy and unfocused.

Petra came to his side and stroked his arm. She laid the basket of pastries on his nightstand.

"Are you hungry, *Opa?*" she said, using the German word for grandfather.

"Hungry *Opa*," said Werner Kunze. His cheeks, a pale gray, sank into the cavity of his mouth. "*Opa*'s always hungry."

She pulled the blanket up to his chin, hiding the lumpy plastic covering his mattress. He was frail and wizened, his skin spotted with bruises and bedsores.

"Do you know who I am?" Petra asked.

The old man's head rolled and began to quake.

"*Opa*'s always hungry," he said.

Petra turned to Kate and Moritz. "When we were kids, he used to tease and pretend he was a bear that would come eat us. That's what he would say."

She unfolded the napkin covering the pastries and served him one. When he wouldn't eat it, she brought it to his mouth so he could take a bite.

Kate walked around to the other side of the bed.

"It's a pleasure to meet you, Herr Kunze," she said, caught in a moment of déjà vu. Something about him looked familiar. "I'm Katharina, and this is Mr. Dahl."

She wasn't sure what possessed her to use her old name.

He furrowed his brow, the creases on his forehead forming a grid as if he, too, were recalling someone from his past.

"Do you know who I am?" she asked.

Please let that be yes, she thought. Please let there be a connection.

There was a pause before his response.

"*Opa*'s always hungry," he said.

"His condition keeps getting worse," Petra said, combing his hair with her fingers.

"Petra," Kate asked, "you don't by any chance have a picture of Werner when he was younger?"

"There, on the nightstand. He was in his early sixties."

Kate leaned close to the framed portrait and blew the dust from its glass cover.

"My God."

"What is it?" Moritz said.

The younger face of Werner Gottfried Kunze dislodged a memory she had filed away two decades ago, one that had been burned into her by the trauma of October 10, 1942. He had been wearing spectacles and a tweed coat then, on a train pulling away from a railway platform.

"I saw this man twenty years ago," she said, "at a train station in Berlin. Moritz, about that night I escaped Germany, when Karl Decker drove me to an escape sub—remember how I said that before leaving for Wangerland, he delivered the Bouguereau forgery to a passenger on a train leaving Berlin? This man was the passenger."

"You're sure?"

She scrutinized the photograph a good half-minute.

"Yes, that's him."

"Are you saying you've met my grandfather before?" Petra asked.

"We never met, but I did see him as a child," Kate said, doubting this man was the saint Petra believed him to be. As a colleague of Karl Decker's, and possibly her father's, he at least could have picked better company.

"He must have made an impression if you remember him after so long."

"Everything made an impression that night."

Werner Kunze began to quiver in his bed, as if the temperature in the room had dropped.

"He's going to try to kill me," the elderly man said.

"Who?" Moritz asked him.

"I don't know," he sputtered. "One man turned them in. He wanted out. He turned them in. He's going to try to kill me."

"What are you talking about, *Opa?*" Petra said. She ran a hand along his shoulder.

"The man who wanted out."

"What are you trying to tell us?" Kate said. "Go ahead, try again."

Werner said, "How many artists were there?"

She was taken aback. He had directed the question at her in an apparent moment of clarity, as if he knew exactly who she was. Was he talking about the artists in her father's workshop?

"Seventeen," she answered.

"Oh, yes," Werner said. "Oh, oh, yes. One man turned them in."

"What do you mean, one man turned them in?"

"They found fifteen bodies in the house."

He had to have been talking about the night the SS had invaded her home and killed her father and his painters. If there had been fifteen bodies, and one for Karl Decker, who had died in Wangerland, that meant one artist was missing.

"So, someone is unaccounted for," she said. "Is that what you're saying?"

"He's going to try to kill me," Werner said.

"Herr Kunze, did you work with my father? His name was Ralf Speer," Kate asked him. He quaked harder and did not answer. "Were you making a delivery that night?" His eyes began to drift again, to mist over and lose concentration. "What did you do with *The Little Marauder*? How did it reach Iris Taha? Can you explain any of this?"

Petra stepped in. "He gave Iris the painting when she interviewed him fifteen years ago. I remember that much."

"If that's true," Kate said, "then he never delivered the painting to anyone. Maybe Werner was a customer of my father's, who thought he was purchasing the real Bouguereau piece. But then, why would Decker risk our lives to make the delivery? What made it so important?"

"Speckles on the pear," Werner said.

"Sorry?" Moritz said.

"Speckles on the pear—the pear that saved an army."

"He's not making sense," Petra said. "I told you this might happen."

Moritz asked him, "What do you mean, 'speckles on the pear'?"

"I gave it to Horace," Werner said. "Horace had to run to the gray pillars. Ask Geoffrey Barkas."

"Who's that?"

"I told you, he's completely delusional," Petra said. "I know you came looking for answers, and I'm sorry to have raised your hopes. The doctors think he suffers from vascular dementia caused by a series of strokes. Or it could be Alzheimer's. He gets more irritable and paranoid every week, more prone to nonsensical outbursts."

"If only for a moment, there seemed to be a spark of coherence," Moritz said. "I think he recognized Kate."

"Whether or not he did, he seems agitated. I don't want him to have another stroke. This would probably be a good time for you to leave."

"We don't want to cause him harm," Moritz said as she gestured toward the door. "Can you interpret anything he said? 'Speckles on the pear,' 'the pear that saved an army,' 'Horace,' 'the gray pillars,' 'Geoffrey Barkas'—"

"Only the last bit," Petra said. "Geoffrey is a close friend of my grandfather's. He's a veteran of the World Wars, and a filmmaker."

"What kind of films?" Kate asked.

"Documentaries, primarily. Among others, he codirected *Wings over Everest*, a movie that won an Academy Award for Best Short Subject, and *Q-Ships*, a film about decoy vessels. But he's done fictional work, too, like directing the African exteriors of Robert Stevenson's version of *King Solomon's Mines*. When work in the film industry disappeared in the late 'thirties, he was guided into military camouflage and became an important figure in the Desert War."

"How did they meet, Barkas and your grandfather?"

"I believe it was Iris Taha who introduced them," Petra said. "My memory isn't the best after fifteen years, but I think Ms. Taha had also interviewed Geoffrey on her search."

"My mother must have seen a connection if she introduced them," Moritz said. "Do you know what it was?"

"I never knew my grandfather well. His started to lose his mind while I was still a teen. He didn't write any memoirs, so I couldn't tell you what brought him together with Geoffrey. But Geoffrey did visit recently, when he learned of Werner's broken hip."

"Do you know how we could find Geoffrey?" Moritz asked.

"When he came by, he said he was filming a documentary in Croatia, interviewing families about conditions in Dubrovnik during its occupation by the Italian and German armies. He might be there still."

"Thank you for your help, Petra," Kate said. She turned to the bedridden man. "*Auf Wiedersehen*, Herr Kunze."

As they left the hospital, she felt encouraged.

"So, Dubrovnik," Moritz said. "We're in for a drive. I say we leave tomorrow and spend this afternoon trying to decode Kunze's words."

"That could be a waste of effort," Kate said.

"We won't know unless we try. He did have his moments of clarity."

"How long do you think the drive will take us?"

"A few days."

She realized her time with Moritz had no clear end. She had lied to her parents and fled Paris to travel with a stranger. Not even Colette knew where she was, and by the looks of things, she wouldn't for some time. Strangely, none of this bothered Kate.

As a teenager, she had dreamed of running away from school and hitchhiking her way to Scotland. The current trip she was taking was crazier and even more exhilarating, and though it served a practical purpose, it also answered the inner voice of rebellion that she ignored as a rule.

There was something else, too. Though he was far from earning her trust, Moritz knew exactly who she was and didn't judge her for it. He was the first person in whose company she could be her real self and not fear the consequences. Being around him helped her believe that someday, with effort, she could unhitch herself from her past and live a normal life.

"In that case," she said, "let's get some rest in the comfort of our hotel and start early tomorrow."

"Where's our reservation?"

"The Monte Rosa."

"Posh," he said. "I could get used to traveling with you."

Lona and Yehuda

Lona jammed her foot on the accelerator, pushing it to the floor. Speeding along Holyhead Road, she could only hope to spot a police car, but if not, the station was less than three miles away.

In her rear-view mirror, she could see Yehuda Uzan's car veering off the Menai Bridge two hundred yards behind. Her palms began to sweat and lose their grip on the wheel as she replayed the two murders in her head—first Clive's, then her husband's. They were gone. Lives ended with the flick of a knife blade. Who was this barbarian, why was Colette with him, and what did he want with Kate? She could only guess that his arrival had something to do with Kate's telegram. And with Ralf Speer.

A sob rose to her throat as she realized that Kate had lost her father, had lost two fathers. She remembered how the matron at the orphanage had dutifully told her the story of Kate's Austrian parents dying in a Luftwaffe bombing. But the young translator who had helped her communicate with Kate for the first time had seemed unsure.

Months later, on a trip to London, she had gone back to the orphanage early one morning and waited outside for the young woman. Lona invited her to tea that afternoon and told her how well Kate was doing, how she had learned English and had made new friends, that she had prodigious artistic talent. Only then had she asked the woman if she knew anything more about the child she had helped. At first the translator had said no, but eventually she admitted that she thought Kate's story wasn't true. The child had never been able to tell her anything more specific about her deceased parents. More important, her dialect had been German, not Austrian.

Over the years, when Kate had recognized certain paintings, when the truth had come out about some of the more insidious deeds of Nazi officers, Lona had suspected that Kate had had some sort of firsthand experience in Speer's workshop. There had never been a comfortable way to ask her more about what she remembered, and besides, what good would it have done Kate to have known the excruciating details of Speer's crimes? She had thought she was being protective by keeping what she knew from her beloved daughter, but now she wasn't so sure. Even if Kate still didn't know, others did, and she was in danger.

Lona traversed a section of the road shaded by a canopy of naked oak, ash, and sycamore branches. The road through the Menai Woods was gravelly and covered in twigs and soil that had blown over in last night's winds. She slowed to avoid popping a tire. The road ran northeast, parallel with the strait. Looking out the window through the woods, she could make out their chateau on the other side of the water.

She rounded another corner and slammed on the brakes. A fallen sycamore, blown down by the recent gale, blocked the road. Forced to weigh a new set of options, she wondered if she could plow through it. The odds were slim to none. She could abandon the car and run around the tree for help, but it was doubtful she'd find anyone before Uzan caught her. It seemed she would have to give up on the police station.

But there was a third option: Drive to Kate's cottage in Snowdonia, where she could barricade herself and radio the park rangers.

She yanked the wheel and slipped the gears into reverse. Then she spun the wheel the other direction and lurched forward. She did it again, completing a one-eighty. Uzan's car was coming at her head on. He might wonder why she had reversed course, but regardless, she expected him to try to ram her or obstruct her path.

She was right. He swerved, causing his vehicle to fishtail and run perpendicular to the street. He stayed parked, trapping her between roadblocks. She put her full weight into the gas and aimed for the rear of his car, hearing the pebbles smacking and scraping her vehicle's undercarriage as she accelerated. At the last second, she turned up into the dirt banks as the right side of her car crashed into his rear fender. Though she had braced herself, the impact sent a whiplash of pain through her spine and caused her face to slam against the steering wheel. Her nose started to bleed.

The collision rotated Uzan's car, giving her the space she needed to squeeze past it. Please, she thought, please let my own car still work. She accelerated again, clearing his obstacle and getting back on the road. The nerves in her neck were still tingling from the hit. In her rear-view mirror, she saw Uzan reversing direction. She had hit him hard and even shattered one of his windows, but he was still coming. He aligned himself with the street. She put the distance between them at around a hundred fifty yards. Damn that fallen sycamore—if there had been a way through, she easily would have beaten him to the station. Instead, she'd lost a quarter of her lead, and the cottage was a long way off.

As she took a new road bearing southeast, the terrain climbed into stony plains and sparse patches of forest. The peak of Snowdon soared higher than the clouds up ahead. The road took her through a small village, where she searched for signs of a police or ranger station. She saw none. She kept driving onto a still-narrower road of an even steeper grade, getting an occasional view of the surrounding massifs.

It was a bumpy ride, tough on her tires. The road wound along a semicircular ring of ridges, bordered by precipitous drops—nothing to break the fall of a careless driver. She had gained a thousand feet in elevation by now. Fortunately, she knew the national park well, having driven to Kate's cottage so often, but she had always taken her time, negotiating the turns cautiously.

She rounded a bend, skidding on a sheet of ice that flung the rear of her sedan toward the cliff's edge. A chopped, inadvertent scream, and she regained control. She squinted, inspired. If she could turn a corner and keep out of view, all she needed were a few seconds to step out of the car and hold down the gas. The sedan would roll over the edge, and she could hide. As he drove nearer, Uzan would see her car tumbling down the mountainside. Best case, he would think her dead and leave. Worst case, he would check that she was in the vehicle, wasting time while she scaled the rocks up to Kate's cottage.

There would be challenges. For one, it would cost her a way out. She would be stranding herself here, and she had to be realistic about her age. She was seventy, not the limber mountaineer she used to be. The climb would be arduous.

But what better option did she have?

Still on an incline, she spotted a sheer rock wall ahead, around which the road snaked to the right. She followed the curve, seeing that from the approaching angle, a good ten-yard section of the path remained hidden. If there were an ideal spot for her plan, this was it.

Uzan was still a hundred yards behind. Momentarily out of view, she slowed the car and turned the wheel toward the edge of the canyon. She got out, searched the ground for sticks, and used one to push the accelerator, running with the sedan until it had broken through the weak barrier between the road and the ravine.

Knowing she couldn't afford the seconds to watch it fall, she jogged toward the inner side of the rock wall and crouched behind a boulder, planning her path of ascent up the mountain. The slope was steep, but the cottage wasn't far.

. . .

"Look at that!" Colette screamed.

Yehuda watched as Lady Atwell's car arced through the air and landed in a gorge a hundred feet below.

"Damn you, stupid old crone," he said. "We need you alive."

"There's no way she survived that. Besides, we don't need her. We know Kate is in Switzerland."

"That's not enough to go on. More importantly, she's leverage." He followed the road, winding his way around a steep face of stone banked in snow. After making the turn, he slowed to a halt and got out of the vehicle. He knelt beside the damaged barrier.

"That's funny," he said, ignoring Colette. "A car sliding on ice would have struck the metal along its side, making a longer dent. The dent in this barrier is only a few feet wide."

"What does that mean?"

"She went through it headfirst."

"Maybe she committed suicide to keep us from getting to her."

"It's possible. Let's climb down and see what condition she's in."

. . .

Lona felt a rush of elation. The stunt had bought her time. She waited for Uzan and Colette to disappear below the edge of the road before attempting to scale the slopes of the Snowdon Massif. Her feet sank deep into the snow. It was a fine powder, glittering like diamond dust, and this made the trek more exhausting.

Her nose still hurt, and the smarting in her hips had dulled and spread down her thigh. She imagined the bruising would be ghastly. On top of that, the pain in her joints limited her range of motion and weakened her balance on the already-slippery incline. Each step through the snow took dedicated effort, and she knew she had to be swift or they'd spot her from below.

God, was it ever a cold place to be wearing gardening clothes. Her cheeks stung. She couldn't feel her chin anymore. A steady wind coiled around the mountain, making her wish for thicker pockets. Seconds passed like minutes until Lake Glaslyn came into view, at an elevation of two thousand feet or so. The landmark told her she was close. George had built the cottage by the lake; it was beautiful in summertime.

Panting, she sidestepped a rivulet and found a footpath zigzagging up the slope. Finally, ground made for walking. She shielded her eyes from the sun and looked out over the lake. There it was, sheltered between the sharp crest of an intermediate mountain and the peak of Snowdon—Kate's old painting sanctuary, a quarter-mile away.

. . .

Yehuda squatted near the wreck at the base of the gorge. Staring into the empty driver's seat, Colette looked puzzled.

"But where did she go?" she said.

"Not far," he said. "She's only had a few minutes on foot." Standing, he added, "She's a brave old bag to pull this trick. She wouldn't have sacrificed her only way out unless she had a refuge in mind."

"Maybe she thought we wouldn't search for her body."

"She may have hoped, but she wouldn't have bet her life on it."

He craned his neck, searching the wall of the canyon they'd just descended.

"You think she's still up there?" she said.

"Has to be."

"Then let's hurry back. She may stop a passing vehicle and hitch a ride out."

"You stay here. Shout for me if you see her scrambling about the ravine. I'm going up."

. . .

Lona clambered through a field of boulders skirting the banks of the lake. She had not come prepared for this terrain. Without proper boots on, she'd slipped a number of times, landing on the slanted rocks and picking up cuts and abrasions that gave her an extra sting in the cold. It took her eight minutes to cross the field and reach the door of the cottage.

She turned the handle. Locked—damn it—but she remembered Kate saying she kept the key somewhere nearby. Where? She lifted a mat at the door—nothing there. It was nowhere under the base of the porch, either. Where was the bloody key? If this took too long, she would have to break a window and risk cutting herself as she squeezed her body through the jagged panes. She walked around the cottage, looking for any nooks and crannies Kate might have used as hiding places. A pot dangled from the roof, one usually filled with flowers during the summer. Now it had only soil. She reached inside, feeling around the perimeter. Her fingers touched something metallic. There it was. She grabbed the key, not allowing herself a moment's relief, and slipped it into the lock, wiping away an icy crust that had formed around the hole. After two tries, the door swung open. She stepped inside and swung the deadbolt into place.

It was a small log cottage with a bed, kitchen, and fireplace. The interior was decorated with snow scenes and gem-encrusted triptychs Kate had made as a teenager. She found the radio transceiver sitting on the dining table. There was also a shotgun hanging on the wall, which she lifted from its mount. She read the make: James Purdey and Sons. She had never fired any gun before, let alone one this size. It was ornate, with twin barrels. Was it loaded? She didn't know how to check, and hoped she wouldn't have to, but noted the box of ammunition on the floor in case she found the gun empty.

She pulled a chair from the dining table and switched on the radio.

. . .

Yehuda finished the climb back up the ravine and stood in the middle of the road, studying its curvature. He searched the area for any hiding spots the woman might have used and discovered a concavity in the bluff ten yards ahead. He jogged over, stooping in the snow. If she had been here, she'd left no trace. So where could she have gone in the past few minutes? He had seen the way she'd run out of her own home, slowed down by her age and a good thwack to the hip. The woman had fight in her, but she couldn't have gone far.

There was a boulder nearby, wide enough to conceal a human body from the right angle. The snow behind it was trodden upon. Someone had been crouching there.

Up the slopes, he spotted a footprint. He hoisted himself onto a plateau for a better view. Now he could see a whole trail of them, fresh depressions in the snow. He scrambled up the incline, following the tracks on the most even ground he could find. They took him to a field of rocks surrounding a lake, where a small cottage could be seen on the northeast banks.

Clever woman, he thought.

. . .

Lona's fingers were useless, trembling little icicles. For God's sake, take control of your hands, she told herself, rubbing them together and breathing warm air on her skin. If only she had time to kindle a fire, this would be a lot easier.

She fumbled with the transceiver, a puzzle of switches, buttons, and dials. Not sure what to do with it, she memorized the starting positions of all the levers and then picked a dial to rotate. The box emitted a steady stream of static.

"Hello?" she said into the machine. "Hello, can anyone hear this?"

She picked another dial to adjust, causing a needle to move along a series of numbers. Was there an emergency channel? She moved the first knob back to its original setting. The static mellowed. She spoke again.

"Help! This message is for the park rangers, or anyone who hears me. Help! Help! I'm in a cottage by Lake Glaslyn, hiding from an armed attacker!"

She knew it was probably for naught. She had never used this machine, and it was too complicated to figure out in a minute or two.

"This is a distress call!" she shouted into the transceiver. "Please, somebody help! I'm stranded in a cottage by Lake Glaslyn, being chased by an armed man! Can anyone hear this? Please, help! Help! Help!"

No response.

"Mayday! Mayday! Mayday!"

She wasn't sure if "Mayday" was the appropriate distress call, or if it was meant for mariners and aviators. It was urgent, and that's what mattered. She tried it again three times into the microphone, still hearing no answer.

Were there no instructions for this bloody box?

Maybe there were.

She tried the kitchen drawers, finding only silverware. There was a cabinet by the bed. She opened it, finding a pile of papers leaning against the folded stacks of clothing. She spread the papers on the dining table, most of them sketches—Kate's rough outlines of paintings. But there was also a booklet inside. A manual!

For the transceiver?

She checked. *Yes.*

She skimmed the contents for the words "distress" and "emergency," then jumped ahead and began reading. She slipped on the pair of headphones lying by the box, and pulled the microphone close, flipping two switches and matching the arrangement of the dials with a diagram in the book.

"I need *help!*" she screamed into the microphone. "This is a distress call! I'm stranded in a cottage on the north banks of Lake Glaslyn! Can anyone hear this? Mayday! Mayday! Mayday!"

More loud, grainy white noise through the headphones.

"An attacker killed my husband and estate manager!" she said. "I'm stranded in a cottage on the north—"

There was a violent yank at the front door handle. God, he'd found her! The door shook in its frame as he applied force from the other side.

She left the radio and snatched up the Purdey. Now how did *this* thing work? She examined the weapon and engaged the barrel breech lever. The gun broke open, and she stared down its twin hollow tubes—that must be where the ammunition should go. She lowered the barrel away from the body of the shotgun and seated two fresh shells in place.

The door rattled until the man on the other side gave up. After a few seconds of quiet, she realized he was formulating a new plan to break into the cabin. She swung the barrel back up and heard a reassuring click. The gun felt heavy and unwieldy, but its use seemed self-explanatory.

The window shattered as a rock hurtled through. She aimed at the broken panes and fired in reflex.

The blast left a high-pitched ringing in her ears, and the blowback knocked her against the dining table. She had fired prematurely, not finding firm footing or seating the stock into her shoulder. There had been more power to it than she'd expected, and she wasn't sure whether that would help or hurt her. She reassumed her position for the second shot, waiting this time for the intruder to show his face. Instead, all she got was another rock, bigger than the first, which missed her head and struck the kitchen wall behind her with a thud. Then came another, pebble-sized, hitting her in the groin. Startled, she pulled the trigger again, a bit more prepared this time, but nevertheless wasting the shot.

She reached for the packet of shells on the floor, trembling ever more when all she needed were nimble fingers. Where was that lever that made the gun break apart? She searched the area connecting the stock and barrel.

Yehuda appeared outside the window and began to climb in. He must have peered through a crack in the exterior and seen her reloading.

Then—a faint noise from the headphones on the table. She listened as a voice crackled through:

"This is the Snowdonia National Park Authority. We are having trouble hearing you."

Not letting go of the shotgun, she held down a button on the transceiver and spoke into the microphone: "I'm at Lake Glaslyn and I need *help!* Emergency at Lake Glaslyn! Emergency at Lake Glaslyn!"

She directed her attention to the Purdey, once again pushing the breech lever. She tilted the barrel, and the two spent casings landed in her palm.

"Ow!"

They were searing hot.

This was taking too long. She wouldn't be able to reload before he was inside. She looked around the room, considering every object as a defensive weapon—pots, pans, a candelabrum. Frantic, she dropped the shotgun and ran to the kitchen, opening drawers. No knives. The candelabrum would have to suffice.

She charged toward Yehuda and swung it like a bat. He pushed through the window, catching the bludgeon with two hands. As his feet landed on solid ground, he shoved her back and kicked her to the wood floor, then used the candelabrum to smash the transceiver.

"Where's Kate?" he snarled.

She held his gaze and spit at his feet.

He removed a candle from the holder. Finding a matchbook in the kitchen, he lit the wick.

"Take off your shoes," he said.

"No."

He bent down and untied them for her. She tried to kick him away, but he held her still with little effort by leaning on her bruised hip. Holding the candle in one hand, he clutched her left foot and brought the flame close to the skin of her little toe.

"I'll burn one at a time," he said, "until they've shriveled into little black flakes."

"You'd do better by the fireplace," she said. "Save time and roast the whole foot."

He brought the flame closer. She felt the prickle of heat.

"I'm warning you, Baroness," he said. "Don't test my patience."

"Go ahead. Test a mother protecting her child. There's no limit to the pain I'll take."

She kicked her head back, thrashing, as he swept the flame slowly across her little toe.

"That was four seconds," he said. "Imagine a full minute."

Her skin began to blister.

"Yehuda!" came a voice.

It was Colette, looking in through the window.

Yehuda sounded furious as he said, "I told you to stay in the canyon."

"I know, but I climbed up to get you when I found this," she said.

"Found what?"

"A note." She handed him a paper through the window. "It was in the car."

He read the paper. No, Lona thought—God, no!

"Interesting telegram from your daughter, Baroness," he said. "I wonder what she's doing in Zermatt."

He let Lona go. She clamped a finger over her seared toe. Yehuda opened the front door for his accomplice.

"Colette," Lona said, her voice cool, "what do you think you're doing with this man?"

Colette stepped close to Lona and stared down at her. "Your daughter isn't who you think she is," she said. "You'll hear it straight from her soon enough."

"Colette, think about what you're doing. We've been family to you. Our home has been your home. Kate's your best friend."

"That's a lie."

"I can't imagine what this monster told you to make you think that."

"The truth," she said. "You don't know the first thing about the girl you brought up. She's fooled you like she did me."

Yehuda used a kitchen towel to gag Lona, then said to Colette, "Help me carry her to the car. Quickly. We have to get out of here."

Using a pan from the kitchen, he knocked Lona unconscious. With one hand, he took the Purdey shotgun and put the remaining shells in a pocket. It took them fifteen minutes to lug the baroness down to the road, where Yehuda opened the trunk of his car and stuffed her inside, along with the weapon, which he made sure was unloaded. He slammed the lid shut and sat behind the wheel. Colette took the passenger's seat.

He fired the ignition and began to turn the car around, when a park ranger's truck rounded the bend and parked. A heavy man got out and hailed them.

"Don't say anything unless he speaks to you," he murmured to Colette, lowering his window.

The ranger said, "Hello."

"Afternoon," Yehuda said. "Everything okay?"

"Sorry to bother, but we've heard what could be a distress call. Didn't come through clearly, so we're not sure. We think it came from around Glaslyn. You didn't happen to come from there?"

"I don't think we did."

"You don't think? You're close to Glaslyn now."

"Sorry, we don't have a map. We've been driving for the scenery. What kind of distress call? That's scary."

"We don't know. The transmission was muffled. May I ask why you chose to park here?"

"For the view."

"There are pullouts nearby. This isn't a stop."

"We thought it made for good photographs," Yehuda said. "And there seemed to be a decent hiking path from this spot."

The ranger paused, spotting the broken barrier and the wreckage of Lona's car down the canyon.

"Bloody hell!" he said.

"What's the matter?" Yehuda said.

"Someone's gone over the edge!"

"My God," Yehuda gasped.

"You didn't see this happen?"

"Of course not. We'd have called for help."

"Come on, let's see if anyone's alive down there!"

Yehuda opened the car door. As he did, a shotgun shell slipped out and landed on the ground.

The ranger looked at him, a question forming in his head as Yehuda stood up, but it didn't have time to develop. Yehuda's hand shot to the boating knife in his pocket. Before the ranger could react, the blade came down on his neck.

Yehuda dropped him in the snow, where a dark stain began to spread. Then he got back in the car and restarted the engine. As they began the long, twisting drive down the mountain, Colette looked shaken, but not as badly as before.

She asked him, "Was that necessary, or do you enjoy bloodshed?"

"He suspected us and would have wasted our time. He was also going to call in more rangers. They might have asked us to stay around or open our trunk."

"Why are we bringing Lady Atwell with us in the first place?"

"Kate has Moritz Dahl on her side," he said. "He's smart. A Sayeret Matkal veteran. It helps our position to have a hostage."

"Sayeret Matkal?"

"An Israeli special forces unit."

"I thought your government was working to bring Kate in."

"We are," Yehuda said. "Dahl is a traitor. He's turned rogue."

Katharina

In a lobby decorated with vintage snowshoes, mountaineering photographs, and other Alpine memorabilia, the receptionist at the Monte Rosa handed Kate and Moritz a room key. They thanked her and relaxed in a nearby salon, where he began scribbling notes in his mother's book.

"What are you doing?" she asked.

"Jotting down every phrase that came out of Werner's mouth."

She saw that he was the type of person who wrote things in random places and connected them in a web of lines and circles. This was a pet peeve of hers; she preferred ordered lists. Nonetheless, she read the sentences he had written: *He's going to try to kill me. ... One man turned them in. He wanted out; he's going to try to kill me. ... Speckles on the pear. ... Speckles on the pear—the pear that saved an army. ... I gave it to Horace. Horace had to run to the gray pillars. Just ask Geoffrey Barkas.*

"Do you think there's more to it than gibberish?" she said.

"No clue, but I want his words on paper before we forget them."

"I've been thinking about something he said. How there was one body missing at my father's house, after the night of the raid. At least, that's what I think he was talking about."

"What do you come up with?"

"This was twenty years ago, mind you, and I was only eight at the time—so my memory's weak—but there was someone missing that night."

"One of the forgers?" he said.

"Yes. I remember one of them saying he was going to pick up a treat for me. He never came back. I think I even remember his name. Heinrich ... what was it? It sounded like the name of an animal. 'Jaguar'? No ..." She concentrated. " 'Jackal'! It sounded like 'jackal.' Heinrich ... *Jecklyn.* That was his name. Heinrich Jecklyn."

"An employee of your father's?"

"He was an artist in the workshop, but he wasn't there during the night of the raid. He left a few hours before it happened. I never thought about him before. Guess I always figured he'd been tracked down and killed like the others."

"Seems plausible that Werner was talking about this Heinrich Jecklyn as the 'man who wanted out' and who 'turned them in.' "

"Maybe Jecklyn ratted out my father and his fellow forgers. But it always seemed strange to me that the Nazi authorities would react by slaughtering everyone involved, including a valued vice minister."

"They must have seen your father's workshop as a threat. Think about it. A high official in the Reich Ministry of Public Enlightenment and Propaganda, responsible for the underground proliferation of degenerate art, would undermine faith in the Nazi Party."

"If he worked with my father and Karl Decker, Werner may have worried he'd be snitched on, too," she said. "Maybe his dementia has brought back the old fear and paranoia. Hence, 'He's going to try to kill me.' "

"Interesting theory," Moritz said. "Any idea what Werner's other words might mean?"

"It's all nonsense to my ears."

"Mine, too. 'Speckles on the pear—the pear that saved an army.' Does that sound like a literary reference?"

"Could be. Horace was a Roman poet during the time of Augustus. But what about 'gray pillars'?"

Moritz underlined the words in the notebook. "And what does any of it have to do with Geoffrey Barkas?"

Kate massaged her temples. "I say we sleep on it."

Closing the notebook, Moritz nodded agreement.

"I could also use a drink. Any interest in a mug of mulled wine?"

"I'll never turn that down," she said.

They went into the dining room and placed their order from a sofa by the window. A waiter served them a concoction of cinnamon, cloves, citrus, red wine, and port. Kate watched Moritz gaze outside, wondering what in the village had caught his eye. He looked pensive. A Christmas fair had come alive with music and lights. The streets bustled as skiers came back from the slopes. A sleigh came by the window; the passengers were two pretty blondes in fur coats.

"Penny for your thoughts," Kate said.

"I'm not that cheap."

"Then how about another *Glühwein?*"

"Sold. I was watching some children building a snowman, feeling sorry for myself that all I had in my childhood was sand."

"You poor, deprived child."

So he hadn't been looking at the women in the sleigh. Or he'd come up with a good excuse. She reminded herself she didn't care either way.

"You know, Moritz," she said, "for someone who's saved my life, accompanied me from Paris to Zermatt, and racked his brains with me over the ravings of a crazy old man, you haven't told me much about *you*."

"There are two sides to that coin," he said.

"I asked first."

"What do you want to know?"

"Something interesting."

"All right. Ask away, and for each question, I get to ask you one."

"Fair." She pretended to think a moment, having already decided on her first question. "How'd you become interested in the military?"

He looked at her in shy amusement.

"I'll tell you only if you promise not to laugh at any part of this."

"I promise. Start talking," she said.

"When I was seven, I had my heart set on buying a camel, so I could cross the Sahara like a Bedouin chief, find my own African princess, and fight the Axis. There was a homeless man who taught me to play checkers, chess, and backgammon. I used to make pieces out of bottle caps and challenge drunken soldiers to games for money, so I could buy that camel."

"If you're one to take advantage of drunkards, should I worry you suggested wine this evening?" She suddenly felt embarrassed. It wasn't like her to be flirtatious, but then, it wasn't like her to drink her wine so quickly.

"Some games shouldn't be cheated at," he said, though she was too self-conscious to think about what he meant. "Anyway, one day I was bringing my small wad of cash to a camel salesman, thinking I could afford one, when a gang of bullies waylaid me and smacked me in the stomach with a cricket bat. They took my money, and I cried my way home to my mother, who was at the time tending to a customer, a British officer named Alfred Paxton. I'd seen this man before. He came by her shop frequently. I realized he was trying to court my mother. Paxton was nice, but I knew he would never earn her affections. She still loved my father, Rasmus Dahl, wherever he was.

"That day I came crying home, Paxton sat me down and asked what the matter was. I told him. He said he was an intelligence officer—someone who could find things out. He said maybe he could help get the money back. To the penny, I told him how much I'd lost. Days later, he came back with a wad of cash for me. I was inspired to learn more about intelligence officers. They did the work of justice!"

"What did you do next?"

"That's question two," he said, winking.

"No fair. I'm allowed follow-up."

"After my eighth birthday, Paxton set me up as a delivery boy with a bicycle, so I could deliver low-urgency telegrams and documents among British officers to and from GHQ. I didn't understand the war's motivations but knew the effort was important. I took my delivery duties seriously, and I made more money than I had playing games. If I made enough to buy a camel, I could fight and help defeat the Axis. That was the master plan."

"Did it work?" she asked with a grin.

"I started to feel like an important 'intelligence officer,' but learned it could be easy for others to take advantage of my services."

"How so?" she said as he shook his head no. "Come on, you can't end with something like that."

"I looked up to Paxton as a mentor for a time. Then one day he asked me, 'Does your mother ever talk about me? Why don't you go home and mention my name, and see if she smiles at all, and see if her cheeks turn red. And you could say you miss having a daddy around.' I told her about Paxton's maneuver, and said it made me lose confidence in intelligence officers. She told me love can make people do strange things, and that while we can't always know whom to trust, there *are* many good spies—Rasmus among them. I was excited to learn my father was a good spy."

"Iris must have finished things with Paxton after that."

"She said it was time to stop delivering telegrams for Paxton and his men, and that I would begin language studies at a school in Zamalek. I was reluctant to give up my telegram delivery post, but I went along with Mum's wishes and never saw Paxton again after the war ended. By that time, she was taking regular trips to Denmark and other places in Europe, looking for Rasmus, not knowing if he'd survived the war.

"The First Arab-Israeli War started when I was thirteen. One evening, while I was out with friends, sneaking around a nightclub after hours, I discovered the club was used as a meeting place for some Muslim Brothers fighting with the Arab Liberation Army. By accident, they'd left a loaded pistol behind. I took it with me and slept with it under my pillow. I felt safer with it. Besides, I was often home alone and might need to protect my mother's hat shop from burglars. I wanted to learn how to use it, so sometimes in the early mornings I went out into the Sahara, far from the city, to set up targets and practice shooting."

"And that's how you learned to fire a gun?" Kate said.

"Right. Figured if I could teach myself to shoot, maybe I could make a decent soldier."

"Later, in the Israeli Special Forces, did they teach you to fly?"

"Of course. Why?"

"I've taken lessons, but couldn't be called a pilot just yet," she said. "I want to finish learning."

"Flying is absolute freedom," he said. "I could finish your lessons, once we get through this mess."

"I accept."

"Good," he said. "Now, your questions are answered. I get to ask, what, a dozen?"

"Just one."

"Oh, come on!"

"Not my fault you answered in a roundabout way!"

"I'll be more thrifty with my words next time." He searched her face as if to gauge her sensitivity. "Remember, I get to ask anything."

"Within reason."

"That little scar on your left eyebrow. How'd you get it?"

"Now it's your turn not to laugh."

He held a hand to his chest and looked at her slyly. "Fair is fair."

"Really, though."

"Tell the damned story."

"Fine," she said. "My parents live at the edge of Snowdonia, a national park in Wales. My father had a cottage built for me up by a lake called Glaslyn. During the winter of 'fifty-one, I set up my easel somewhere along a route leading to Mount Snowdon. The weather got bad fast. I wanted to stay and finish the work, but a blizzard swept in and forced me to pack up and head for the cottage. I didn't leave soon enough and got lost in the whiteout. I felt like I was going to die, but a ranger found me and helped me back to the cottage. Along the way, I fell and nicked my eye on a bramble. The whole thing was so embarrassing."

"How long were you stranded alone?"

"A few days, but not alone."

"Not alone?"

"I invited the ranger in."

"For days?"

"It was a harsh storm, and his station was miles away. I said he could stay with me until it was over. He worked most of the time, anyway."

"So, it was out of the goodness of your heart that you spent those days in an isolated cabin with a handsome ranger."

"Did I say he was handsome?"

"I read between the lines."

"We fell in love, and we were engaged for a time."

"But you didn't marry?"

"When he found out who my father was, he broke it off."

"You told him?"

"I've kept secrets my whole life. From my parents, from my friends. I didn't just want a husband. I wanted a sweetheart, a partner, a confidante. But I suppose in my case, that's too much to ask."

"Your father shouldn't determine your destiny. The ranger was mad to break it off because of that."

"That's enough about Alfred. My turn to ask again." She took a deep breath. "I want to know what brought you to Israel."

"A girl."

His answer surprised and even startled her, though it really shouldn't have. She tried not to let it show.

"Really?"

"During the thick of the war beginning in 'forty-eight, I met a Jewish girl named Nava Laslo. She came into my mother's hat shop wondering if she could afford something pretty for her sister. It was sort of a 'love at first sight' thing. She was beautiful. I asked if she wanted to go fishing on the Nile that night. She said yes. We cooked our catch on the open desert, in view of the pyramids. Then we started spending more time together. Nava would sleep over while Mum was busy looking for Rasmus. I fell head over heels for her. Occasionally I'd take her into the desert, where we'd shoot my pistol, practicing just in case we needed to protect ourselves. In 'fifty-one, after the resolution of the war, Nava and her family were among the hundreds of thousands of Jews to move to Israel. I told Mum I had to go with her. Mum didn't want to be apart from her only son, especially after having lost Rasmus, so she packed up her hat shop and moved with me to Beersheba. Two years later, when Nava's father learned that I had a gun and taught Nava to use it, he forbade her from seeing such a 'violent warmonger,' not to mention a goy. She disobeyed him for a while, but it got too hard for her. She broke it off in 'fifty-three. That's when I changed my name and joined the military."

"Sounds like you were pretty heartbroken," Kate said.

"I was."

"How did you settle on 'Moritz'?"

"The homeless man who taught me games—that's what people called him. And now it's my turn," he said. "There's something I'd really like to know."

"Oh?"

"Remember, anything is fair game."

"Within reason."

"I'll be the judge of that. Tell me, why have you kept your heritage a secret from everyone you love, including your adoptive parents?"

The question put her on edge. "Well, the one person I told *did* stop loving me," she said.

She set her glass down, wondering why it made her so angry that he'd asked. It was a perfectly reasonable question.

"I don't think everyone else would," she said. "But I'm afraid they might."

"You shouldn't be afraid. You don't choose your blood."

She knew that, of course, but she wondered who would still see her in the same light after knowing the truth. Every relationship she cherished might take on a different tone.

"I know," she said.

"Then stop letting the ghost of Ralf Speer haunt you."

. . .

When morning came, Kate and Moritz packed their bags and put them in the car. Moritz hadn't said anything else about Yehuda, but she had noticed how cautious and alert he had been the entire time in Zermatt. Both of them were ready to leave Switzerland behind so that no one would know where they were. Kate had learned her lesson from the telegram, so she was careful when she went down to the lobby to speak to the mustachioed concierge.

"Good morning," she said. "My husband and I are planning a drive. We hope you might suggest a route to Yugoslavia."

"Of course," he said, reaching under his desk and handing her a sheet of hotel stationery and a pen. "Which part?"

"We'd like to take a route along the Adriatic and stop at little towns along the way. If you could direct us to the nearest border."

He played with his mustache, thinking. "I can tell you how to get there directly, but for that kind of trip, you'd probably be better off looking at a map. Check the lounge down the hall to the right. There's a bookshelf full of them."

"Thank you," she said.

She took the pen and stationery to the lounge, finding the shelf beside a wood table. The shelf was packed with cartographic and pictorial booklets covering the globe. She skimmed the spines and pulled out a volume on East-Central Europe. Taking a seat at the table, she flipped through the pages and settled on an illustration that stretched as far west as Geneva and as far east as Sarajevo.

She set the stationery over the map and traced their route in a dotted line. The line took them north to Visp, then east to Brig, and zigzagged through the Simplon Pass all the way to Domodossola in Piedmont, Italy—a twisting road between the Pennine and Lepontine Alps. From Domodossola, her line continued southeast to the outskirts of Milan, then east under Verona, and around the Gulf of Venice to Slovenia. Eventually, it connected all the way down the Dalmatian Coast to Dubrovnik, which she circled on her sheet.

On her copied map, she labeled the key motorways and wrote down a list of directions with approximate distances. Then she closed the book and slipped it back into its place on the shelf.

"Honeymooners?" the concierge asked her when she gave the pen back.

"Right," she said quickly.

"Bon voyage to the handsome newlyweds. Enjoy your drive."

Colette

"We can rest there for the night," Colette said, pointing off to the side of the road.

Their day crossing through France had been so long and tiring that the drive from the ferry in Le Havre early that morning felt like a week-old memory. Yehuda parked outside a motel by Lake Geneva, a few miles from Lausanne. Its claim to luxury was a small, outdoor whirlpool tub in the shape of a Swiss cross, giving off wisps of steam into the night air.

Yehuda checked in at the front desk and instructed Colette to give Lona a dose of chloroform before they sneaked her through the door and tied her up. The room smelled of cigarettes. The bathtub was cracked, the curtains tarnished by sooty streaks. A monochrome television stood on four legs near the foot of the single bed. Folded on the nightstand was a handwritten notice indicating that all sheets and towels were washed daily.

Colette took off her coat and lay back on the bed while Yehuda shaved in the bathroom. She looked at herself in the mirror beside the television and smiled at the reflection. She felt proud of herself. Yesterday morning, she had felt like a whimpering teenager and a burden to Yehuda. Then she had swallowed her cowardice. She had seen that flicker in Yehuda's eyes when she'd proved herself an asset. No longer would she be questioning or timid when they had work to do. And though she couldn't explain why, she'd felt unbelievably attractive again, like the beauty the Parisian fashion world had fawned over in her modeling days.

She'd forgotten what that felt like, having been away from the photographers these past few years—but now, she admitted, the young woman in the mirror looked hard to resist in her pleated scarlet skirt. She played with her hair, holding it up, curling a few strands around her finger, and then letting it flow down her back in a silky stream of dark red. The color of a fine merlot, she thought, emboldened.

No man she'd been with could handle the woman she'd become in the last twenty-four hours. She thought of Philippe. Suddenly he seemed like an adolescent—an idiot with a paintbrush next to Yehuda. Never mind the photographer she'd lived with in Paris, that fat old lard. She was traveling with a real man now, a man with worldly skills. There was a fearless energy about Yehuda—the kind that conquered continents—and an intelligence she could only describe as erotic. He came out of the bathroom, the edges of his short beard now groomed into hard angles. Detecting a leathery fragrance, she wondered whether he had spritzed out of habit, or whether it had been for her. She stood up and meandered toward the bathroom, stretching, ostensibly limbering her muscles after the long day of sitting, and caught him eyeing her. She had to say something.

"This place is far from five stars," was all she could think of.

"We'll be gone soon."

His presence made her aware of all the things that should have been automatic. Was she standing straight? What was she supposed to do with her arms—fold them, let them dangle? For God's sake, she was fidgeting like a bundle of nerves.

"How far are we from Zermatt?"

"A few hours."

"I suppose you have a plan for when we get there."

"We'll see if Kate and Moritz are still at the Monte Rosa. If so, I will find their room number and stage a surprise."

"If not?"

"I'll think of something."

He was not the kind of man who needed to fill silence with conversation. It was a relief sometimes, being with someone who didn't mind minutes or hours of peace, but it could also make the air heavy, and heavier still when he was looking at her. She saw neither approval nor disapproval in his stare, just the recognition that she was there, like a piece of furniture. If he was mentally undressing her, he did not show it in his eyes. She wanted so badly to get inside his head and learn whether he was truly as indifferent toward her as he looked. She reminded herself that a man who wants a woman rarely knows what to do with his eyes; he will usually reveal too much, or too little, and though too little was more interesting, it also could be maddening.

Tonight, she did not want to have to interpret signals. She had made up her mind about his attractiveness. There was a good chance he felt the same way about her. She was an *asset*—valuable to him. He didn't know much about her, or she him, but it was exciting that way, and they had gone this distance together, even carried a woman down a mountain together, so they weren't exactly strangers anymore.

Her thought as she turned to face him was: Kate would never have the nerve to do this, not to any man.

She edged closer to him, centering her lips an inch from his ear. "I see you're not one for small talk," she said. "Stop staring and take my clo—"

Her sentence ended with a light yelp: He hadn't waited for the permission she was about to give. She could feel his hands digging into her hips, molding into their shape, working their way up to the buttons of her sweater. He spun her around, holding her at the edge of the bed. There was force in his grip, and even more, there was patience. He slid the sweater off her shoulders. His fingers traced their way along her arms and down her torso, not in any rush to unclasp her bra.

She tried to back away a few inches, not because she wanted to, but because she was curious to see if he would let her. He did not. She'd known it! He'd been thinking about this all day, sitting in that cramped little car with her in the passenger seat, wondering what kind of tramp she was . . . and now she could feel the hunger in his touch. It was time to test that patience of his.

She grabbed his belt and undid the buckle, untucked his shirt, lifted it, flung it off. She took in his physique, admiring the peaks and valleys in his musculature as she removed his pants. His hands explored her back, gravitating toward her buttocks and teasing her skirt line. She undid her own buttons until she was now in her stockings and underwear.

Her skin tingled wherever he touched her, especially where he *barely* touched her. She glanced into the mirror again, seeing how her hair had spilled into her cleavage. She delighted in the vision of herself. He inched closer, and she finally lost her balance, tripping over the footboard and falling onto the mattress with a heavy gasp. He fell after her, landing with his legs apart, and glided her underwear off, moving his fingers along her thighs. That made her shiver. Oh, please, don't stop there, she thought. She closed her eyes as began to feel the warmth of his breath on her skin. He began kissing her abdomen, making his way down to her mound, a thick, blonde bush she had not dyed to match her red locks. Pausing a moment, apparently surprised by the color, he then began to kiss her more violently, exploring her upper legs with an occasional bite. Pleasure swelled within her, a wave on a run, rolling and building.

Please, you know where to kiss me, she kept thinking. You know where I want it, and I'm burning down there. She could feel his lips winding tension into her spine, making her back arch and her body writhe. She was hardly aware as her moans became louder, higher-pitched. Stop wasting time, she thought. You know exactly where I want you to kiss me. Oh, God, do it, kiss me there, I want your mouth, and if you don't give me yours I'll give you mine first.

She opened her eyes. He had stopped.

What was the matter?

"I want you," she said, running a hand through his hair. "I've never wanted a man's body like this."

She tried to push his mouth into her, but he moved her hand away.

"Oh, baby, don't stop!" she begged. What was the matter with him? She reached down and felt the bulge between his legs. He was hard for her. She could feel him pulsing. He looked her in the eye, and though she liked the sight of his face buried between her legs, she could tell his mind was only half there, and that he was thinking about something else he wanted. She took her bra off, hoping it would help. Her nipples were on fire, and he hadn't even touched them.

He looked enticed, but he did not feel her there. He laid a hand on her crevice and moved his fingers in a slow circle.

"You look like you're tight," he said.

"Why don't you find out?"

He pushed himself off the bed and leaned over her naked body, running a hand over her hip, before lifting her up into his arms. She let out a soft, helpless whimper.

"Where are you taking me?"

He didn't answer; she found out soon enough. In the bathroom, he set her down in the basin of the tub, plugged the drain, and turned on the hot water. Steam began to rise, and he removed his few remaining garments.

"Ow," she said, drawing her feet away from the stream. "Make it cooler." She watched as the edge of the rising water inched closer to her body. "That's scalding."

"You'll like it."

As the water lapped against her thigh, she reached for the cold faucet and tried to turn it on, but not before he climbed in on top of her, blocking the way. She was about to complain when he reached into the running water and splashed his face with it. If he could do that, she could get used to the heat. She winced as the water began to climb up her calves and buttocks, but she said nothing, not wanting to look weak. Not when he was this close to her, supporting himself with two hands on the rim of the tub and lowering himself onto her.

Bestriding him from beneath, she could feel her lips parting as his hips brushed against hers. The bath water, which had begun to make her sweat, no longer seemed so uncomfortable. The stings of heat felt satisfying, making her ever more aware of her body and the solidness filling her. The tension in her spine began to coil again as his pelvis rolled forward and back, winding her like a clockwork doll.

"Ahhh . . ." she said. "*Oui . . . oui . . .*"

She wrapped her legs around the rim of the tub, propping herself higher, enabling his thrusts. The sound of the running water slipped her into a trance as it always did. She loved the sound, and often when she took baths, she would let water out when the tub got full, just so she could run another stream and hear the splashes. She felt protected within the walls of the basin, even if the water was hot enough to turn her skin pink.

Closing her eyes as the fire between her legs grew violent, she felt a short, sudden surge of intensity, then a long, burning wave of pleasure, and a satisfying gush of wetness. The sensation spread throughout her body, relieving the tension in her spine, causing her to bend and moan and shudder, until finally there was only a throb and a sensitive feeling between her legs.

Yehuda pulled himself out of her, and as she sank back into the water, he bent down toward her and whispered, "You'll do what I ask, whatever it takes to get Kate."

She wasn't sure if that was a question or a declaration, but she nodded.

"Good," he said.

He kicked his head back, grunting as he spurted on her breasts. Colette lay still in the steaming water, wondering why there weren't more men like Yehuda, men who weren't afraid of whatever it was they wanted. She had felt a crisis of meaning with other men she had slept with. She had felt no different before and after, aside from the physical satisfaction.

Yehuda had given her a purpose: to put everything in his hands and discover the pleasure of unconditional surrender.

Moritz

Twisting their way through the Simplon Pass, Moritz and Kate took turns at the wheel, stopping only occasionally to stretch and admire the white panoramas of the Pennine and Lepontine Alps.

All through the mountains, his mind had been re-creating scenes from history books. Smugglers had marched through the pass in the 1600s with Mediterranean sea salt; carriage roads were built so Napoleon could transport cannon between Italy and the Rhône Valley; and the Swiss had made the pass impenetrable to the fascist south during World War II, tunneling fortresses into the canyon walls of Gondo. Now the mountains looked peaceful, and the centuries they had witnessed still alive in books and stories.

Moritz was an aficionado of history, so it bothered him that he knew so little about his own past. He had seen his father only once, and he hardly remembered what Rasmus had looked or sounded like. If he were to hear a recording, the man would sound like a total stranger. He had no photos. All he remembered was the reassuring feeling, at the age of five or so, that he actually did have a father, even if it was the first and last time he ever saw him.

He had far more vivid memories of his mother, Iris. She was the most meticulous woman he had ever known, and the most tenacious, never satisfied with her work and never giving up until she was. She spent hours centering squares of moist felt over her hat blocks, running steamers over the fabric, stretching it, molding its shape, steaming again, inserting pins that would hold the felt steady while it dried. Her hat shop had been their home in Cairo; it overlooked a nightclub that drew customers to her business. She'd had a wide view of the traffic outside. She would watch all the goings-on with keen eyes and say that all the heads in the streets looked naked as robins without her creations.

Yes, he remembered the shop very well. He would sit on the floor making game boards out of cardboard and bottle caps, and listen to the radio while his mother worked. Sometimes she would ask him to serve tea to customers. Other times, she would insist he go run and play.

Usually, he'd been given the freedom to do as he pleased. She never spoke to him as though he were a child, so he had never really felt like a child in her eyes. She had treated him as an adult whose cup of knowledge had yet to be filled. Not that she wouldn't reprimand him when he misbehaved, as she had been known to do, sometimes in the most humiliating ways—but he had felt respected in her household, as so few Egyptian children were in theirs.

He pictured her long, triangular face, her steep eyebrows, the olive hues of her complexion. Iris had been as mysterious as she was beautiful, and he had always believed there was more to his mother than she let on. He was never quite sure what was in her mind. She was unpredictable—happy one moment, agitated the next—and there were times when she would send him out, not to any particular place, but because she needed the space. There were also times when he would see her running through the streets of Cairo like a maniac, dodging in and out of the lorries and motorcars and farm animals to get where she was going. He never found out why or where she was going. It was impossible to keep up with her, and she would get flustered when he asked, using the excuse that she had important meetings with clients.

Aside from occasional help in the shop, she had never asked anything of him in life. Her first request had come in death. Leaving a painting to a total stranger, and one who could have been on any continent, was without a doubt the most puzzling thing his mother had ever done. It was her in a nutshell: She was a passionate woman who took painstaking care in everything she did—and who never explained her reasons.

Moritz would curse his mother if he didn't love her so much. If it weren't for her, he wouldn't be on this wild goose chase, trying to uncover her connection to a German World War II refugee, and his Mossad colleague would not be trying to kill him. But then, if it weren't for her, he'd never have met Kate.

Kate was an enigma all her own. Only days ago, he'd believed she was helping war criminals. He had looked into her dark brown eyes at the Christmas soirée and seen everything Yehuda had told him to see: a menacing individual bent on carrying her father's torch. He hated her, feared what she was capable of, and had been forced to pretend otherwise. Now he realized she wouldn't hurt a fly. If there was anyone she had chosen to harm in her life, it was herself, by continuing to believe she owed something to anyone, that she owed restitution for Ralf Speer's crimes.

He looked at the sky through the windshield. The setting sun drew a dark blue curtain over the apricot hues. They had traversed a range of geographies today, having driven the first day through Domodossola, then on past Milan and Verona to the outskirts of Trieste. The highway had taken them into the People's Republic of Croatia, where they were now driving south along the Dalmatian Coast.

He pulled over by the roadside. He and Kate got out and climbed a hill that overlooked the bluffs and coves.

"I miss the mountains," Kate said.

"Must be that cold German heart of yours."

"*Das ist eher möglich,*" she said. *That is more likely*.

"Hard to believe you'd take the icy summits over this. I don't think anything holds a candle to the Adriatic."

A thin crescent of the moon waned above them. His camel-hair overcoat had begun to flap in the wind. Kate's hair blew across her shoulders, resting between gusts. Now and then a few strands of hers would brush the side of his face. He tucked them back over her ear in a useless attempt to fight the breeze.

"Katharina," he said. He liked her original name. It was a regal one, and he figured it was good for her to get used to hearing it, even if she objected.

"Yes . . . Anwar?"

"I'm glad we're doing this together. Looking for answers to the puzzles we inherited."

"It only makes sense to put our heads together."

"Yes, but I had no idea what you'd be like. After the lies I'd been told about you, when Yehuda was using me to find you, the thought of trusting you seemed crazy."

"How do you know they're all lies?"

He returned her canny smile, glad she was finally demonstrating a sense of humor.

"Come to think of it, I don't. For all I know, you could be a serial murderess."

"Yet you tag along."

"Danger and mystery make for strangely alluring females. Haven't you read *She*?"

"I'll gladly accept the comparison."

"Don't expect me to call you 'She-who-must-be-obeyed' or anything like that."

She paused a beat. "I'm glad we're doing this, too." She touched his arm. "Come on. Let's keep driving. We're almost there. If you look far enough south . . ."

He did, and saw the walls of Dubrovnik jutting out over the ocean.

Isabel

Filing purchase records for Pendelfarr International was not how Isabel de la Fuente had envisioned spending her evenings this close to Christmas, but she needed the work. Even more, she wanted to impress Conrad. It was a miracle he'd hired her as his executive assistant. She was underqualified to take such a bold step into the world of art, but he'd opened the door for her. She was typically a realist, not an optimist, but she felt good enough about this job to let herself hope the experience might pave the way to her dream of attending art school someday.

This was no boutique auction house, after all. Pendelfarr International had a fine and far-reaching reputation. She had been introduced to collectors from around the world and might soon have a chance to do a little traveling herself on assignment. It would be an excellent way to build credentials.

Sitting in her office in Conrad's Bariloche mansion, she gazed out the window at the snowcapped Andes, remembering the life she had left behind on the other side of the mountains. She was glad the range was there for her to see every day—a tall, jagged barrier between the past and the present. She was twenty-two and had come from Port Montt, Chile, but she would never speak of this to Conrad Pendelfarr.

The door opened. As Pendelfarr walked in, Isabel began shuffling through the papers on her desk to look busier than she really was. She had been working nearly fourteen hours straight and was getting weary.

"Still working?" he said.

"Almost finished."

"I think that's enough for tonight. It's getting late. Surely you have someone to go home to."

If that's what he believed, she wasn't going to tell him otherwise. Lately she'd had the feeling he was trying to pry into her personal affairs. A few other employees had begun doing the same, and she suspected he might be the reason. The questions were never uncomfortable or inappropriate in themselves, but she didn't like talking about herself, even with friends.

She said nothing, but he pressed: "Or don't you?"

"Thanks for asking," she said. "You're right. I'd love to get home early."

His pause told her that he had noted the evasion.

"Come spend a few minutes with me," he said. "I've prepared some yerba mate."

She left the papers on her desk and followed him into his sumptuous but garish living room. He handed her the drink in a calabash gourd.

"*Bueno?*"

"*Sí*," she said. "Nice and warm."

He took off his sport coat and laid it on a sofa. The room was overdecorated and uncoordinated—a mishmash of bronze statuary on pedestals, silk embroideries from the Orient, Moroccan rugs, and Art Deco furniture. She wondered whether the blend was the work of a sentimentalist or a man without taste. The latter seemed unlikely of an eminent art broker.

"What do you think?" he said.

"An impressive international collection . . . but too much for one room."

He sipped from his gourd, apparently nonplussed.

"Oh, no," she said. "I'm so sorry. I shouldn't have said that! It's beautiful, really. But . . . maybe better if it were spread out across two or three rooms instead of one."

Damn you, Isabel, she thought—you can't keep your stupid trap shut for thirty seconds, can you, even when you need this job?

He was quiet a moment, and then came an outburst of laughter.

"First honest answer I've ever gotten to that question," he said. "I like that you have an opinion and you're willing to share it."

"I didn't mean to suggest—"

"That it's a dreadful hodgepodge? You'd be right. Everything in here has special meaning to me. I like to have all my favorite treasures in one place."

He took her on a brief tour of the room, describing where he had acquired the various items. Each had a story that he shared in extravagant detail. She nodded and smiled, sneaking glances at her watch as her evening disappeared. While discussing a piece from a collection of netsukes, he set down his drink and loosened his tie. It came off a few minutes later. He flung it across the couch.

"Have all you like," he said, refilling her yerba mate.

"Thank you, but I'd better head home soon."

"Why don't you have a seat first, Isabel? There's something on my mind."

She felt guilty about making him forgo the small talk.

"All right," she said, settling back on the sofa, attentive.

"Do you know much about economics?" Pendefarr asked.

"Some basics, I guess," she said. "Supply and demand, that sort of thing. Why?"

"I'd like to talk about bargaining power. Let's think about a simple, hypothetical market."

"Okay."

"Say you have a merchant selling an apple to a customer," he said. "They'll negotiate and agree on a price, right? Now what if the customer discovered the apple isn't fresh, and that the vendor next door is offering a nice, succulent apple straight from the tree? What do you think will happen to the first guy's price?"

"It will probably drop," she said.

"Sounds reasonable. Now, going back to the first case. No competition, and the apple's fresh. What will happen to the price if the seller learns his customer hasn't eaten for days?"

Isabel figured he was drawing an analogy, but she wasn't sure what kind.

"It will go up."

"Why?"

"The customer values the apple more. He's hungry."

"And because he's hungry, he loses bargaining power?"

"Sure."

"I suppose most customers wouldn't want to reveal how hungry they are, then," Pendelfarr said. "They would try to keep that information private. Wouldn't they?"

"Yes," she said.

"Then consider another market, not for an apple, but for a job. The participants are an employer and a worker."

Suddenly she had an idea where this was going, and she felt a prickle of panic.

"Suppose the new employer were to do a background check," he said, "and contact the company in Buenos Aires where his new worker ostensibly had been working the past few years, only to discover no one at that company had ever heard of her—or of the executives who supposedly wrote her glowing recommendation letters."

She sat frozen on the couch.

"How do you think this information might affect the employment contract?" he said.

"*Madre de Dios*," she whispered. "I'm so deeply . . . I am so sorry, Mr. Pendelfarr. Please let me explain."

"You don't need to," he said. "I asked an accountant to do a little digging. Your picture was recognized at a brothel not far from here. One of your friends there explained your circumstances to him."

She was speechless.

"You are not Argentinean. You're Chilean," he said. "A few years ago, your brother spent your family's savings on a treatment for your mother's pneumonia. To prevent an eviction, he got involved with a group of drug traffickers. He was caught running a business on the side, diluting the traffickers' cocaine and selling the loot. You tried to bail him out of trouble with quick cash you could earn by advertising yourself as a high-class prostitute. Your friends at the local brothel say you told them you never went through with it. You would take your clients' money and slip away before performing the services. It was a short-term tactic, and one you tried one too many times, as it led to your arrest and sentencing to a women's detention center. You later learned in jail that your mother passed away, and that your brother was killed by the traffickers. You determined to start a new life for yourself. You escaped while being transferred to Santiago and crossed the border into Argentina with nothing but the lint in your pockets. Am I right?"

She nodded. It was all she could do to hold back her tears.

"You searched for jobs and were homeless for many weeks," he said, "until you approached the local 'massage parlor,' where my accountant met your friends. You gave up that line of work quickly. Faked a résumé and some referrals, and applied for a job as a secretary in response to a job vacancy posted by my company."

"Yes, it's true," Isabel said. What was she going to do now? The thought of being unemployed again was too much to bear. She had nothing, and she couldn't think of going back to that awful place. Yet she knew what he had to do. "I know you have to fire me now. You don't have to explain."

"I'm not finished," Pendelfarr said. He removed his cufflinks, getting comfortable. They clinked as he set them on a table. "Returning to my original question—*How do you think this might affect your employment contract?*—well, for most employers, that would be a simple answer. You'd lose your job. The full context, however, makes things a bit more complicated for me. You're not a criminal in my eyes, or a whore. You're a good person. Desperate, but good. You're resourceful and hardworking and good at what you do. You're discerning and opinionated. Most of all, you're passionate. If there's one true aspect of your résumé, it's your love of art. I know that because my accountant tells me you regularly borrow, and devour, the art history textbooks in my personal library. He tells me it's your dream to attend art school."

"Yes," she said, finding his compassion difficult to understand.

"You falsified your referral letters because you needed to survive. Am I right?"

"Yes," she said again, "but I'm still ashamed."

"There's no need to be. When we are facing forces beyond our control, we go into survival mode. I understand this. I want you to know that I don't only forgive you. I empathize with you, and I want to help you in the best way I can. By sending you to art school on scholarship."

She must have misheard. "Sorry?"

"Isabel, you'll begin studying during the autumn of next year. Paid for by my company."

"I . . . what? I'm confused. I don't understand—*why?*"

"One option was to fire you and turn you in as an illegal immigrant. You'd be deported back to Chile and incarcerated with an even longer sentence." He smiled, and she wondered if the remark was a delicate reminder of his position in light of his spiel on bargaining power. "But it seemed more beneficial to invite you to become the inaugural scholar in a philanthropic program I'm developing. A program designed to fund the studies of young, aspiring artists."

"But . . . I don't have any background in—"

"After a few more months at my company, you will." He bowed his head. "Besides, I'm connected with lots of top educational institutions. My company often consults with professors. Getting you into the school of our choice will not be an issue."

"So, I'll no longer be working for Pendelfarr International?"

"Not after you take the scholarship. You'll be studying. Rigorously. All your expenses will be covered. Unofficially, you'll still be working for me, as a media liaison. Your only obligation will be to give press interviews. As many as my publicity team can schedule. They'll train you in media relations. You'll express your gratitude for the opportunities afforded you as the first Pendelfarr Scholar, and you'll encourage other students to apply for similar scholarships."

"There will be more?"

"That's the idea. This doesn't benefit only the students. It benefits me. Good press on philanthropic efforts is good for business. Brand recognition attracts clients. I'll make no bones about the self-interest underlying my generosity."

"I understand this is a business decision, and I truly appreciate what you're doing, Mr. Pendelfarr."

She understood well enough why she had been selected. Conrad Pendelfarr needed a puppet. He had a credible threat against her, one he was openly expressing, and he could use it to influence her messages to the media. Still, she was bursting with gratitude. He was aware of her passion for the field and probably thought she would make a motivated student and exemplary inaugural scholar.

"You'll accept the scholarship, then?" he said.

"Yes," she said. "A thousand times, yes. Thank you!"

It was unprofessional, but she didn't care: She leaned over and hugged him tightly. He was offering her more than a stepping-stone toward her dream. He was handing her the dream itself, at essentially no cost.

"Let's celebrate in my office," he said. "I've got some champagne cooling."

She felt like she was floating as she followed him in, and if there was anything she'd worry about in the coming days, it was the moment she'd wake up from this dream, or hear him change his mind. But right now, this was *real.*

He lifted a bottle from an ice bucket that was propped on his desk beside a small sheaf of papers.

"Please read and sign these," he said, handing her the papers. She looked them over as he popped the cork and filled her flute.

Seeing her name already printed in the scholarship agreement gave her a rush of excitement. But she took her time reading through the pages before signing and dating them.

"To the first Pendelfarr Scholar," Pendelfarr said, and they clinked their glasses.

She looked through his window. He had a nice view of a Patagonian lake and the Andes beyond. As the evening grew darker, they looked taller than ever, forming a boundary that seemed truly impassable.

"I've reviewed your summary of auction results," he said. "This has been our most profitable winter in five years."

"I'm glad to hear it, Mr. Pendelfarr."

"The news has me feeling munificent; with Christmas four days away, your check this month includes a 20 percent bonus. You've been a fine assistant."

He reached into a drawer and handed her the check.

She looked at the numbers.

"Truly, I . . . I don't know what to say after tonight!" she said. "Thank you, from the bottom of my heart. For everything. For understanding. For helping me. *Thank you!*"

"I make it a point to keep my employees happy," he said. "By the way, have we received any more messages from Europe?"

"You mean, from Professor Maxence or Mr. Uzan?"

"Right."

"No, we haven't. I've been meaning to ask you, Mr. Pendelfarr."

"Yes?"

"Who they are, what that's about. This 'girl who got away,' I mean, I imagine it's some sort of code for an art piece?"

Pendelfarr downed his flute.

"Yes, a special piece," he said. "A painting of a very special girl."

"I hope you find her."

"Good wishes are always appreciated." He looked at his watch. "It's quite late. You must be itching to get home."

"Some sleep would be nice."

"I'll call a driver to meet you in the porte-cochère. *Feliz Navidad*, Señorita de la Fuente."

"*Feliz Navidad*, Mr. Pendelfarr," she said. "And again . . . thank you."

Yehuda

Yehuda's car was zipping along the mountainous road toward Zermatt before sunrise. As he preferred, he drove in silence. Lona remained bound and sedated in the trunk, and Colette was still a bit too stunned to carry on a conversation after last night. It was better that he remain a mystery to her. He had no intention of telling her anything, but he allowed himself to think back, as he did practically every day, on where he had come from and what he had done. Remembering where he had been was what kept him going.

He had been born in the Aden Settlement of the Bombay Presidency to a family with three sisters. His mother and father operated a shelter for neglected and exploited children. They were atheists, but they named him after a Jewish child who had died of typhoid fever under their care.

The Uzans were hostile toward religion, believing that man's way of learning was through reason. At ten, Yehuda had grown curious about the meaning of his given name. His parents had told him of his namesake—a brave child whose life had been stolen from him—but not of his name's biblical origins.

He had followed a man wearing a *tallit gadol*, a prayer shawl, to a synagogue, and had begun asking the questions his parents would not or could not answer. The man brought him to his study and begun to speak of Jacob, third patriarch of the Hebrew people, and his fourth son, Judah, whose name was sometimes transliterated as "Yehuda."

The man, Yehuda discovered, was a prominent Yemenite rabbi and mystic, founder of a growing Jewish tribe in Aden, and an interpreter of the Zohar, the sacred text of the Kabbalah. Enthralled by the rabbi's stories, Yehuda returned for more lessons and kept his visits secret. His parents, sure to disapprove, were not to learn of his budding interest. He had lied to the rabbi, telling the man that his parents didn't care about him, even that they beat him. He had discovered that this earned him sympathy, as his namesake's wounds had done. The excuse to stay close had proved effective, as the rabbi had taken him under his wing, teaching him to speak Hebrew, read the Torah, and understand the Jewish principles of faith.

In his early teens, Yehuda was welcomed into the tribe and considered an important member. In his mind, his new friends had replaced his blood relatives; he felt too intellectually independent to bond with them. He had chosen the path of the rabbi's teachings and knew his family would look down on his faith if he spoke of it at home.

A physically frail child, he'd been bullied often, but he was never a coward. At one point, one of his fellow students, an Arab, had learned of his trips to the synagogue and threatened to tell the Uzans unless he swallowed a live baby cobra whole. Without hesitation, he had reached into the sack, pinched the snake's fangs shut, and swallowed it tail first. The respect he earned that day put an end to the bullying.

At the time, there were around 55,000 Jews living in Yemen, and several thousand more in the British Colony of Aden. After the 1947 vote by the United Nations on the partition plan for Palestine, Muslim rioters—assisted by the local police—had initiated violence against the Jews in what was the 1947 Aden pogrom, triggered by false accusation against Jews for the murder of two Muslim girls. The pogrom devastated Jewish communities in Yemen and the Colony of Aden. At least eighty-two were murdered and seventy-six others wounded; over half of Jewish stores and businesses in Aden were robbed bare; four synagogues, including the rabbi's, were burned to the ground; and hundreds of Jewish homes, and even a girls' school, were destroyed and looted by the rioters. In response to the economic paralysis and increasing dangers brought on by the catastrophe, a majority of the Adeni and Yemenite Jews emigrated to Israel as part of Operation Magic Carpet.

As he grew older and began adhering more strictly to Jewish religious laws, Yehuda found the issue of concealing his faith increasingly problematic, particularly at mealtime, when his mother served her usual nonkosher dishes. His parents had begun to worry about his new habits, and finally, when he was twenty, they learned the truth. His father followed him to the synagogue one day and confronted the rabbi, discovering his son's second life, secret faith, and hurtful fabrications. His father had lashed out at them both, beating them, earning himself a two-month prison sentence; during that time, Yehuda did not visit once. When released, his father discovered that Yehuda had left home with the rabbi's family.

They all had been airlifted from Hashed Camp, an old British military post in the desert about a mile from the city of Sheikh Othman, but a midflight mechanical failure caused the plane to go down in the Red Sea a mile off the coast, near northwest Saudi Arabia. The rabbi and his kin did not survive. Yehuda did, but he was alone now; the family he'd left would no longer embrace him, and the family he'd chosen was gone.

Bruised, battered, his arm broken, Yehuda nonetheless had escaped the plane and swam to shore along with a few other survivors. A group of hostile, roving Muslims had discovered them to be Jews; he'd concealed himself under the waves while the others were slaughtered. Unable to swim far or well with a broken bone, he spent hours shivering in the surf until sunset, watching from the water as the killers built a bonfire on the beach. While they slept, he crept into their encampment and found a dagger. Despite his injury, he roused them and held the dagger to their leader's throat to demand food, water, and a camel.

God had not given him an easy pilgrimage to the Holy Land. Maybe, he'd thought, this was punishment for betraying his father. But he would not betray God, even if God had left him with nothing. He would continue his journey at whatever cost. After leaving the camp and heading north, he stripped his hostage naked, donned his thobe, and slit the man's throat. He was so angry at what those men had done that he stabbed the naked corpse dozens of times with the dagger, leaving the body in the sand for the winds to bury.

He traveled between villages, stealing what supplies he needed, never sharing his real name. He knew theft was forbidden by God, but God would excuse him, for he was only trying to reach the Holy Land. For his sadism against the Muslim leader, he wondered if he could ever be forgiven. Perhaps God would think he had turned against the rabbi and his Jewish principles. To make things worse, he was forced to break other rules. When his camel finally collapsed from exhaustion, he'd killed the animal and cooked its meat, guiltily recalling Leviticus 11:4—*There are some that only chew the cud or only have a divided hoof, but you must not eat them. The camel, though it chews the cud, does not have a divided hoof; it is ceremonially unclean for you.* Continuing on foot, he came to accept that the tenets of faith were not always practical.

In time, his arm became more painful, and his skin blistered from the sun. The trip exhausted him. But after forty days, in late October of 1949, he reached Israel.

The experience helped him become even stronger physically. When members of the IDF learned that he had traveled over five hundred miles to come to Israel, he was vetted by and conscripted into the 7th Sa'ar Armored Brigade, which was formed during the 1948 Arab-Israeli War. His strategic talents were recognized, and soon he was reassigned to the "Central Institute for Coordination"—later called Mossad—becoming one of its first agents during its reorganization as part of the prime minister's office.

In 1953, though most Jews had evacuated Yemen and the Colony of Aden, more violence erupted. Yehuda was assigned to lead Operation Nest, a covert operation in the Colony designed to rescue the families of Jews who had not fled during Operation Magic Carpet. But the mission failed when a group of demonstrators discovered his fellow agents. Machine gun fire rattled against them in a town square, inspiring a wave of riots that killed hundreds of civilians in the crossfire. The incident proved catastrophic to his first family. Among the deaths were his mother and father, two of three sisters, and five children under his parents' care.

He returned to Israel depressed, realizing that his failure represented a second betrayal of his family. This time, he'd gotten them killed and robbed those children of a shelter, all because he rejected his mother and father's values in his youth. As a boy, he couldn't have known better. That's what he told himself. His mind had been vulnerable to all sorts of ideas. That faith had seduced him.

He came to reject the religion he had spent so many years studying and learned to loathe its practitioners—especially the rabbis and the academics. The thought of them, with their beards and curls and precious Torah, was enough to make his blood simmer. Their teachings had led to the destruction of his family. Only one thing could replace his beliefs, and that was hatred—of Judaism, Israel, and Jews, and of his own stupidity for having counted himself among them.

He kept his post at the agency, waiting for an opportunity to undermine Mossad and redeem himself. Two years ago, he'd been handed a way to do it.

Now he looked at Colette in the passenger seat, seeing a callow twenty-five-year-old in the midst of self-discovery. Perhaps she'd had her hardships, too, but not like his. She didn't have the experience to understand his motivations, and if she ever learned how he felt about the Jews, she'd group him with the people who killed her parents, and he would lose her help tracking Katharina.

The less she knew, the better. As long as she remained attracted to him, she would be putty in his hands. Her loyalties had been easy enough to manipulate.

"There it is," Colette said, breaking her silence. "The Monte Rosa."

They had reached Zermatt. Yehuda parked a block away and got out of the car.

"Wait here," he said. "Keep your head down."

He saw the receptionists were busy as he walked into the lobby, and instead approached the concierge desk.

The man asked, "Can I help you?"

"I'm with a car rental agency based in Täsch," Yehuda said. "Recently, we rented a car to customers named Kate Atwell and Moritz Dahl. The car is overdue by four days. They told our company they would be staying in this hotel. We have no other means of contacting them. If you wouldn't mind, I'd like to ask if those two are still checked in."

"It is our policy to keep guest information private."

"We intend to contact the police as long as you can verify the information we already have. We aren't asking for a room number. Just hoping we have the right hotel."

The concierge looked worried as he rubbed his mustache. "You said the names are Kate and Moritz?"

"Yes."

"A married couple? Honeymooners?"

So that had been their story.

"I think so," Yehuda said.

"Pretty, dark-haired lady and a tall, swarthy man?"

"That's who we're after."

"Bad news. They checked out two days ago."

"What do you remember about them?" Yehuda asked.

"The young lady was asking for directions to Yugoslavia."

"Which part?"

"She didn't say."

"You're sure? Nowhere specific?"

"She asked for the nearest border, and that would be Slovenia. I directed her to our shelf of maps."

"Where is that?"

"Down that hall, first room on the right. Those two really had me fooled! She seemed like a nice lady, and he a nice man. Would you like me to call the police for you?"

"I'll take care of it," Yehuda said, "but thank you."

He found a row of booklets in the lounge and read the titles. The collection spanned geographies from around the world. Half the volumes covered Asia and Africa. There were only two contenders for modern Europe.

He adjusted the window blinds to let more light into the lounge, illuminating the layer of dust—a fine, gray blanket of disuse—coating the empty space on the shelf. The dust was uniform, built up over a month or two, broken by a streak in front of a volume covering East-Central Europe.

Carefully, he took out the book that he assumed had been removed not long ago. He set it on a table, scanning the contents and identifying any maps that might have informed a route from Switzerland to Yugoslavia. He flipped to each of these pages, feeling for creases in the binding that might show where the book had been opened. It was too hard to tell, but he noticed something else: One of the maps was rutted. The borders of the countries were not only marked, but finely depressed. Someone had traced over them.

The map covered a region of Europe bounded by Geneva on the west and Sarajevo on the east.

He got a blank piece of paper from the reception desk, and asked the receptionist to sharpen a pencil for him. As sharp as she could make it. Then he came back to the lounge. Laying the blank sheet on top of the map, he placed the flat edge of the graphite on his paper and began shading lightly. Intelligible markings started to appear, bit by bit, until he could see everything that had been traced over the map.

A route had been drawn from Zermatt. The final destination had been circled.

Dubrovnik.

The motorways had even been listed, step by step.

He felt a lurch of excitement. All this from a swath of missing dust and some scratches in a book. Still, taking a trip to Dubrovnik without knowing it was Kate who had written in the map book seemed extreme. He needed to test his theory.

He put the book away and brought his decryption of the markings to the concierge.

"When guests check in at this hotel, do they fill out a form?" Yehuda asked him.

"Yes."

"Would you show me the one for those two honeymooners?"

"As I said, we do not reveal private information, sir."

"It's not the information I need. Just a handwriting sample."

"For what purpose?"

"To help me track the stolen car."

"I'd still be uncomfortable."

Yehuda heard the hesitation of a man who respected the policy of his hotel but was nonetheless eager to help catch delinquents.

"That's understandable," Yehuda said. "But if you show me a few words on the form and hide the rest, you won't be breaking your rules."

"That's never been done."

"You have the chance to save my company the time and trouble of involving the police. If you help us act now, we can still catch the runaways."

The man sighed, thinking it over.

"Okay," he said. "If it'll help you get your car back, I'll show you a sample."

The concierge searched through a folder in his cabinet and pulled out a document. He let Yehuda see some of the words on Kate and Moritz's check-in paper.

"You're sure this is the right form?" Yehuda said. "Belonging to the brunette traveling with a swarthy man, both in their mid-to-late twenties?"

"Yes, absolutely."

They had used false names, and as he compared the penmanship on the form with the letters traced over the map, he decided that they did not match. The letters on the map swirled and flourished, written by someone with an artistic flair. The letters on the check-in document were boxy and plain. This was not enough to disprove his theory, however. It was possible that one of them filled out the form and the other wrote over the map.

"Thank you," he said to the concierge with deepening frustration.

"Good day. Hope you get it back."

As he went back to the car, he had another idea, one that should have come to him earlier:

"Colette," he said, "have you ever seen Kate's handwriting?"

"I'd say so. We've known each other ten years."

"Can you tell if she's written something?"

"Probably."

"How about this?"

He showed her the page of tracings. She took a quick glance and handed it back to him.

"Yep," she said. "Very Kate."

"Okay," he said. "Buckle in tight."

Within two hours, they were rounding the curves of the Simplon Pass.

Katharina

Kate's eyelids felt heavy. She hadn't slept much; they had arrived and rented an apartment only six hours ago, but she was anxious to see the sunrise. The tiled roofs of Dubrovnik were turning their brightest shades of orange as she watched from their balcony in Old Town.

"Have some breakfast," Moritz said, tossing her a peach as he joined her outside.

"Thanks."

"I went downstairs, asked about Geoffrey Barkas."

"What did you find out?"

"Some locals say they've seen an English filmmaker doing interviews at Bokar Tower along the western walls. He starts at about eight o'clock each morning."

"Let's get moving."

She got dressed and followed him down an alley of stairs full of ivy and bromeliads. The alley fed into the limestone-paved Placa, the city's main street, from which they had a good view of the circular Minčeta Tower in the northwest—the highest point in Dubrovnik's stone defenses. Moated and armed with cannon, the city's walls had been built and strengthened over centuries and remained unbreached all through the Middle Ages. There were three main fortresses aside from Minčeta: a detached Revelin Fortress to the east, Saint John Fortress to the southeast, and Fort Bokar to the west. Also defending the city's western gates was the freestanding Lovrijenac across a small inlet. Old Harbor sat beyond the walls on the east side.

Kate and Moritz followed the Placa through a fruit and vegetable market, passing many a church, monastery, and palace. The thousand-yard esplanade had a fountain and a bell tower on each end, and the street sparkled as if it had been rained on, with a waxlike finish so smooth that it could almost reflect a human face. On the west end, they reached a small iron gate to an enclosed stairway and climbed to Bokar Tower.

"Looks like Barkas's people beat us here," Moritz said.

The enclosure at the top was bustling with film crew moving boxes, cables, and dollies. At the edge of the wall, two makeup artists were powdering an actor's cheeks. Beside her, two sound technicians were busy attaching a microphone to a pole. One man stood at the center of the platform, directing his production assistants and occasionally peering through a camera mounted on a tripod.

Kate admired the composition of the scene. The walls cut down into the rocky bluffs at the edge of clear, aquamarine waters. The sea was so close she could smell the salt, and the green slopes of the nearby island of Lokrum were visible from certain angles.

Two production assistants spotted them standing there.

"Oi'm sahrry," said one. "With permission frarm city, we're filmin' a document'ry for t'next few hours. During that toime, the tower is aff limits to public."

"We'll be finished working within a few hours," said the other. His Norfolk dialect was more subtle, one Kate guessed had been polished away by years spent elsewhere—but there was no mistaking the way "few" had become "foo," and "working" had become "wurreken."

She was about to speak when the director at the camera trotted over—a man of sixty-five or so, his hair combed in a part over a kind, inquisitive face.

"There's no need to send anyone away," he said, extending a hand to Kate and then to Moritz.

"We don't mean to interrupt," Moritz said. "We're looking for a man named Geoffrey Barkas."

"You're looking at him," said the man. "And you are?"

They introduced themselves. He told them they were wrapping up a few scenes, and asked that they wait until noon so he could finish, which they did. At twelve, the crew began packing supplies, and the three of them took a seat at the wall.

"Thanks for making time for us," Moritz said. "You must be very busy with this film going on. It sounds interesting."

"Tell that to my crew," Barkas said. "They leave for the beaches earlier and earlier each day."

"Hard to begrudge them in a place like this."

"I wouldn't mind if we didn't have so much work left. We're still collecting interviews of people who lived through the Italian and German occupations. But you didn't come to hear about my film. Please, tell me what I can do for you."

"It's an unusual story."

"I've made a living of unusual stories."

"This one starts after the capture of Adolf Eichmann in Argentina," Moritz explained. "I helped track him down in the Israeli Defense Forces. When I got home, I learned my mother had passed away. She'd left me a letter with instructions to find a bank vault and bequeath what was inside to Kate here. Strange thing was, I'd never met Kate before. Had no idea who she was."

"Did your mother leave an explanation?"

"Not much. Something about appreciating Kate's family legacy."

"Ironically, not something I'm particularly proud of," Kate said. "So that's still a mystery to us."

"What was in the vault?" Barkas asked.

"A copy of a painting, *The Little Marauder* by William-Adolphe Bouguereau. My mother also left me a notebook detailing her travels to find Kate and my father, a Danish sailor who never came back to her after the war. I was able to get in touch with Kate on my own. We went to the home of Werner Kunze together. His address was in the notebook. He was too sick to give us anything, but he did say your name. His granddaughter, Petra, told us he's a friend of yours."

"A good friend, poor chap," Barkas said. "In fact, the woman who introduced us sounds very much like the one you describe. Your mother, searching for her Danish lover . . . was she by chance Iris Taha, the milliner of Cairo?"

"Yes!" Moritz said. "Did you know her?"

"She was also a dear friend. A vivacious spirit. I'm sorry to hear she's passed."

"Thank you," Moritz said.

"It's no coincidence we were friends," Barkas said. "Still, it's quite remarkable to be approached by her son so many years after I last saw her. Tell me, when Werner mentioned my name, what exactly did he say?"

"There were some strange phrases. Things like: 'Speckles on the pear—the pear that saved an army.' Then, as if in reference to the painting, he said, 'I gave it to Horace. Horace had to run to the gray pillars. Just ask Geoffrey Barkas!' We aren't sure if that means anything, or if it's as random to you as it is to us. We hoped maybe you could tell us what you do know."

"Werner, poor chap. He's lost a lot with age, but he hasn't gone completely mad."

"You mean there's some sense to those words?" Kate said, encouraged that nothing Moritz had said seemed to surprise Barkas.

"As for the 'pear' and its 'speckles,' I couldn't say," he told her. "As for the rest, I have some ideas. Like yours, it's an unusual story."

Kate waited impatiently as Barkas looked out over the sea. The waters below had frothed as small waves rolled up to the bluffs.

"During the war," he said, "camouflage played an important role in our victory in the desert. Many deceptions were used, ranging in scale. In a scheme called 'Shadow Houses,' entire airfields were disguised by giant murals painted on the roofs of hangars, fields, and runways. Local women and children were recruited to make dummy airfields, complete with antiaircraft defenses and realistic equipment, to divert attention from the real ones. During the Siege of Tobruk, camoufleurs led by my good mates set up a giant Hessian screen that would draw over two thousand German shells. For the Royal Navy in Tobruk Harbor, the same team hid naval landing craft and stores ships under false dummy jetties and sunken barges. Fortress Tobruk's only three Hawker Hurricanes were also concealed in hangars dug into a *wadi* and covered with netting, while a dummy airfield complete with false 'ack-ack guns'—manned by strawmen using dummy rangefinders—had drawn actual fire from German fighter aircraft. I could go on, citing the victories of camouflage. During my time, perhaps the grandest success was Operation Bertram."

He paused to organize his thoughts. Kate could hardly wait for him to continue.

"My job in the desert was to lead the Middle East Command Camouflage Directorate," he said. "On the sixteenth of September of 'forty-two, my deputy and I were called into a meeting with a man who worked for Dudley Clarke, the famous architect of military deception. We were briefed on a large-scale ruse devised by Clarke to fool Rommel about the time and location of an upcoming attack by our Eighth Army.

"The trick was to be composed of a real attack in the north of the Alamein line, with a feint twenty miles to the south. We were asked to hide hundreds of tanks and field guns, and thousands of tons of other material, all to be used in what would be one of the largest desert battles of the North African campaign." He chuckled. "I'd been hoping this kind of opportunity would present itself. Being there with Clarke's man, and then sitting out on the dunes to mull it over, I was terrified as we considered the plan. But there was a lot of sense in it. We already had proven tools at our disposal. A stage magician had developed 'Sunshields' to disguise tanks as lorries, and vice versa. We thought of creating a dummy water pipeline, inspired by a dummy railhead with proven results at Misheifa, which could help our efforts.

"The plan went forward. Entire armored brigades, complete with soldiers, were conjured from calico and palm-frond hurdles. The phantom army was realistic enough that German recce planes would fly back to their bases and report that an attack was looming to the south. Meanwhile, elaborate devices were used to hide the transport of the real army materials to the north."

"How do 'Horace' and the 'gray pillars' enter the picture?" Kate asked.

"I'm leading to that," Barkas said. "As you can imagine, absolute secrecy was crucial to Bertram's success, even at GHQ Cairo. With so many delicate processes in the mix, including false radio traffic intended to support the operation, indiscretion could ruin everything. As it turned out, one of the biggest threats to Bertram was working close to me. An Irishman named Damien Bray had been sent over from the camoufleurs' training center in Britain. Little did we know, he'd gone mental after his wife had been wounded terribly in the Coventry bombings. Serving as a fighter pilot, he crashed his plane near Malta, where, believing England had betrayed him, he handed himself over to the Germans. They put him through Abwehr spy school and later planted him near Farnham Castle back in England. He wheedled his way into camouflage as a mole."

"How did he manage that?"

"He was an experienced Saharan archaeologist and stained-glass artist before the war."

"So he had the right skills," Moritz said.

"And no shortage of funds. As was later discovered, he murdered a businessman aboard his ship to Egypt. Stole the man's money. Bray also made a convincing camoufleur. I remember his arrival at Eighth Army headquarters near Borg-el-Arab. He came into my hut. I briefed him personally. He sounded enthusiastic. I had no idea I'd handed over our plan to beat Rommel, wrapped in a bow."

"What happened to Damien Bray?" Kate asked.

"He stayed with the Eighth Army a few weeks. It was only just before the culmination of the plan at El Alamein that he tried to leave headquarters on a BSA bike and inform the *Panzerarmee*."

"How did you stop him?"

"With the help of a mysterious spy living in Cairo," Barkas said, placing a hand on Moritz's shoulder as if to brace him. "On the outside, an ordinary business owner selling hats to the Egyptian elite. In reality, she was an agent of the Allies—a smart, relentless woman operating under the name 'Horace.'"

Moritz paled. "You can't be serious!"

"I am," Barkas said.

"My mother was a spy?"

"Iris Taha was intercepting and relaying messages from a secret room in her hat shop."

"That's impossible. There were no secret rooms."

"Not even behind the carpet hanging on the second floor?"

Moritz paused, then said, "She would have told me."

"She would have told a child, during the war, that she was a deep cover agent?"

"What about after?"

"She chose not to revisit that part of her life," Barkas said. "Not with anyone."

"I can't believe it. That's . . . madness!"

"Then why did she move from Alexandria, where she had a thriving millinery studio, to Cairo?"

"I don't know," Moritz said. "I was five."

"And incidentally, wasn't that the same year you met your father, Rasmus Dahl, for the first and last time?"

"How do you know these things about my family?"

"As I told you, Iris was a dear friend. She saved the operation I was leading."

"What does her move have to do with my father?" Moritz said.

"He was part of an Allied information network, a top-secret organization with agents throughout Europe. He brought her in. She started her espionage work soon after he visited in 1940. That was the purpose of his visit: to recruit her in the hope that it would bring them closer together. She had a well-developed cover as a milliner for the Egyptian elite and technical experience with radio technology. She agreed to the work not only because she supported the Allies, but because she hoped she could marry Rasmus when the war ended. So you'd have a father."

"Again, impossible. Rasmus served in the Danish navy."

"That's not all he did," Barkas said. "I confess, I don't know much about the network itself—only that an encrypted message of vital consequence was channeled through your mother on 21 October 1942, days before the battle. As soon as she learned that an Irish spy named Damien Bray had infiltrated our ranks, she delivered a message to GHQ Cairo—which, incidentally, we all called 'Grey Pillars.' The report made its way to us, and we detained Bray before he could contact Rommel."

"Hence, Kunze's words," Kate inferred. "*Horace had to run to the gray pillars*."

"Right. Now, none of us were silly enough to think the Desert War had been won by conjuring tricks alone. But we couldn't have been more delighted when Churchill himself acknowledged the deception in a victory speech to the House of Commons. 'By a marvelous system of camouflage,' he said, 'complete tactical surprise was achieved in the desert.' It saddened me that Churchill never learned how Iris had saved the operation. After the war, I met her for the first time. She was trying to identify other individuals in the information network, hoping to locate Rasmus. She introduced me to Werner Kunze, who she discovered had also played a role in saving Bertram."

"What did Werner do?" Kate said.

"He was never willing to tell me. All I know is, he was part of the network."

Kate wondered: If Werner had been on a train leaving Berlin not two weeks before Bray was foiled, what had transpired in that time?

The conversation was interrupted when one of Barkas's production assistants appeared on the tower platform and called out to him, "Geoffrey?"

"Excuse me," Barkas said to Kate and Moritz, and then to his crew member: "Yes, Rossa?"

"We've found another potential interviewee for tomorrow. She'd like to speak with you."

"I'll be down in a moment," Barkas said. He turned to Kate and Moritz. "My film duties beckon. That's about all I have for you, anyway."

"You've been a tremendous help," Moritz said.

"It's a lot to take in," Barkas said with another clap on his shoulder. "I wish I could stay longer." As he shook their hands, he had an idea. "There's someone I know who may be able to assist you. She's a private person, a bit of a recluse. But I'll contact her on your behalf. If she's interested in talking, she'll need a way to find you."

"I live in Paris," Kate said. She jotted down her address. "We'll take all the help we can get. Thank you for trying."

"Very good," he said.

He left them and waved goodbye from the bottom of Bokar Tower.

Sitting on the wall, Moritz found a pebble and flung it toward the ocean, watching it skip. Kate saw disbelief and something like exhilaration on his face.

"It's too shocking," he said. "I thought my mother made hats."

"She did," Kate said. "She also happened to be a spy, and a bloody good one. I worry, though. Barkas was our final lead. We still don't know a thing about whoever wants us dead."

"Or what Werner meant by the damned *speckles on the pear*. That phrase has been a thorn in the flesh."

She thought for a moment, squinting. "Unless, wait a minute," she said.

"What?"

The corners of her mouth quirked up. "Speckles on the pear . . . speckles on the *pear* . . . oh, my God."

"What is it?"

"We've been bloody idiots," she said, running down the steps of the tower.

Yehuda

"We'll park here and bus to town," Yehuda told Colette. "Moritz may recognize my car."

He switched off the ignition near a patch of forest in the Lapad peninsula. They had broken up the long drive from the Simplon Pass with only a few stops and were now minutes from Dubrovnik. Kate and Moritz would soon be within reach, unless they'd left town, in which case Yehuda knew there was a chance the trail had gone cold.

"Let's go," he said. "Quickly."

"Where to?"

"The marina. Be quiet and follow. Keep a low profile."

Colette wrapped her head in a scarf from her suitcase. "What about the baroness?"

"We'll come for her later. After her last sedation, she won't be waking any time soon."

Yehuda watched Colette closely. The first few days, she clearly had felt guilty and nervous about sedating the older woman, but now she walked away from the car without looking back. A bus arrived and took them to the Buža Gate, on the north side of the walls. Yehuda kept to the sides of the street as they walked through the city, scanning the crowd for either target. He knew Kate by her size and shape, but not well by her face. He could more easily recognize Moritz.

He led Colette out a gate on the eastern side of town, crossing a stone path between two fortresses—from Revelin down to St. John's, whose ramparts jutted out over the water and marked the boundary of the marina. A breakwater jetty protected the open mouth of the Old Harbor from southeasterly waves. Yehuda looked out over the several dozen yachts and pleasure boats moored in the harbor, weighing his options. He spotted one with the characteristics he needed. It was close to dock, with a sizeable cabin: a masthead-rigged sloop, twenty-eight feet in length, with an eight-foot beam. The swirly letters on the hull read *Lady Louise*.

It would do.

"What are we doing here?" Colette said.

"Finding a place to stay."

"There are apartments within the walls."

The girl was becoming a pain, but he would put her to use soon.

"We'd be seen inside the walls, and on a boat, we can escape town quickly. Now take my hand and smile like we're in love."

He wrapped his fingers around hers, feeling little reluctance on her part. As they approached the yacht, he could hear the squeaks of a rag rubbing its guardrails. The owner stood by the pulpit, a can of polish in hand. The man was broad and muscled, sporting a jungle of a beard down to his chest. He was well into his sixties, Yehuda figured, but fit enough to tussle with any man a third his age. His ship gleamed, its pearly white hull an object of pride.

"Come for a stroll by the marina?" said the man, noticing Yehuda's interest. "Good day for it."

Yehuda sensed a gentle soul—an enjoyment of people, a friendliness toward strangers—but the yacht owner would be protective of his property. By the looks of it, he cared more about the appearance of the *Lady Louise* than he did his own. The bottom of his left earlobe had been sliced off, perhaps in a fight or a boating accident. His shirt was ripped in three places, his dungarees smeared with grease stains. A life under the sun had given him leathery skin.

"Beautiful boat," Yehuda said.

The man beamed, dropping his rag. "She's not your bog-standard sloop, that's for sure. Come take a *shufti* round the cabin."

The owner took Colette's hand and helped her board.

"Thank you," she said.

"You two come in for Chrissy?"

"That, and we're on honeymoon," Yehuda said, recalling how well Kate and Moritz's story had worked for them at the Monte Rosa.

"Good on ya both! Cigarette?"

He held out a box.

"Please," Colette said.

"I'm knackered. Time for a smoke." He lit up with her and took a drag. "Name's Oliver Gibney," he said. "Friends call me Ollie."

"I'm Christopher," said Yehuda, shaking his hand. "This is my wife, Agnes."

"Pleasure."

"You're not from around here."

"Nooo," he said, inflecting an invisible *R*.

"Australian?"

"Kiwi, mate."

"What brings you to Dubrovnik?"

"My wife and I'd always talked of sailin' the Mediterranean together. But we never did, and then she got sick. When she went to heaven, I said to myself, we ain't waitin' no longer. So I painted on *Lady Louise* and took her in spirit. This nice spot here in the Adriatic suits me fine."

Ollie showed them down a narrow set of stairs. The cabin had an interior of varnished mahogany and crimson upholstery. There was also a small kitchen down there. The room was immaculate, and perfect for their needs.

"You know," Yehuda said, "Agnes and I were hoping to find a yacht to sleep in. It's more romantic than a hotel. Would you consider renting her out a few nights? We'd take care of her."

Ollie pursed his lips. "You have to understand, this boat's my last love in the world."

"Agnes is mine. I'm willing to pay a premium. Five thousand dinara a night."

"Ain't got no anklebiters with ya, eh?"

"No children, if that's what you mean."

Ollie thought it over.

"Six thousand and we're good as gold, mate."

"All right. Six."

"I'll stay with a friend in town in the meantime. Long as you don't mind if I come by during the day to tend to a few things."

He did mind, but he'd deal with one problem at a time. "Of course not," Yehuda said.

Ollie tossed him a key to the cabin.

"My sloop is your sloop."

Katharina

Kate's idea had become a full-fledged theory. Anxious to test it, she took Moritz's hand, trying not to lose him as they negotiated the Placa's crowded marketplace.

"What's gotten into you, Kate?" he asked, muttering soft apologies to the people they jostled.

"Keep moving!"

They passed an antique store, where Kate spotted a magnifying glass in the window; she bought it before continuing east through town and turning south on a crooked street lined with steep steps.

Plants and greenery climbed up the slope, some dangling from hooks, some growing from pots. Stray cats slinked around the restaurants and cafés, drawn to the smells of fish and grilled squid. Echoes of church bells could be heard over the gurgling of fountains. Kate tuned it all out. She hardly registered the faces around her, heard the musicians, or noticed the street performers.

She turned left and passed under a stone tunnel feeding into their residential street, Zvijezdićeva. More steps. Their apartment was located on an incline in the south part of Dubrovnik's Old Town, in an alley of zigzagging clotheslines and cascading bougainvillea.

Inside, Kate unfurled the forgery of Bouguereau's *The Little Marauder* and set the painting in the sunlight. She stared at the painting, looking deep into the brown eyes of the little girl and following the sweep of her dark hair and the contour of her white dress.

"I can't believe I didn't think of this earlier," she said. "In the little marauder's right hand, she's holding a pear."

"Why don't you tell me what's going on in that loony head of yours?"

Kate hunched over the canvas and held the magnifying glass over the fruit clutched in the girl's fingers. "Yes, yes, *yes!*" she said. "Lean in. See for yourself."

He took the magnifying glass by the handle and peered through it. "What am I looking for?"

"Speckles on the pear," she said.

"Seriously, though."

"I'm not kidding. Teeny tiny dots."

He looked harder. "My God, you're right. I see them on the skin of the pear! A series of them . . ."

"They're incredibly small," she said. "Little microdots. If you look closely enough, they seem to be arranged in a pattern."

"I see! They're not all dots. Some of them are . . . lines. Short lines, all spanning the same interval."

"Yes, dashes. It's Morse code!" Kate said with delight.

He got a pen and paper. "Read off the characters while I transcribe."

Kate examined the pear with her naked eyes again. It was remarkable: The microdots were almost imperceptible without magnification, blending with the spotted texture of the fruit.

"Okay, ready?"

"Go ahead."

"Dot dot, dot dash dot, dot dot, three dots, four dots, slash . . ."

She continued reading until he had copied all eleven words:

·· ·–· ·· ··· ···· / ·– –··· ·–– · ···· ·–· / ––– ·––· · ·–· ·– – ·· ···– · /
·– – / · ·· ––· ···· – ···· / ·– ·–· –– –·–– / ···· ––·– /
–· ·– –– · / –·· ·– –– ·· · –· / –··· ·–· ·– –·–– / ··– ·–· ––· · –· –

"That's it?" he said.

"That's it. What does it read?"

He wrote a letter above each Morse character:

IRISH / ABWEHR / OPERATIVE /
AT / EIGHTH / ARMY / HQ /
NAME / DAMIEN / BRAY / URGENT

"Damien Bray—that's the name Geoffrey Barkas told us!" she exclaimed. "He was the spy who nearly exposed Operation Bertram, whom your mother stopped after intercepting a message in Cairo. Does this look like . . ."

"Like it could be that message?"

"That's what I was thinking. This is unbelievable!"

"It's perfectly believable," Moritz said. "Barkas said Werner was part of the same information network as Iris. You said Karl Decker, the artist who drove you to Wangerland after your father's home was raided, first stopped at a Berlin train station to deliver this painting to Werner. You said you could never figure out why it was so important the painting be delivered. Decker put you both in danger by making the delivery. Now we know why."

"Decker must have been part of the network, too, working to undermine the Nazis!"

"Delivering this forgery was his last effort to convey information on the Desert War. After getting his hands on the painting, Werner made sure the information got to Horace—my mother—before Bray could give the Bertram plan to Rommel."

A prickly heat flushed through Kate's cheeks, ears, and nose. She turned the color of a warning beacon.

"So, all along, Karl Decker was working against my father," she said.

"No, Kate. It's grander than that."

"How do you mean?"

"Decker had to have been working *with* your father. I'll bet Ralf Speer was the ringmaster in this intelligence circle."

"That's not possible. He was Vice Minister of—"

"Propaganda, I know. That's how he learned Hitler's secrets, including the one about this Irish operative. The forgeries weren't for profit. They were a way to move information through Germany without risking radio interception. I think your dad organized a workshop of artists and used paintings as a medium to send coded messages. He may have worked closely with Goebbels and other high-ranking Nazis, but I'll bet he hated those men with every fiber of his soul."

"I guess it's plausible, but—"

She stopped; it was also insanity.

"It's more than plausible," he said. "It's the only story that makes sense. If your dad truly had been a Nazi loyalist, let alone in his position of proliferating propaganda, why would he have gone against the very tenets of Nazi 'enlightenment' by organizing painters to distribute more 'degenerate' art? Those artists must have been working for your father to hide messages for the Allies. And then, someone turned them in. Like Werner said, there was a man who wanted out. Maybe it was Heinrich Jecklyn, the artist you think got away."

Maybe he was right, and her original theory had only scratched the surface.

"That would explain the Nazi raid on our home," she said.

"It would also explain my mother's appreciation of your family legacy. Though they probably never met, your father and my mother would have been distant partners. Ralf encoded and disseminated secrets he learned at his ministry—presumably across Europe and the Western Desert—using art forgeries. My mother's information came from this *Little Marauder* painting. She brought the warning to Grey Pillars in Cairo."

"So, this little dark-eyed girl saved Operation Bertram, thanks to my father and your mother, and Rasmus and Karl, and all the artists, and everyone else involved in their spy ring."

"And Werner Kunze, whose words make sense now. 'Speckles on the pear' are indeed the Morse code microdots. The 'pear that saved an army' refers to the British Eighth Army in the Second Battle of El Alamein, where the phantom brigades of Operation Bertram were created."

Kate's eyes began to well up. There was no denying Moritz's logic, or the appeal of his story. The pieces of the puzzle did fit best with her father as orchestrator of the spy ring. *The Little Marauder* had almost certainly been used to warn the Eighth Army of an infiltrator.

All at once, the hatred she had felt for Ralf Speer was replaced by an emotion more powerful than anything she'd known. She let a moment pass, trying to identify the feeling. She realized it was the most acute form of guilt she had experienced: guilt that was the sum of twenty years spent renouncing a good man, and treating his choices as if they had been her own.

They were choices she had not even understood.

She'd loved her father once, as a child. Then she'd grown up and seen him as a monster and learned to fear the blood in her veins. He had lived on as her darkest secret.

It seemed she had been wrong about him.

His voice returned in her head, comforting her for the first time in two decades. She could hear him whisper in her ear: *Are you happy, my good little marauder?*

The voice was gentle.

I'm so sorry for hating you, Papa, she thought. How could I have known you deserved my affection all along?

You have it now!

She brushed away the tears in her eyes.

Lona

The transition to consciousness was gradual. Lady Atwell cracked her eyelids open to darkness, unable to tell if she was still curled in a fetal position. The repeated sedations in a confined area had worn away the sense of effort it took to move her limbs. It was a feeling she had gotten used to these past few days: an awareness of thought before body.

A wave of fatigue washed over her. She resisted, willing the chemical out of her system, grasping at lucid thought, which had escaped her for . . . how long?

She couldn't say when the darkness had started, but there had been breaks now and then every few hours—days?—as she lay there, and slowly an awareness of the world, a bumping and rumbling world, would come back to her and last a while. She'd feel like she could think again, or almost think—and she'd wonder where she was—when suddenly the rumbling would stop and a sudden light would blind her. They gave her water and bits of bread and dragged her to the washroom, but then a human form would descend, administer more of whatever it was that made her sleep, and stuff her back in the trunk.

Yes, this had been happening for a while. There had been a pattern. A cycle between consciousness and sleep, and throughout she'd been conscious of this rumbling vibration beneath her that would shake her bones and then stop before she went under again.

Right, of course. Her memory was coming back. She was in a car, locked in a trunk. They were driving somewhere. She'd been tranquilized by one of her captors. Yehuda or Colette. Probably Yehuda.

She lay in the stillness. There was no rumbling now. The car must be parked, with her still in the trunk. Maybe she was about to get another dose. Her mind felt like an old tool. Thinking had already helped rehone the edge, and the more alert she became, the more disturbing it was to consider losing the edge again.

Her hips tingled. And her knees. She could feel them, too. The tingling felt unpleasant, then downright painful after a minute. She was glad for the pain. Better to feel something than nothing.

She realized she was indeed curled into a ball. She tried moving, scoping out the boundaries of the trunk. It was cramped. Just a few inches in any direction.

Her mental haze was clearing. She was able to multiply numbers in her head. Two times three was six. Three times four was twelve. Four times five was twenty. If there was ever a doubt, that was her test.

Enough arithmetic. She needed answers.

Is Kate all right?

Where is she?

Where am I?

Lona kicked the inside of the trunk, heard a thump. She did it again, and again. Loud thumps, possibly audible from outside the car if they were parked in public. Could someone hear her? She kept at it, aware of the risk, knowing she might only earn herself a higher dose of the drug if Yehuda heard her.

"Hello?" she rasped. "Can someone hear me?"

She cleared her throat and tried again.

"Hello! Is there someone out there? Help! I'm trapped in here!"

She kicked and kicked and kicked. Risk be damned.

"Somebody! Bloody hell! I'm trapped in here!"

When her foot began aching, she banged with a fist.

Minutes passed like hours. What sounded to her like thunderclaps, she realized, might have been the gentlest of thuds heard from outside. She continued to scream, kick, pound, feel for any release mechanisms, and *wonder*: What did he want with Kate?

I'll stop the bastard, she thought. Kick his testicles when he opens the trunk.

The pain in her joints was terrible, but she did her best to ignore it as she maneuvered herself parallel with the long axis of the car. She put her feet by the lid, ready to spring at her captor when the trunk opened. She waited in this uncomfortable position, minute after minute, knowing it could be hours before Yehuda returned.

She would be ready for him.

An hour passed.

Voices. A click of the latch.

Light flooded the trunk as the lid opened. She shot her legs out, thrusting in what seemed to her a powerful kick to her captor's groin. Neither the attack nor the surprise seemed to have any effect on Yehuda, who grabbed her feet, held them down against the rear of the car, and slammed the lid on her exposed shins with enough force to subdue her. God, did that hurt. This was the second time he'd almost broken a bone of hers.

She wailed, but he opened the trunk lid again and lifted her out of the car. She should have expected her plan to fail. What chance did an arthritic, tranquilized woman of seventy have?

"Do it again," she said, spitting on him. "Shatter my shins. I'm not going to help you."

He didn't say anything. Colette was with him. She closed the trunk, then helped Yehuda carry Lona by one of her arms.

"You deceitful whore," Lona hissed at her. "After all Kate's been to you. What do you think he's going to do when he's finished with you? Give you a pretty wave goodbye?"

Colette leaned in and whispered in her ear, "Kate's not who you think she is. She's been lying to you her whole life. I'm going to help this man uncover that lie."

"He's going to bury you, you stupid tart, after he's rogered you silly." Colette was leering at her. "Is that what you want?"

"Enough talking," Yehuda said, readying a rag of chloroform.

"Don't you dare!" Lona said. She squirmed, trying to free herself.

"Stop moving."

He steadied Lona's head and forced her to breathe a few whiffs—enough to make her woozy, but not to put her under. Lona tried not to inhale. Don't let it near you, she thought. His grip was too strong, and eventually she had to give in. She could feel her thoughts going blunt as the chemical took over. Fight it, she said to herself. Fight it, Lona, you fight it . . . think . . . what was that trick? Multiply two numbers. Pick two numbers . . .

She couldn't think of two numbers.

She stumbled forward, and they caught her.

Yehuda slipped the bottle of chloroform into his pocket.

"Walk," he said, putting Lona between himself and Colette. They wrapped their arms around her for support.

Lona tried to take in her surroundings. Where were they? It was getting dark, and the world was blurry again, like something seen through unfocused binoculars. The car was parked near a forested hill. She smelled salt in the air. To the southwest, she could see the ocean, beyond which the crown of the sun had sunk minutes ago.

They dragged her to a bus stop. A shuttle arrived. It dropped them off a couple miles down the road. From there, they helped her walk through a stone gate, to the other side of a wall. The sounds and shapes melded together as they entered a public place. Some kind of town. People ambled about the streets. She could see their fuzzy profiles.

I can shout out to them, she thought. Someone will help me.

"I've been kidnapped!" she tried to say.

Her words came out a slur.

She tried again, louder: "I've been *kidnapped!*"

Why did people keep drifting along? Why didn't they stop? Couldn't they understand her? What was this place?

She tried more simply: "Help! Help me!"

She was then vaguely aware that someone was stopping them on the street. Finally, a concerned citizen. She tried to look at the person. Her head felt too heavy to lift.

"Help," she croaked once more.

Yehuda and Colette started laughing. Why were they laughing?

He began to say something, and she only heard a clip of it: ". . . Bottle of chardonnay, after the champagne. She'll be fine."

"Don't . . . listen to them," Lona managed to say. "Kidnappers! Help!"

"Let's go to bed, Grandma," Colette said, patting her head.

They kept moving. This was hell. Could no one grasp her situation? Her captors must have been first-class performers.

The crowd thinned as they brought her southeast through the city. Which city was it? The stone path took them into a marina. They went to a dock with rows of yachts and little boats covered in fishing nets. She tossed a glance at the town behind them, seeing thick ramparts and towers. The stronghold looked familiar. She must have seen this place in pictures.

As they carried her along the dock, she spotted a boat on whose sails were emblazoned the words: *Non bene pro toto libertas venditur auro*. She was educated in Latin, but this was not the time to search her memory banks. It didn't matter, because just then two sailors passed them on the dock, and she heard one of them say "Dubrovnik."

She realized that's where she was, and connected the Latin phrase to its meaning—*Liberty is not well sold for all the gold*—which had been the motto of the Republic of Ragusa.

Hence the city walls, the forts . . .

Yes, they had taken her to Dubrovnik. But, why?

"Here," Yehuda said, pointing to a yacht moored to the dock. The swirly writing on the side indicated her name—the *Lady Louise*. "Climb aboard."

Were they going to sail somewhere?

The trek from the car had taken a few minutes, and she could tell by the sharpening of the pain in her shins that the sedative was wearing off again. She tried not to let it show. If only she could find her voice.

She didn't like the idea of boarding the yacht. An idea came to her. He needed his live bait, a hostage to draw Kate in. If she jumped into the water, he would be forced to rescue her. She would kick and scream, and the noise would attract help.

There was no time to think it over. She threw herself over the edge of the dock, landing belly-first and kicking up a shaft of water that splattered the yacht's hull. What first seemed like a hand yanking her down, she realized, was the drag of her soaked clothes. Fully submerged, she lost her sense of up and down. The plan felt foolish in retrospect. She thrashed about the marina, blowing out a small stream of bubbles, and came to the surface, wondering why this was so difficult. She had been a good swimmer once. Now she could hardly tread water, and she hadn't expected the pain that her flutter-kick would cause her hips and knees.

"Help!" she gurgled.

The water in her throat stifled any attempt to cry out. She swallowed a mouthful as she struggled to stay afloat. The water tasted disgusting—sandy, full of engine oil and flakes of weeds and barnacles.

"Some . . . body . . ."

The pain in her shins got worse as she kicked the water like a blender. It was as if the edge of the trunk lid kept slamming down on them. She knew she couldn't keep it up, but how would she stay at the surface? She was too lean to float. And her clothing gave her too much drag. She slipped her shoes off and tried to wriggle out of her sweater by sliding it over her head. Her elbows got caught, and she panicked, sinking again . . .

An arm clamped around her waist, hoisted her from the water, and set her on the dock. She collapsed on her elbows, spewing water and spittle on the planks.

"Don't be stupid, old trout," Yehuda said to her, helping pull her sweater off.

Reining in a bout of coughs, she glanced around the marina, hoping her plan had worked, that someone had heard her tumble and her splash. No one came. Yehuda put a gag over her mouth and carried her into the sloop's cabin, where he tied her arms behind her back and her feet to the legs of a chair. He closed the door.

Damn, damn, damn, she thought.

She sat still, making no attempt to undo her binds as she recovered. She would muster energy for that later. Instead, bringing her pulse from a gallop to a trot, she took in her surroundings. The crimson upholstery made for an attractive interior. A bronze mackerel hung on the door, strewn with medallions belonging to the yacht's owner, presumably from fishing competitions. There was a small window next to it with a view to the deck. The bedside table had a collection of items, including a mariner's compass, a spyglass, and a tackle box.

She slumped in the chair. Why had he taken her here? Where did he plan to sail?

What did he want with her daughter?

Another hour passed, and night fell, leaving her shivering in her wet clothes. In spite of herself, she began to wonder if Kate had kept secrets from her. What could she have been hiding? Life had been quiet all these years, without surprises. Then, suddenly, a strange telegram had arrived. This man had come knocking at their door and murdered her husband and majordomo. Colette had been complicit. Surely it wasn't Kate's fault, but Kate had to know something. What had her daughter been keeping to herself?

Lona knew she had a good relationship with her daughter. She understood her daughter better than George ever had; she was more perceptive than he had ever been. He'd never comprehended the extent of Kate's sense of isolation growing up, and he'd never bothered to try to get to the heart of whatever she'd been grappling with as a teenager. "Ordinary youthful angst," he'd called it, as if all young people were cut from the same mold.

Still, Kate had always felt closer to him. There were things she would whisper to George, but not Lona; funny glances she would toss in his direction, but not hers; late-night talks she'd have in his library, and never in Lona's bedroom. This had started only a few years after Kate had learned to speak English. At twelve, she had asked George questions about getting boys to notice her, flirting, carrying herself like a lady—and even about the red stains in her underwear, which was a conversation meant for mothers. Of course, there were things Kate would ask Lona, too—about history, about art, about her past, her interests—but these were never the questions she'd hoped to answer as a mum. Looking back, she wondered if she had somehow missed something, if Kate's questions about art and art history had been about more than just the subjects themselves.

Lona had always been glad for the closeness between George and Kate, but it was hard not to envy it. She was, after all, the parent who had so dearly wanted to adopt when she and George couldn't have their own child. Once or twice, she had sneaked down from her bedroom to listen in on their conversations. She only ever heard them talk about frivolous things. Their giggles, which usually carried into the wee morning hours, had always made her smile and yearn for what she was missing.

Maybe she was too heavy a person herself. George always had been lighter in spirit. His favorite book was *The Hound of the Baskervilles*, for God's sake. Or maybe Kate had felt a greater need for a father. She didn't know.

But whatever secret her daughter might have harbored, and however lethal it might be, Lona would have to learn the truth. Could it have to do with Colette's strange comment, that Kate wasn't who Lona thought she was? Odd as it sounded, Yehuda seemed to have convinced Colette it was true.

Lona's attention turned to a shuffling sound outside the companionway. Yehuda had risen. He was moving, quickly. She heard the shout of a friendly voice she didn't recognize:

"Agnes, Christopher! Ow ya goin', mates?"

She wondered who it was and heard Yehuda answer, "Evening, Ollie."

"Takin' precious care of m' sloop, are ya?"

"As if she were our own."

"Figured I'd check on ya both."

"Thank you. We're well."

A gleam of hope—a dim one, but nonetheless, a gleam. This had to be the yacht's owner. The prospect of rescue seemed to chase away her cold shivers. He couldn't have been more than a few yards away.

She looked through the tiny window. It was dark out, but she could see the man Yehuda had called "Ollie," a bearded giant in his sixties. Please look this way, she thought. Over here! She tried to scream through the gag. It came out a mumble.

"Had tea yet?" she could hear Ollie ask them.

Outside, Colette backed against the window, blocking the view into the cabin. Smart girl, Lona thought, but I'll outsmart you.

"We did have supper," Yehuda said.

"Where'd ya go?"

"Just to the market."

Lona thrust her body upward, shifting the chair a few inches toward the door. She did it again, this time making an audible thud. Soon she'd be able to make a rap at the door.

"Try the swordfish?" Ollie said. "It's delicious."

"Next time."

Within a foot now, Lona launched herself at the door and hit it with her shoulder. It rattled. She did this a second time, and a third time. Outside, Colette turned around, throwing daggers her way.

Lona returned the glare.

"Beautiful sunset," Ollie said. "Did ya catch it?"

Yehuda was beginning to sound impatient. "Yes, from the beach."

"Went for a stroll, did ya?"

"Yes. Right, well, thanks for stopping by, Ollie."

No, you can't go!

Lona flung herself at the door once more.

"What was that?" Ollie said. "From the cabin."

"Sorry, that was me falling against the door," Colette said.

Lona could hear the owner taking a step closer to his sloop.

"Help!" she tried to squeal through the gag. Over the sound of the boats rocking in the harbor, she doubted she could be heard. Gathering her strength, she once again sprang up from the chair and struck the inner side of the portal with an elbow.

"There it is again," Ollie said.

Again and again Lona cried, "Help! Help!"

"Yes, I definitely hear something," Ollie added.

She could feel the slightest cant of the boat as he boarded. He was standing by the companionway, feet from her, but Colette still blocked the window.

"I thought we agreed you would only come by during the day," Yehuda said.

He's desperate, Lona realized.

Ollie sounded offended. "This here's my sloop. I'll come by when I see fit."

"That's not going to work for us," Yehuda said.

"Don't like the rules? You can bugger off," Ollie said, growing stern.

"We're paying for privacy at this hour. It's part of the deal."

"The deal's off, unless I have a look in my cabin."

"Like I said, that's not going to work," Yehuda said.

"Like hell it won't. You're on my property."

Lona heard him take another step closer.

"You, Agnes, out of m' way," Ollie said.

Colette didn't move.

"Now!" the man demanded.

"Don't listen to him," Yehuda said.

Lona drove her shoulder into the door one final time.

"Who's there?" Ollie shouted, shoving Colette aside.

"Get your hands off my wife!" Yehuda said.

Lona felt a rush of elation as the handle shifted and the portal opened. As Ollie stood there, the doorway could hardly handle his broadness.

"Help!" she stammered through the rag in her mouth.

She wasn't sure which shone more plainly on his lopsided grimace: the disgust at having been used by criminals, or the shock of seeing a hostage in his cabin. There was sympathy, too, and an urgent desire to help her.

His two big paws curled into fists, and he whirled around as if to flatten the offenders. Yehuda's hand made a sweep along the plane perpendicular to Ollie's neck, and Lona saw a flash of the familiar boating knife. But Ollie ran at him, apparently unharmed, and drove a punch into Yehuda's stomach. Yehuda fell back—hard, as if tackled by a bear—but rebounded with nimble feet and hard focus. He looked eager to fight, despite having gotten the wind knocked out of him. Colette leaped out of the way, looking terrified.

Charging again, Ollie rammed a knee into Yehuda's groin. Yehuda's face twisted with pain, though he made no sound. The yacht owner was relentless in his attacks, landing one punch after another, but never managing to strike Yehuda in the head. His opponent was agile and swift enough to deflect the blows downward. Yehuda was a powerful man himself, with youthful reflexes. Nonetheless, he had a smaller build, and Lona doubted he was a match for Ollie's raw strength. Ollie had him on the defensive. Unable to counterattack, Yehuda retreated toward the stern of the ship, dipping under the yacht's boom and clambering around the tiller for better footing. He's running, not fighting, Lona thought with glee. Ollie went after him. He crawled his way around the starboard side, using the rails for balance, chasing Yehuda toward the bow. Yehuda stood by the forward pulpit, bracing for another storm of fists.

Then Ollie stopped. He grabbed the boom once again. It pivoted along the boat's gooseneck and moved under his weight. He seemed to teeter on his feet. Go at him, Ollie, Lona thought. You have him. Take him! Why won't you finish him?

The yacht owner collapsed onto his knees, then fell limp, rolling into the companionway. He lay still.

Only then could Lona see the slit in his carotid artery.

She realized what had happened. Yehuda had been quick with his knife at the beginning of the brawl; Ollie had been losing blood. The man had had only a minute or so to take Yehuda's bait and fight.

"Go get some large stones from the nearest beach," Yehuda said to Colette. "Then help me wash the deck off."

Colette nodded.

"First," he said, "give her another dose. Make her hibernate this time."

He tossed Colette the bottle of chloroform. She doused a rag.

"*Bonne nuit, Madame la Baronne*," Colette whispered to her. "*Dormez bien.*"

Lona refused to breathe for as long as she could, staring straight into Colette's eyes, which were hard and wide. She returned what she saw in them until the need to inhale finally overwhelmed her, and the world went dark.

Yehuda

The next morning, Yehuda had a lot to prepare.

He shaved his beard, bought a vested gray suit, and paid for an expedited tailoring job. Then he visited a camera shop and purchased a professional instant camera imported from the United States, along with a roll of film.

He returned to the yacht and propped up Oliver Gibney's body at the bow of the sloop. Careful to frame the scene so neither Gibney's face nor the location would be recognizable, he snapped a photo. Next, he weighed the corpse down with Colette's rocks, rigged the sloop, and took the ship about a mile out for an inconspicuous dump into the Adriatic before returning to the marina.

In the cabin, he took several items out of his bag: a generic-looking badge, a thin copper plate, and a bag of steel-cutting tools. He spread the tools on a table, including a burin, a diamond-shaped V-point graver used for cutting straight lines, and a burnisher. Planning each cut, he clutched the heel of the burin and began to glide the tip along the copper plate in the contour of Serbian Cyrillic letters. Occasionally he used a whetstone to grind and hone the graver's edges as microscopic chips broke away from the face. After two hours of work, he laid the finished engraved plate into the badge, which now marked him as a member of the State Security Administration, the secret police of Yugoslavia.

He donned his new formal attire and put the badge in his pocket.

"Stay in the cabin until I come back," he told Colette, who had been staring through the window as he changed.

She gave him a bitter look. "Why?"

She was fishing, but there was no harm in his saying: "It doesn't take long for a face like yours to become familiar in a small city."

"We'll only be here a day or two."

"That's all it would take."

"Fine."

She gave him a pouty grin, one that went away too quickly for his liking, as it made him realize she was getting impatient with him. Despite her rampant sexuality, he had remained strictly professional after their first night of intimacy. If he gave her too much of himself, she might get attached and start behaving irrationally, but if he gave her too little, she might lose her incentive to cooperate. She was the type of girl who felt bruised when a man didn't respond to her overtures.

"How do I look?" he asked her.

She flattened the wrinkles of her checkered skirt, looking pleased that he had asked her opinion.

"Like a man who gets what he wants."

Colette had proved helpful last night, he thought. Cleaning up the spattered deck must have been unpleasant work for someone unaccustomed to the sight and smell of blood. A small tease wouldn't hurt.

He took a step toward her, pulled her in by her blouse, and wrapped her hands behind her back, lifting her onto the kitchen countertop. He placed his lips on her neck and gave her a hard bite while his fingers reached down her skirt and brushed through her curly mound. He wasn't sure whether it was the rocking of the yacht or her apparent rush of pleasure that caused her to reach up and brace herself against a cabinet for balance. He kissed his way along her neck and shoulders and continued to stroke her, letting her get wet.

She kicked her head back, panting, whispering in indecipherable French as two of his fingers glided into her.

"Oh, yes," she said. "Oh, oh . . ."

She squirmed to his touch as he rotated his fingers. Soon she dropped to her knees, one hand on his belt and the other reaching into his zipper while he played with her red hair.

"This is what I want," she said, feeling him, trying to pull him through.

He pushed her head back against the wall, sliding his fingers into her mouth, but then zipped his pants again with his free hand.

"There's still work to do," he said. "I need to find Kate and Moritz before they move on again. And then it will be your turn to do something important."

She bit down on his middle finger.

"Ouch!" he said.

He slapped her.

Colette fell back, landing on the tiny bed, gasping, more excited now. Her knees drifted apart, and she began to rub her legs and move her fingers higher up her thighs.

"What's wrong with you?" she said. "Aren't you a man?"

He refastened his belt buckle.

"We'll finish what we started after you've done your task."

"What task?"

"I'll explain once I've found Kate and Moritz."

"What am I supposed to do here while you're gone looking for them?"

"Keep an eye on the hostage." He added, spanking one of her open legs, "And whatever else pleases you."

He closed the door to the cabin. Crossing from the dock to the stone path, he decided not to tease her too often, and to give her what she wanted next time.

He followed a group of fishermen carrying baskets of fresh catch. Reaching the Placa, he paced the road several times and explored the smaller streets and alleys, mentally mapping the seaport and its landmarks, working through the logistics of his plan. Returning to the main thoroughfare, he looked up at Minčeta Tower, Dubrovnik's highest point, with an idea of what to do once he learned where Kate and Moritz were staying.

He walked into the nearest shop, a bakery, and waited for the patrons to leave before approaching the owner.

"My name is Deputy Svetozar Jovanović," Yehuda said. "I was sent from Belgrade. Can we speak in private?"

Yehuda got out the badge from his pocket and set it on the counter. Reading the inscription, the baker asked, "What's this about?"

"This man," Yehuda said, showing him the photograph of the mortally disfigured Oliver Gibney.

The baker winced. "Who was he?"

"A close friend of an advisor to President Tito. I'm investigating his murder. The prime suspects are a couple. The woman has dark hair, brown eyes. Approximately 175 centimeters tall. Speaks English with a North Welsh accent. The man is swarthy, also brown-eyed. Approximately 188 centimeters. Often wears a camel-hair overcoat. They travel together. Our intelligence tells us they're here in Dubrovnik. Have you seen them in your shop?"

"I don't think so. And I couldn't help anyway. If it's political, I wouldn't want to meddle in anything that—"

"Tito's advisor grieves the loss of his friend. He will be indebted to anyone who helps," Yehuda said, flashing a wad of bills. "He's a good man to have owe you a favor."

The baker looked troubled. "What do you want me to do?"

"If you think you've seen these two—if they come into your shop, for instance—I'd like you to alert me."

"How?"

"I'll be standing under the arches of the Rector's Palace between five and six, today and tomorrow. Remember to act naturally if they come in."

"Lots of people come and go. I don't see them all. And Christmas is coming. We're very busy."

A policeman walked into the shop and began whiffing the fresh loaves of bread by the counter. Yehuda knew it was time to leave.

"Do your best," he said. "The offer stands. You know where to find me."

Swiping the badge and photograph from the counter, he left the shop and went to the next, telling the same story.

Within hours, he had eyes throughout Old Town.

Moritz

"Shoes off," Kate said.

Moritz took her advice, leaving them by a pile of rocks.

"Socks, too," she said as she jogged to the water. Her dress billowed behind her, diaphanous in the fading sunlight, a close match to the aquamarine of the Adriatic.

As his feet sank into the sand, he couldn't help but think her idea had been a grand one. It was two days until Christmas, and they had come for a walk along the waterfront outside the city walls. The locals had gone home in the late afternoon, leaving them a private stretch of beach.

"How many Christmases have you spent like this?" he asked her.

"This makes twenty," she said. "Our home in Beaumaris is by the water."

She looked out at the horizon, where a string of clouds appeared to be lined with gold. The highest point in the sky had turned a dark purple.

Moritz pretended to gaze out to sea with her, but was instead captivated by her profile—the slight upturn of her lips, the arc of her lashes, the fluttering of her narrowed eyes, the swirl of her hair. She closed her eyes and turned toward him as if she knew he was watching. How statuesque she looked, and how different from the woman he had first met. She seemed to have found the peace that had eluded her for twenty years. An understanding must have finally settled in: She was her own person, proud of her values and choices, worthy of the happiness they brought her.

"It's funny," she said.

"What's funny?"

"I've spent most of my life trying to get free of him. Ralf Speer, the fascist, the intellectual thief. The day I learn who he really was, the first day in twenty years that I feel proud of my biological father, is the day I realize I'm not him."

"It's a good thing."

"You think so?"

"It helped you give up the idea that he, or anyone, ever had any authority over your mind because you're related. Now you can be an independent woman and stop torturing yourself."

"And you? Knowing your mother was a spy? Does it make you feel proud to be her son?"

"It doesn't make me feel any different about myself. It deepens my love for her, and my respect for who she was. But I'm still me."

"That's how I feel," Kate said. "But I never knew he was a good man to begin with."

"The 'speckles on the pear' must have come as a more dramatic revelation for you."

"Guess so. It's strange, feeling so much the same, after being so wrong about Ralf. Everything should feel different now."

"But it doesn't?"

"No."

"That's the point. Nothing about you has changed. It's all been in your head."

She took a few steps toward the surf line, and he followed her. A wave washed over their feet.

"Ooh!" she said, tensing.

"Christ! Cold cold cold . . ."

They laughed.

"You're more of a wimp than I am, Mr. Sayeret Matkal," she said.

"Sorry, I hail from the swirling sands of the Sahara, not the icecaps of Snowdonia."

"Does that mean you're prone to spontaneous freezing?"

She kicked the water at him.

"Careful," he said. "I retaliate."

He rolled up his pants and then swept her up in his arms in one smooth motion.

"Put me down!" she squealed.

"Let's see how far into the sea I can walk before a wave knocks me over."

"No! My dress!"

"Since when do you care about your *dress*?"

"Let go, let go!"

"One step . . . two . . ."

"Nooo!"

He set her down, keeping his arms at her waist while she caught her breath. Then she ran a hand through his hair, and he leaned in, closing his eyes, to kiss her.

He was no longer conscious of the waves washing over his feet and shins, or of his heartbeat as it quickened; he felt only the warm, soft urgency of her lips and the tickle of her fingers as they moved down his chest and abdomen. She ran her hands along his back, which he imagined was rough with goosebumps from the cold, but to his relief, she didn't seem to mind. Her grip on him only tightened, and she tensed and relaxed and tensed again, changing the pace of her kiss but never the fervor.

For the first time, she was behaving like a woman who deserved to be happy; it was the selfishness of her kiss that made the rest of the world disappear. Half an hour passed in seconds, and his awareness of everything else came back to him, gradually, as the rising tide climbed his knees. A breeze whistled between them as their lips parted.

A distant marine bell was ringing in the harbor. The walled city had become a silhouette in the setting sun. He ran the backs of his fingers along her cheek, sweeping past the scar at her left eyebrow, and he might have swept a few errant tendrils of her hair into line had they not so attractively caught the sun's glow, little nets of light flapping with the wind.

"Shall we begin celebrating Christmas early?" he asked, taking her hand as they waded their way ashore and dried their feet.

"As long as there's an opulent dessert and a roaring fireplace," she said. "And you."

"Mmm. I'll go along with that. What kind of dessert?"

"Let's see what we can find in the market."

Jogging to town, they found most stores closed, though a few stalls were still serving food on the Placa. They approached one that seemed to be full of sweet aromas. Behind the stall, a chef was tossing a pan over a flame on a guéridon.

"Merry Christmas," Moritz said to him. "What are you making?"

The chef, a pudgy man with sideburns, looked startled at the sight of them. His eyes darted from Kate to Moritz and back; then, after a moment, his expression changed, as if he was reminding himself to remain calm.

"I don't think he speaks English," Kate said.

Moritz pointed to the pan, making an exaggerated shrug.

"Crêpe Suzette," said the chef.

"One of my favorites," Kate whispered.

Moritz pointed to the pan and gave a thumbs-up, then pointed to Kate and himself and flashed two fingers. "Two, please," he said. "And extra sauce."

The chef flicked butter into the pan, and it sizzled, melted, and thickened when he added vanilla sugar. Sprinkling in a handful of orange zest, he sliced open a fresh orange and lemon and squeezed in the juice. He dipped the crêpes into the sauce, coating and folding each one. Fire erupted in the pan as he added the Grand Marnier.

Moritz paid the chef, who handed them their dessert.

"Smells delicious," Kate said to the man. "Thank you."

The chef nodded.

"Now," said Moritz, "what do you say we head back to our apartment and get that fireplace roaring?"

Yehuda

Standing beneath an arch outside the Rector's Palace, Yehuda felt his patience wearing thin. The streets were nearly empty now. His watch read five fifty-six. Four minutes, and his window of opportunity for the day was over. He dreaded the worst: If Kate and Moritz had left the city, or if they hadn't come here in the first place, tracking them would be impossible.

He scanned the streets, and as the minute hand of his watch approached five fifty-eight, he spotted a familiar figure walking his way. It was one of his scouts: a squat, chubby man wearing a chef's hat and apron.

"Do you have something?" Yehuda asked.

"Young couple you say," said the chef, talking quickly. "I think I find them. Her, dark hair, dark eyes. Him, tall. Ordered crêpes, speaked English."

"Where?"

The man rattled off a phrase in Serbo-Croatian and pointed down the Placa.

"When did you see them?" Yehuda asked him.

"Now, just now," said the chef. "Two mee-noot."

"Show me."

He followed the chef to his stall. "Here."

"Where did they go?"

The chef gestured toward a corner. Yehuda handed him his payment and took off toward the intersection. It was getting dark out. He rounded the corner, avoiding the light of the lampposts. The street was empty but for two people, a young woman and man, holding hands and climbing a set of steps. He recognized the man's voice as it echoed through the alley.

It was Moritz. He followed them up the stairs and through a stone enclosure. They turned right onto the street Zvijezdićeva. Yehuda stayed back as they slid a key into the door of their apartment. The two went inside.

Holding back his excitement, Yehuda left the alley and headed to the marina, where Colette was waiting in the cabin of the boat.

"They're here," he said to her. "I've found them."

She was sitting in front of the mirror, brushing her hair. The news dispelled her gloom.

"Where are they?"

He spread a map on the kitchen counter and circled their building, tracing a path from the boat to the apartment.

"Here, on the second story," he said.

"What are you going to do?"

He looked at her, making a final evaluation of her trustworthiness.

"This is where you come in," he said. "It's the two of us against the two of them now. We have the advantage of hostages. The baroness is one. The other is you."

"I'm not a hostage."

"Kate doesn't know that. You'll pretend I've brought you here against your will. Give a good performance, and she won't know you're helping me."

"What exactly is your plan?"

"First I'll take out Moritz. As long as he's alive, he will protect her. You will get Kate to hand him to me."

"That won't be easy."

He smiled, then untied Lady Atwell's bonds.

"Just listen."

He spent the next few minutes sketching his proposal on the map. When he had finished, she nodded her understanding.

"You'll need this," he said, handing her the telescope on the night-stand. "Now get ready. We start at ten tonight, and you may want to practice your delivery."

Katharina

Having found a collection of vinyls, Moritz put a record on the phonograph. The voice of Dooley Wilson began to sing "As Time Goes By," and he crooned with it: "Da dai, da dai, da dum . . ."

He curled up with Kate by the fireplace, where she had made a bed of pillows and cushions. She took a bite of the crêpes, scooping the orange butter sauce into her spoon.

"Still warm?" he asked.

"Try it."

"Ouch, yes, hot. But, mmm."

She leaned into the fire, letting the heat warm her shoulder blades, and wished he would hurry and finish his crêpes and take her in his arms. She felt safe with him, even with a man out there who wanted to kill them, and what was more, she could be herself with Moritz.

She listened to the voice on the phonograph. He was talking about moonlight and love songs never going out of date, and hearts that were full of passion and jealousy and hate. She wondered if Moritz was listening, too. He had to be, for he had begun to sing along.

"It's still the same story, fighting for glory . . ." he hummed, not quite confident in his version of the lyrics. Her mind drifted a moment, carried away by the occasional pops and crackles of the vinyl. All that mattered to her in this moment were Moritz's presence and the warmth of the fire. Everything else was irrelevant, and she wanted to tell him that she wished they would never leave Dubrovnik.

She was hardly aware she had begun to lean on his shoulder. He set down his plate and drew her in, tasting the sweetness on her lips. She tugged at the buttons of his shirt. His hands were already inside her dress, sweeping it off. Her hair fell over her bare shoulders and down her back in a black cascade. Sitting on a pillow, she stared at him by the fire, daring him further.

His hands traversed the full length of her back and unclasped her bra. He reached for her breasts as they dangled freely, and she gave them to him, her hands on his, helping him fondle her, urging him to massage her harder. She slid his pants and underwear off as he laid her back against the pillows. He took hers off, too. She was only a few feet from the fireplace, and God, did the flames burn on her skin, a pleasurable burn that made her sweat and writhe under his body as he entered her. She could hardly breathe fast enough as her hips dug into the pillows, her hands moving from his abdomen to his pectorals to his thighs, discovering every ridge and crag of the man she had wondered about ever since seeing him in his full-length overcoat. She reached for his shoulders again—delighting in their firmness, their hard angles—and pulled him in closer, so close she could feel the tips of her nipples jouncing against his chest as he gently thrust. He pulled away a moment, reaching for something, a devilish look in his eyes that made her wonder what he was planning, and when he came back, he spilled a spoonful of orange butter sauce over her breasts. Ooh, was it hot, almost painful, but she laughed despite the sting. He took her erect nipples in his mouth, one at time, swirling his tongue in little circles. He did it again, this time on her stomach—it tickled—and again on her thighs, tasting the sweetness, and soon she could feel a rivulet of sauce trickling down between her legs and . . . oh, God, was he really going to?

. . .

She cuddled in his arms by the hearth, feeling his breath on the nape of her neck. He was probably asleep now. They had lain there for hours. The fingers that had been stroking her back were still, and his breathing was slow and deep, but she couldn't sleep yet, not when she felt this good. It was hard to believe Moritz had been a stranger only two weeks ago. In some ways, she felt he had never really been a stranger; their lives had been tied together at birth by threads of resistance and espionage. The connection had taken them ten days to discover, and over the course of those days, she had learned to do more than trust him. She had begun to fall for him.

She wondered how long it could last, and whether he felt as she did, or if she was simply the fulfillment of a promise to his mother. Then her thoughts took a morbid turn. How long would he protect her from the killer—and, God forbid, should they soon part ways, how would she learn to protect herself? She decided to ignore these questions for now. This was too perfect a night to be wasted.

Gradually, sleep reached for her, but not before she heard a rapping at the door.

She paused, listening. Ten seconds, and there it was again. Definitely a visitor.

"Wake up," she said to Moritz. "Someone's here."

He was already awake. He had heard it, too, and she could see in his eyes that he had switched on his senses.

"I'll get the lights," he said, rising.

"It's probably singers, or kids selling treats."

He looked skeptical.

He palmed a knife from the kitchen before she opened the door a crack . . .

. . . and froze in place.

"*Colette?*"

After a moment of paralysis, she rushed forward with open arms, embracing her friend.

"Oh, Kate, I'm so happy to see you," Colette said, sniffling.

"What on earth are you doing here?"

Kate released her. Colette lingered a moment, then withdrew, and Kate could see her expression in the light now. Her friend's eyes were glassy and bloodshot, her cheeks moist.

"Colette, tell me everything," Kate said. "What's the matter? How did you find us? What's going on?"

Kate glanced at Moritz, who had zeroed in on Colette's every gesture. Relax, she wanted to say. Even if something is amiss, this is my best friend.

Stifling a sob, Colette said, "Kate, I need to talk with you alone."

"This is my friend Moritz. You can trust him."

"I'm sorry," Colette said. "I need privacy."

What on earth was the matter with her? Kate wondered. Something was terribly wrong.

"Okay. Come inside. Sit by the fireplace."

Colette shook her head. "I have to show you something out here."

"Outside? Why?"

Kate wiped Colette's cheeks.

"Just come! I'll explain everything."

"All right, all right."

Kate closed the door, leaving a disapproving Moritz inside, and followed Colette down the stairs and toward the Placa, where Colette leaned on her shoulder and began to cry. Her sobs were broken by quick, desperate gasps for air.

"Start explaining, Colette!" Kate said. "What's going on?"

"I've been kidnapped."

"*What?*"

"Back in Paris, there was a man waiting for me on the Rue Dauphine. He drugged me and threw me in his trunk. We've been driving for days. He keeps threatening to kill me."

"Who is this man?"

"He says his name is Yehuda Uzan. Do you know who he is? Is he the reason you disappeared?"

Kate felt remorse. She hadn't warned Colette, and he had gone after her!

"Oh, Colette, I'm so sorry! I—I didn't think he . . . I never thought about the possibility he'd hurt you! The night of the soirée, that man Yehuda tried to kill me in our apartment. Moritz stopped him. We've been on the run from him since then, trying to learn his motives. I should have told you everything, but there were risks, and, God, now look what I've let happen!"

"Kate, I'm so confused and terrified. He says you stole a painting from Maxence. A Klee. He's using me to get to you and this man Moritz. *J'ai peur.* I'm so scared."

"That painting's a forgery! Maxence is worried I'll go to the police," Kate said, trying to connect the dots. "But you've escaped Yehuda!"

"No. He has your mother."

Her stomach twisted into a knot. "Impossible!"

"Unless I go back to him tonight, he'll kill her."

"Where are they?"

"I'm not allowed to tell you," Colette said.

Kate shook her. "Tell me! It's me and you here."

"He'll kill us both if I do."

"How did he find us?"

"He has spies throughout town."

"I mean, how did he track us to Dubrovnik?"

"I don't know. Tonight, he told me to deliver a message to you. Just you. Moritz must not hear."

"What message?"

"Kate, I'm so sorry." Colette handed her a telescope and said, "Look at the Minčeta Tower to the northwest."

She peered through the spyglass, focusing on a crenellation in the wall about a half-kilometer away, where she discerned two human figures standing at the edge. The area would have been shrouded in darkness if not for the oil lamp one of them was holding. She could see who they were: Yehuda and, unbelievably, her mother.

He was peering down from the ramparts, holding Lona in a headlock. The lamp made something in his hand shimmer. A blade pressed to her cheek. The lamp went out, and their two forms receded from the tower's edge.

"I'll kill him!" Kate said to Colette. "Tell me where he's going."

"I told you, I can't, or he'll kill us!"

"We'll bring the police."

"Don't even think of it. You can't say anything to the police, or he'll murder Lona!"

"What are his demands?"

"He's going to kill me, and then your mother, unless you turn Moritz over to him."

"Oh, God."

"He wants you to find a way to get Moritz to Lokrum. It's a forested island less than a mile from the harbor. Make sure he arrives at noon, two days from now."

"On Christmas Day? And he'll let you both go if I do this?"

"No. Just me."

"What about Mum?"

"After Moritz crosses to the island, you're supposed to follow in a rowboat. Then he says he will release Lona."

"I see."

More tears poured from Colette's eyes as she glanced at her watch. "I don't know what's going to happen to us. But I have to go. He'll start hurting her if I don't go back soon. Don't follow me. Don't do anything stupid. I'm telling you, he's sick."

"I won't let him touch either of you," Kate said.

"Whatever you decide, your mother wanted me to say how much she loves you. And you know I do, too."

Colette hugged her once more, and then she broke into a run, disappearing down a side street.

Kate's heart raced. Suddenly she felt claustrophobic. The alley had the illusion of shrinking as she walked back to the apartment, trapping her within contracting walls.

She had no idea what to do. The deal was clear: Moritz for Colette, she for her mother. If she didn't turn him over, they would both die.

In each case, she had to choose. Was there any way around this but to decide whom she valued most?

With a swell of anger and fear, she picked up a rock from the ground and threw it against the wall, just to hear the crack.

What was she supposed to tell Moritz when she got home? He had only known her for ten days; what was to say he wouldn't cut and run if she told him the deal? She couldn't tell him. She couldn't! What would she do without Colette and her mother?

She should have warned Colette back in Paris, told her to move away and hide. She should have given her parents a stronger warning, too. Maxence had invented the whole story about the stolen painting to have a reason to come after her once she knew it was a fake. Her blood ran cold. He was clearly willing to do anything to protect the gallery and its reputation.

And what about George? Was he safe?

She began to imagine life without her mother and her best friend, knowing she would be to blame for their murders. But what about Moritz? She cared about him, too. He had saved her life, persevered with her, helped her become a new person. She was falling in love with him. How could she send him to the slaughterhouse?

She resolved to say nothing for now, and to invent a story while she decided what to do.

Returning to the apartment, she said, "I'm back."

There was no answer.

"Moritz?"

Still nothing. She checked every room. In the living room, fresh smoke rose from a recently extinguished fireplace. The embers were still burning. He was gone.

Colette and Moritz

Jogging back to the marina, Colette felt proud of her performance, and tonight, Yehuda would reward her for it.

Around her, families were preparing to celebrate Christmas in their homes with feasts, presents, and songs—but Kate's merriment was through, she thought exultantly. Kate had bought her story and now faced quite a dilemma. Colette felt certain that she would think it over for twenty-four hours and conclude that her new companion's life was tradeable.

Colette turned into a series of streets, following a zigzag pattern to a gate through the eastern walls. The way was lit by torches and gas lamps.

She stopped, hearing a crunching noise. Had Kate been stupid enough to follow her? She whirled around, more nervous than she cared to admit, searching the street for a pursuer but seeing no possibilities. Just a homeless man lying under a shelter of newspapers and palm fronds, who probably had moved in his sleep. If she'd seen anything, it must have been the shadows cast by the fluttering torches.

She relaxed, taking the stone path around the harbor toward the *Lady Louise*.

. . .

Squatting behind a frond, Moritz rose to his feet slowly so as not to wake the vagabond. He removed his shoes and tiptoed after Kate's friend as she crossed through the gate into the marina.

There was no way that Colette could have found them alone. All signs pointed to someone who knew what he was doing. Someone like Yehuda. Apparently, he and Kate hadn't covered their tracks as well as he'd thought. Yehuda must have threatened Colette and taken her hostage, intending to manipulate Kate. If that were the case, Colette would lead him straight to Yehuda.

He had left through the back door of the apartment and followed her cautiously, at all times ready to stop and dart away or crouch down. She seemed paranoid, constantly checking her shadow.

He ducked behind a dumpster and watched as she boarded a sloop at the dock. The walkway was empty and dimly illuminated by the glow of a lamppost. When she disappeared into the cabin, he scurried after her, keeping low. The cabin had one window. He stayed out of view and hid behind the hull of another yacht to plan an approach. The marina was quiet but for the lapping of water against the dock and the creak of a lantern swinging from a chain on the *Lady Louise*.

The cabin door closed as Colette went inside. He dashed across the planks of the dock, keeping his knees bent to pad his steps. He winced as a few splinters poked through his socks. The lights were out on the ship next door. He grabbed hold of the neighbor's gunwale and swung himself aboard, then edged around to the starboard side, careful not to wake any sleeping passengers who might have spotted him. Using a chainplate as a balancing handhold, he extended his legs and jumped over to the *Lady Louise*, landing with a soft thud.

Too loud.

The cabin door opened and Colette came out. He ducked down behind a pile of rope on the port side, and watched her. Inspecting the deck, she said nothing as she removed the lantern from its chain. The shadows around him shifted as she moved the light, searching for signs of an intruder. Satisfied after a half-minute, she went back inside. He wondered why she was so obsessively careful not to be followed. Yehuda must have threatened to hurt her if she revealed this spot to anyone, deliberately or not.

He found firm footing by the companionway and peeked through the window into the cabin. She was taking her clothes off—her cardigan, her blouse, her pants, her underwear—revealing a graceful body sprinkled with freckles as she stretched out on the bed. Now completely nude, she rested her head in her hand. So, she's really a blonde, he thought guiltily. Why hadn't she put on a nightgown? He found her behavior strange as she lay across the pillows, sensually, experimenting with positions, posing as if for an artist. He understood why, as Kate had mentioned, she'd been asked to leave her bucolic home and model for fashion magazines. Perhaps it was true what they said about Parisian women becoming bolder these days, but he had to be missing something. She seemed to be expecting a visitor.

He dropped to his knees, hearing a scuffing sound from the harbor's stone walkway. Two people approached. He scrambled to the bow of the ship and watched as the silhouetted forms strode along the dock. One was Yehuda. The other was an older woman, and judging by the way he dragged her, a prisoner. Her steps were short and sluggish. Perhaps he had abused or sedated her. Whoever she was, Moritz guessed Yehuda had found another person Kate cared about.

The boat pitched as they boarded. Moritz watched from behind the coils of rope as Yehuda opened the portal to the cabin and shoved the woman inside, following her in.

Moritz crawled to the top of the cabin, beneath the boom, and pressed an ear against the hatch, listening for their voices, catching a few phrases:

"... Waiting for me, are you?"

"... Know that I ... several days, and I won't do ... any longer."

He heard fabric rubbing on fabric. Yehuda taking his clothes off, probably. The conversation continued:

"And you did what I said?"

"Yes."

"And she ... to every word?"

"Every word."

Moritz couldn't help but notice the familiarity between them. They weren't speaking to each other like captor and hostage. They sounded like colleagues.

Silence lasted a good while. What was going on in there? He heard a faint whimpering noise, and a thud, then heavy breathing and a rhythmic creaking.

A totally illogical scene, he thought. Colette had been waiting for Yehuda, making herself look provocative, as if she wanted to please him ... and be pleased. Did she see Yehuda as her enemy?

He revisited his doubts. Kate had insisted Colette was her best friend, whom she had known since Oxford. It was inconceivable that Colette would help Yehuda unless she had been threatened. But as much as he wanted to believe in her innocence, what could explain her luxuriating on the sheets for Yehuda?

Most likely, Moritz thought, it was a ploy to seduce him. She was trying to earn his trust so she could sting him and end all this madness while his defenses were down. There would be logic in that, and if true, he could help her *now*, by sparing her an encounter that was practically rape.

He climbed his way down to the deck again and peered through the window into the cabin. He had to act. He would burst through the door and kill the bastard with his kitchen knife, catching Yehuda naked and defenseless . . .

He stopped himself as he spotted the Purdey shotgun near the bed's headboard. That tipped the odds the other way. His attack would have to be fast if he were to seize the element of surprise.

He took a step down toward the cabin, ready to lunge through the door. The stair squeaked as his sock slipped on a damp step. He stood still, listening. Through the window, he could see their bodies were no longer moving as one.

"What was that?" he heard from inside.

Damn it, he thought, stepping back. There went his chance. Inside, he could see Yehuda reach for the shotgun and approach the door. There was nothing he could do to help Colette any more. Not now, anyway.

Raising his arms above his head, Moritz arched his body and dove quietly into the marina.

He took three strokes while fully submerged, propelling himself toward the bow, thinking: Old friend, at least I've found you.

Katharina

Kate paced the living room.

If Yehuda killed Colette or her mother, he would lose his leverage. But he was a psychopath, and there was no telling what psychopaths would do.

Horrific as the idea was, she had to consider capitulating to Yehuda's demands and sacrificing Moritz—if she could find him again—to save Colette's life. As quickly as she was falling for him, she hadn't known him long. She had known Colette for years, and despite her quirks, she loved her like a sister.

Where had Moritz gone? Had he left through the back door and eavesdropped on her conversation with Colette? If so, did he expect her to betray him now? Had he abandoned her and fled to save his own life? She didn't know how she could get him to the island of Lokrum, anyway. She would have to lie to him, convincingly, knowing how he picked up on the smallest signals when something was wrong. She wondered what it would feel like to deceive a man she admired, knowing it would be his death sentence; then she shuddered, repulsed by the thought, feeling terrible for considering it—but there was no alternative, if her mother and best friend were to be saved.

There was another trade to think about: her own life for her mother's. The thought of losing Lona to this murderer was excruciating. Her mother took center stage in all the sweetest memories of her youth in Beaumaris. She loved Lona so deeply, every bit as much as she loved George. She only wished she had shown it. Growing up, she'd thought she needed a father more than a mother and hoped, somewhere in her hindbrain, that spending time with George would purge her of Ralf's evils. How wrong she had been, on so many levels. And to think of all the time she had wasted brooding and sulking and agonizing over nothing. Time that she could have devoted to a relationship with Lona. She hadn't wanted any sort of distance between them, but if there was, it was her own fault.

Who would it be? Lona, or herself?

She paused. Maybe there was an alternative. Not only for her mother, but for Moritz and Colette. If she told him everything when she saw him next—that was, *if* she saw him again—maybe they could think of a way to trump Yehuda together.

The door opened soon after she had the idea, and she heard a series of soggy, squishing footsteps. "You're back!" she said.

Whether her relief at the sight of him was well informed, she could not say. He was dripping wet from head to toe and looked pained to see her.

"Where were you?" she asked. "And what happened? You're soaked."

"Yehuda's here," Moritz said. "He's staying in the marina on a yacht. I followed your friend back to the harbor. He's got a second hostage. An older woman."

"I know," Kate said. "That's my mother."

"Kate, I'm so sorry to have to tell you this, but I saw something horrible. I wanted to stop it and almost found a way, but he had a shotgun on the boat, and he almost discovered me. I had to get out of there."

"What did you see?"

He described the scene at the yacht, and his belief that Colette had been threatened into submission and was using sex as a survival tactic.

"He'll suffer for what he's doing to them," she said after hearing his story.

She decided that she had imagined his moment of discomfort, that there had been no flash of uncertainty in his eye, that there was no alternative explanation he could be considering.

"What did Colette want to talk to you about?" he said. This time she knew she hadn't imagined the edge of accusation in his tone that seemed to regard Colette as a potential wrongdoer rather than a victim. She held her breath a moment. There was no going back after she told him. Here goes . . .

"She came to deliver a message from Yehuda," Kate said. "He knows you're protecting me, so he wants to kill you first. I'm supposed to get you to the island of Lokrum at exactly noon on Christmas Day. After he's murdered you, he claims he'll release Colette. I'm to go next, in a rowboat. In exchange, he'll release my mother."

She studied the softening of his expression as he came into the light, and felt grateful that he seemed to understand the scope of her dilemma.

"Seeing that you told me," he said, "I suppose you don't plan to deliver me to the devil?"

"No, but I don't have a better plan yet. I thought maybe if we put our heads together, we could think of something."

"Let me change out of these sopping clothes first," Moritz said. "I think better warm."

He came back in his pajamas, after having wrung out and pinned up his clothing in the bathroom. She had a kettle of tea waiting.

They sat at the dinner table, where Kate had plopped a pile of blank papers and a handful of pencils and erasers. She taped a half-dozen sheets together to form a large rectangle, on which she began sketching a map. At the edge of her peninsula, four sharp lines demarcated the walls of Dubrovnik. She added a few circles and squares for the forts, shaded in the island of Lokrum to the southeast, and drew a series of ships in the Old Harbor.

"We're here," she said, adding a pointed star to the end of the map where the sound was and tracing a dotted line to the forested island. "This is where he wants to take us."

Moritz leaned over the drawing. She could tell his mind was busy.

"I'm guessing he doesn't want to kill us on the island."

"Why not?" Kate said.

"He wants you to think that's his plan, that he picked a remote place where it would be easy to hide our bodies and exit. But the island is full of trees and hiding spots. It's a soldier's terrain. He knows it would be hard to finish me off there, and that I'll be suspecting foul play to boot."

"What do you think his real plan is, then?"

"I'll bet he wants to take us en route."

"Over the water, before we get to Lokrum?"

"Yes. I think he wants to sail right up next to us and take us by surprise, then sail straight out of Croatia. Clean kill, and a very clean getaway."

"Seems like tough maneuvering."

"He's a good sailor, and he has a shotgun."

Kate's eyes narrowed. She took a few clean sheets from the pile and began sketching a series of lines, circles, and intersecting arcs.

"What are you doing?" he asked.

"I have an idea. Give me a second."

He watched with interest as the sketch took on detail. In two minutes, he began to recognize a few shapes, all of which looked to be part of some floating contraption. Her fingers jittered faster as she fleshed out the image and gained confidence that her plan might work.

"It's our own miniature Operation Bertram," she said. "If we can get a water scooter and a dummy, can you figure out a way to blow it all up?"

"I'll need electronic components," he said. "Solenoids. Coils of wire that generate a magnetic field with current. And a remote control. What's the dummy for?"

"Our phantom friend will divert attention from the real attack."

"Sounds like we owe Geoffrey Barkas and his camoufleurs a big thank-you for the inspiration," he said. "Now, let's get to work."

Isabel

In the three days since her conversation with Conrad, Isabel had filled a notebook with a list of art colleges and their descriptions. She researched the schools in her hours off work, detailing what she liked about each. She had yet to pick a top choice, though she was confident she had narrowed the cities to London, Edinburgh, Paris, Düsseldorf, and Chicago.

Her only travel experience to date had followed her flight from a transport vehicle between detention centers in Chile. Hungry and cold, she had escaped to the border and crossed the Andes on a string of ramshackle buses and lake ferries, and even gone part of the way on foot. In her twenty-two years, she had never seen beyond the southern parts of Chile or Argentina. The distant cities on her list could have existed only in photographs, and she would not have known the difference.

For the past few hours, she had caught herself doodling, making sketches of Big Ben, Edinburgh Castle, and the Chicago skyline, wondering how close her imagination was to reality. She usually found it easier to focus in good spirits, but today her spirits were overflowing. It was Christmas Eve, and never in her life had she been given so much to look forward to. Now and then a daydream would whisk her off to a foreign place until the ticking of the clock would snap her back to her office in Conrad Pendelfarr's mansion, where she would resume her work, sorting and filing accounting documents.

She looked at the time. One more productive hour, and she could go home.

She skimmed through a couple of spreadsheets listing recent acquisitions and sales, and then stored them in a file cabinet organized by date and geographical region. Her next task was to update an address book with information on some boutique auction houses in Europe and North America that had done business with Pendelfarr's company. Working efficiently for the first time that day, she had neared the end of her stack of papers when she noticed a document called "Pendelfarr International Scholarship Program."

The document had a preliminary estimate of costs, as figured by Pendelfarr accountants. Scanning the page, she spotted her name next to the words "inaugural scholar," and felt a rush of pride. Then she noticed a puzzling sentence toward the bottom of the page, in fine print:

Pilot scholarship program to be funded through revenues from Inventory Zero.

She didn't know what to make of that. The company had offices in many countries. Each office operated several warehouses, called "inventories." The pieces comprising each inventory were either acquired locally or shipped from another location to maximize the probability of sales, given the regional statistics. Inventories were named with three letters and a number, specifying the region and the warehouse. The most valuable acquisitions typically shipped to the Pendelfarr headquarters in Bariloche and were stored in a warehouse called "Inventory BAR-1."

Having worked at the company long enough to know the location of each warehouse by heart, she was surprised to see one she didn't recognize. To her knowledge, there was no such thing as "Inventory Zero." It seemed her scholarship was to be funded through sales from an inventory off the books.

She would have asked Pendelfarr for clarification, but he had left hours before to host a local Christmas auction, so instead she picked up the phone and dialed a number by heart.

"Pendelfarr International, accounting," said the voice on the other end.

"Hi, this is Isabel de la Fuente, Mr. Pendelfarr's personal secretary," she said. "Quick question here."

"Go ahead."

"I'm updating addresses and realize I don't have any information on a warehouse called Inventory Zero. Would you mind giv—"

Click.

She set the phone back in its cradle, wondering if they had been disconnected by accident. When she tried calling again, there was no answer.

Why had they hung up on her? If the source of scholarship funds was in question, this was personal, and urgent.

She needed access to the full list of warehouse addresses. That would be in a cabinet in Pendelfarr's office. She let herself in using a spare key and went straight to the file. In it was a paper listing several dozen inventories and corresponding addresses.

Inventory Zero was the last entry, and the only one with no address listed. No normal address, anyway.

In place of an address was the word: *Guesthouse*.

She said the words aloud, trying to give them meaning, until it dawned on her. This could mean right here, in Bariloche: the cottage in the property's rear gardens—Pendelfarr's guesthouse. He had spoken of it, but she had never seen it. As far as she knew, it had not been used in a long time, at least not while she had been working for him. When Pendelfarr had overnight guests, they were given bedrooms in the main house.

She returned the study to its original state before going downstairs and entering the gardens at the south end of the Pendelfarr estate. During the summer, she'd have heard the gurgling of fountains and seen the red blaze of Patagonian flowers. Now the garden was silent and white, except for bits of green poking out of the frosted hedges. She passed under a vine trellis, feeling guilty for violating her employer's trust a second time. Not only had she faked her résumé and recommendation letters, but now she had entered his office without permission and was about to break into his guesthouse.

Nonetheless, she knew this was no regular inventory, and she had to find out about it. Spotting the Spanish-style cottage on the lower grounds, she checked first that she wasn't being followed—a silly move, because she knew no one else was even on the grounds—and walked down to the next level. She knocked on the door, knowing this was also senseless. He had no visitors, and even if he did, they wouldn't have been staying here. Her knock went unanswered. The lights were off, the curtains drawn. A window near the entrance was open an inch. Using a stick from the garden, she used the opening to swing the bolt on the front door.

She turned on the light. It was a small habitation, one that might have looked elegant with a little care. Dust on the bed and rocking chair suggested they hadn't been used in years. The portraits on the walls of the bathroom and breakfast nook had begun to slack and sag in the changing humidity. The most commanding presence in the room was a monogrammed upright piano outside the kitchenette.

Isabel sighed. Big surprise—a *guestroom*. What else had she been expecting? There was no inventory here. She surveyed the space a final time, almost ready to give up, but then she decided to check out the closet first. Sliding it open, she figured she'd find clothing.

What she found was a door of thick steel. She immediately started breathing faster. In a matter of minutes, her suspicion had evolved into something more.

What was this? She realized she hadn't been told everything. Pendelfarr had kept this from her, a secret that was supposed to finance the education he had promised her.

Laying a hand on the steel surface, she saw that it was part of a vault. The door was as tall as she was and secured by a fifty-digit combination lock.

"I'm glad you've made yourself at home."

She jumped, startled, and turned around to see Pendelfarr entering the guesthouse.

"Mr. Pendelfarr!" This was an utter disaster. How would she explain herself?

"I see you've discovered my hidden stash," he said.

"I . . . got curious when I saw a file specifying the source of funds for the scholarship," she said.

"So I hear." He was wearing his usual tranquil, benevolent expression, a face that promised that nothing could ruffle his calm.

There wasn't anything physically intimidating about Pendelfarr. He reminded her of an aging elf, with his pointy ears and diminutive, bespectacled features. Still, she was shaking. She did not want to disappoint the man who had treated her mistakes with generosity.

"I thought you were hosting an auction tonight?" she said.

"It ended."

"Oh."

"You have quite a sense of daring, Ms. de la Fuente."

"Please forgive me," she said. "Please, I hope you can. I had to know. I have a good memory, and I know all the inventory codes, but this was one I hadn't heard before. The accounting people wouldn't tell me anything. There was a sheet in your office that said 'Guesthouse' for the address, and I figured maybe there was something here. So I checked." He didn't say anything. She added, with guilt, "I would have asked if you had been there. It was just me being too curious."

"No such thing as 'too' curious," he said, taking a step closer. "Curiosity is a good thing. Unless you're a cat." He grinned.

Though he had a reputation for a mercurial temper that kept people off balance, she had never seen it. Pendelfarr had only ever been kind with her, and he had an uncanny way of putting her at ease, even when he caught her breaking rules.

"You're not upset?" she said.

"No. If anything, this proves how much you value your art education."

He entered the combination. The steel door swung open to reveal a steep staircase.

"Come inside," he said. "I'll show you Inventory Zero."

She followed him into a basement encased in reinforced concrete. The room was filled with leaning stacks of canvases, some removed from their frames and stuffed into cardboard tubes. There had to be at least three hundred paintings down there. Most were small, not three feet in either dimension.

The stacks of works astounded her as she thumbed through them. A lily pond in Giverny, one of many by Monet. A Renoir of two young girls reading on a sofa. Several Degas ballerinas rehearsing. A bar scene by Toulouse-Lautrec. A portrait of a young woman in the style of Greuze.

"That's just the French section," Pendelfarr said. "Have a look around."

She tried a different stack, this time recognizing a dark, nightmarish scene by Goya, a court painting by Velázquez, a gathering of street urchins by Murillo. The more she wandered, the more painters she recognized.

"This is unbelievable," she said, overwhelmed. "You have an entire museum's worth down here."

"Everything you see here has profound historical significance."

"Shouldn't these be . . . well, in a gallery somewhere? I mean, wouldn't you expect—"

"You might not think treasures like these could be found in an art broker's collection, but you'd be amazed what careful scouting can accomplish."

She returned to the French section and continued to flip through the canvases.

"So, this is where you keep your most prized pieces."

He nodded.

"Occasionally, our warehouses get broken into," he said. "This underground vault was built specifically for Inventory Zero, and the guesthouse was built to contain the vault. No one has ever spent the night there. It's for show."

She now understood why his accounting office had hung up on her. Most likely, they had been instructed to protect the secrecy of this inventory, a trove of inestimable value, to keep its existence unknown to anyone, and therefore, to thieves.

"I won't say a word about it," she promised, feeling honored to have been invited inside.

"I appreciate that," he said. "Now if you're all finished, I'd like to close up shop."

Still thumbing through the paintings, she saw a piece that grabbed her—and then he hit the light switch.

"One minute," she said as the room went dark. "Would you turn that back on?"

"I think we've spent enough time down here."

His convivial tone had taken on a sharp edge. She had tested the limits of his patience these past few days with her brazen remarks and false employment history. Breaking into his guest cottage was no different. She knew she should let it go, but something about what she'd glimpsed had struck a note of discord, and she needed to know why.

"Please, Mr. Pendelfarr. I really like this one."

Reluctantly he obliged, and the light went on.

The focus of the painting she'd noticed was a woman in a white dress, standing under a parasol in a sunny garden.

"I've seen this before, in one of the art history textbooks I borrowed from your library," she said. "It's a Monet. A study in the interplay between shadow and color." At once she realized what was wrong. "This is supposed to be at the Hermitage Museum in St. Petersburg!"

Conrad folded his arms.

"And this Goya piece," she said as another memory fired. "I recognize it, too. It's at the Prado! I read about its acquisition! What are these? Copies?"

"Yes," he said.

She did not understand.

"But if they're copies, then why would you keep them so safe in—you mean, copies as in *forgeries*?"

"Yes," he said.

"How many?"

"Everything in this room."

She could feel her face getting hot.

"What are they doing here? How did you get them?"

"That's a story for another day."

"You said they all had profound historical significance!"

"I assure you, they do."

"But that file said you're going to use revenues from Inventory Zero to fund the scholarship."

"I am," he said.

"What revenues? You're going to sell these? These fakes?"

"Right again."

Madre de Dios, she thought. She could feel her beliefs about the man turning upside down.

"But they're not real!"

"That's hard to argue," he said, his voice soft and even. "They were made by masters."

"But not the right masters. Do you expect . . ."

"Expect what?"

She knew what she wanted to say: *That I'm going to ignore this?* But it would sound like a threat. She played out the rest of the conversation in her head. He would insist that the integrity of his company would not be questioned, seeing as Inventory Zero's revenues were to sponsor philanthropic causes. He would argue that his scheme was a win-win for everyone—that he had found a cost-effective form of publicity, that his buyers would never know the difference, and that she was being handed her dream on a silver platter.

If she pressed the issue and threatened to expose him, he would ask her if she truly believed anyone would listen to an *illegal* immigrant and a convicted *thief*, who left a local *brothel* by faking her résumé and reference letters. It wouldn't matter that she had only stolen from lowlife scoundrels who had done worse things. It wouldn't matter that she had done it because her mother was dying. It wouldn't matter that she'd faked those letters because she was hungry and needed a place to work where she wouldn't be choked and beaten and slapped like someone's dog.

Nor would it matter that she hadn't misrepresented her abilities in those letters. She *was* a good worker. He had said so over and over. One of his best. Was it wrong, what she'd done? Yes, and she'd learned her lesson. But his crimes were of a whole other magnitude. He was committing fraud on an epic scale, asking her to take this scholarship on stolen money. She couldn't do it. Not at the expense of the people he swindled.

She played out the conversation a bit more. He would tell her she had signed a contract. She'd say it had been without full information.

Then he'd give her the alternative: Go back to some Chilean jail, and rot.

She had a bit of leverage. She didn't know exactly what he was up to, but he was clearly crooked enough to hide behind a corkscrew, and he had some dirty business deal in Europe. After tonight, she could no longer believe that "the girl who got away" was merely an artwork. She had seen the telegrams between Pendelfarr, Maxence, and Uzan. Her boss was trying to kill somebody. She could inform the police on him.

What good would that do? He'd call her a lying, thieving whore, and he could prove it. Discredited, she'd be whisked off to prison.

There was one threat he might find credible. She had memorized the names and addresses of his millionaire clients. If she were to write every one of them from prison and share her perspectives, perhaps Pendelfarr would lose their business. She could credibly threaten him with this.

But then she would never make it to prison. His hired goons would find her first.

There was no way out for her.

"Expect what?" he said again.

She steadied the tremble in her voice. "Never mind."

"Do you have a problem with this?"

"I was surprised at first, but I see the sense in it."

"The scholarship is your gateway to an exciting intellectual dimension of life," he said. "Think about what's in store for you. The students, future colleagues with ambition and promise. The professors, mentors for life."

These were no longer on her horizon. She would not be attending art school after all, but she couldn't tell him that without endangering herself, maybe even her life. She had to play along, even as her head was spinning and her eyes were welling up.

"And an exotic foreign city to call home," she added, looking away.

"I knew a girl like you was smart enough to see the value here."

Girl like you. She knew what he meant: liar, thief, whore.

Pull yourself together, she thought. She would get away from this man as soon as she could, but that time was not now. Right now, her life depended on an income stream, and his trust.

"I understand," she said. She took a step toward him and set a hand on his shoulder. "Opportunity is made, not found. But I have one problem."

"What's that?"

"You shouldn't have let me into this room without knowing whether I'd keep your secret safe. Maybe you thought you could hold my illegal status over my head if I took issue. But it was still careless. No one else can learn about this vault." She leaned in close to his ear and dropped her voice to a whisper. "Now that you've given me my dream, I don't want to lose it because you couldn't keep a damned lock on a door."

He was sizing her up with an amused look.

"I'm glad you feel so strongly," he said, switching off the lights. "Let's head to the house."

She walked ahead of him so he wouldn't see her eyes tearing up.

Moritz

"It's Christmas Eve," Moritz said, nudging Kate out of bed. "Rise and shine. Time to get supplies. Today we honor Operation Bertram with a trick of our own."

She rubbed her eyes, then practically sprang from beneath the covers. "What time did you get up?" she asked.

"Five."

"You hardly slept."

"Working on the supply list." He handed her a sheet. "I've added some embellishments."

She read the items out loud. "Category one: mannequin, paint set, long-sleeved shirt, pants, gloves, cap, cardboard. I'm guessing that's for the dummy?"

"That's right. As artist extraordinaire, you are going to use the paint set to give our phantom soldier a face that looks like mine."

"A few blotches should do."

"I envisioned subtle shading for my masculine features, with neoclassical influence."

"I'm thinking realism. Let's keep that ego in check."

"As long as it's convincing through a telescope."

"What's the cardboard for?"

"You're going to cut out the shape of a rifle and paint it black, so he thinks I'm armed."

"Got it," she said. "Category two: a pair of solenoids, five yards of electric wire, radio transmitter and receiver, two four-foot dowels."

"For the remote steering device. Next?"

"Category three: five inches of steel water pipe, two brass caps, match heads, drill, glow plugs, fuse. What for?"

"A pipe bomb."

"He has my mother and Colette as hostages. They could get hurt."

"It won't go off anywhere near them. And we're not after killing power anyway. We want a loud bang, so he thinks the dummy is firing the cardboard gun at him."

"Okay. Category four: stone weights, one can of gasoline."

"Dramatic pyrotechnics for our phantom soldier's death. After a few shots from Yehuda's gun, you'll trigger a gasoline explosion remotely, creating a ball of flame on the water scooter and making him think he's hit the fuel tank. The weights, connected to the mannequin, will fall overboard and drag the dummy with them. That way there's no floating mannequin left over to give us away."

"All right, last items. Category five: scuba gear, water scooter, rowboat."

"Our marine equipment," he said. "We'll rig the water scooter with your dummy and my remote steering device. As for the scuba gear and rowboat, you know the story."

"Who's going to get what?"

"I'll take categories two through four. You take care of the rentals and get the supplies you need for the dummy soldier." He tore off her sections of the list and handed them back to her. "We've got twenty-four hours to put this together. Let's not take too much time scrounging for supplies."

"Meet back in four hours?" Kate said.

"That should do it. We'll need the rest of the time for construction."

"See you soon, then."

. . .

They reconvened at eleven in the morning.

"Find it all?" Moritz asked her.

"Everything for the dummy," she said. "There was no scuba shop, but I found a diver willing to rent us his stab jacket, regulator, tank, fins, and mask." She gestured toward a duffel bag full of the gear. "The rowboat and water scooter were easy. The owners will have them ready for us tomorrow morning, waiting in the small inlet between the western walls and Fort Lovrijenac."

"On Christmas Day? You're sure? There's no room for mistakes."

"At their price, they'd better be there. How about you?"

"There was no electronics store, but I did manage to find a hobbyist who had the solenoids, glow plugs, and radio components," he said. "The gasoline was a bit tricky. I had to run a siphon from someone's car."

"You rotten thief."

"Guilty as charged."

"What about the rest?"

"There was a small hardware shop for the water pipe, drill, and dowels. Everything else was fairly easy to scavenge."

Kate set the mannequin on the kitchen floor and opened a set of acrylic paint tubes.

"Hey," said Moritz. "Our phantom soldier looks female."

"It's all the clothing store had," she said. "Don't worry. I'll distribute some pillow fluff under the shirt to hide the bust."

"Don't forget the handsome face."

"Oh, don't worry."

She began mixing paints, while Moritz got to work on the bomb. Threaded on both ends, the metal water pipe was a half-inch in diameter and six inches long. He drilled a small hole in the center, screwed a brass cap on one end, and then poured several dozen severed match heads into the pipe. When finished, he screwed on the second cap and plugged a fuse into the hole.

"What a nice complexion our soldier has," he said, with a glance at Kate's progress. She was texturing the cheeks and forehead.

"Quiet, or he'll end up with a black eye."

Moritz began wiring the remote steering mechanism, first testing the solenoids.

"How do those work?" she asked after a few minutes.

"Inside each coil is an iron rod used as a plunger. Current running through the coils creates a magnetic field, causing the plungers to accelerate through the cylinders of wire. The plungers will be attached to the dowels, which will be fastened to the throttle of the water scooter. As the iron rods push and pull depending on the direction of the current, the scooter will turn left and right."

He began dissecting the radio signaling devices, studying the internal circuitry. By late evening, he had glued the dowels to the plungers and integrated their function with the receiver.

"It's working," he said.

Standing across the room, he activated the solenoids at the flick of a switch, causing them to jitter on the floor.

"Amazing!" she said. "And so is our dummy, dressed and painted. Have a look."

She leaned the phantom soldier against the refrigerator. It was wearing pants and a shirt now, stuffed with feathers around the lower torso, as well as a cap and gloves. The mannequin's face, painted a dark copper, featured a wide-eyed stare that was almost frightening in its intensity.

"Well done," Moritz said. He pretended to shake its hand. "Greetings, fearless rider. Tomorrow you shall conquer the Adriatic. I hope you are as skilled a soldier as you are a cross-dresser."

He gave Kate a peck on the cheek.

"Sleep time?" she said.

"I need a few minutes to attach the glow plugs to the fuses."

"Be quick," she said. "Tomorrow comes early."

Yehuda

"This is it," Yehuda said. He checked his watch. It was eight on Christmas morning. "Time to tie you both."

"Do you really have to tie me up?" Colette said.

"Soon Moritz and Kate will cross the waters. If she sees into our cabin, and only the baroness is bound to a chair, she'll suspect you."

"She'll never suspect me."

"I won't take the risk. Give me your hands."

She sat down, the backs of the two chairs flat against each other. He wrapped her arms and legs together, elbows to quadriceps, and bound her calves together with several tight coils of rope. Colette and Lady Atwell were now stuck together, facing apart.

"It's too tight," Colette said.

"Uncomfortable? Try a thousand miles in a trunk," Lona retorted.

"Quiet, both of you." Yehuda spun two handkerchiefs into gags.

"What are you doing?" Colette said.

He tied the first handkerchief around her neck and mouth.

"What did I tell you he'd do once he was done using you?" said Lona.

Colette resisted, trying to shout.

Lona shook her head. "You stupid girl." She did not fight him as he slipped on her gag.

Yehuda left them in the cabin. Outside, he began to prepare the boat for sailing, pulling the lines out of their cleats and off their winches. He checked that the proper stopper knots were in place to prevent any lines from yanking through the mast or sheaves. He secured the tack of the mainsail to its shackle, then did the same for the jib, and raised both sails.

Within minutes, the *Lady Louise* had begun to creep out of the marina. As the yacht passed the breakwater jetty and sped up to fifteen knots, Yehuda drew a mental line from the seaport to Lokrum. He slackened the sails and dropped anchor at the midpoint.

He scrambled himself a half-dozen eggs. Reclining over the closed hatch, he rolled up his cargo pants and enjoyed breakfast under the sun, keeping the telescope and the Purdey within reach. It was a good place to camp—one that afforded a clear view of the harbor and of every craft within miles. His targets would not suspect he'd be here, positioned to ambush them. Occasionally, he stared at his watch and panned the seascape. Only a few hours to go.

As nine o'clock drew near, he began to feel nervous. Two full years had passed since he'd been given a way to find personal redemption, in an act as simple as taking the life of a twentysomething girl. And now, on top of protecting people and beliefs he held dear, he would be rich. The greatest challenges in his life—crossing vast regions of the Arabian Desert on foot, stealing supplies from roving barbarians while he had a broken arm, leading a failed rescue operation in his hometown—should have been experience enough to help him control his anxiety. But he needed his plan to work today, and his nerves had a will of their own, coming and going as naturally as the swells rocking the yacht.

Katharina

The cove between the western walls of the city and the triangular Fort Lovrijenac, or "Dubrovnik's Gibraltar" as it was sometimes called, concealed a dock where Kate and Moritz found the two watercraft they had rented. Sporting a twin-cylinder engine, the scooter, a British propeller-driven model called *Amanda*, manufactured by Vincent Motorcycles, had a T-shaped throttle and a narrow cushion for seating. Kate watched as Moritz ran a hand along her burnt-orange finish and white underbelly, admiring the way she glistened beside the other craft, a plain, wooden rowboat.

They dropped a pair of duffel bags on the jetty and unloaded their supplies. Kate extended the arms of the mannequin and taped its gloves to the throttle of the scooter, seating the rest of its body on the cushion. Moritz rigged the steering device by sliding the tops of the dowels into the dummy's gloves and fixing the solenoids to the floor of the craft. Next, he attached the gasoline can and fuse and tied a bag of heavy stones to the mannequin's feet at the rear. He fixed the pipe bomb to the port side of the fiberglass hull. Each fuse was connected to a glow plug, while the glow plugs and solenoids were wired to his signal receiver.

He handed Kate the transmitter.

"This controls direction," he said, pointing to a switch. "It has only three settings. Left, straight, and right. Since I had less than a day to rig this, I had to sacrifice maneuverability for simplicity. You won't be able to adjust the steepness of your turns. I suggest you practice with the controls here in this inlet for a few minutes. Get used to the sensitivity, and don't crash, please. This is our plan A, B, and C."

"Tell me about the other switches."

"Each of those can only be used once. The first is the pipe bomb. Use that when steering straight at him, when you're within fifty yards. When he starts to fire back, that's when you hit the second switch . . ."

"Which will eradicate our dummy?"

"Right."

"I'll use it wisely."

While she experimented with the controls, he changed into his wetsuit.

"What time is it?" he asked her.

"Eleven."

"Time for me to go," he said.

He secured the tank to his buoyancy compensator and tightened a weight belt around his hips, adjusting the position of the iron discs. He slipped his arms through the vest. The mask on his forehead was a one-piece wraparound with a tempered glass lens. He fastened a depth gauge to his wrist and strapped a titanium knife to one calf.

As he jumped off the dock, his splash was swept away by the mounting winds. He put his fins on in the water.

"We're going to rescue your mother and Colette," he said. "This is going to work."

Kate looked out at the sea, then back at him, wordless for a moment. She reached into the water and took his hand. He held onto it.

"I should get into position, and you should go," she said.

"Right. Good luck, Kate."

He gave her hand a final squeeze, then let go. Reducing his buoyancy, he sank a few feet. The water was cool, but not cold. He stiffened his body, catching a current that pulled him along the rim of the shore. The waves crashing against the bluffs of the inlet threatened to cast him into the rocks, but he kicked, struggling against a surge, and was soon free of the cove.

The sun shimmered over the water, and Kate watched Moritz's black, suited shape fade into the depths. She was on her own now; if anything went wrong, there would be no way to communicate with him.

She untied the scooter's mooring lines, oriented the craft seaward, and then spent a few minutes playing with the transmitter's controls, careful to avoid the switches for the explosives. Left, straight, right. She toggled among the three, watching the solenoids push and pull on the dowels, which in turn shifted the orientation of the throttle and the dummy.

At eleven forty-five, she powered on the *Amanda* and rammed the stick forward. The scooter zoomed away from the dock. Using the transmitter, she turned the throttle in both directions, executing a few circles and then a more ambitious figure eight, at all times keeping the craft within the cove. It was almost as natural as driving a car. Maybe a bit sensitive to starboard turns, but the rigging was bound to have quirks.

She moved west, scouting a trail for herself. Leaving the duffel bags on the jetty, she sprinted to the beach and followed a steep, gravelly footpath through a carpet of foliage. The path connected with another, this one pointing south along a headland, which she followed to Fort Lovrijenac at the tip of the promontory. A pole and sign, held down by a cluster of sandbags, blocked the entrance. She ducked under the barrier and raced up the steps to the top of the stronghold, emerging a hundred and twenty feet above sea level.

Her hair whipped her face. There was quite a gale up here, but it was worth the clear view of the inlet from the eastern rampart. The *Amanda* was still doing circles. Kate set the transmitter on the wall and eased the scooter into a straight line out of the cove.

The craft entered a swath of aquamarine waters separating the Dubrovnik peninsula from Lokrum to the southeast. Kate studied the panorama, spotting a tiny, fluttering speck of white halfway to the island.

A yacht.

There they were.

Her mother, Colette, and Yehuda would be aboard. She angled the *Amanda* toward them.

Yehuda, Moritz, and Katharina

Yehuda's watch read noon. Any moment now, he thought, cradling the Purdey.

He wondered what he would do if Kate hadn't convinced Moritz to visit Lokrum. Today's sail would be for naught; he would have to find another way to finish them. Brute force was the best alternative—he knew where they lived, and he had the firepower—though the kills would not be as clean, and he might end up with the police on his tail.

The current plan was much more promising; it took advantage of his hostages and the secrecy of his location. He knew he shouldn't worry. With Kate's mother and friend in captivity, he had every reason to trust in the young woman's conscience. She would respect his ultimatum and trade Moritz, practically a stranger to her, to protect them. Whether she turned herself in to save the baroness was irrelevant. Without Moritz to look after her, he would have no trouble tracking Kate.

He had thought over his next move after they were dead. Though he had earned the trust of his superiors, trust was a fragile thing in Mossad. He would not be able to deceive the agency indefinitely. They would begin piecing together a collection of facts suggesting that he had been pursuing his own agenda. He would try to deflect suspicions by framing Moritz, but they would come after him if this failed, and he would spend his life as an international fugitive, albeit a hundred thousand British pounds richer. It was a good thing he knew how to disappear.

He had decided he would return to Tel Aviv, gauge the severity of Mossad's suspicions, and vanish if necessary.

He smiled, thinking about the place he was about to earn in history. An anonymous place, no doubt. His name would not be remembered, but he would be the man who protected a hero—the man who saved the destroyer of the Speer spy ring from a girl who never learned that she alone could bring him down.

He hoped to meet Pendelfarr after this, not because he worked for the man, but because he admired his act of bravery in 'forty-two. Yehuda wondered what it must have been like to stand as a soldier of truth among those Jew-loving resistors, to know that any day he could be discovered and murdered. Whatever his aspirations had been, and whatever his vision for the globe, they were Yehuda's now, too. Defending the man was an honor, not to mention a good way to twist the knife into Israel's wounds.

He wondered what Conrad Pendelfarr looked like. Maybe he would find the man in Argentina and pay his respects. He could tell Conrad that his desire for a clean world lived in him, too, and that he would fight for it, and one day bring together others who shared the vision.

A buzzing noise pulled him from his ruminations. Feeling a flutter in his ribcage, he looked northwest through the telescope. A craft was zooming toward him at about fifteen or twenty knots, skipping over the swells. An orange scooter. He studied the rider, seeing a man wearing a cap and gloves and leaning into the throttle with an inflexible shoulder line. There was a kind of static determination on his face, a determination that seemed to hold his spine rigid.

The girl came through, he thought, pulling on the anchor lines. Moritz was crossing to Lokrum.

. . .

The water was so clear, Moritz would have been able to read a newspaper at a depth of eighty feet if he'd wanted to catch up on the morning headlines. Fluttering his fins, he held his body in a streamline, his arms and head in line with his torso to reduce resistance.

Below, tiny gobies with salt-and-pepper markings flittered over the rock pools. He remembered how, having grown up in proximity to World War II and the First Arab-Israeli War, he had spent many days of his childhood looking at birds and other critters immune to the complexities of human life. They hadn't a real concern, he'd thought with envy; they only needed to worry about food. He was thinking the same thought again now.

He breathed in through the regulator and let out a stream of bubbles that trailed behind him in an ascending line. Covering this distance on one tank, with a pulse raised from exertion, would not be easy at depth. He'd been careful to control his oxygen intake and keep to shallow waters, never below ten feet.

Somewhere in the mid-fifties Fahrenheit, the sea had begun to chill him, even through his wetsuit. He kicked harder, working up his body heat. Now and then he would surface, careful not to show much of himself, and he'd adjust his direction toward the yacht. After a few course corrections, he went down a final time. Yards ahead, he could see the shape of the keel, and he propelled himself onward with renewed stamina.

He was close enough now that Yehuda might have been able to spot him at his shallow depth. Planning to rise from beneath, he angled himself toward the sea floor and kicked hard. The sun cast its rays onto the rocks, sand, and coral below. Reaching thirty feet, he leveled off and swam parallel to the rock bed until he glided into the yacht's shadow.

He could hear the drone of an engine. Kate was early. He tilted his mask and blew air through his nostrils to clear away the water. Then he glanced up, just in time to see an anchor disappearing above. To the south, a small craft was zipping through the water toward the sloop, which would soon begin to drift and sail away. He shot toward the surface with outstretched arms, reaching for the yacht's keel.

. . .

From the fort, Kate toggled her steering switch to the right and watched as the *Amanda* executed a starboard turn at fifteen knots. She squinted, trying to see what was happening aboard the *Lady Louise*. It looked as though the sails were being drawn taut. The yacht had begun to slice through the water and follow the scooter. Yehuda was taking the bait. She could imagine him leaning over the gunwales, fixing his telescope on the dummy, waiting to get close enough to fire.

She straightened the *Amanda*'s path and took her to port, following a broad arc toward the stern of her target. She could only hope that she had given Moritz enough time to reach the yacht. The scooter took on a straight path when she flipped the switch to its center position. She placed a finger over the detonator that controlled the glow plug attached to the pipe bomb's fuse. Allowing the scooter to approach the *Lady Louise* from behind, she waited for the distance between the two vessels to narrow. Sixty yards, fifty, forty . . .

Any more than thirty yards, and Yehuda might see the dummy for what it was. The *Amanda* had reached the ideal distance. She pushed the button.

. . .

Yehuda heard a loud bang.

Peering through his spyglass, he made out the shape of a rifle in the approaching rider's clutches. The bastard was firing at him. He felt a tinge of worry. Had Moritz lost his mind? There were hostages aboard, and Moritz had no way of knowing they were sheltered in the cabin. He had emerged from the cove between Fort Lovrijenac and Bokar Tower and come zooming toward the *Lady Louise* on a shooting rampage.

Realizing he had lost the element of surprise, Yehuda wondered how Moritz had known he'd be waiting here, and how the man had found such a powerful rifle. Kate must have told him everything. She'd made a fatal mistake. Seating the stock of the Purdey into his shoulder, Yehuda took aim at the orange scooter. He still had the advantage. Moritz was exposed.

Still, something told Yehuda this was too good to be true. He knew his opponent to be smarter than to make himself such an easy target. Did Moritz really think he could win by skipping across the waves, without cover, in a blaze of glory?

Something was wrong, but whatever it was, Yehuda couldn't risk losing his shot. He fired off the stern.

. . .

The explosion of the pipe bomb could be heard echoing off the ramparts of Lovrijenac. It must have been earsplitting closer to the water, Kate imagined, watching as the *Amanda* trailed behind the sloop under her directives. Seconds passed, and there was a second crack, just as she'd hoped. Yehuda was firing back.

A voice from the bottom of the fort startled her. Something had been said in Serbo-Croatian. She cursed. Two policemen standing on the rocks below had seen her. They were banging against the lower wall and shouting for her attention.

"I don't understand," she called back. "Do you speak English?"

The police exchanged glances.

"You cannot be there," one yelled up at her from ground level. "The fortress, it's closed on Christmas Day."

"A few photographs, and I'll be right down," she said.

"Come *now*."

"Just two minutes, please!"

"You have ignored obvious barriers."

Two minutes was more than she really needed.

"It's for a photo album," she said. "I'm almost finished."

"You are trespassing. We apprehend you if you not comply immediately."

She said nothing. The officers did not look pleased, and she could see they had begun scrambling about the rocks toward the fort's entrance. God, they were about to ruin everything, and all she needed was the right opportunity to set off the gasoline. Fire, Yehuda, she thought—fire again, fast! Apparently, he was taking careful aim.

Footsteps resonated in the chambers below until the policemen came out at her level.

"Let's go," said one, striding alongside her and grabbing her arm.

Her spirits sank when the other asked, "What's in your hand?" He pointed to the transmitter. "That's not camera. What are you doing?"

"This gadget helps me get a read on the light and conditions. I had hoped to come later with my camera and tripod and take some photographs to bring to my family."

The first officer looked skeptical. He took the device and began to inspect it.

"We hear talk of an agent from Belgrade who has come to town looking for Welsh woman," he said. "The agent has been saying she and accomplice murdered someone in government."

"I don't know what you're talking about," Kate said, trying to sound American.

"We will sort this at the station."

She searched for another excuse. "I'm with Geoffrey Barkas," she said.

"Who?"

"He and his crew have been filming a documentary here. I'm one of his production assistants. Just ask him."

"Ah, film director." The officer shook his head. "How you propose we ask him if he left town yesterday?"

"Ask any of the other production assistants who have stayed behind to take photographs," she said, reaching for the device in his hand. He pulled it away and strengthened his grip on her arm.

"Don't try anything," he said. "You come with us now."

From over the water came the distant boom of a second shotgun blast.

"What was that?" said one officer.

"Who cares?" answered the other, escorting Kate down the stairs. "We have the suspect. Let's go."

. . .

Swimming along the underside of the yacht, Moritz hooked his elbow around the fin keel as the craft began to accelerate. The sways of the boat nearly shook him off, but he held tight, flexing his abs to keep his body in a streamline. If the current claimed him, he knew he would not be able to catch up with the *Lady Louise* again.

He checked his pressure gauge and found he had a modest twenty bars remaining. Given his heavy exertion in these cool waters, he was consuming air at an elevated rate. He guessed he had a minute or two. He tempered his breathing to conserve oxygen and fought to bring his pulse down to double digits.

How would he ever make his way to the upper deck while the boat was slicing through the water? The hull was slick and offered no handholds.

The yacht tacked, veering to port, and Moritz heard the clank of his cylinder on concrete as his body slammed against the ballast. His bent elbow began to hurt like hell. The pressure was so great he almost wished his joint would just snap already, but he couldn't let go. Yehuda was only a few feet away, on the sloop's deck.

. . .

Yehuda fired a third shot and watched as the scooter peeled off on a diagonal trajectory, no longer riding his wake. At last Moritz was showing some sense. He must have realized he was about to be blown to bits.

"Come on," Yehuda muttered. "Come at me. One more time."

Was Moritz going to keep running? He was no longer within shooting range. Would he circle back and continue the gunfight?

Oddly, the scooter tilted sideways and began zipping about in a circle. Yehuda watched him complete one loop after another, each about ten yards in radius. What was he doing? Was this some kind of bait? He couldn't imagine how. This didn't look like a trap.

He looked through the telescope again, training his view on the other craft's lateral movement to study the rider, who appeared to be leaning into the wind. As far as he could tell, Moritz was unharmed, though there was something awkward about his stance. His legs and upper body looked uncannily still. Yehuda would have expected to see movement, a shift of weight as he maneuvered the craft. He hadn't changed the position of his rifle, either.

He wondered: Did I hit him? Is he conscious?

What am I missing?

He tacked the sloop again, beating to windward to stay on the scooter's tail.

. . .

This can't be happening, Kate thought. Sixty seconds more were all she had needed. *This cannot be happening!*

Without her steering, she could only wonder what strange figures the *Amanda* had begun to trace over the water. If the scooter behaved too erratically, Yehuda would know something was amiss, and if he sailed too close, he would see the dummy for what it was. She had only one hope: that Moritz had already climbed aboard the yacht. Not likely. He'd hardly had enough time to reach the keel from below.

The officer's grip was making her bicep sore. She listened to the cadence of the nearer policeman's footsteps as the two uniformed men escorted her down a stone stairwell through the fort's antechambers. Learning his rhythm, she kicked her leg forward a microsecond before the man's foot could make contact with the ground. He tripped, dropping the transmitter. It landed on a step. Damn—had it broken? She dove for it, snatched it up, and ran.

"Hey!" the fallen officer bellowed. "Stop!"

She didn't look back as the man clambered to his feet. She knew what she would see; both men would be charging after her. She was also aware of the consequences of fleeing. Soon authorities throughout Dubrovnik would be after her. These two were already on her tail, at most five seconds behind.

She took the steps three at a time, careful not to trip over her feet. That would surely be the end of her escape. She ducked her head to avoid scraping the low ceiling. There was a door at the bottom. She pushed through it and slammed it shut, then spotted the sandbags holding down the sign forbidding entrance to the fort. She wedged two of them against the door, impeding its swing.

Make that thirty seconds of lead time. Maybe a little longer if they didn't see where she was running.

There was a bang at the door, followed by a stream of shouts she could not understand. She moved east through the shrubs and took a footpath toward the cove, where the rowboat was docked. She threw off the mooring lines and ran the boat to the end of the jetty, where she leaped inside, dropping the oars into the rowlocks.

Facing astern, she pulled the oars to her chest with all her strength. She was clumsy at first, but her coordination improved with the first few rows. The boat wobbled less with each stroke, and soon she reached the mouth of the inlet.

She glanced back. The officers had found a way out. They were seventy yards behind, scanning the rocks and brambles for their escaped captive. She crouched down, holding her head beneath the gunwales, waiting for the boat to drift behind the promontory of Fort Bokar.

As soon as she was out of sight, she looked out at the open sea. The *Amanda* was spinning in circles. Her view at sea level was not optimal, but she would manage. Please, please, don't be broken, she thought as she handled the transmitter. She flipped the steering switch and heaved a sigh of relief as the scooter straightened its path.

The yacht was headed straight for the *Amanda*. She stood up on two legs for a better view, finding her balance, and steered the scooter after the *Lady Louise*.

There was a sharp crack as the paths converged. Yes! Yehuda had fired again, but she hadn't been quite ready. She was now. Her finger hovered over the switch to the gasoline can.

"One more shot," she whispered. "Come on, take it!"

. . .

Yehuda loaded the Purdey with another shell, took aim, and fired at the oncoming scooter. There was a deep growl over the water as a ball of flame erupted from the small craft and sent a column of smoke into the atmosphere. The scooter sputtered to a stop, leaning on its side like an injured animal. Yehuda sailed closer, jockeying the sloop alongside the wreckage, seeing a cracked and shattered hull. He decided he must have ruptured the fuel tank.

He searched the water for Moritz's body but didn't find anything, figuring the corpse had drifted away or snagged a heavy piece of debris. Shaking his head, he felt the adrenaline in his veins subside.

So that was it. It had been a pathetic way for Moritz to go, sacrificing himself for a girl he hadn't known more than a few weeks, so she could live a few hours longer at most.

The hard part was over. He set down the Purdey, let out the sails, and dropped anchor again. To the northwest, he saw a rowboat approaching. Through the telescope, he saw the only passenger was Katharina Speer herself. She was rowing toward him. *It was working.*

. . .

Still clinging to the keel, Moritz felt triumphant as he watched the stone-strapped dummy sink to the sea floor.

The pain in his elbow became manageable as the yacht came to a halt. An anchor dropped from the surface, trailing behind it a rope. He breathed in a final lungful from his regulator, then released all the air from his buoyancy compensator, unstrapped his vest, and removed his weight belt. He swam along the sloop's hull and came up beneath the bow quietly—no sudden gasps.

Slipping his fins and mask off, he spotted Yehuda at the stern, studying the destroyed scooter. This would be his best opportunity to climb aboard. He looped the anchor line around an exterior cleat and hoisted himself aloft, grabbing hold of a gunwale, and then unfastened the loop to hide his trace.

He concealed himself behind the elevated roof of the cabin and peered out to see if Yehuda had noticed him. The man seemed oblivious. Perhaps he should attack now, he thought, but he discarded the idea when he saw the man was still clutching the Purdey.

He crab-walked along the starboard edge as Yehuda circled around the port side toward the bow. Through the cabin window, Moritz could see Colette Fossey and Lona Atwell gagged and tied to chairs, back to back.

Their eyes grew wide at the sight of him. With a few extra seconds, he might have been able to free them, but Yehuda was moving again.

Moritz opened the door a crack and slid his knife along the floor toward the women. He then backed away, keeping out of Yehuda's view.

Lona

Lona didn't know who the man was, but he did not look like a policeman. What mattered was that he was apparently on her side—and didn't seem to realize Colette was not.

She thrust her weight upward, letting her foot come down on the knife before Colette could nab it. Behind her, Colette began jumping in her chair, fighting against her bonds, making as much noise as she could manage through the handkerchief over her mouth. Lona knew she was trying to get Yehuda's attention so she could tell him he had an unbidden passenger.

"Stop it," Lona tried to say through her gag.

Colette kicked her head back, landing a blow to Lona's skull. The girl continued to scream and thrash. Yehuda must have heard something. Lona could hear his steps along the companionway . . .

She had to hide the knife. She pinched it between her ankle bone and the leg of the chair, feeding it up to the tips of her stretching, wiggling fingers. Though the movement in her feet and wrists was limited, she managed to grab the handle on the second try.

"You will not warn him!" she tried to tell Colette. Her voice was unintelligible.

Yehuda pushed the door open.

"What's going on in here?" he said.

Colette wriggled in her bonds, her eyes fluttering. She squealed through the handkerchief in her mouth. He regarded her like a child throwing a tantrum and did not make an immediate move to untie her. Lona could imagine what was going through his head: Colette had protested when he gagged her, so he would just see this as rebellion.

He looked angry to have been disturbed.

"Is there a problem?" he said.

Lona shook her head calmly, while Colette nodded a vigorous *yes.*

Colette's wrist was inches away from Lona's. Lona had a greater range of movement on her right side. She had worked a bit of slack into the rope, which was why she had taken hold of the knife there. She was far from freeing herself, but she at least could rotate her hand a few degrees. The knife was wrapped in her palm, concealed.

"I'm getting contradictory answers," Yehuda said.

Colette made a gurgling noise and began heaving, apparently in the midst of stomach convulsions. The girl was trying to make him think she would vomit, so he would remove her gag and prevent her from choking. He still needed her alive and well.

Her little trick worked. Yehuda slipped the handkerchief off her mouth. Lona felt a clamp of fear as her hope of rescue was about to be exposed.

Thinking quickly, she pushed the tip of the blade into Colette's wrist and used her thumb against the underside to drive it in further. She applied enough pressure to break the skin. Colette straightened, startled by the pain. She tried to move her hand away, but the bonds were too tight, her forearm immobile.

"What's going on?" Yehuda said, no less furious.

Sensing Colette's indecision, Lona drew the knife's edge along the girl's ulnar vein. Surely Colette would realize she was of little value to Yehuda out at sea with a slit wrist.

"Say something, dammit!" Yehuda said.

"I have to piss," she said.

"Then piss."

"And . . . I was suffocating," Colette said. "I thought I was going to throw up."

"Breathe through your nose," he said.

"That's not all. I saw . . ."

Lona pushed the knife in harder, drawing blood. Anything to help Colette reconsider.

"I saw . . ." Colette went on stammering, all the while wincing, and Lona could feel her weighing the risk, wondering whether Lona had it in her to make a lethal vertical incision.

"Stop wasting time," Yehuda said.

"I . . . heard gunshots, and wanted to find out if you killed Moritz Dahl."

"Yes," he said. "Now Kate's on her way."

"Then untie me," Colette said.

"When the job is done."

"Are you sure you saw him die? What if he's still—"

Lona held her breath, digging in deeper, twisting the blade.

"Still what?" Yehuda said.

"Out there."

"He died in an explosion. I watched it happen."

"You're sure?"

Yehuda smacked her face with his knuckles, hard enough to leave a welt on her cheek. He seated the gag over her mouth again.

"Don't waste time when I'm this close."

He went back outside, and Lona began to slice at her own bonds.

Katharina

Kate knew she might be rowing to her death.

With a high probability, any number of things could have gone wrong. Moritz might never have reached the yacht. Yehuda may have gotten suspicious at the sound of the pipe bomb or the sight of the gasoline explosion. The stones may have detached from the dummy. The list went on. Then again, there was a chance everything had worked. She could only trust that the pieces had fallen into place. Turning back now would mean the death of Colette and her mother.

A siren blared somewhere behind her within the walls of Old Town, giving her even more reason not to turn back. The officers must have reported back to the station. A full-fledged search would be underway soon. She had no desire to run into any authorities again and wondered if they would dispatch patrol boats. The thought made her stroke faster.

She looked ahead, not more than a hundred yards from the *Lady Louise*. Yehuda was waiting for her, his arms folded. He was leaning against the guardrails. Her stomach wrenched at the sight of him. She began to remember her terror during that night in Paris when he had tried to murder her. She had only been more afraid once in her life, during her escape from Germany. Paris had been a close second.

After a few minutes, she was close enough for him to hear her.

"I did what you said," she shouted. "Now let one of them go."

"Keep rowing and they both live," he said back.

"Release one first."

"You are in no position to make demands."

"We had an agreement."

"We never 'agreed' to anything."

"I want to see my mother," she said. "I'm not going anywhere until I do."

Yehuda lifted the shotgun.

"I suggest you stay the course."

She took several more strokes toward the *Lady Louise*. Moritz, she thought, you had better be aboard that sloop, or we three women are as good as dead.

She maneuvered the rowboat alongside the yacht. Yehuda helped her aboard.

"It will be less painful this way," he said as she flipped over the gunwales and landed on deck.

She looked him in the eye, sensing his excitement. He must have worked hard for this.

"Aren't you going to tell me what this is about?" she asked. "Why you've been trying to kill me? This can't be about the painting that Maxence said I stole."

"It's better you don't find out."

"For whose sake? Mine, or yours?"

"Neither. A man you met once, long ago. Someone you've forgotten."

"Fine," she said. "All that matters to me is that you hold up your end of the deal."

With a glance about the deck, she began to wonder where Moritz could be hiding if he was here. There was no sign of him. Had he made it?

Yehuda pushed her into the cabin. Her heart quickened when she saw his two captives bound to each other.

"Mum! Colette!"

Lona groaned beneath the handkerchief, looking wide-eyed at Colette and then at Yehuda, shaking her head. Colette was fighting the ropes that restrained her, squealing.

"Free them!" Kate said. "It's my life for theirs."

"Not anymore," he said. "Time's up for all three of you."

Kate tried to strike him. He grabbed her by the torso and flung her down to the floor. She fell on her knees, and then rose to embrace Lona and Colette.

Yehuda took a step forward, setting down the shotgun. He produced his blade.

"So that's your plan?" Kate roared at him. "Slit our throats and dump us?"

"Shhh," Yehuda said with a finger to his lips. "It'll be quick."

Kate pulled the gags below the chins of both Lona and Colette. At once, they began to scream over each other.

"There's a man onboard!" Colette said.

"She's working with him!" Lona said.

Kate could make no sense of what she was hearing. But she saw a knife in her mother's hand. As she listened to them both, she reached for it and cut Lona free. First a leg, then an arm . . .

Lona grabbed the knife from her, pivoted in her chair, and shoved the blade into Colette's chest.

Colette let out a shrill cry.

Kate herself shrieked.

"MUM! What—are—you—*doing?*"

Tears streamed from her eyes as Colette bled.

"Stay away from my daughter!" Lona shouted.

Colette was hardly moving. Kate knelt beside her, seeing terror and shock in her eyes. She untied one of her friend's arms.

"Why did you? What's going on?" Kate shouted at her mother.

"She's with him!" Lona shot back. "You can't trust her!"

Kate shook her head. "What are you talking about? He *kidnapped* her!" She took Colette by the shoulders. "Stay here, Colette. We'll find you a doctor! I don't know what's gotten into Mum!"

Colette was no longer looking at her. Her gaze had drifted to Yehuda.

"Listen," she tried to say through a hacking cough. "There's a . . . man onboard . . ."

He leaned closer: "What did you say?"

Kate paused. Had Colette actually tried to warn him?

She whispered into her friend's ear, "No, Colette . . . if you saw a man—he's with us."

"That girl is a treacherous whore!" Lona bellowed. "Can't you see, Kate? She's working with this monster! She stood back while I watched him kill Clive Mountjoy and George!"

Colette shook her head. "Your mum has gone mad," she said, her voice a labored whisper. "Don't just stand there while I have a knife in my chest. Help me!"

Kate stood frozen, watching her mother, and said, "What did you say about George and Clive?"

"Yehuda killed them both! Your father is dead!"

"That's ridiculous," Colette said. Her eyes widened. "Yehuda . . . watch *out!*"

Summoning her energy, Colette pointed at the door, and Yehuda spun around.

He was too late. The portal smashed open, and Moritz dove into the cabin, knocking Yehuda to the ground. Yehuda tumbled backward, landing a foot from Lona.

"Give me that knife, Colette!" he said.

Kate could hardly believe her ears. Yehuda had *asked* Colette for the knife.

Colette tugged at her wound and tried to free the blade. Lona hit her in the stomach. She screamed with pain, unable to remove the weapon. Kate realized that she was trying to give it to him.

"Colette, *now*!" Yehuda said.

Dear God, she *had* been helping him.

Face contorted with anger, Moritz struck Yehuda in the neck. Yehuda tried to pull himself away. He reached for the shotgun, but Moritz snatched it first and held the barrel against Yehuda's chin.

"Everybody freeze!" Moritz shouted.

Kate looked Colette in the eye. "What have you done? You *helped* this man? Are George and Clive really dead?"

Kate saw more terror than physical pain in Colette's expression. And there was something else there: loathing.

Colette hawked up a wad of blood and saliva and spat it in Kate's face. "Stay back, bitch."

Kate was mystified. It was as if there were a demon in her friend's body.

"Colette . . . how can you do this to me! Is George really . . . ?" She couldn't bear to finish.

"George wasn't your father," Colette snapped. "Your father died twenty years ago. I know who he was. I know what his people did to my parents. I know everything. And I'm about to reveal it all to this worthless, pampered hag you call your mum!" Her face was drained of color. "Oh, no, you better stop me before I reveal your secret!"

Kate felt helpless as Colette proved herself to be an utter stranger. An ocean of heartache seemed to leak up through the yacht's floorboards; she was sinking in it.

"Go ahead," Kate said. "Tell her. Please."

Colette looked to Yehuda for help, but he was still pinned by Moritz, the shotgun at his chin. Cornered, she bared her teeth at Lona. "How many times did I say your 'daughter' isn't who you think she is, *Madame la Baronne*?"

"Do explain," Lona said acidly. "I'm sure it will shatter my universe."

"She never told you much about her real father, did she? An Austrian farmer? Hah! He was a German executioner. Ralf Friedrich Speer, Vice Minister of Propaganda under Joseph Goebbels. You heard me. A high-ranking Nazi minister!"

Lona's face twitched briefly before she fell back into her calm.

"I'm sorry," Lona said, shrugging, and looking directly at Kate. "I've suspected as much for years, but I missed the part where you told me something important about my *daughter*."

Kate felt a burden lift. All this time, she had been guarding her identity from her parents, hiding her true self from the people who loved her most, and her mother already knew. She had been a fool.

"She's *still* a Nazi sympathizer, helping ratline escapees," Colette said, groaning as she bled out into her clothes. "Yehuda has all the evidence."

When Yehuda tried to sit up, Moritz struck him in the cheekbone with the shotgun barrel, digging a gouge that made him bleed.

"I'm sure it was good enough for you to believe," Lona said as she yanked the blade from Colette's wound and finished freeing herself. She then held the edge to Colette's trachea.

"You won't," Colette said, though the certainty of her words belied her pleading voice. "You're a baroness. A woman of refinement. You are *Lady* Atwell."

"No, Mum," Kate said, imploring. "Don't!"

"Listen to your daughter!" Colette said.

"You haven't seen what I've seen, Kate," Lona said. "She betrayed our family. She stood by this monster after he killed George and Clive. She washed away the blood after he murdered the owner of this boat. She helped him find you. I've been with them every step of the way."

"But—" Kate started to say.

"She betrayed you, Kate. She wants you dead." Lona leaned into Colette's pale, freckled face, practically nose to nose. "No one threatens my child."

Colette threw her head back to try to free herself. Her hand shot out, going for Lona's knife.

Lona slapped her hand down, and flicked the knife across Colette's throat.

Kate fell into her mother's arms and began to sob.

Katharina

Twilight fell.

Moritz sailed the yacht to the southernmost tip of Lokrum and dropped anchor in a cove hidden from the view of Old Town, keeping Yehuda sedated with his own chloroform. They swam ashore, dragging him in tow, as the stars began to peek out.

Kate and her mother buried Colette deep within the island's thicket of evergreen oaks and bushes. Lona did not stay at her grave, though Kate spent minutes standing in silence over the mound of dirt and brambles, doubting she could ever comprehend the reasons for Colette's deceit. Kneeling in the underbrush, she picked a little white flower, whose shape and color reminded her of the snowbell Karl Decker had given her on the night of her escape.

"For the times I had hoped we would share," she said, holding it over the mound of soil where Colette was buried, "and for the times I was foolish enough to cherish."

Her hand quaked, and she closed her eyes. An image of Clive Mountjoy came to mind—his bald head, his folded arms, his courteous yet opinionated smile. He saluted her, and the vision of him blew away, replaced by a scene with George. He was leaning back on his chaise longue, whiskey on the table, pipe in hand, a Conan Doyle book in his lap. She breathed in his distinctive scent of Scotch and tobacco and listened to his jolly, gravelly laughter. He knocked back his whiskey and blew her a kiss. Then he, too, disappeared.

She did not drop the flower; she tossed it away.

Kate headed back to shore and found Moritz and her mother on the beach. Lona was kindling a campfire using matches, dried leaves, and sticks. Soon it was blazing. Moritz stripped Yehuda and sat him on the ground with his ankles tied and his arms bound behind his back. He slapped Yehuda's cheeks with one hand and took hold of the Purdey with the other.

"Wake up."

The man cracked his eyes open and stammered, "Where are we?"

"Lokrum, at your suggestion," Moritz said. "Lean back. Slowly."

When he tried to do so, Yehuda jolted upright, feeling his shoulder blades scrape the edge of the campfire.

"Now that you understand your position," Moritz said, resting the barrel of the shotgun on his captive's chest, "you will answer my questions."

Yehuda smirked. "This isn't your style, Moritz. You're too soft for this."

Kate shuddered through the silence that followed. There was a glint in Moritz's eye that suggested a side of him she hadn't seen yet.

"The last time I came out of sedation," he said, "I was at the bottom of the Seine with my feet tied. Look at me and tell me if you see much pity. Why have you been trying to murder Kate Atwell?"

"I think we all know by now that's not who she really is."

"Did Mossad send you?"

"No."

"Did anyone in the Israeli government?"

"No."

"Who hired you? Give me a name."

"*Hero*. That's his name."

Moritz pushed harder. "Quit stalling."

Yehuda stared back at Moritz, saying nothing. Moritz pushed on the handle of the shotgun, forcing him closer to the fire.

"Her employer," Yehuda said, scrunching up his face.

"Maxence?"

"No. He thought we were just going to keep her quiet about the forgery. But she had to be shut up about . . . *everything*."

"Who had to shut her up?"

"I assume you've learned about Speer's spy ring by now," Yehuda said. "The information network that helped win the Desert War for the Allies."

"We have."

"Ralf Speer had sixteen artists working for him in his basement, making copies of paintings that were ostensibly being sold to collectors. The business was a cover, a way for him to disseminate the secrets he picked up as a confidante of Hitler and Goebbels." Yehuda grinned. "One of the sixteen ratted on him and his fellow Jew-lovers."

"Who?" Moritz said.

"A man named Heinrich Jecklyn."

So, it was true, Kate thought.

"Explain," Moritz said, pushing him toward the flames again. Yehuda's back must have been searing. Kate wondered if his skin would crackle. She'd never have imagined she could stand to watch something like this.

"Jecklyn made a deal with the Nazis," Yehuda said. "He would hand over the artists in Speer's resistance network. In return, he would be allowed to leave Germany and bring the remaining forgeries with him. Goebbels accepted. Jecklyn left Germany with the paintings."

"What happened to Jecklyn?"

"He changed his name to Conrad Pendelfarr." Kate and Lona took in a sharp breath. Pendelfarr. Kate's employer, indeed, at the highest level, whom she had never met, whose reputation in the artistic world was legendary. He was the man who betrayed her father. And now he was after her. "Started an international art brokerage firm after the war ended. Some of his most profitable pieces over the years have been these forgeries."

"Why is he after Kate?"

"After Speer's artists were slaughtered, there was only one person who knew Jecklyn's face, who could piece things together and destroy his new life if they crossed paths. That was young Katharina. He might have left her alone if she hadn't suggested going to the police about the forgery she'd discovered. After that, he figured he could kill two birds with one stone."

"He found you to help him kill her. How?"

Yehuda tried not to answer, hoping Moritz would think he had answered enough. He was wrong. Moritz tipped him into the fire again. Kate could see the blisters forming along his spine. By all appearances, the man had a remarkable pain threshold—even as his body shook, he did not cry out—but everyone had a limit, and the idea of being pushed closer into the fire seemed to agitate him.

"After Mossad's capture of Adolf Eichmann," he said, "Jecklyn worried he'd somehow be found and tried for war crimes. He needed a way to monitor Mossad. He sent a team of private eyes to Israel, looking for moles to put on his payroll. They found me two years ago, in Tel Aviv."

"What kind of monster betrays Mossad to work for a Nazi?" Lona interjected.

"You don't know the first thing about my life, old crone."

"I know what you've done."

"How did you find Kate?" Moritz said.

"I've told you enough."

Moritz struck him again across the face with the Purdey's double barrel. Yehuda took several moments to recover, still saying nothing.

"Guess you prefer fire, then," Moritz said.

"Wait."

"Start talking."

"Maxence is a partner in the company. In 'fifty-five, he was invited by Pendelfarr to become the French regional director of Pendelfarr International. His job was to find new clients and art purchases in Paris."

Kate was astonished. "Victor Maxence knows who I am?"

"He knew Pendelfarr was trying to find you. When you came to his office asking about Ralf Speer, he got suspicious and made some calls. He thought he'd found you. At the same time, I had befriended Moritz within Sayeret Matkal, and he shared the unusual task his mother had left him—to locate Katharina Speer."

"So, you used Moritz to find out if Maxence was right that he'd found me?" Kate said.

Yehuda's smile gave her the answer.

"And Maxence had no trouble turning me over," Kate said, "knowing Pendelfarr wanted me dead?"

"His reputation was in danger, as was his income from Pendelfarr International."

"Where's Jecklyn now?" Moritz said.

"I wouldn't tell you in a thousand years."

Moritz thrust him into the flames. He yowled at last, twitching and squirming as the fire scorched his skin. Kate was surprised she felt no need to cover her eyes anymore. Eight seconds later, Moritz relented and said, "Tell me."

Yehuda spat at him. "Why, so you can kill him?"

"We haven't decided."

"You'll have to burn me to cinder before I give him up."

"Whatever he's paying you, you aren't going to see the money," Lona said. "You're not getting off this island alive."

"Money was a perk."

"What was this about, then?" Kate said.

"Honoring Jecklyn's bravery."

"Bravery?" Lona said. "He sent sixteen resistors, all good men and women, to their deaths!"

Yehuda's face flushed, his forehead moist with sweat.

"Those artists conspired to poison our race. All the resistors were guilty of it, guilty of saving the Jews who . . ."

"Who what?" Moritz said.

"Who brainwashed me, took me from my family, and later forced me to kill my parents and sisters!"

"Everything you've done here has been an effort to absolve yourself," Moritz sneered. "You blame the entire Jewish people for things that only you have done."

"You don't know me!" Yehuda yelled at him, attempting to hurl himself at Moritz and knock the Purdey from his hands. Moritz backhanded him and then held the barrel to Yehuda's crotch.

"Go ahead, try that again," Moritz said. "Give me a reason me to shoot your manhood into the flames."

"You on your high pedestal. You'll never understand why I—"

"I already do," Moritz said. "You think helping Jecklyn redeems you."

"No. You're the guilty one. For helping the daughter of that Jew-lover, Ralf Speer."

Moritz added pressure again, tilting him closer to the fire. "You'd murder Kate, me, and countless others. At the cost of your own life, you won't give up Jecklyn's location. You're a danger to this world and no longer any use to us."

Yehuda looked up at him and said, smiling, "I die a knight."

The blast resounded through the forest. Yehuda's wails were subdued as he buried his head in the fire.

. . .

"I'm sorry you two had to watch that," Moritz said. "As difficult and exhausting as this day has been, we should keep moving and start the drive back to Paris."

"I imagine you'll be having a similar chat with Victor Maxence," Kate said. "He'll be the one to take us to Jecklyn."

"Do you know where Maxence lives?"

"No, but I can find out."

"Good. Now let's get ourselves back to the mainland."

They swam to the yacht and sailed a short distance northwest.

"I can't show my face," Kate said. "The police are looking for me."

She filled him in on the reason, and they took caution to keep her out of view on the way back to the Renault parked outside the city walls.

Kate and Lona waited in the car while Moritz ran back to their apartment to fetch their belongings and the Bouguereau.

Kate took her mother in her arms.

"Mum, I can't believe what you've been through. I am so sorry. For everything."

"From the moment we adopted you, I've always said you were our best Christmas present," Lona said, kissing Kate's cheek gently. "You were then, and you always will be."

"You know I love you, too. And I realize it may not have always seemed . . . I mean, I wasn't the most affectionate, as I was with George."

"You wanted a father in whose goodness you could trust. You never realized you had always had it. Neither did I. Now, we'll be strong together," Lona said. "But between the two of us, you must be stronger. This is the second father you've lost. My darling, about that—I hope you know that through all your years growing up, it wouldn't have mattered a whit to us if we'd known exactly where you came from. Even before you knew Speer was a good man. We love you for the remarkable soul that *you* are. That's all that matters."

Kate held her cheek against her mother's. "We have the rest of our lives."

"We do," Lona said. "And if it's your wish to find and finish this Heinrich Jecklyn, I want you to know that I'll stand behind you. All the way."

Katharina

They could see the Eiffel Tower in the distance. The City of Light was glowing through the rain on the windshield.

Kate stared through the window, mesmerized by the patter of the rain and the swishing of the windshield wipers. Moritz was behind the wheel. They had spent December 26 through 30 driving back to Paris. Along the way, they left Lona in Milan, where she took a plane to Wales to arrange a proper burial of George and Clive. The drive had been more or less continuous, broken only by breaks for food in cities and villages.

Kate yawned and might have fallen asleep, but Moritz had asked for her help navigating as they approached from the south. She knew the city better than he did and guided him to the Rue Dauphine, where he parked and followed her to her apartment.

"It's going to feel empty inside," she said. "I don't know how I'll go through Colette's things, or what to say when I contact her relatives."

"You don't have to think about that now," Moritz said. "Save that till after we've had our tête-à-tête with Maxence tomorrow."

As they went upstairs, they found a woman waiting for them at the top of the stairwell. She was sitting alone in a chair outside Kate's apartment. The lady looked to be in her early sixties. A white cane was folded on her lap. Her eyes were shut, her expression peaceful and somber, like a woman in prayer. Her face had begun to take on the wrinkles of age, though in places her skin was taut, contracted, and discolored. Her left eye drooped a bit, pulled down by what Kate realized were old burn scars.

"Hello," Kate said. "Can we help you?"

"Are you Katharina Speer?" the woman said.

Kate paused in surprise. "Yes."

"Then it is I who have come to help you. Are you traveling with your new friend, Anwar Taha?"

Kate looked at Moritz, who nodded permission for the disclosure.

"Yes, though he goes by a different name."

"Call me Moritz," he said.

"I see," said the woman.

"And you are?" Kate said, noting the woman's Galway accent.

"A friend of Geoffrey Barkas," she answered. "He sent me a message saying you were curious about the spy ring in which your father, Kate—and your mother, Anwar—were key players. His message included your address in Paris. I got here a few hours ago."

"Where did you come from?"

"London."

"My goodness! You could have called or sent a telegram."

"I prefer to speak with someone in person and hear a voice. It's my best means of perceiving people, and in this particular case, I was especially curious."

"What is your name?"

"Evanna," said the woman. "Evanna Bray."

"Bray, as in . . ."

"Geoffrey told you about my late husband, Damien."

"Please come inside," Kate said, trying to stay even-keeled. Was she *really*? "It's chilly here. Do you like tea?"

"How kind. I do."

The woman took Kate by the arm, and Kate escorted her to a sofa inside. Kate gathered some fruit cookies on a plate and prepared a kettle of Earl Gray. She could hardly believe that sitting on her couch was the wife of the man who had nearly handed the Desert War to the Germans. What did the woman want? Could she even be trusted? Damien Bray had been a traitor to the British, and Evanna ostensibly had been in love with him.

At least she looked harmless enough to have in for tea.

"You have nothing to fear," Evanna said almost telepathically. "I may have loved the man at one point in time, but I am not my husband."

"Of course you aren't," Kate said politely, thinking it remarkable how far the blind often could see without their eyes.

"Geoffrey said you are intent on uncovering the truth about Speer's resistance network."

"We are."

"I might know a thing or two."

"I am also curious about you, Mrs. Bray. Geoffrey Barkas didn't tell us you were still alive. In fact, after hearing his story, I assumed you hadn't survived the Coventry Blitz. I thought it was your death that drove your husband, Damien, to the Axis."

The teacup jiggled against the saucer as Evanna took a sip. Kate watched her cheeks draw tight, perhaps touched by a sorrow that had weakened with time and acceptance but had not altogether disappeared.

"I didn't want to join the war effort," the woman said at last. "The two of us had a happy life in Ireland and a beautiful home by the water. We had each other. I didn't want to change any of it. I loved the simple peace. He insisted the only way we could keep that life was to move to England and fight. The Allies, too, had drawn up plans to invade Ireland despite Irish neutrality. War was coming, he said, so we'd best join the effort and do our part rather than get swept away by the tide."

"So you left?"

"Damien gave up his lecturing post at University College, Galway. He became one of the five thousand Irish soldiers to join the British military. A pilot. I was a linguist myself and found work at Bletchley Park as a cryptanalyst. Toward the end of 1940, I was assigned to work with a team in Coventry and was injured during an air raid, blinded by shrapnel. But by then I had come to believe we could make a difference. I wanted to help, and I volunteered to be a German interpreter."

"How did your superiors respond to that?" Moritz asked.

"It really shook them. It might have gone over well if, before the accident, I hadn't kept secret my ability to speak the enemy's language. I was afraid they wouldn't trust me enough to have me work there. But it would have been better to tell them, because when they found out, they sent me to an internment camp on the Isle of Man under suspicion of espionage."

"How terrible," Kate said.

"War is terrible, my dear. My superiors at Bletchley could never be too careful. I understand now what they had to do. Didn't then, oh, no! I remember being so angry. I had only wanted to help, to volunteer, even after losing my vision. But instead I was confined and got very little care for my wounds. Not saying I blame them. They had higher priorities. That's simply how it was."

"Did your husband come to visit?"

"Oh, yes. Too frequently. And when he did, I wasn't fair to him. I blamed everything on Damien. Trapped in my little cell, I shouted through those metal bars that it was his fault I was a prisoner. His fault

I couldn't see. His fault, because he had wanted to leave our home in Galway so badly and I hadn't wanted to. I told him . . ."

She shook her head.

Kate took her hand and said, "What did you tell him?"

"That I didn't love him anymore, and that I never wanted to see him again. Oh, what a nasty little shrew I was."

"What did he say?"

"He said he was sorry, he had been wrong, he loved me more than anything in the world, and there could be no greater pain than his that I'd been harmed and detained. As the weeks went by, he came to visit whenever he could. But, oh, I couldn't get past my self-pity and my regret over having left home. I shouted all my anger at him whenever he came. I told him I had moved on from him, that I was leaving him, so damn it, stop visiting. I didn't think I loved him anymore. And then, toward the end, something changed in him. I must have driven him mad."

"It couldn't have been you," Kate said.

"Oh, but it was. One day he showed up, and I cried as usual. He was dead silent. Of course, I couldn't see him, but I knew he was there, standing on the other side of those bars, watching me in my misery. Finally, you know what he said?"

"What?"

"He said, 'Evanna, why did you die?' "

Kate could only imagine the woman's shock. "That's what he said?"

"I told him I didn't know what he was talking about. I was right there. But he said, 'They've killed you. They've refused you treatment. You aren't my wife. Evanna is dead.' And then he left, and I never saw him again."

Moritz said, "No offense, but he sounds like a bastard. And a coward."

"None taken," she said.

"He must not have understood what you were going through," Kate said.

Evanna went on, "He blamed the British for my mistreatment, and he blamed himself for getting us into that situation. He was the one who had wanted to leave Ireland. He couldn't handle the guilt. It must have twisted something in his mind. I later learned he had actually convinced himself I was gone, that I'd died of diphtheria or something."

"There's one sick sort of denial," Moritz said. He added to Kate, "Like Yehuda's."

"The war went on," Evanna said, "and eventually I managed to convince them to let me go back to Bletchley. I later learned Damien's full story. He'd crashed a plane near Malta and given himself to the Germans. During his recovery, he was trained by the Abwehr. They sent him back to England, where he gave them a convincing story to explain his absence. As a former Saharan archaeologist and stained-glass artist, he had the skills needed to be a camoufleur. He took his course at the Camouflage Development and Training Centre at Farnham Castle, then sailed aboard the RMS *Andorra* around the entire African continent, all the way to Egypt. They stationed him at the Eighth Army headquarters at Borg-el-Arab, where he worked with Geoffrey. He learned about a top-secret operation there called Operation Bertram. During his attempt to escape west and tell Rommel about it, he was shot dead on his bike by one of Geoffrey's men. As Geoffrey told you, the Eighth Army received word of his true mission from Cairo. The milliner Iris Taha—operating under the name Horace—had learned of his presence through Ralf Speer's information network. A forgery of Bouguereau's *The Little Marauder* carried a message warning the British of Damien's presence in Africa."

Kate wondered if the woman felt any bitterness, knowing that her father and Moritz's mother had enabled Damien's death. She didn't think so. Evanna seemed relieved that he had been killed.

"How did you learn all of this?" Kate asked her.

"Some of our best intelligence at Bletchley came through Speer's network. It was a tragic day when Hitler ordered the deaths of your father and his team of artists. After the war, I went to Berlin with some colleagues. We managed to contact some of the operatives who had been involved in transporting the forgeries from Speer's workshop. From these people, I learned the names of the artists who were killed that night. In the years that followed, I tracked down the children, spouses, and other relatives of the murdered artists. I wanted to grieve with them, to tell them about the heroes their fallen relatives had been. I wanted them to know that thanks to their sacrifices, my husband was stopped."

Kate had an idea.

"Mrs. Bray," she said. "Do you still have the names and addresses of the relatives of the deceased artists?"

"At home in London, I do."

"The artists were turned in by one of their peers. A man called Heinrich Jecklyn. Do you have anything on him?"

"Oh, no. Nothing. He was the missing one. The one who disappeared."

"We have a way of finding him. And when we do, I suspect the families of the betrayed would like to be notified, if not there to see him . . . well, taken down."

"What do you have in mind?"

"I don't know yet," Kate said. "That will depend on his location. But if you'd be willing to give me the contact information you've gathered for the fifteen families, there may be a way for them to see justice."

"How do you intend to find Jecklyn?" Evanna asked. "I've been trying for almost twenty years now."

"He calls himself Conrad Pendelfarr now," Moritz said. "He's working with one of Kate's professors at a fine arts school here in Paris."

"Tomorrow, we are going to have a visit with that professor," Kate said.

Evanna nodded and said, "My dears, you have my cooperation. I will mail you the names and addresses in a letter when back at home. I had better scurry back to my hotel now. My plane home leaves early. When you're my age, you don't do well without sleep."

"You're welcome to spend the night here," Kate said.

"Again, very kind, but my luggage is in the room."

"At least let us drive you back."

"A taxi will do," she said. "I'm no longer the helpless bother I was in my youth."

Evanna stood, clutching her cane. Kate and Moritz helped her to the door. She turned toward them.

"Dearest Katharina and Anwar," she said after a moment. She reached out with a hand and felt their faces, slowly drawing her fingers along their foreheads, cheeks, and chins. Then she took them in her arms, one at a time. "I am happy to have met you. Your father and mother would be proud of what you are doing. Look for my letter in a few days."

Then she left them, guided by the steady metronome that was her cane, tapping a path down the stairwell.

Katharina and Moritz

It was December 31.

Moritz and Kate had watched the gallery until Maxence finally appeared. Moritz had trailed him to his house. It was located in Passy of the sixteenth arrondissement of Paris, one of the city's most affluent residential areas.

Evening found Kate wearing a scarlet dress and a red-feathered cocktail hat. Moritz was wearing a suit and his favorite camel-hair overcoat. They took the Renault to the professor's address and stood by his door, listening. It was a modest home with a courtyard, manicured garden, and view of the large public park to the west, the Bois de Boulogne. They heard music inside, a din of conversation and laughter, and saw bright lights through the windows.

"Sounds like a New Year's Eve party," Kate said.

Moritz nodded. "And we've just been invited."

He knocked, and after a few seconds, Victor Maxence himself opened the door.

Kate felt a dark delight as the expression on his face flickered.

"*Bonjour, Monsieur,*" she said.

"*Mon Dieu,*" he said. "Kate Atwell?"

He looked even taller and thinner than she remembered, standing there in a checkered shirt, blinking rapidly as if to question his spectacles. Behind him, guests were milling about with flutes of champagne and plates of hors d'oeuvres, some peeking toward the door to see who had arrived.

"It was generous of you to invite us to your party tonight," Kate said. "Moritz and I have been looking forward to attending."

Maxence stiffened, drawing his shoulders together.

"Invited . . . yes, of course, though . . . I seem to . . ."

"I don't imagine you invite many employees," she said. "Mostly family, I presume?"

She brushed past him, stepping inside.

He looked embarrassed as he said, "Ehh, yes."

"I say, Monsieur," Kate remarked, "you look surprised to see me. Not just here at your home, but . . . living and breathing?"

"That's a strange thing to say," he replied. "Come in. Have some food and wine."

"Please, introduce us to your loved ones," Moritz said.

It wasn't long before a lady wearing an apron came out from the dining room and greeted her two new guests ebulliently.

"*Bonne année et bonne santé!*" she said.

"Happy New Year to you, too," Kate said. "You must be Madame Maxence."

"Yes, dear, call me Brigitte," she answered, heavily accented. She looked at her husband disapprovingly. "And who did you fail to mention was coming?"

Maxence said, "A young woman who works at the gallery, Kate Atwell, and her boyfriend, I presume."

Kate smiled.

"I'm sorry, Monsieur, but not quite," she said. "You must have me confused with someone else." She turned to Brigitte and said with a wink, "Shall we give him another try to get my name right?"

Maxence soured. "That is your name. Kate Atwell."

Kate chuckled, directing her words at the fear she knew to be growing in him: "Here's a hint, *Monsieur le Professeur*. It's a German surname."

"Come on now, Victor," his wife said, poking him. "Unless you're going senile, you must remember the name of someone you invited to our dinner party without telling me."

There was another pause.

"Katharina," he ventured. "Katharina Speer. That is her name."

"Very good," Kate said, sensing his discomfort. "I thought you had it in you."

"I must watch the oven," Brigitte said, "but why don't you come and meet everyone? Victor's sisters, nephews, and cousins are here, and many of my relatives." She held up a mitt. "You know where to find me. Now fill your glasses!"

"Thank you, Brigitte," Kate said, and Madame Maxence returned to the kitchen.

"What a lovely wife you have, Professor," Moritz said. "Does she know what you're doing for Pendelfarr International?"

Maxence whispered, "What do you want?"

"How about your other relatives? Do your sisters know?" Moritz pointed at two little boys sitting by the fireplace, who were playing with toy soldiers, talking in French. "How about your nephews? Do they know who you work with?"

"I didn't invite you into this house, and I don't know what you're talking about. Now I see you have hostile intentions. If you don't leave, I'll call the police."

"Good idea," Kate said. "We can tell them about the forgeries. Not to mention what we learned from Moritz's former colleague. You wouldn't happen to know him?"

"Who?"

"A fellow named Yehuda Uzan, though he's no longer with us."

"Shhh," Maxence said. "Please . . . keep your voices down."

"Is there something you don't want them to hear?"

"No—well, that name, and the other name."

"What other name? Pendelfarr? Or should I say Jecklyn?"

"Keep it *down!*"

"I guess you haven't told your wife," Moritz said.

Kate saw Victor eyeing the telephone.

"Go on, call the police," she dared. "You can tell them I stole a painting, right after you tell them about your boss."

"You know I'm not going to do that now."

"Then perhaps you could excuse yourself from the party for a few minutes," Moritz said, "so we can have a chat in the other room."

Maxence made a grumbling noise as he led them to his office. He shut the door with a flick of the deadbolt.

"Now," he said in high dudgeon, "you'll tell me what this is all about and get out. You are not welcome here."

"Victor," Kate said, "shut up and listen."

"You can't just—"

"We know about my father's resistance network—that he was fighting against the Nazis, not with them. We know Jecklyn made a deal with Hitler and Goebbels, earning safe passage out of Germany in 'forty-two, with all the remaining forgeries, in return for betraying my father and the artists. We know he changed his name to Conrad Pendelfarr and started an art-brokering business, for which you consult as a partner. We know you are the one who identified me and told Jecklyn I was here, so he could use his mole within Mossad to hunt me down. You helped try to get me killed, and now you have the audacity to tell me to get out. Let me explain something. You don't have any chips left. We do. Big ones. We know everything about your involvement with Jecklyn. So shut up and listen, and do everything we tell you, or we tell your family about your activities. Understood?"

Maxence stared off at the wall. "What is it you want?"

"Yes or no?" Kate said.

"Tell me what you want!"

"Yes or no?"

He sighed. "Yes."

"Good. Now that we understand each other, you will give us Jecklyn's location. It better be right, or we will deliver on our promise."

"I don't know where he is."

"You're partners."

"It's the truth."

"I don't believe you."

"Is that my problem?"

"Yes, I think it is." She unlocked the door and called down the hall, "Brigitte? Are you there? Your husband has something to tell you."

"Shhh, stop!" Maxence said. "Close the door."

"We don't have time to waste," Kate said. Then, down the hall again, "Brigitte?"

There was a reply from the kitchen. "Yes, dear?"

"Would you come here please?"

"Just a minute."

"You won't!" Maxence said to Kate.

"Watch me," she said.

They waited.

When Maxence heard his wife's footsteps coming down the hall, he could bear it no longer.

"Bariloche," he whispered to Kate. "San Carlos de Bariloche, Argentina. That's where Jecklyn lives. Now get my wife out of here!"

"Never mind," Kate shouted out to Brigitte. "We'll be out soon." She locked the door again and faced Maxence. "Address."

"I don't remember offhand."

"You have thirty seconds to remember."

Maxence pulled opened some drawers and leafed through his folders. He took out a stack of papers and copied an address down from one of them, handing it over to Kate.

"You do understand what happens if this is the wrong address," she said. "Your wife learns the truth."

"Yes. I know."

"Good. Item number two. Where does Jecklyn think Moritz and I are?"

"Somewhere in Europe, following a trail to learn about Speer's spy ring."

"Does he think Yehuda's found us?"

"The last time we made contact, he told Uzan to follow and kill you."

"What was to happen when he did so?"

"He was to transfer one hundred thousand pounds to me, which I was to then deposit into an account in Paris in Uzan's name. How did you . . . you said Uzan was dead?"

"Buried on a little island called Lokrum, next to a former friend," Kate said. "Tell me, does Jecklyn generally communicate directly with Yehuda?"

"He communicates through me."

"I see," Kate said. "That leads us to item number three. You had better take notes. Tomorrow is going to be a busy day for you."

She handed him a pen and a blank paper from his desk.

"I'm not doing anything for you after tonight."

"You really must be going senile, Victor. Do I need to remind you, yet again, of the consequences if you don't?"

He rubbed a knuckle into his temple, seeing no way out. "What do you want me to do?"

"Send Jecklyn a message. Tell him Yehuda has reported success; Katharina Speer and Moritz Dahl have been eliminated. When he transfers the money, you will give it to us."

"So that's what this is? A robbery? You're doing this for cash?"

"It's what that cash is going to buy that matters," Moritz said, "and it's all made sweeter coming from Jecklyn's own pocket."

Maxence began scribbling on the paper.

"Item four," Kate said. "In your message to Jecklyn, you will tell him—on an unrelated note—that you have found a new potential partner for Pendelfarr International by the name of Anwar Taha."

"Who?"

"Jecklyn left Germany too early to have ever heard that name—my real name," Moritz said. "You will tell him you have been doing business with this man, Anwar Taha, and that you trust him, and that he is connected to several dozen wealthy art collectors who are interested in flying to Bariloche for a private auction."

"Why would I do that?"

"You are going to help arrange an auction for us."

"Who are these 'collectors?' "

"Not your concern. Just do as told. Have you written it all down?"

"Yes, but now, before—"

"Good," Kate said. "Last item. How many others work at Jecklyn's company in Argentina?"

"I don't know the exact number."

"We need someone on the inside. Do they all know who he really is?"

"Most do. He pays them to keep quiet. But . . ."

"But what?"

"He does have a personal secretary, a girl named Isabel de la Fuente. She's a recent replacement for his prior assistant, a woman who learned who he was and threatened to expose him. Since Isabel's predecessor left the picture, I believe Pendelfarr has been careful not to say too much around his secretaries."

"So, you don't think Ms. de la Fuente knows who he really is?" Moritz said.

"That's right."

"Then here's what you'll do," Kate said. "Tell Jecklyn that your new associate, Mr. Taha, will be coming to town in a few weeks. Set up a meeting. Let us know what is decided, and we will buy our tickets to Argentina when you give us the date."

"This is absurd. You're actually going?"

"Yes." Kate opened his office door. "That is all we needed to discuss. And remember, if you as much as hint to Jecklyn that he's being played . . ."

Brigitte's voice carried from the kitchen.

"Victor? What are you doing? What's going on in there? Come out and help me serve the soup."

Kate whispered the remainder of her thought: "Then I invite your wife to afternoon tea. Now, again: Do you understand all your instructions, yes or no?"

"Yes," Maxence said. He looked at her, struggling to make eye contact. "I want you to know something." She watched as the fear in his eyes softened, becoming a plea. Whether it was for understanding, mercy, or something else, she couldn't be sure, nor did she care. "I was invited to become the French regional director of Pendelfarr International because of my position at the national fine arts school. My job was to bring in clients and scout for worthy purchases. It wasn't until years after that I learned who Conrad really was, and that Ralf Speer had been a resistor, and that Conrad—*Heinrich*—had turned him in . . . but it was too late. I had already been doing business with the man. My career and reputation were on the line. I had to help him keep his secret. My livelihood depended on it. My family's well-being. Surely you see that."

"I see a man who knows how to tell a good joke, Victor."

Brigitte appeared in the doorway.

"Victor, I've been calling for you. You vanished."

"That's our fault," Kate said sweetly. "How rude of us to corner your husband during his own party!"

"That's okay, dear. Come eat."

"We really should go," Kate said, to Maxence's obvious relief. "We came to say a quick hello, wish you a Happy New Year, and leave you to celebrate with family."

"Oh, but you don't have to! Victor's students are welcome here any time."

"You're very kind, really. But we'll leave you with the ones who matter most." Kate caught Maxence's eye. "Though perhaps we'll have tea someday, Brigitte?"

"That would be lovely." She hugged them both. "*Au revoir.*"

"*Au revoir.*"

As his wife went back into the living room, Maxence said, "You won't get away with whatever it is you're doing. Jecklyn is too powerful and too clever."

Kate bowed her head and spoke softly on her way out.

"*Bonne soirée.*"

1963

Isabel

Early spring

Isabel trotted down the steps of Pendelfarr's mansion and walked faster beyond the gate. It was her favorite time of day, going home after work and leaving that wretch behind.

Today, a visitor flew in from Paris, an attractive man called Anwar Taha. An associate of Victor Maxence, he had been introduced as the head of a successful art-brokering business, with an impressive client list, and was looking to start a partnership with Pendelfarr International. Eager to expand his loyalty base, Pendelfarr had been receptive to the idea and had agreed to host a private auction in Bariloche this fall for Mr. Taha's collectors.

Isabel couldn't help but be suspicious of the foreigner's motivations. Having spent months handling Pendelfarr's finances, she had built up a sizable mental registry of names in the art world and had never seen Taha's. There was also something less tangible. Whereas Pendelfarr had seen an honest gentility in the man, she had sensed machination, and wondered if he was really some sort of thief. Guiltily, she hoped he was. It would be delicious to see Pendelfarr robbed clean. She had fantasized about Mr. Taha breaking in at night, looking dangerous in a mask and suit; in her dream, she would catch him and threaten to turn him in but eventually choose to help him.

A breeze blew through a row of trees that were beginning to grow leaves. The Andean foothills were green again, and she no longer had to bundle up in scarves. Bariloche had begun to bloom with color, while keeping its alpine character. Isabel enjoyed the scenery on her walk home every day, and the chance to be alone with her thoughts. She felt safer outside the mansion, being farther from Pendelfarr. Still, she was careful to look over her shoulder every few minutes. If Pendelfarr really had been involved in a murder plot, as she suspected, he was just as capable of doing *her* in should he ever question her desire to preserve his secret.

This evening, as she looked back, she saw she was not alone. There was a young woman on the other side of the street, who looked to be in her mid-twenties, walking in her direction with purpose. She had never seen the woman before, and since her near altercation with Pendelfarr, she had gotten nervous about strangers approaching her. Malice was generally her most charitable interpretation of their motives; she had no way of knowing who was on his payroll. She also wondered from time to time whether the old brothel would hear of the growing hostility between her and Pendelfarr and send an envoy to bring her back. Something about this woman's clothes and bearing, however, made Isabel think she had come on her own.

"Excuse me," the young woman said. "Are you Isabel de la Fuente?"

Not knowing whether this would be wise to confirm, Isabel kept walking.

"The man you work for, that Conrad Pendelfarr," the lady said. "He's not honest."

Isabel heard confidence in the woman's voice. She paused and turned to face her follower. The young woman was tall and lithe, with a porcelain face and dark hair. A scar cut through her left eyebrow.

"To answer your question, yes, I'm Isabel," she said to the woman.

The stranger extended her hand.

"My name is Katharina Speer. Will you walk with me a few minutes?"

"What's this about?"

"Your employer."

"What do you want?"

"Open ears, and the possibility of your help."

"I don't even know you."

"Not yet, but if you give me a few minutes to share my story, you will. Then you can decide what to do."

Isabel stopped, mulling over the allegation of Pendelfarr's dishonesty. Was this woman an investigator? What did she know? Had the Argentinian government sent her? If so, where were her credentials?

Isabel reminded herself that she lived paycheck to paycheck and needed the work. Any involvement with this stranger could disrupt her income. Then again, she also needed to be safe once and for all. If this woman could prove Pendelfarr to be more dangerous than she realized, Isabel wanted to hear it.

"There's a coffee shop nearby," Isabel said. "Follow me."

Conrad

Autumn

Glancing in a mirror in the lobby of the Llao Llao Hotel, Conrad cinched his necktie and awaited the arrival of his new associate. Anwar Taha came through the doors at 6 p.m. and shook his hand, at which time Isabel showed them to the Grand Salon.

"You sure know how to pick a venue," Anwar said.

"I hold an annual auction here for top clients," Conrad said. "If all goes well, the collectors you bring tonight will be welcome at future events."

The first guests began to trickle in at seven. It would be a successful evening, Conrad thought, judging from the surge in traffic during the first few minutes. A line of men in tuxedos and women in dresses had formed. They were a punctual group. He stood at the door to the salon as Anwar introduced him to each of the arrivals and pointed the way to the banquet tables, where they took their seats.

"Thank you for making the trek," Conrad would say as guests ambled in. "It's a pleasure to meet you, Mr. and Mrs. Ott. . . . I hope your taste in art is half as sharp as your taste in fashion, Ms. Carlebach. . . . Mr. Taha tells me you have a keen eye for Dutch landscapes, Mrs. Decker . . ."

And they would say things like, "I have looked forward to this evening, Mr. Pendelfarr. . . . We hear you have some true treasures in your collection. . . . Thank you for your gracious hospitality, Mr. Pendelfarr . . ."

Conrad turned to Anwar after a few minutes and whispered, "Is it just me, or do most of these guests have German names?"

"I do most of my work in Germany," Anwar said.

Soon the room had filled with several dozen of Taha's collectors.

"They seem quiet," Conrad said.

"Their anticipation abounds."

By seven-thirty, chatter filled the room, and every seat was taken. The waiters arrived with champagne, and guests were invited to choose an appetizer—prosciutto-wrapped asparagus or seared scallops.

Conrad took the stage.

"Greetings, friends and collectors," he said. "You've come a long way to be here this evening. I would like to thank Mr. Anwar Taha for introducing me to all of you, and to welcome you to the family of Pendelfarr International. A former painter myself, I began this business in the late 'forties and have spent the last decade connecting with collectors and artists from around the globe." He paused with a practiced modesty. "The company now has twenty offices in ten countries, offering clients a remarkable opportunity to see our galleries and exhibitions, attend auctions, and discover the world's leading artistic talent. Of course, we also have an extensive collection of classics created by names you'll recognize from history. I would like to introduce my assistant, the lovely Isabel de la Fuente"—she bowed her head in acknowledgment—"who will unveil the first piece featured in tonight's auction."

Isabel removed a lace sheet covering a sculpture mounted on a pedestal. Conrad listened for a reaction but heard none, and he wondered if he should worry that the debut piece had been a dud.

"What you see before you is *Philetas*, a terra-cotta original by Jean-Baptiste Carpeaux. Those who know his most famous works will surely be familiar with his *Daphnis and Chloe*. The latter is named after the characters in a second-century Greek story by the novelist Longus. In the story, a boy named Daphnis is raised by a goatherd, and a girl named Chloe by a shepherd. When they fall in love but are too naïve to understand romantic attraction, they are advised by a countryman named Philetas—the subject of the present sculpture—who tells them of the good that will come from kissing. It is a lesser-known but charming piece by a renowned artist. It is signed 'Carpeaux' and twice stamped '*Propriete Carpeaux*.' The bid will open at ten thousand dollars."

All at once, seven hands shot up around the room.

"One at a time now," he said. "That's ten thousand from Mr. Ott. . . . Twelve thousand from Mrs. Schleck. . . . Fourteen from Mr. Kramer. . . . Sixteen from Mr. Ott. . . ." After a few minutes: "Sold for thirty thousand to Mr. Ott."

An auspicious start after all. Four suited men carried the sculpture away and replaced it with a covered easel.

"Isabel," he said, "once again, would you do the honors?"

She lifted the sheet away to reveal a watercolor of a ship listing in a gale in the style of Turner. There were a few mutters from the audience this time. Conrad sensed a growing energy in the room. It looked as though this would be a profitable night after all.

Waiters had begun to carry the appetizers away and were now serving duck breast as the first entrée. Conrad finished his exposition of the painting, and it sold to a middle-aged single woman named Inga Hovde for forty thousand dollars. Price points only went up from there.

After an hour, he took a break. A sorbet was served, and the mellow arpeggios of a harpist could be heard. Conrad prided himself on producing elegant affairs like this one. He mingled from table to table, congratulating the successful bidders, telling them that he hoped they would come back next year. When the second entrée came around, he returned to the stage. The music faded, and he resumed his role as auctioneer, selling an oil with an exuberant rococo style, reminiscent of a Fragonard, for fifty thousand—followed by an obscure still life for sixty.

The night had exceeded his wildest expectations.

He clapped his hands.

"Ladies and gentlemen," he said, "that concludes tonight's auction. The way I see it, everyone is a winner. Many of you have added magnificent pieces to your collections. Others have now seen the kinds of pieces we offer here at my company. I would like to extend the invitation to all of you to come back to this hotel next year, where we will hold—"

He was interrupted: "Mr. Pendelfarr."

It was Anwar, now jogging toward the stage.

"Yes, Mr. Taha?"

"You've forgotten the final piece."

"I believe you're mistaken. What piece?"

"There's still one to be sold."

The suited men came out from behind the curtain, carrying a covered painting on an easel. They set the easel down, bowed, and walked away.

Conrad was confused. There had been twenty works for auction this evening. He had hand-selected them. What had he missed?

"It looks as though I have indeed forgotten the last piece," he said to his audience. "Forgive me. Isabel, once again, I leave it to you."

She pulled away the sheet.

He felt a violent thump in his chest.

On the canvas was a little girl, her obsidian eyes full of mischief. She was sitting on a stone slab in a field somewhere, holding a green fruit in one hand, barefoot among the weeds, sweeping the other hand through her hair. He could feel her in that moment, a specter of that child escaping her painted form, leaving the canvas to wrap her cold fingers around his heart. He looked into the eyes, seeing not oil or texture or color, but a real person, after more than twenty years.

"Christ . . ."

A hand was raised in the audience. Conrad fell quiet.

"Mr. Pendelfarr," Anwar said, "you have a question."

"Yes, of course," he said, pointing to the woman who had raised a hand. "Mrs. Decker?"

She asked, "What can you tell us about this one?"

"This piece . . . forgive me, I had forgotten I'd selected this one—in fact, I'd forgotten it was even . . . that it was in my collection. The fact that I—yes, please give me a second . . ."

What was it doing here? He knew the painting had never been a part of his collection. This one had gotten away that last fateful night.

Dozens of eyes were watching him. The audience's silence was louder than a thunderstorm.

"This piece is one I haven't seen for some time, and you'll have to forgive my short memory on the details. I believe this is an original by William-Adolphe Bouguereau."

"An original, Mr. Pendelfarr?" Anwar said. He pulled a magnifying glass from his pocket. "Mind if I have a look?"

"Please . . ."

He watched, mortified, as Anwar knelt before the painting and, as if for dramatic effect, leaned in to inspect the brushstrokes.

Who was this Anwar, really? A competitor who had set him up to be discredited in front of dozens of wealthy collectors? The man would hang for this.

"Interesting," Anwar said. "How do you explain those speckles on the pear? They almost look to be arranged in a pattern of dots and dashes."

It was getting harder for Conrad to hide the quaver in his voice or the dryness in his throat. "Like I said, my memory is short on this one. It's more likely a lithograph. I'd take as little as a few hundred for it."

Mrs. Decker raised her hand and said, "I'll start the bidding at fifty thousand dollars."

He gawked at the woman, not sure whether to be embarrassed or elated.

Another hand shot up in the back of the room. "Sixty."

Perhaps he hadn't been altogether humiliated?

"Seventy," said another.

"Eighty."

"Ninety."

What was driving the bids so high?

Mrs. Decker countered, "One hundred thousand."

He couldn't believe what he was hearing!

"One ten."

"One twenty."

The bidding went on until Mrs. Decker won the item for two hundred thousand dollars.

Anwar Taha started to clap, and the audience followed.

"Congratulations, Mrs. Decker," Anwar said, turning to face Conrad. "And to all those here tonight who have come to see the finish."

Suddenly Conrad felt as though he had swallowed a liter of acid.

"What are you talking about?" he said.

Anwar joined him, center stage.

"Do you recognize any of the surnames of your guests, Mr. Pendelfarr?"

Conrad thought for a moment. "I may have known others with those names, but other than that—"

"Maybe from the time you lived in Germany?"

"But I never—"

"Take a good look at everyone here," Anwar said. "Tonight, they've taken a good look at you. Remember these faces."

Conrad felt the heat in the room reach a peak. They were all watching him closely.

"Who are you?" he said to Anwar.

Anwar continued, "On 10 October 1942, you informed on a team of artists whose paintings were used to convey messages as part of a Nazi resistance network. Led by Ralf Speer, the artists were slaughtered by SS guards after you turned them in. Tonight, the families of those artists have gathered here to meet you and see what you have done with many of the pieces their loved ones created."

"You mean . . ."

"Everyone here tonight is a dear friend or family member of the sixteen artists you handed to the Nazis."

The spectators began to stand, one by one.

"Hello, Herr Jecklyn," said one. "My name is Leopold Ott, and this is my sister, Hanna. Our other sister was Kristina Ott."

"Good evening, Herr Jecklyn," said the next. "My name is Greta Carlebach. My husband was Emil, now deceased."

One by one, they continued to introduce themselves. The new owner of *The Little Marauder* spoke last.

"Good evening, Herr Jecklyn. My name is Clara Decker. My husband was called Karl. He painted what's on that easel and helped win the Desert War. He and his friends died heroes."

"I don't know what you're all talking about!" Conrad exclaimed.

"Don't bother with that," Anwar said. "We know that you know. I have yet to introduce myself. My birth name was Anwar Taha. I later changed it to Moritz Dahl. You hired someone who tried to use me, and then tried to kill me."

Conrad was sweating in his tuxedo. Christ, oh, Christ, how had they found him? Moritz was supposed to be dead. What was their plan? Were they going to call the police?

He walked to the side of the stage and whispered into Isabel's ear, "Drive me out of here."

"Where to?" she whispered back. "And what are they talking about?"

"It doesn't matter. There's an airfield nearby. I always have a pilot on call during these events."

"Show me the way," she said.

No one tried to stop him as he bolted out of the Grand Salon through a back door with Isabel.

Conrad

"Turn left ahead!" he barked at Isabel.

Conrad pointed down a road that climbed to a plateau in the hills. Isabel did as she was told.

"What about your property, your company? Your home, your things?" she asked. "You're going to leave it all? Leave the country?"

"I don't know what those people have planned," he said. "I need to get out of here. Then I can figure things out."

She stopped the car, and he raced away, dashing across a field of grass toward a small runway. A Cessna 172 stood ready for takeoff. He waved at the craft. The pilot leaned over and opened a door.

He entered, strapped himself in, and allowed the whir of the propeller to ease his nerves. The Cessna traced a loop and was soon sprinting across the asphalt. When it nosed into the air, he let his muscles relax and looked out the window at the shrinking Llao Llao Hotel, perched in the forest between two lakes.

Dozens of people had begun to pour into the gardens below. Either they were watching his plane, or he was being paranoid . . .

The Cessna banked northeast.

"You know where you're going, right?" he said. "Take me to Montevideo."

"That's one idea," the pilot said.

He looked up at the sound of a female voice. All his pilots were men, he'd thought. He hadn't noticed her face under the headgear.

"Are you new?" he said.

"Yes," she answered.

"I should have been notified of any new pilots on call."

"You're in good hands. I've spent the last few weeks taking flight lessons from a former Sayeret Matkal man."

Sayeret Matkal?

He did not like surprises. There already had been too many this evening. And he did not like hearing the words *Sayeret Matkal*.

"I've never seen you before," he said, trying not to overthink things.

"Think back twenty years."

He looked at her more closely. She was a beautiful young woman, resembling a mature version of the peasant girl in *The Little Marauder*, with her dark hair and dark eyes.

"The last time we spoke," she said, "you told me you were going to pick up a treat for me. Do you remember? I was a child, and you had a full head of hair then."

Had she not sounded so certain, he might have laughed at the idea.

"I think you're wrong."

He was paying little attention to her, his heart still racing from the episode at the hotel. What occupied his mind was the question of how his past had caught up with him.

"Are you sure, Heinrich?"

There was a flash of heat in his veins. He lost his train of thought.

Since Eichmann's capture in Buenos Aires, he had known he was at risk. He'd tried to ready himself for the day someone might use his old name. Despite his efforts, it was jarring to hear it pronounced. The name "Heinrich" sounded like a threat. It *was* a threat.

He couldn't say who this woman was, but if she had been a player in this day's string of revelations, she was no friend of his.

He studied her chin, her nose, her cheeks. Her features were beginning to look more familiar. He had seen them on a man once, and on his little girl.

Could it be? Could it *really* be?

"Katharina?" he said, incredulous. "Is that you?"

The plane banked again, now bearing southeast.

"I knew you'd remember."

"But you're supposed to be . . . Yehuda was supposed to have . . ."

"Your man is buried in Croatia," she said.

This was impossible! "How?" he managed to get out.

"Don't worry. The money you sent Victor Maxence, as payment for Yehuda's services, went to a good cause."

"What cause?"

"Airfare for your guests at the Llao Llao this evening."

"*You're* behind all this?"

He didn't know what her intentions were—revenge, justice, intimidation—but it was no use denying his identity. Katharina knew who he was, and he would never convince her otherwise. But maybe he could make her think differently about him. He tried to conjure up a way to deal with her. He would have to address his actions candidly. No mincing words. His honesty would surprise her. She would see that he felt pain for what the war had forced him to do. He would stress his friendship with her father, paint himself as an integral part of her family. How impossibly difficult that decision had been twenty years before.

Yes, maybe he could change how she felt about him.

"I'm guessing you're here to punish me for my actions on 10 October 1942," he said. "I don't begrudge your feelings. But you have to understand how chaotic a time it was. There was no trusting anyone. I didn't even know if I could trust your father or his colleagues. The feeling was mutual. Any of the others could have just as easily betrayed the whole lot of us."

"Of course," she said. "It would only take one rat, so it might as well be you."

She could moralize all she wanted, he thought, but she hadn't lived through war as an adult. This young woman didn't have the experience to know that right and wrong were different when the world was in upheaval. In wartime, the ethics of peacetime were a death sentence.

He had acted out of self-preservation. By turning in the others, he had made sure he wouldn't pay the ultimate price for all the good he had done as part of the artists' collective. If he was guilty of one thing, it was of the desire to live.

That argument would be his last resort, he decided. A youthful idealist like Katharina, reared with absolutist platitudes, would not understand. He could expect more sarcasm than sympathy from her, and would have better luck showing her how difficult his actions had been for him, as a devotee of Ralf Speer.

"Doesn't mean I wasn't a champion of our cause," he said. "It was a noble cause."

"I'm sure it was a real passion for you."

"Do you know how I met your father?" he asked.

"No."

Conrad lifted his chin as he looked at her. "During the early 1920s, I was one of Ralf Speer's first admirers, particularly of the paintings he created during his depression after World War I. Your father had been in a POW camp, you know."

"I read that in Victor's biography of him."

He sensed he had begun to pique her curiosity, though she was trying to hide it.

"His depictions of tormentors and the tormented fascinated me. His art suggested that men were naturally masters and slaves. That some groups were destined to be controlled by others, as history suggests."

"In light of his resistance efforts," Kate said, "I'd say his art was a repudiation of that idea."

"Regardless, I was drawn to his content and style. So much so that he inspired me to complete my doctorate in art history in Vienna. After that, I met your father while he was teaching a master class at the Städelschule Academy of Fine Art."

She was listening intently, he could tell. He had known her father much longer than she had. Kate's memories of the man were vague. Her little brain had hardly begun to mature when she'd watched him die. His own memories, on the other hand, were clear and resonant. He knew he could draw from them and invoke her sympathy by glorifying Ralf's life.

"I was starstruck," he said. "We kept in close touch. I spent years lecturing at the Bauhaus before I was hired as a professor of art history at the Prussian Academy of Arts in 'thirty-three. There, I watched as the Nazi government declared a number of famous German artists to be 'cultural Bolsheviks' and creators of 'degenerate art,' seizing thousands of pieces from galleries and exhibitions across the state. I adapted by preaching my opposition to the degenerates. Do you know how your father's network formed?"

"No," she said.

"Would you like to know?"

He was glad to be taking control of the conversation. She would look small if she said no and silly if she said nothing.

"Tell me," she said.

"Hitler became Chancellor in 'thirty-three. At the time, his regime was popular with the German people; in their eyes, the failures of the Weimar Republic had discredited democracy. Nonetheless, your father met a few underground members of the banned Social Democrats group—the SPD—and the *Freie Arbeiter* Union, who were attempting to organize resistance."

He saw apathy in her expression, but suspected it was more likely sheepishness in disguise. She had to realize that the gaps in her knowledge made her look ignorant.

"Ralf also learned of a resistance network within the German Army, the Foreign Office, and the Abwehr," he said, trying to sound paternal but not pontifical. "But he was worried by the lack of coordination, the high arrest and execution rates. So he set up a clandestine network of his own to unite the efforts. He called upon friends within his art circles. In Berlin, he organized them into a painting workshop. The paintings would contain codes in microdots. Embedded in several of the first of his workshop's paintings were messages to exiled SPD leadership in Prague, who would publish reports of events inside Germany."

He wondered how aware she was that he had gained the upper hand.

"In 'thirty-eight," he said, "your father was contacted by Hans Oster, deputy head of military intelligence, who was organizing his own network of resistors. Oster had learned of Ralf's activities and told him that given his fame as an artist, he could get Ralf a job as Vice Minister under Goebbels. He took the role at the start of the war and hired me to manage his workshop. I'll always be grateful to him for that."

He paused, hoping she would find the veneration in his voice sincere. He was speaking of her father in a tone he might use to describe a religious figure.

"Over the years," he went on, "your father became a trusted member of the Party and a confidante of Goebbels and Hitler. Meanwhile, he continued developing his network of artists and spies throughout Europe, dispersing some of Hitler's most precious secrets within the forgeries. Ralf's members used the airwaves in combination with traditional transport, from radio centers to railways. The messages went from continent to continent. Berlin to Cairo, for example, was not uncommon."

Kate asked him, "Did you aspire to my father's position as Vice Minister?"

This caught him off guard. The woman was perceptive.

"I admit I did, much in the way an apprentice often wishes to take after his teacher."

"Was it offered to you?"

"Despite my qualifications and outspokenness against the degenerates, no. It was not. Even after I turned in your father and his artists."

"Though you did manage to bargain for safe passage out of Germany and bring a large stash of paintings with you."

"That I did. Goebbels got me a fraudulent *laissez-passer* issued by the International Red Cross. I fled with an inventory of forgeries to

Bariloche, knowing that you—who had escaped to England—would be my only liability. That is to say, should you ever learn of my actions without context and misjudge me as a cold-blooded traitor. And then you revealed yourself. I couldn't believe my luck."

"I fail to see the misjudgment."

"There was no ideology behind what I did. I didn't do it for the advancement of fascism or my career. There was no opportunity for me to climb the ranks within the Nazi Party. I was only trying to survive."

"At whose expense? The heroes you say you admired?"

He had no good answer.

"You have to believe my admiration was real. Your father was a great man."

"Why did Hitler cover up the incident and paint him as a national hero?"

"To avoid encouraging other resistance movements. That is why the history books came to regard Ralf Speer as a prominent Nazi loyalist."

"After all these years," Kate said, "did you really think you were safe?"

"When the war ended, I thought so. But when Eichmann was captured, I had to be sure."

"So you found Yehuda Uzan to monitor Mossad."

He was beginning to feel exposed and decided to ask a few questions of his own.

"Yes, he was my man. Now I'd like to know something, Katharina: How did you track down the families of the artists?"

"I had help from a woman named Evanna Bray."

"I don't recognize the name."

"She was the wife of the Abwehr agent, an Irishman named Damien Bray, who nearly exposed Operation Bertram. The last painting to leave my father's workshop had a message bound for Cairo. That's what stopped him."

"I see. And as for getting me here on this plane . . ."

"Isabel told us you keep a pilot on call. She helped with the arrangements."

So he had been fooled, sabotaged, by a couple of twenty-something girls.

"And next?" he said. "What are you doing here, Katharina? I assume it was to humiliate me in front of those families. Send me to the stocks, scare me a little, ask me to repent, ask me why I snitched on your father. What happens now? Or have you thought this through?"

"This has nothing to do with disgracing, intimidating, or understanding you," she said.

"What, then?"

"It's about giving you a choice."

"You'll have to explain."

Having completed a wide circle, she eased the Cessna into a southwest bearing.

At first, she did not answer him.

"Where are you taking me?" he pressed.

"To the Andes, if you choose."

"Across, to Chile?"

"Did I say that?"

The calmness in her voice told him she had made up her mind about him long ago. The woman was as stubborn as her father.

"Katharina," he said, more than a little uneasy. "Ralf's greatest sadness was having to rear you with the belief that he was a true Nazi adherent. He couldn't trust an eight-year-old with his secret, and he longed for the day he could explain everything to you, in his own words. Because of me, that day never came, but can you understand, I was just trying to survive?"

Kate stared through the windshield, silent. He was starting to feel desperate to reach her.

"It is the weak who cannot forgive," he added.

"You're responsible for the death of both my fathers, biological and adoptive—both good men," she said. "You sentenced fifteen resistors to death. Handed them to their executioners, so you could profit from their work. What, exactly, would forgiveness mean for a man like you?"

"It would mean understanding. Understanding that I had to, to be safe in a chaotic time. A time when we were all surrounded by evil. Your understanding would be a gift to me."

"I already have a gift for you."

She reached between the seats and pulled out a plump, green pear. She handed it to him.

"There are dots and dashes penned in on the skin," he said, holding the fruit in his palms. "You've written something?"

"You remember Morse code, don't you?" she said. "You used it back then."

"It was long ago." He twisted the pear in his hands, reading slowly. "It says: *From . . . a . . . good . . . little . . .*"

He trailed off, more aware of the drone of the engine and the buzz of the propeller. She was heading due west toward the mountain range. He could see the jagged line of snowcaps.

Suddenly she took out a bent steel pipe from under her seat and jammed the tip into the controls, over and over, shattering the protective glass on the gauges, breaking the throttle, damaging the control column.

"So that's how it ends?" he said. "All those people down below will watch us crash together into the side of a mountain?"

She had no reply.

"You know," he added, "we could have put the past behind us. You're a talented artist, I hear. An aspiring art consultant. You could have come to work for me. I would have embraced you. We could have honored your father's legacy together. Given our love of the canvas and paintbrush, we aren't so different, you and I."

"There's one important difference," Kate said.

"What's that?"

"I'm wearing a parachute."

She opened the door. Wind rushed through the cabin.

Panic took hold of him.

She fastened a pair of goggles over her eyes.

"You have one, too," she said. "Behind your seat. If you strap it on and jump, you'll be picked up on the land below and transported to Nuremberg, where you will be put on trial at the Palace of Justice. That's your choice."

He glanced out the nearest window again and tried to gauge the plane's altitude.

When he looked back, she was gone.

He grabbed the yoke—unresponsive. She had destroyed the controls.

His options were indeed limited to two. For a reason he could not explain, they were a relief to him. His options made him forget about Conrad Pendelfarr. He was Heinrich Jecklyn again, living in reality.

He reached for the pack behind his seat. It was military green. There was even a helmet for him to wear. Goggles, too.

He strapped in, finding the ripcord.

The icy air whooshed through the cockpit. Flakes of snow swirled around. He could feel them on his cheeks, little stabs of cold.

He thought about the terrain below. He would never be able to escape down there. Even if he didn't break a limb when he landed, he would not be able to move quickly enough. They would find him hobbling through the snow without trouble.

He imagined the courtroom he would face in Nuremberg and thought of the men who had been tried there. Men he had helped. He would walk the same halls.

He positioned himself in front of the open door. The air felt as though it would suck him right out. He kept a solid grip on the frame, not ready to let go.

The pack felt heavy on his shoulders. Very heavy.

He didn't like the way it felt.

Heinrich Jecklyn took the parachute off and tossed it out the door.

He sat back down in the passenger seat, gazing ahead through the windshield at the approaching Andes. They were beautiful. In the daytime, they were clean and white, glistening in the sun. Now they looked like dark rumples on the earth. He would have enjoyed painting them just after sunset.

EPILOGUE

Katharina and Family

The jeep rolled over the side of a dune and stopped at the edge of town. A wide-eyed little boy came leaping out the back:

"Cairo! Can I go?"

"We'll walk together, Ralf," his mother replied. "Take my hand, rascal."

"My feet are hot."

"Soon, all of you will be hot! Let's go see Grandma and your godmother."

Moritz put an arm around Kate's shoulders. As they meandered through the marketplace, she watched her husband taking in the commotion—chickens darting about the street, dogs barking and cats slinking, traders bargaining, carts wheeling, bikes and motorcycles weaving through traffic—and she wondered if he was hearing the sounds of the present or the past.

She asked him, "Is this how you remember it growing up?"

"Just as vibrant," he said, "minus the topees and Tommies."

"Does it still feel like home?"

"I could get used to it again, but one step at a time. I'd like to get a handle on managing the Beaumaris estate before having a second home here."

"Mum, Daddy," said the boy, "that looks good!"

He was pointing to a man carrying a tray of freshly squeezed mango juice. Moritz handed the vendor a few bills and said, "Does it ever. You can bring one to Grandma, too."

Ralf sipped and smacked his lips.

"Delicious," he said.

They explored the streets a bit, stopping to watch the performers, buy pastries and chocolates, and show Ralf the animals. Soon they reached a shop with a sign that read:

HORACE HATS
In memory of Iris Taha
And her millinery company
Managed by Lona Atwell and Evanna Bray

Kate pushed the door open, and Ralf rushed inside: "Grandma!"

Lady Atwell was arranging a display of fascinators in the window. She dropped what she was doing and took the little one in her arms.

"Darling, how are you?" she said.

"Here," he said, handing her the drink.

"How thoughtful!"

They heard a tapping noise and looked up at the stairwell to see Evanna feeling her way down with her cane. Ralf ran to greet her next.

"Auntie 'Vanna!"

"Hello, dearest."

He gave her a peck on the cheek as they embraced.

"The shop looks great," Moritz said.

"It's been in the works a few months now," said Lona. "I find the vintage hats and get them here. Evanna does the marketing."

"How are things with the art consultancy?" Evanna asked Kate.

"Going well, thanks," Kate said. "My colleague, Isabel, is well connected in the art world. We keep growing. We're looking to develop in the Orient, but she'll be taking a few years off for art school. She's been accepted at the Royal College of Art." She gestured toward the stairs. "Now, we've been dying to see the radio room. Mind if we have a look?"

"Upstairs," Lona said.

Moritz and Ralf followed her.

"I remember this place like it was yesterday," Moritz said. Patting his son's shoulder, he said, "This is where Daddy grew up."

"I like it," Ralf said.

Hanging from a wall on the top floor was an Egyptian rug. Moritz lifted it away, revealing a secret, office-sized room beyond. Inside were two desks full of decades-old electronic equipment: cables, receivers, transmitters, and other odd-looking silver boxes dotted with switches and buttons.

"In all my years here as a kid, I never thought to look here," he said, wiping the dust from a receiver. "Did you ladies find it like this?"

"Your mother had smoothed the wall and covered the hole before she moved away with you," Evanna said. "Once we took the wall down, the stuff was all there."

"Come here, Ralf," Moritz said, taking a seat in front of the desk. The boy sat on his father's lap and studied the electronics with interest. "A little more than twenty-five years ago, your other Grandma sat in this chair, and she heard a message from Mommy's Daddy—your Grandpa—in Germany. Grandma Iris bravely took the message to the headquarters in town and helped win an important fight in the desert. It was called the Second Battle of El Alamein."

"She was a soldier like you?"

Kate raised an eyebrow. "Careful what you encourage."

Moritz winked at Ralf and whispered, "A fierce one!"

. . .

When dusk fell, Kate and Evanna took a drive southwest toward the Pyramids, parking the jeep by a mound of grass. They walked a distance through the sand and lay back against a dune. The warm wind tickled Kate's arms.

"Kate, dear," Evanna said. "How many stars do you see?"

The sky had a wide palette of colors, from a yellow topaz to a deep magenta, but no stars yet.

"It's too early," she said. "Well, actually, there's one I can see."

"Only one?"

"A bright one."

"That's no star. That's Venus. Tilt my head toward it, would you? I'd like to pretend I can see it." Her expression was unusually serene.

Kate lifted Evanna's head to the side, supporting her neck as the woman looked through sightless eyes at the only twinkle up there. Kate wondered what seemed to be giving Evanna such peace.

"Thank you, dear," Evanna said, turning away. She then murmured, "For the times it mattered to me."

Kate decided not to ask what she meant.

. . .

They all came back to the edge of the Sahara after breakfast the next morning.

Ralf, running through the sand, shouted: "Look! Mum, Daddy, a *camel!*"

They were approached by a dark-skinned man wearing white robes and a keffiyeh scarf. He was tugging the animal along with him, offering rides. Saddled with decorative bags, the camel stopped, planting its hooves in a dune. It let out an exasperated bray.

"One pound," the owner said. "Ride far."

"I always wanted one of those," Moritz said.

"Me, too," said Ralf. "Always."

Moritz glanced at Kate, who nodded her agreement.

"Then, little rascal, why don't you ask how much to buy the damned beast?"

Recommended Historical Nonfiction

The camouflage operations of the North African campaign that are described in this book, including Operation Bertram, are real. Geoffrey Barkas was a real person; Damien Bray was not. While the book references a number of real British and Israeli military leaders, German artists, prominent Nazis, and other historical figures, Ralf Speer's character and position within the Third Reich are fictional. All geographical locations exist except for the town of Trefwyn. Other fictional entities include the RMS *Andorra*, Operation Nest, and the No. 4 Camouflage Course. Although I strive for authenticity of backdrop and character, this is a work of creative historical fiction and should not be viewed as an infallible source of fact. For readers who wish to learn more about the Camouflage Unit and military deception in World War II, I recommend the following literature.

- Stroud, Rick. *The Phantom Army of Alamein: How the Camouflage Unit and Operation Bertram Hoodwinked Rommel.* London and New York: Bloomsbury, 2012.

This book tells the full story of the British camoufleurs who banded together and harnessed their artistic creativity against Rommel's army in the Desert War. The history culminates with their most dramatic feat of military deception, Operation Bertram, whose success proved vital to the North African campaign.

- Barkas, Geoffrey, and Natalie Barkas. *The Camouflage Story (From Aintree to Alamein)*. London: Cassell, 1952.

This firsthand account was written by the director of camouflage in the Middle East during World War II, the filmmaker Geoffrey Barkas, who appears as a fictionalized protagonist in this novel. Illustrated by Brian

Robb, also a member of the Camouflage Unit, the book documents the growing importance of military deception in the Desert War and details camouflage techniques used in Operation Bertram.

- Sykes, Steven. *Deceivers Ever: Memoirs of a Camouflage Officer*. Tunbridge Wells, UK: Spellmount, 1990.

This memoir, written by a stained-glass artist and another member of the Camouflage Unit, describes a wide range of concealment devices, from small-scale projects to large-scale military deceptions such as the dummy railhead mentioned in this novel.

The following titles, several of them classics, are suggested for readers interested in a general history of camouflage and military deception used in World War II:

- Cave Brown, Anthony. *Bodyguard of Lies*. New York: Harper and Row, 1975.
- Crowdy, Terry. *Deceiving Hitler: Double Cross and Deception in WWII*. Oxford, UK: Osprey, 2008.
- Cruickshank, Charles. *Deception in World War II*. Oxford and New York: Oxford University Press, 1979.
- Dobinson, Colin. *Fields of Deception: Britain's Bombing Decoys of World War II*. London: Methuen, 2000.
- Goodden, Henrietta. *Camouflage and Art: Design for Deception in World War II*. London: Unicorn Press, 2007.
- Holt, Thaddeus. *The Deceivers: Allied Military Deception in the Second World War*. New York: Scribner, 2004.
- Reit, Seymour. *Masquerade: The Amazing Camouflage Deceptions of World War II*. New York: Hawthorne Books, 1978.
- Young, Martin, and Robbie Stamp. *Trojan Horses: Deception Operations in the Second World War*. London: The Bodley Head, 1989.

www.ingramcontent.com/pod-product-compliance
Lightning Source LLC
Chambersburg PA
CBHW030547310726
48979CB00010B/2063/J